Indigenous Cultural Groups Pronunciation Guide

There are 65 distinct Indigenous cultural groups living in Canada and at least as many languages. A few of them appear in End of Innocence. (Phonetics where given are approximate.)

Anishinaabe (uh-ni-shi-nah-beh)
Nehiyawak (what the Cree people call themselves)
Gits'ilassu one of five groups belonging to the Tsimshiam (chim-shē-an) Nations
Hesquiaht (hesh-kwee-at)
Ixil-Maya (eesheel-Māyǎ) an Indigenous cultural group living in the Guatemalan highlands.
Nisga'a (Niss–gaa)
Secwepemc (Seck-wep–um)
Sts'Ailes (known as Chehalis an independent band)

Much of the novel is set in Vancouver, BC and surrounding area, on the traditional, unceded territory of the *Musqueam, Squamish,* and *Tsleil Waututh* (Slail watooth) First Nations.

For Lisbeth Porteous and Marcelle Birgeneau

The Evil Among Us

1

The soccer team from Kitimat were really good and every time #19 got the ball, she tore down the field with Carey Bolton right behind her. Carey was a forward and her and Emma had been chasing #19 since the beginning of the game. She'd already scored twice and they weren't going to let that happen again. The coach called a time out and put Roxanne in the game and Carey came off for a break. That's when she first noticed her new friend was on the other side of the field. He was an older guy who had just moved to Terrace with his mom. They were living in Thornhill, not far from Terrace. He was really cute, but Carey knew he was too old for her. Her mom wouldn't even let her date yet, never mind let her date a guy his age. Still, it was nice to get attention from an older guy and he was a sweet guy, kind of like an older brother. Kelsey had just scored a goal and they needed that goal to tie the game. She noticed he was clapping with everyone else.

By half-time, Carey's knee had started to ache, just a bit. If coach noticed, he wouldn't let her play, so she was careful not to limp. It worked and she took to the field for the second half with the rest of the team. #19 was relentless and she could run like the wind. Carey would have given anything to be able to run like that. She did her best to keep up but it wasn't long before she started to limp and coach noticed, so he sidelined her, much to her embarrassment. She didn't like to be treated like a baby.

Carey was coming off the field when she noticed that her new friend had moved to the bleachers behind her team. He gave her a friendly wave and she waved back. After a while, he came and stood behind her and asked her why she was limping. She told him her knee was sore. She definitely didn't tell him that she'd worn a leg brace for years. He would think she was so uncool. He quietly offered to drive her home when the game was over. She felt her cheeks go red and she hoped he didn't notice.

After the game, Carey's cousin Beth asked her if she was coming over for dinner, like she usually did after their Tuesday game. Beth was on her team and her family lived close to the soccer field.

"My knee's pretty sore, Beth. I'm getting a ride home. She nodded in the direction of her new friend. Mom's working late tonight and I'll be able to get dinner ready for her." Her brother was staying at a friend's tonight and it would be just her and her mom. She'd be getting home from work soon.

"Mom's making mac and cheese," said Beth, eying the guy behind Carey with interest.

"Oh no! I love Auntie Estelle's mac and cheese! Tell her I'll take a rain check."

"Your loss, Carey," said Beth, with another look at the young man. She leaned over and whispered, "Who's the guy? He's cute."

Carey flushed again. "A new friend," she whispered back. "Just moved to town. I'll tell you about him tomorrow."

"Okay. See you at school." Beth headed for home with

End of Innocence

A Novel

Valerie Van Clieaf

Porteous Publishing

End of Innocence / A Novel

Copyright © 2017 Valerie Van Clieaf.

Porteous Publishing is a registered trademark.

Library and Archives Canada Cataloguing in Publication data is available upon request.

Book and Cover Design by Marcella M. Reay

Published in Canada by Porteous Publishing
ISBN-10: 197966885X
ISBN-13: 9781979668859

anticipation. Her mom's mac and cheese was one of her favourite meals.

Amelia Boudreau lived in residence on Burnaby Mountain at Simon Fraser University in Vancouver. She was two weeks into her first semester. It was the first time she'd lived away from home but she'd really lucked out with her roomie, Taliah. She was *Hesquiaht* and had grown up on Vancouver Island. It was her first time away from home too.

It was close to midnight when her mom, Estelle called. According to Amelia's sister Beth, Carey had taken a ride home after her soccer game with some guy that no one knew. She wasn't home when her mom got home. That was about 8:00 pm but Rosaline wasn't worried because Carey usually went to Estelle's for dinner after soccer. It was only two blocks away. When Carey wasn't home by nine, Rosie called over to Estelle's to tell Carey to shake a leg. She had school tomorrow. But Carey wasn't at Estelle's. She didn't come over after the game. Rosie called everyone she could think of but no one knew where Carey was.

The game ended five hours ago, and everyone was worried. Carey was everyone's ray of sunshine and unstoppable in her enthusiasm for all things. She was only eleven, but she was a smart, responsible kid and Amelia knew that she hadn't just wandered off and gotten lost, or decided to visit a friend or forgotten to call.

"Carey seemed to know the guy she took the ride from. Beth didn't know him, but said he seemed like a nice guy and that Carey was going to tell her about him tomorrow."

"Did Auntie Rosie call the police?"

"Cpl. Cumberland dropped by a while ago. He was very reassuring and the fact that she seemed to know the guy."

"Meant no amber alert?" guessed Amelia.

"No amber alert. Not till she's been missing for 24 hours."

"How could she know the guy when no one else seems to know who he is?"

"I don't know honey."

"Geez mom. This is scary. How's Auntie Rosie?"

"Not so good. I'm staying with her tonight. She doesn't want to leave the house, in case Carey comes home."

After Amelia got off the phone, Taliah made a pot of tea and sat up with her for awhile. When she couldn't keep her eyes open any longer, she begged off and went to bed. Amelia curled up on the couch but sleep wouldn't come, so she got up and brought her laptop back to the couch. She did a search on missing kids in BC. Clicked on the RCMP stats on missing persons. This led, inevitably, to looking at the stats on missing and murdered Indigenous women and girls in Canada and more clicking as she followed the links calling for a federal inquiry.

Amelia was thinking about majoring in Criminology, maybe becoming a police officer or working in the justice system in another way. She admitted to herself that maybe she wanted to pursue a career in criminology so that the statistics wouldn't twist her gut into a knot like they always did. Like they were doing now.

It was about 8:30 am and Amelia was still awake when Taliah's cousin George Evans dropped by to see if she wanted to go for breakfast. George was a sophomore at SFU, majoring in business and he lived in another residence on campus. He'd been spending a lot of his free time with Taliah and Amelia. He was fond of his cousin, who he'd basically grown up with, but it was Amelia that had him showing up at their door like a homing pigeon.

Taliah didn't have any classes this morning and they didn't want to wake her. Amelia and George walked over to the student building for breakfast. She told George about her cousin's disappearance the night before. If Carey wasn't found by tonight, Amelia had already decided she'd get the midnight bus up to Terrace, but George offered to drive her up instead.

"You'll get there sooner if I drive you up," he insisted. "And you won't be so tired. That bus ride would be brutal." It was a very kind offer as it was a long, 18-hour drive up to Terrace, close to the coast — in British Columbia's north. By bus, more like 24.

"It's a long way. Do you think your car will make it okay?"

"No problem," said George.

"That'd be great. But only if she isn't home yet."

Amelia called her mom at supper time. Still no sign of Carey and the RCMP had put out an amber alert. She told her mom she had a ride and was coming up that night and to let Auntie Rosie know they'd be there by tomorrow late afternoon. George had some errands to run and couldn't pick her up till 10:00 pm.

Amelia had made sandwiches and filled up her water bottles. George had a large thermos of coffee and snacks, so they only had to stop for gas. As the miles stretched behind them, they found they had a lot to talk about. He told her stories about his summers working on his uncle's fishing boat. Like the one time they'd all nearly drowned when an ocean liner came within a few feet of them late

5

one dark night, full out, but no lights and how its waves had rocked their boat from side to side like it was a toy and they'd had to fight like hell to keep from sinking and them screaming at that fucking liner for all the good it did. They talked about their families and growing up stories. George encouraged her to talk about Carey and how she was feeling and he totally understood that she was shit scared by now and couldn't help it when she started crying.

By four in the morning, they were past Prince George. Amelia was so tired she didn't remember dozing off. When she woke up, she had a blanket over her knees. They were in Hazelton and George had stopped for gas. They drank some of George's coffee which was still warm and a little sweet. Then they took off again. After a while, they talked about university life and George shared war stories about finding his path through real and imagined white expectation and genteel and not so genteel racism. Amelia listened to these stories closely. She'd just started down that path and had already dodged a few curve balls and watched other brown folks dodge them too — or not. It was different for the sisters and brothers.

Amelia told him about the *Nisga'a* student in her Spanish class, picking up a breadth requirement so she could graduate and how the prof was trying to get them all to say '*I am Canadian*' in Spanish and Sharon says '*I am Nisga'a*' and the prof stops her because she's not sure what she's talking about and the prof says '*Aren't you Canadian*' and Sharon says '*I'm Nisga'a first. Sometimes I'm Canadian too*.' And how the prof was cool about it, and nodded her head like she'd just learned something. But how Amelia was surprised some of the other students were kind of embarrassed.

"Oh. You mean like we're not one big happy family, us

Canadians," said George. And they both laughed. When they weren't talking, the silence was companionable.

They arrived at Amelia's parents in time for dinner on Saturday.

"She's been gone for two days George. I don't know what to say to them," Amelia said, hanging back in the mud room, trying not to cry; afraid of her own feelings — afraid for all of them. He gave her a careful hug; their first.

"Your being here is what counts," he whispered as they hung up their coats.

George was right. What was hard was everyone seemed so lost and she wanted to comfort, but the helplessness in the room stole the air. She gave everyone a hug before taking a seat beside George at the table.

Auntie Rosie had dark circles under her eyes and her skin was blotchy from crying.

"They wouldn't listen to me. I told them, she's only eleven years old. She would never just take off with a boy. Who is this boy, this stranger that took my girl? I can't believe that nobody recognized him! Someone must know him! All those people at the soccer game and he just took my girl! It's been two days. She could be anywhere!"

Elwin sat beside his mom. He was Carey's younger brother, normally quite rambunctious and a real joker. He was sad and scared and picked at his food. Beth was sitting beside him. Amelia watched as a few lone tears slid down her sister's cheeks.

"I'm so sorry Auntie," Beth said, so quietly she could barely be heard. "I shouldn't have let Carey get into his car. I didn't know he was a bad person."

"No, no honey. It's not your fault," said Rosie.

Her dad was nearly in tears himself. "Beth, sweetie,

please don't cry. There's no way you could have known."

By now, Beth's tears were an uncontrolled flood. Estelle took her into the living room and sat with her, holding her close until her tears were spent.

Uncle Michael arrived soon after and Amelia got up to give him a hug. She was so glad to see him. Uncle was a lawyer who lived in Vancouver. His area was intellectual property rights and he worked with a lot of artists and musicians. He sat down across from Amelia. Her dad got up to get him some food.

"Hey, Amelia, I called you last night, but your roomie said you were already on the way. I was going to fly you up this morning, but I see you have the situation in hand." Michael smiled at George, quiet and a little shy next to her.

"Uncle, this is my friend, George Evans."

"Michael Bolton. Good to meet you, George. Thanks for bringing our girl up."

"My pleasure. I mean, no problem," said George. "Good to meet you too Michael." George was more than a little flustered. Amelia stole a glance at him.

"Try to eat something Michael," said Geoff. "Amelia and George, you as well. You must be hungry after such a long drive."

"Where were you, Uncle?" Amelia asked.

"At the RCMP detachment."

"Who'd you talk with?" Geoff asked.

"Cpl. Graziano initially, then Cumberland. He was helpful, but I didn't find out much that we don't already know."

"The RCMP did a house to house search in the area surrounding the soccer field where Carey was taken. They went to St. Jerome's the next morning and talked with the principal, teachers, some of the students. There is one thing, but they're not sure if it's connected to Carey's disappearance. She was seen talking with a young Indigenous man on the school grounds last Tuesday. One of the teachers, whoever was doing yard duty that afternoon, didn't recognize him, so approached them both, but he left before the teacher could question him, though not in a hurry, she said. He kind of ambled off, got into a car and drove away. When the teacher asked, Carey told her the guy was new in town and just talking."

"Bill Cumberland told me about him yesterday," said Rosie.

"We asked Beth," said Geoff. "Whoever he is, she didn't see him talking to Carey in the school yard, so she didn't know if he was the same boy that took her."

Beside Amelia, an exhausted George was falling asleep over his plate, so her dad hustled him off to the spare bedroom for a nap. She picked at her food and listened to the others talk, saying little; strung out on too much coffee and a lot of fear. While she waited for George to pick her up last night, she'd once again pulled up the statistics on missing children in British Columbia. Over 7,000 children were reported missing last year. 65% of these reports were removed within 24 hours; almost 90% within the first week. After the first week, about 950 children — most of them runaways or missing for unknown reasons — were still missing. Eight children were reported as abducted by strangers — like Carey. But did the police really know? What about all those kids missing for unknown reasons.

Women were targets of violence everywhere, but Indigenous women and girls were targeted in numbers that scared Carey — by close family members, but also by men they only knew in passing and so many by strangers. Not just in Canada. It was the same for sisters in the US. And African-American women too — so many missing.

She looked at her Aunt's haunted face. No one would know these stats better than Auntie Rosie. For eight years she'd been the Director of a shelter for Indigenous women and their children fleeing violence.

"Did she have her cell with her Auntie?" Amelia asked.

"It's not here, so she must have had it. It goes to voicemail."

Michael put a protective arm around Rosie. Nobody voiced the obvious. If Carey wasn't answering, her phone was most likely lying on a roadside somewhere. Cells are easy to track.

"It's gonna be okay, Rosie. They're going to find her and bring her back to us, safe and sound." Michael's words, hollow, bounced off the walls. Bill Cumberland hadn't mentioned Carey's cell. Michael would call and ask him about it after dinner.

Amelia had always felt safe, even when she moved to Vancouver, on her own for the first time in her life. The pressures of university life aside, it was exhilarating, not scary. But Carey had been taken in a public field, surrounded by her teammates, Beth right beside her, her mom at the women's shelter only three blocks away! And they didn't even know the name of the guy she got in the car with. She knew this kind of thinking wouldn't help Carey. She had to do something. But what? She decided to go see Kate Brennan as soon as she got back to campus. Kate was a PhD Criminology candidate and the lecturer for the Introductory Crim course she was taking. Kate was awesome and really smart. She'd have some idea what Amelia could do to help find Carey.

2

"I'll pick Amelia up first, then we'll swing by and get you, Morgan" said Kate. I should be there in an hour."

"I'll be waiting." I met Amelia Boudreau for the first time when Kate brought her to our cottage to meet Lucas and me. That was five days after her cousin Carey Bolton was abducted. Time was still on their side that they'd get her back safe. Nearly 90% of children reported missing in BC return home within a week. Kate knew this, as did Lucas. They're both criminologists. But everything changed when four days later, Michael Bolton spotted Carey getting into a car behind the *Clarendon*, a private members club in downtown Vancouver. He saw two other children in the car and was sure there were three men altogether. He reported the sighting to the Vancouver Police that night.

Kate, Amelia and I had coffee with Michael the next day. He was still badly shaken because he'd only realized it was Carey as the car sped past him. The last place he expected to see her there was the private members' club he belonged to. It's almost 1,400 kilometres from Terrace to Vancouver. Carey was a long way from home.

We had dinner with Michael at the club a few days later. He wanted us to have a look at the place. I only have one black dress — really all a woman needs — and that's what I wore. When Lucas and I walked through the front door of the club, I felt like a pretender to the throne, now that I have first hand experience of what that means. '*So, this is how the other half lives*', dad would have said. '*You mean the top 1%*', Kate would have corrected.

Michael was there to meet us, looking every inch the high-roller that he is. He signed us in and took us up to the second floor for drinks. Amelia was already there, sipping on something pink and we settled in with scotch and sodas, single malt. The club started off as a white enclave and the times might be a changin', but I didn't spot many brown folks enjoying the amenities. I'm sure the four of us turned a few heads that night.

After drinks and dinner in a private dining room, Michael took us on a tour of the place — and not to show it off. He'd been doing lots of snooping around since spotting Carey behind the club. We gathered our things — like we were leaving — and hopped an elevator, but instead of taking it down to the basement and parking access, we took it up to the fifth floor, where the overnight accommodation is. Once there, we made our way back down to the main floor by way of a labyrinth of old stairwells. Michael didn't need to point out that we didn't encounter a single person coming down. From there we took an elevator to the basement. Before picking up our cars, we followed Michael out the club exit to the street. He showed us where he was standing when he saw Carey and we all huddled around him as he described, once again, exactly what had happened.

After a dinner meeting with clients, he decided to walk home through Gastown. He was leaving the club via the pedestrian entrance when he noticed a young girl getting into a *Suburban*, off to his left. As the car pulled away from the curb and drove past him, he realized the young girl was Carey. He pulled out his cell as he ran after the car, trying to get a picture of the license plate, but all he managed was a blurry shot as the car turned at the next side street. I'm a filmmaker and have access to excellent equipment. I played with the file, but no luck.

It's been a week since Michael saw Carey behind the *Clarendon*. Then late this morning, there'd been a call to Carey's mom, by a man who told her he'd seen Carey enter a house on Franklin Street. She called the Vancouver Police and Det. Cpl. Hermes from Missing Persons paid a visit. She phoned Rosaline back and told her that it appeared no one was living there. The caller had been so specific about the location that Rosaline just couldn't believe Carey wasn't there. She asked her niece to please visit the address again — just to be sure. She wanted Amelia to take George with her, but he'd already left the university for a weekend visit home. Amelia left messages for both Kate and me.

Amelia had gone to Kate in the first place because she has a reputation for going to bat for women's rights on campus. What Amelia doesn't know: back in Ireland, Kate ended a relationship with a guy who became physically abusive. He didn't take no for an answer and began stalking her. In Ireland, stalking isn't grounds for a safety order. He showed up at her home, her school, the homes of her friends — a *'friggin' eejit'* was how she described him to me. She finished her last year of high school and a few years after that, looking over her shoulder. I spent more than a few years looking over my shoulder as well.

Thunder Bay is my hometown, and too many young men and women from my community have died under suspicious circumstances. I was in my final year of film studies when I took a semester off to work as a production assistant on another filmmaker's documentary about our missing and murdered Indigenous women. Our missing. Our murdered. I will take my memories of the interviews with their families to my grave.

Greenwood Lake Reserve is where some of my family still live. I'm more beige than brown because of my Irish dad, who never left the house without a sunhat and a liberal dose of sunscreen. Some folks think it's oh so romantic being mixed race these days. Then there's the folks that wish we'd go away. Then there's the folks who think we're the answer to the race problem. But I don't think we are, not yet anyway. My last name's O'Meara and no one ever asks me if I'm Irish.

Canadians are some of the most analyzed people on the planet. The non-Indigenous ones that is. The government did a big study a few years back, wanting to capture illusive information like where everyone comes from and who they're hanging with. I looked it over. There were lots of boxes and you could tick where you came from and your language and whether you married one of your own and they also wanted to know if you didn't. Now the government can talk about how many of who made it here and from where and who speaks what language at home. How many are visible; how many aren't. Kate would say boundaries and borders are pointless in a world were millions have been on the move — *mixing it up* as they say, for centuries now and what's happening in Canada is happening everywhere. She's right. But how we're different is very important to a lot of people.

And then I remember Ray, a friend of my older cousin Maynard, an African-American from Buffalo, NY. They met in Toronto. Ray came up to Thunder Bay a few times to visit Maynard. He loved coming to Canada. *'No heat on us niggers up here. You Indians take our place,'* I remember Ray once saying with a big grin. And my cousins all nodding and Maynard saying, '*He's right about that.*' I was just a kid and I still play that conversation in my mind.

Lucas spent the first ten years of his life in the Guatemalan highlands. He never talks about it. I wish he would. Maybe some day. I've done the reading and I know that part of his childhood included dodging bullets and witnessing atrocities that are difficult to read about, never mind experience. After he finished his masters, he worked for a few years in Vancouver's Downtown Eastside. For lots of the folks he worked with, histories of trauma, individual and collective, fueled addiction and mental illness. People went missing, women, children, men. In some cases, it was years before the VPD would even consider letting the family file a report. When news of the case against serial killer William Picton hit the papers. Lucas was devastated. 49 women dead. Half of Picton's victims were identified as Indigenous and Métis and he'd worked with some of those women, and when they disappeared — their families. He'd tried and often failed to get the attention of the police.

A muffled honk interrupts my thoughts. Kate's here. I quickly don a rain jacket and grab my umbrella. The rain is pouring down and in my dash to the car my pants and shoes get soaked. Kate cranked the heat, but no real chance to dry off because not ten minutes later, we pulled into the curb in front a fish wholesaler, a nondescript, cinderblock building next door to 168 Franklin Street.

As soon as Kate killed the engine and the wipers came to rest, rain coursed across the windshield in waves. The rain had been a constant for days, a grey that matched the sky and those patches of ocean visible only a few blocks away. It was the kind of day where you're happy to see evening come, with its warm, welcoming lights.

168 Franklin Street has a grimy stucco facade and

faded green trim; the only holdout in this dreary, light industrial area — the high windowless walls of a computer parts distributor on one side and on the other, thick trees and the back-alley entrance. If Carey had been brought to this desolate house, what must Amelia be thinking.

"Thank you both for coming," Amelia said, looking sideways at the house. Her face said it all.

"I'm glad I could be here, Amelia," said Kate.

"Me too."

"Auntie Rosie is so hoping that Carey is here," she said as she got out and quickly opened her umbrella against the pouring rain.

Kate's glance caught mine in the rear view, the steady thrum of rain on the roof an unneeded counterpoint. I reached for the wet umbrella on the floor at my feet and exited the car, quickly popping it open. Kate got out and ducked under mine and we followed Amelia back to the address and up the wooden stairs to the front door. I noticed the stairs were a fairly new addition, at odds with the rest of the house. Newer stairs could mean the house was in use. Amelia knocked and we waited. Nothing. Amelia moved to the left of the door and was trying to peer into a grimy side window.

"The curtain is pulled shut," she said.

"Maybe we should go around to the back door," suggested Kate.

"I'll try one more time." I knocked again. We all heard it — the sound of something hitting the floor.

"Someone's in there," said Amelia, reaching for the front door knob. "It's locked."

"Wait. I hear footsteps," she said, her ear to the door and sure enough, moments later, the latch was released and the door opened a few inches to reveal a young woman in her late teens or early twenties.

"I din't order anything." It was hard to miss: the slurred speech; how she had to work hard to stay standing. She was high.

"We're very sorry to bother you," said Amelia.

"We're not delivering anything," I said.

The young woman nodded, like that was a good thing and gave us a faint smile.

"T'at's good, cause I'm not 'ungry." She moved to close the door, so I jumped in quickly.

"We're looking for a young girl. Her name's Carey. Carey Bolton. Is she here?"

"Carey?" she said, looking from me to Amelia to Kate. The smile disappeared. She looked confused.

"That's right," said Amelia. "Carey. She's my cousin. She's 11 years old, about this tall," and she indicated the top of her shoulder. "Have you seen her?"

"No ... No one here. Jus' me," and she tapped herself on the chest. The hand remained there, fingers splayed, like they needed a resting place.

"But she *was* here, wasn't she? Before today I mean?" Amelia tried again, voice full of hope.

"No. Not here," the woman said, shaking her head vehemently. "Like I tol' you. Jus' me."

"But a man called Carey's mother and told her she was at this address," I said.

"He made mist'ke," she said, trying hard to focus as she turned to me with a vacant, hooded stare.

I persisted. "Carey's been missing for more than two weeks and her family is desperate to find her. Please! If you can help us in any way. Was Carey here recently? Maybe she here before but now she's gone?"

"No one here." She'd been leaning against the door jam for support, but now stepped back into the room.

"Please. Wait. You live here alone?" asked Amelia.

The young woman moved to close the door but I applied pressure to keep it open.

"Are you here by yourself?" Kate asked. "It's a big house for one person."

She moved to close the door again, but I moved faster and positioned my foot to prevent her closing it.

"We'll go to the police," I said. "They think no one is living here. We'll tell them you're here."

Her eyes flew wide in confused alarm. She struggled as best she could to close the door.

"Best to let her go, Morgan," said Kate. "You'll not get a thing out of her, not right now anyway."

"But what if she knows something, Kate!"

"Let her go," Kate said again.

Reluctantly, I stepped back and the door slammed in our faces. We heard her struggle with the deadbolt, finally sliding it into place.

"She's not going to give us anything," said Kate. "She's too stoned."

"Kate's right," said Amelia. "I think she's an addict. I don't think she knows anything about Carey." Kate gave Amelia's shoulder a squeeze. "Auntie's going to be so disappointed," she said, heading down the front steps.

Without a word, we followed her to the car. As soon as we were in, Amelia pulled out her cell. "I'll leave a message with Det. Hermes at Missing Persons that someone is living here and ask her to check the place out again."

"That's a good idea," said Kate. "Just to be certain."

"Warn her that the occupants are probably drug users," I added.

"Right," said Amelia.

Kate drove Amelia back to her residence on Burnaby

Mountain, then the two of us came back to the East Village and grabbed a bite at the Pemberton Hotel, just down the hill from the house on Franklin. Lucas was away at a prison reform symposium in Victoria till Monday evening. Kate's husband Bart is a psychiatrist. He was settling in a new patient at West Sanctuary, a trauma clinic, one of the programs of the Institute of Mental Health at the University of BC.

"What do you think, Morgan?" Kate asked me over tea. "That young woman was not happy to see us. I wish I hadn't threatened her with the police. It was stupid of me."

"No. It wasn't. We're all starting to feel desperate."

"She was so wrecked though. Hard to tell if she was lying or just stoned."

"True that."

We finished our tea and retrieved the Prius where Kate had parked it, just west of the Pemberton.

"Let's check the house one more time," said Kate, as she turned right on Victoria Street. We bounced uphill along the cobblestones, slick and shiny with rain, which had backed off to a thin, steady drizzle. She turned onto Franklin and parked in front of the house.

We got out of the car, approached the house and stood at the bottom of the porch stairs, looking up. The house loomed dark. We climbed the stairs to the front door, knocked and waited. When there was no answer, we went around to the rear of the house and up the stairs to the back door. We knocked loudly. There was no sign of life: no lights; no sound from inside the house; not a flicker of movement. The only sound was the rain beating a gentle, irregular patter on the porch.

"I don't think anyone's here now," said Kate.

"It's my fault, Kate!"

"No, it's not, Morgan! I think that whatever was going

on here, isn't now. That's my sense of it."

"Damn!"

"Maybe the guy will call Carey's mom again," said Kate.

The visit to the house left me feeling depressed, tense and very useless. Once Kate dropped me off, I puttered around the cottage for awhile, did a load of laundry and checked my email. No word from Lucas yet but I didn't expect to hear from him tonight. He threw himself wholeheartedly into everything he did and this conference would not be an exception. Prison reform was a subject close to his heart. I didn't want to bother him with bad news about a dead-end lead—especially when there was nothing he could do about it. Instead, I decided on a hot bath, my go to fix for most everything. It was about 10:00 pm when I put on some Bill Evans and climbed into the tub with a mug of tea and my relaxation pillow. A glass of wine would have been more to my liking, but I wanted to have a clear head tomorrow. I was sleepy and the water was lukewarm when I climbed out of the tub, pulled the plug and got ready for bed.

I went for a run early the next morning down at New Brighton Park because relentless drizzle doesn't count as rain in Vancouver, not with me anyway and I needed to wind out. I was back at the cottage by 8:00 am. I changed into warm fleece, then had some yogurt and fruit.

I planned on spending my day editing footage at the Cineworks film lab, but the house on Franklin was pulling me back. I couldn't shake the feeling, so real it was almost visceral, that an opportunity was slipping through our fingers. I decided to visit the house one more time before heading to the lab. I put on a rain jacket, grabbed my briefcase and an umbrella, and headed out into the drizzle.

The curtains on the window closest to the front door were pulled tight, same as last night. I tried the front door first, banging loudly, again and again. If the young woman had come back, she might be a heavy sleeper and it was still early. Then I moved around to the back of the house and tried to peer in the ground level basement windows, but they were filthy with years of grime. I climbed the stairs to the back door; knocked and waited. After a few minutes, I returned to the front door and knocked again. The rain was picking up, so I pulled out my umbrella.

It could be that lots of people came and went, like the young woman here yesterday. I figured it wouldn't hurt to leave my name and cell number and a quick note asking if anyone knew anything about the whereabouts of Carey Bolton, to please get in touch. Her mom was worried sick about her. It was raining hard again. I was careful, as I folded the note and tucked it into the mail slot on the door, not to let it get wet.

I headed over to the Cineworks lab to get some work done. I was editing footage for a documentary I'd finished shooting about Canadian Indigenous women scholars. I kept at it the rest of the morning and for a good part of the afternoon, but my thoughts kept returning to the house on Franklin.

I finally gave up the pretense of trying to work and called Kate, to see if her and Bart wanted to take in a movie later, anything to chase away the hopelessness that was closing in. Kate was feeling just as despondent. I arranged to meet them at the Cineplex downtown.

Much later, back home, despair had its way with me.

Sheets of grey rain raced across the Burrard Inlet. The inlet had been shrouded for five days now and counting. Lucas wasn't back till Monday. He texted me earlier that he was going out for drinks with some buddies from Toronto and he'd call tomorrow afternoon if he got the chance. Something to look forward to.

Last week, Amelia had given us all pictures of Carey and I picked up mine, lying on the coffee table where I'd left it earlier. It was her school picture, taken last year, a beautiful kid with a great big smile. Rosaline. Amelia. Michael. Everyone so desperate now. No one sleeping. It would have been wonderful to find Carey at that house, safe and sound. It would have been wonderful to bring her home.

A strong gust of wind blew sheets of rain against the window and for half a minute, I couldn't see the road below our cottage, or the inlet. Only my forlorn face, suddenly reflected there. I pulled my blanket tighter.

3

It was a difficult decision, but he chose the soft white doggie with the black eyes and red ribbon. Perfect for Carey, a beautiful, innocent child, untouched by the ugliness of this world. She wasn't too old for a stuffed animal. She was only eleven and it would help with the loneliness she might be feeling.

This was a big change for her. He could understand that, but eventually she'd come to realize he wanted the best for her and once they were close, she'd know how lucky she was. He'd buy her some clothes as well. The *Hudson's Bay* store, the children's department. He loved *The Bay*, the bustle and excitement and the wonderful smells. Had loved it since he was a boy and shopped there with his mom.

It would be so much fun to bring Carey shopping and let her choose the things that she liked. Silly of him. That couldn't happen. Not yet. Not until she trusted him and knew he was her friend. Once she grew to truly love him and understood that he wanted only the best for her.

Young girls love pretty things, love to dress up. He knew that. Hadn't he raised a daughter, his own little Wilhelmina, nearly a woman now. Winnie had always loved his presents although lately she seemed standoffish, as though she wanted to put some distance between them.

He blamed that on her mother Sarah, such a poisonous bitch. Doing her best to turn Winnie against him.

He didn't really approve of the way Sarah was allowing Winnie to dress. Far too provocative. She'd always been such a sweet, innocent child. It had meant a lot to him to have a close relationship with Winnie. She was so much like him. But she was sixteen now and probably thought her old dad a bit of a fuddy-duddy. She would always be his little Winnie though, and when she got older, she would understand how much he loved her. He knew that Winnie loved him more, but she had chosen to live with Sarah; probably because she felt sorry for her. Sarah was having a hard time with their separation. She was so insecure, but she had always been that way, depending on him for everything, like a child really. Now though, she was mean and ugly and did nothing but yell at him every chance she got. She was so ungrateful for everything that he'd given her. He wanted to just cut her off without a cent but his lawyer said no, you can't do that, there are laws, and so he had been generous because he didn't want Winnie to suffer, but not too generous. No point giving either of them the wrong idea.

If he was to admit it, he could barely relate to Winnie now. So very different than she used to be. An adult really. Maybe he would just have to let her go. The thought made him sad. They had shared so much.

The sales clerk brought him back to the present, pointing out that the stuffie had a secret compartment. That made it an even better gift. Children love that kind of thing. He purchased the stuffie and hurried down the street to *The Bay*. Once there, he headed to the children's section. He would pick out some warm colours to accent Carey's beautiful skin and she would need underwear and socks, new shoes. Melanie said she was a size 12. While he was at it he would pick up new outfits for all the children. He loved shopping for them.

Melanie certainly didn't, but she was young, barely an adult herself. She didn't realize how precious the children were. Joy was good with them, but they were keeping her busy with other things and she wasn't always available. He'd pressure Phineas to find a replacement for Melanie, preferably a mature adult with experience caring for children. Someone like Joy.

Carey had been awake for a while, but found it hard to open her eyes. It was so much easier not to. Rain was coming down hard, right above her head. Like at home, she thought. There was a truck outside her window, making a high-pitched beeping as it backed up. It was so close, as though she could reach out. Touch it ... This wasn't home.

"Leave me alone! I want to get dressed by myself." Somewhere in the house, a boy. Unhappy. Crying. A door slammed. Swearing. Another voice. "Dress yourself then, for Chrissakes! Just get it done."

Carey's leg began to cramp and she instinctively stretched her leg out straight, then bent her knee. She became aware of warmth and wetness. She looked at the young girl, fast asleep beside her, then sat up, lifted the covers; saw the pee stain under her. She shifted to the dry side, snuggled back down and pulled the covers up to her chin. She glanced sideways at the girl, hoping she would wake up, but she didn't move. She has the most beautiful hair, thought Carey, who had always wanted curly hair.

"Don't touch me ... Please don't ... It hurts! Stop! I don't want to!" Another boy, then a woman's voice; quiet. Carey can't hear what she is saying. The crying stops. The door to Carey's room opens and a young woman enters.

"You're awake. Good. You need to have a shower and put on this dress." She laid the dress over a chair. There's more clothes for you in the dresser. The right side is yours."

"Excuse me, please," said Carey. "Does my mom know I'm here?"

"Get out of bed you little bitch! Now! Get downstairs and eat breakfast. It's on the table. Then get back up here. Have a shower. Get dressed." Carey quickly got out of bed and stood beside it, wincing at the coldness of the floor.

"Is it okay if I call my mom? She'll be worried."

"Get moving. Now! Your boyfriend's coming to visit."

"My boyfriend? There must be some mistake. I don't have a boyfriend. Please. Can I go home now?" The woman ignored her as she pulled back the covers on the sleeping child, then, disgusted, threw them back over her and left the room.

Carey went to the dresser and looked in the right-hand drawers. She found some socks and underwear and a pair of jeans and put them on under the nightgown. She crossed the room to the bed and looked at the sleeping child, reached over and touched her shoulder to see if she could wake her up, but she didn't move. She wanted to ask her where they were. She left the bedroom and went downstairs. She was alone in the kitchen. She could hear a bathtub being filled somewhere in the house. There was yogurt and bananas and apples on the table. She found a bowl in the cupboard and a spoon in one of the kitchen drawers. She ate a few spoons of yogurt and reached for a banana. She peeled it half way and started to eat it, but her stomach lurched and she wanted to vomit. That's when she started to cry.

"Shut up down there! Finish eating and get your ass up here."

"I'm coming." Carey got up from the table and moved to the back door. Right there. Quietly tried to open it, but it was locked. She started looking in the cupboards for the key.

"Get your ass up here. Now!"

A man came to visit in the early afternoon. Carey thought he must be important and that's why she had to wear a grown-up dress for him. He brought new clothes and toys for everyone. He had a white stuffie for her. She didn't want to hurt his feelings so she pretended to like it. He'd bought clothes for her too. The dresses he bought were for someone much younger. Not like the one she was wearing which was so embarrassing. Her mom would never let her wear it.

The man who stole her from Terrace went and got food for everyone and the visitor ate with them. Carey was scared when he put his arm around her like he was her father. She didn't know what to do. But he was nice and he told her not to be scared. She tried hard not to be and told him that she wanted to go back home and could she please call her mom. He told her not to worry. They would take good care of her and everything would be okay once they got it all sorted out.

Before the visitor left, he told Carey he'd be back Friday because he was taking her for a special welcome dinner. He told Melanie which dress he wanted Carey to wear that night. Melanie was mad about that, but she didn't say anything. He chose two other kids to come to dinner with them and told Melanie to make sure they were dressed nicely. The girl who slept with Carey was coming. The other girl that he chose started to cry and asked could she please not go, but the visitor said no, it was a special request. Melanie grabbed the girl's arm and took her upstairs to one of the bedrooms but she wasn't nice about it and the girl had to run to keep up.

After he left, a boy named Christopher told Carey that you have to do everything they tell you even if you don't want to and even if it hurts and no one gets to go home and she'd better stop asking or Melanie would hit her. She asked him where they were, but he didn't know. She asked him how long he'd been here but he couldn't remember. A man brought him here and before that he lived in Quebec with his foster parents. But he knew they weren't in Quebec because when they were driving around in the car all the signs were in English.

The kids were watching a movie when Melanie left the house. Carey heard her lock the door. The man who stole her came in and turned off the TV and told them they had to go to bed now. She knew why because she heard the visitor tell him that there would be visitors tomorrow night and make sure the kids were rested. He gave them all a blue pill, like the one he gave her the first night. He checked to make sure everyone swallowed it, then he took them upstairs and told them to get undressed and go to sleep. He told Carey to sleep with Marie. 'She likes you,' he said. Carey got a towel from the bathroom, folded it and put it under the sheet on Marie's side of the bed. Then they climbed in. Marie took her hand and held it tight, but didn't say anything. She hadn't said anything all day although sometimes, she made strange, grunting sounds. She wanted to ask someone why visitors were coming tomorrow night, but no one else asked.

4

My hair is floating free. I'm in the tub. Must have fallen asleep. The water's cold. Why didn't Lucas wake me up, like he always does when I fall asleep in the tub ... Morgan, my lazy princess, let me warm up your tub, your highness ... Lucas. Must have gone out. Something's bunched up under my neck. My bath pillow ... No ... It isn't. Bath pillow is comfortable. I must have used a towel and it shifted while I was sleeping and now it's wet. I'll just turn on the hot water. Then I'll find my bath pillow.

Oops. I slipped off the towel. It's pulling on my neck ... That hurts ... It's tied to my neck ... It's not a towel. It's my hoodie ... Why am I wearing my hoodie in the tub? I'll just shift my head. Damn. Cold water is going into my ears ... Really cold ... I'm not in the tub ... Better open my eyes.

So beautiful. Wow ... the sky's so close. Like I can touch it. Thick with stars ... But it's so cold ... I'm outside ... lying in water ... No ... my head's in water. Running. On the beach ... Fell on the beach. Right ... It's the ocean ... ocean waves. If I roll over ... I can get up. Have to go home. Damn, that hurts. These pebbles are sharp ... digging into my cheek. Get off these pebbles ... I need to get up. Need to use my hands ... Hands ... Feels like they're asleep ... Oh ... No wonder ... I'm laying on them. Need to roll over. Bring them forward ... Can't ... They're stuck. Can't move my hands. They're not stuck. They're tied behind me!

"Shit." Can't hear my voice ... I can't hear my voice ... Can't talk. My throat is sore ... so sore ... hard to swallow. Awful smell? From the rag. He made me breathe it. Didn't want to. Tried not to ... Shit ... I'm scared. No. No. Can't be scared ... Don't be afraid. It's okay Morgan. You need to get up. If I can just stand up. My head hurts. It's bleeding. Must have banged my head. When I fell. My feet are too high. Need to get my head up higher. Higher than my feet. Bend my knees and pull my feet downhill, far as I can. That's better. Now, lift myself. Over the pebbles. Hard to do. Shift up. Up. I'm tired. Really tired. Have to do it again. One more time. A little bit further. Get my head a little higher. Up the slope ... That's better. The sand feels so good under my cheek. Nice and cool. Rest here, just for a little while. Have a nap. On the slope. Very steep. Running near the ocean ... Night time ... Love running at night ... By the ocean. Can't smell the ocean.

No lights ... No boats ... Not the inlet ... Where? Need to get up. Now! ... Get up. Roll over onto my knees ... Damn ... Everything really hurts ... Don't make any noise ... Need to get up ... Get my feet under me ... Stand up. Shift some weight to my left knee. Pull my right foot forward. My runner's caught ... Careful. Don't fall. Bring it forward. That's it. Shit! I'm going to fall. No! Can't fall ... Slower ... Go slower ... Okay. Right foot is under me ... Now. Shift my weight to it. Careful. Nice and slow. Pull my left foot forward. Get it under me. I'm falling ... Not falling ... Just dizzy ... Raise my head and torso ... Wait ... Wait. Find my balance ... Dig in and push up, hard as I can. Fuck ... Nothing is happening! Can't do it. Can't stop shaking ... Wait ... Just wait ... Don't give up. Try again. Okay. Halfway up. Almost there. I can do this. I know I can do this ... Balance ... Lean forward ... Keep legs strong

... Damn ... Hurts ... Push up ... Slow. Nice and slow ... I'm up! ... I'm up! ... Dizzy ... So dizzy ... Wait it out ... I'm gonna fall ... Can't fall. Don't fall. Air is cold ... Hoodie's wet ... Cold against my back. Head hurts ... Can't wait ... Don't wait ... No time ... Move ... Now ... Slow ... Keep your balance ... Climb the slope ... Not far ... A few more feet ... Almost there. Almost there. Okay, you made it! ... Oh no! Shit! The blue truck. He's here! Where? ... Where the hell is he? No. No. I won't get away! He's going to kill me ... Now! Get away now! Those trees ... to the right. Help me. Someone please ... No one here ... I'm weaving like a drunk. Don't fall ... Don't fall. Can't fall. Not now ... So dizzy ... Don't fall ... Keep going ... Shit! He's going to catch me! No ... No. Don't think that. Get into the trees ... Hide in the trees. *You Are My Sunshine* ... It's him! Whistling. Doesn't know I'm getting away! Find a place ... hide ... Can't help ... stumbling ... Keep going... Where's the trail ... here ... It's here ... Damn ... Legs are shaking ... Have to hide ... No where to hide! ... What was that? A flame ... right there. Gone now. Shit! ... I'm hallucinating. No ... there. Another flame, and another, and another. So many! Thick brush. Can't see in. Oh no! My legs. I'm down ... Can't get up. Doesn't matter. Need to rest. Shit. He'll find me ... Wait ... Here ... in here ... A place to hide! Get off the path. Wiggle in, feet first ... Move faster ... Can't. The brambles ... Low ... Ouch ... Hurts. Not enough room. Push ... Harder ... Make it bigger. Pull yourself ... All the way in ... Pull my head in ... Almost ... in ... I'm in ... Is my hair in? Don't know. Thumping. Heavy boots. He's coming. Slivers of light. His flashlight. Blood ... running down my nose. In my mouth ... Salty. Take a few more breaths. Don't make a sound. One last breath ... Hold it.

Shit . . . his boot ... inches from my face. Paint spatters on the toe caught in an arc of light ... His flashlight.

"Fucking bitch!" His voice is deep and guttural and I wince with fear. Feel the pee seep between my legs. But he can't see me! He can't see me! Hold still ... He's moving away. Footsteps are fading. I can't hear them now.

Where am I? Water isn't salty. A lake. What lake? Where? ... So many stars ... No stars in the city. What's that smell? ... On my clothes ... Sweet. Sickening ... Making me sick ... Can't vomit. Can't make a sound ... Need fresh air ... Have to move my head. Just a little. My neck is sore. Hurts ... Box ... I was in a box. Hard to breathe ... Someone yelling ... *Do what you want ... Get rid of her* ... Me ... Get rid of me ... Have to stay awake. Can't let him find me. Have to ... Stay ... Awake ... So tired.

5

Lucas Arenas is a man who turns heads. People are drawn to him. It isn't that he's particularly tall, or wildly handsome, although he does have large, expressive blue eyes, thick lashes; a beautiful smile. It's the intelligence and sadness and hope that invite everyone in. The eyes are his dad's. His smile is his mom's, a tiny 4′ 8″ *Ixil-Maya* woman.

He is staring out on the Burrard Inlet and the Port of Vancouver, watching the rain sweep down on the business and industry that booms, 24 hours a day, oblivious to weather. Ocean going vessels, moored here and there in the deep waters, flash now and then through a rainy curtain.

When he went to search for Morgan the first time, he saw his car parked near the entrance to the trails, but no sign of her anywhere. Then he called close friends Kate Brennan and Bart Morris and the three of them went to New Brighton and searched for her again. They covered the trails by the ocean first, just as he had earlier, then made their way along the thickly wooded Canada Trail which ran beside the inlet — a last resort, just in case.

It was late when Kate and Bart went home, with a promise to return early the next morning. But he knew and they knew. She was gone. He called the VPD. The woman he spoke with was understanding but insisted he had to wait 24 hours before he could file a missing person's report. He knew that. But he was out of his mind with worry and not thinking clearly.

It was still a while before first light. He looked down at Carey Bolton's smiling face, her picture beside Morgan's favorite camera on the table in front of him. He reached for the camera and cradled it to his chest. It was the Canon she took to Guatemala on their trip earlier in the year. Her amazing pictures — his Guatemala through her eyes, a filmmaker's eyes. She'd arrived in his life, laughing and hooting at Kate's side, instantly serious when Kate introduced them. He remembered how eye to eye they took each other's measure — her dark eyes serious, his blue eyes laughing. There should have been trumpets heralding your arrival in my life, he said. People don't arrive in your life, she'd laughed, enjoying how he used language. You arrived in mine, he insisted, like a head of state. I could not resist your eyes, she told him. I have my father's eyes, he said. Her didn't tell her, not right away, that he was the second child born to his parents; that his older brother had been stillborn.

In less than a month they were sleeping together every night. After a few months, they found the cottage and moved in together. There wasn't enough room for all his pots and pans or their libraries or her precious 16 mm film stock and film drafts and shot reels which prompted many trips to Ikea and finally, when they couldn't fit it all in, a storage locker nearby.

They'd been together seven years now. After a while, he'd given up taking pictures altogether. Why bother. Morgan was born with a photographer's eye and a storyteller's soul. In Nebaj, his first time back in Guatemala, he'd taken her to see the Catholic church, so imposing, right on the town square. Lucas wanted pictures and he wanted Morgan to take them. He watched her capture the towering, hand carved front door, then close-ups of the Mayan religious and cultural symbols that adorned it; carved 400 years ago but looking as though they'd been carved yesterday. Then inside the church: All the Stations of the Cross but especially a larger than life Black Christ with Anglo features — on his knees, blood dripping from his crown of thorns, threatening to move right into the room and take over the aisle. And the altar: beautiful angels and the white Virgin floating above them all. It wasn't a trip for pleasure though.

Guatemala City: dry, dusty and hot, the rainy season not yet begun; the trip from the airport to Zone 10, a walled compound and the friendly armed guard; the quaint hotel behind its own stucco walls; the owner who chatted amiably with them while they registered. Lucas remembered now, when his eyes happened on the magazine for army veterans on the registration counter — his frisson of fear, a sucker punch. The owner had been in the army. Lucas had to struggle for composure and when he looked up, the owner was watching him. Over 600 unofficial massacres, over 200,000 murdered — Ríos Montt's reign of terror — genocide, Guatemalan style with American expertise and guns and when some of their citizens started to question that involvement, US client states more than willing to supply what Montt needed. Montt on trial in Guatemala City when they arrived; the country holding its collective breath. Many of his mom's people were in the city, some of them testifying.

He remembered Morgan telling the owner they weren't here to see the pyramids. And the owner telling her he'd never served in the highlands, his eyes on Lucas. The highlands — where most of the killing took place — far away from prying eyes. He wanted Lucas to know that his hands were clean. That he didn't participate in the genocide. But Lucas remembered when he looked in the owner's eyes, how quickly he lowered his gaze and he wondered how clean his hands were.

He closed his eyes and he was on a narrow, mountain path in the Guatemalan highlands, walking behind another man, a tiny procession of Ixil men and women, each of them carrying a small coffin holding the remains of a loved one killed in an army massacre almost 30 years before. His father in the little box he carried in his arms.

The first rays of dawn lit up the underbelly of rain clouds. Lucas was awake instantly. He couldn't wait for Kate and Bart. He pulled on a jacket and left the cottage, ran the short distance downhill to New Brighton Park, allowed himself to hope. Maybe Morgan had fallen and was badly hurt. Maybe she was lying somewhere, unconscious, where they hadn't been able to find her last night. In the rain. In the darkness.

The air was thick with cold drizzle. Oblivious, he passed his car, still sitting in the parking lot where she'd parked it last night — running at full speed now through the pedestrian underpass to the trails along the beach.

6

A shaft of sunlight warms my nose and cheek. Daytime. What day? I'm under brush. It's so thick. Can't move around. The earth is cold under my cheek. Musty leaves. I want to sneeze. The path just inches from my head. Must have come in that way. Feet first ... I'm hiding. Hiding. Man said ... just get rid of her. Get rid of her. Don't care what you do. Get rid of her. Who said that? The man in the truck. Was he there? With the others? Need water. The lake ... I'm so thirsty. . . It's hard to move around. My hands are so numb. Can't feel them. Can't feel my hands! Taped. Need to get the tape off. Need to get out of here. Get my head out first. Don't see him. Maybe he's gone. Wiggle out. Onto path. Get up. My legs. Like rubber. Oh no. Falling back. Ouch ... I'm weaving. A little dizzy. Lean against tree. Wait till my head clears. Not too long. He must be here. Hard to keep my balance. Take it slow. Don't fall. The lake. Already. Sunshine is too bright. Hurts my eyes. The blue truck. Still here! Shit! My heart. Pounding. Can't breathe. I'm peeing. Shit! Get back into the trees! Stay calm. He's not behind me. He's not on the shore ... Can't see him at the truck. If I can't see him, he's looking for me. Need to do something. Don't know what to do. What's that? A motor. Getting louder. A motorboat! To my left, just beyond that point of land. Coming this way!

I have to get down to the shore. My only chance. All downhill. Don't fall. Can't fall now. Take a wider stride. Angle your feet out. There's the boat! It's heading across the lake, right in front of me!

"Help!" I can't hear myself. They won't hear me! They're not looking! I'll wade in. The boat's wake is strong. Hard to keep my balance. Two people. Fishing poles dangling off the back. Get their attention. Wade in further, almost to my knees now. Move sideways. Please look here. Over here ... Damn ... So many rocks. One of them is reaching for a fishing pole. Does he see me? He sees me! He sees me! He's pointing at me! They're turning the boat around. They're heading toward me!

"Leave her alone, asshole!"

"Don't you dare lay a hand on her!"

He's here! Shit! Have to go deeper. Hard to stand. The boat is closing in fast and they're yelling at him at the top of their lungs. He's grabs for me and falls hard on his right arm and knee. He's up again. Swings toward me. Boat's so close now. It's too late. He hauls himself out of the water and sprints toward the truck.

They've cut the motor. He's bringing the boat beside me and I'm crying like a baby but I don't care. It's gonna be okay. They're out of the boat. She puts her arm around me and helps me out of the water and onto the sand. My legs buckle under me and I'm down. She's stays with me, holding on tight and helps me to sit. We all turn to watch as the blue truck spins away up the road and disappears around a bend.

"I couldn't read the license," she said.

"Me neither," he said. He tied the boat up and was quickly pulling stuff out of it.

"Water please," I managed to croak out, my voice barely a whisper. But she understood.

"Alex, she needs water."

He's beside us now and hands her a water bottle and places a first-aid kit on the sand beside her. She opens the bottle and she holds it to my lips. One side of my mouth isn't cooperating, but I manage to get some of the delicious, wet water into my mouth and swallow it.

"Thank you so much, for stopping, for helping me," all of it whispers into a mouthful of cotton.

"Don't try to talk. You're going to be okay honey. Everything's going be okay. My name's Gwen. This is Alex." Her companion is a strongly built man with thick, black hair showing a little grey. He's a brother and I find that very comforting. She's a youngish woman, with warm, brown eyes and her dark hair gleams auburn where it catches the sunlight. He's holding a knife at his side.

"I'll cut that tape around your wrists. It won't take long and you'll be a lot more comfortable. Just hold as still as possible." I nodded gratefully. He moved behind me and worked carefully, cutting the tape where it joined the back of the wrists and then the front, leaving flaps of tape attached to both my arms.

I moved my hands into my lap. It was such a relief to feel the blood surge into my arms and hands, but that was quickly followed by intense and painful pins and needles.

"We'll leave the tape attached for now. When we get you to the hospital, they'll have something to remove it without a lot of unnecessary pain."

"I'm going to clean up the gash on your forehead though, right now," said Gwen. "It's deep and I'm worried about infection."

"That one might need stitches," Alex agreed. "Looks like it's bleeding?"

"Oozing. I'll butterfly tape it for now. They can make a decision at the hospital whether to stitch it."

I must have blacked out. I'm on my side by the water's edge, some kind of a bandage taped to my forehead and a blanket over me. Between them, they helped me climb into the rear of the boat. I settled in, leaning on a wooden seat for support. Gwen climbed in behind me and re-wrapped the blanket around me, then put a lifejacket under my head. Alex pushed the boat clear of the shore. Then he climbed in and he and Gwen took up the oars and started to paddle out, turning the boat around until it faced the middle of the lake. He started the motor then and steered the boat back in the direction they'd come from.

I dozed until the feel of the bottom of the boat shifting up against sand brought me around. We were disembarking on another shore, a small, snug little inlet. The sun was higher now and the air is heavy with the smell of pines. I could see a vehicle on a small access road, about six metres from the shore. It was theirs, a dark green truck with a camper trailer hitched to the back.

They helped me out of the boat. Alex tied it up to a narrow wooden dock. Then the two of them supported me for the short walk to their truck and helped me climb up and into the cab. I sat between them. Alex got behind the wheel and helped Gwen hold me steady so they could tuck a blanket around me and fasten my seatbelt. The last thing I remember was Alex talking on a radio to someone about the guy in the blue truck. When I came to, I was leaning into Gwen's shoulder. She was doing her best to prop me up, which must have been difficult as my body felt like it was made of rubber and at five feet, ten inches, I was head and shoulders over her. It was too much of an effort to open my eyes, so I just listened to them talk.

"This road gets worse every year. Too bad we can't go faster."

"The cowboys don't need roads; they're on horseback

most of the time."

"Cowboys?" I whispered. I love cowboys.

Gwen understood me. "You're in cattle country," she said.

"The cut-off's just up here on the right. We'll be at the hospital in twenty minutes," said Alex.

When we arrived at the hospital, Alex hopped out and fetched a wheelchair and they helped me into it. Alex wheeled me into emergency, Gwen walking along beside us.

Alex, turned out to be Sgt. Alex Desocarras, an officer with the 100 Mile House detachment of the Royal Canadian Mounted Police. As soon as we were at the front desk, he was on his cell, talking with someone about the guy at the lake.

"We rescued this woman about two hours ago at Gustafsen Lake," Gwen told the admitting clerk. "She's been through an ordeal. We've no idea how badly she's injured."

I tried to give the clerk my name, but in the end, I made the universal writing movement and was given paper and pen. Once she knew I was Morgan O'Meara and she had my address in Vancouver, she found me in the health care database. The clerk's face was positively alarmed at the sight of me.

"Morgan, is there someone I can call for you?"

I nodded, took up pen again and wrote: Lucas Arenas, partner, our address on Trinity Street in Vancouver, and phone numbers where he could be reached. Alex watched as I wrote and took note of the information.

"Vancouver is about 450 km away, so about five hours by car," said Gwen.

He looked at his notes. "Does Lucas have a car?"

I nodded yes.

Two nurses moved me to a stretcher and wheeled me to an examination cubicle. One of them prepared a site on my forearm for an IV and quickly hooked me up. The other tucked me in with warm blankets. Then the two of them cleaned up the scratches and abrasions. One of them cleaned my forehead, prepping me, she said, for stitches. I had no idea when the damage to my forehead was done, but the staff were sure it had been less than 12 hours. The cut was deep and still oozing, so they stitched it up. One of the nurses used a solution to ease the flaps of tape from my wrists.

The next few hours went by in a blur of x-rays, doctors and emergency room nurses. I heard one of the orderlies tell another that he was starting his holidays tomorrow, which was Friday.

I beckoned him closer. "What day?" I whispered.

"It's Thursday, October 9th."

Thursday. I shook my head in disbelief. Tuesday, I led a film lab at SFU. then drove to New Brighton Park for a run. It's just 10 minutes from our cottage on Trinity Street. That was two days ago.

"Good news Morgan," said Sandra, one of the nurses. "The clerk reached your partner. He's on his way."

I could feel the tears sliding down my cheeks.

"It's gonna be okay Morgan," said Gwen, touching my arm gently, then getting up to fetch me some tissues.

Sandra had given me something for pain earlier. The attending ER doctor had requested full x-rays which revealed no broken bones. They'd also done a pretty thorough head to toe exam, which I mostly dozed through. After that, they wanted to do a rape kit. I said yes. My hips, my thighs, my vagina, my pelvis were all hurting bad. I couldn't remember what happened, or when, or where, but I knew I'd been raped. After the rape kit, a lab tech took some blood for a toxicology screen. The ER doctor wanted to keep me overnight for observation.

"No," I whispered, and shook my head as vehemently as I could. I was going home as soon as Lucas got here.

The doctor reluctantly agreed to let me travel, but cautioned me to continue with the medication he'd prescribed and watch for any discharge from my right ear, ringing sounds, or uneven pupil size. If any of those symptoms. surfaced, I was to consider myself in very big trouble and get myself to a hospital immediately. I nodded my understanding. For good measure, he wrote all of that down and listed the hospitals between 100 Mile House and Vancouver. Once the hospital staff were done, I went to sleep for real. When I woke up it was nearly 11:00 am according to the wall clock just outside my cubicle and Gwen was with me. She'd made a trip home to fetch me some clothes to wear: a pair of faded jeans and a plaid shirt, warm wool socks, and she'd nabbed one of her husband's old jackets as well. She helped me get dressed. Never had well worn, comfy clothes felt so heavenly.

Gwen told me Alex had asked a nurse to bundle my filthy and torn running gear into a clean, plastic bag. He'd already taken it to the 100 Mile House Detachment office for delivery to the RCMP forensics lab in Vancouver.

Then Alex poked his head in and told me that someone named Cpl. James was waiting at the detachment to take a statement from me. He'd been to the hospital earlier and asked Alex to bring me over when I was ready. Gwen intervened.

"Let's get her something to eat first, Alex. I'll bet she's hungry."

"Good idea Gwen. We all need to eat." They hadn't eaten since 5:00 am, just before they headed out fishing.

We picked up breakfast-to-go from Barney's, a restaurant in town that specialized in all-day breakfast and took ours to the detachment. I didn't have to sit in public and have people stare at me which was a relief. I wasn't really hungry, but I didn't want to refuse their kindness. The first time I used the washroom this morning I was very groggy. I was standing at the sink washing my hands and I raised my head to look in the mirror. I've never suffered physical abuse of any kind and it was a shock to see my bruised and battered face. I held on to the sink and watched the tears well up and trickle down the cheeks of this woman who was me, but not me. My right eye was black and blue and partly swollen shut. Another large, purple bruise took up most of my right cheek. I leaned forward, felt the lump on my forehead beneath the stitches, followed the line of stitches from my eyebrow to my hairline. My lips were dry and cracked open in spots and my bottom lip was swollen and hung down on one side. My neck had some ugly bruises too. I looked grotesque, not quite human. Even so, I couldn't look away, tried to memorize this face — make it real. If I had a camera, I would take pictures. No. I didn't want to take pictures. Maybe they took pictures. They could give me copies. I need pictures ... Maybe not ... Maybe I don't need pictures. It was a few minutes before I got my tears under control and limped back to my cubicle. What I really wanted was to be at home, in bed, away from prying eyes. But this wasn't over yet. There was still the interview. Then wait for Lucas to get here and take me home.

I was surprised by the size of the RCMP detachment building. I'd noticed a population sign indicating this was a small town of 2,000 people, so I expected a police station of two or three rooms with a jail in the back. But it was a modern, spacious structure and no jail cells in sight. Alex led the way to his office in a wing to the left of the main entrance.

We gathered around his desk and they dug into containers of bacon, eggs, hash browns and buttered toast and washed it down with coffee. The coffee was easy to get down and I did manage a little poached egg although it took a lot of willpower to keep it down. Another sip of coffee; try not to vomit.

"You guys are great," I whispered. I could tell they had no idea what I'd just said, so I just put my hand over my heart, and gave them a lopsided smile. There was so much more I wanted to say, but settled on, "thanks." They got that. Gwen and Alex had an easy grace about them, and despite my unease about my appearance, I felt okay with them.

"Well, Morgan, it isn't often one gets a chance to be a hero," Gwen said, with feeling. "As for him," she chuckled, pointing at her husband. "He gets to do that all the time."

That got a grin from Alex. "Not as often as I'd like."

"How are you feeling, Morgan?" he asked.

"Not bad," I whispered. I was sore all over, and my head felt like it belonged to someone else, but the pain meds were working and took the edge off.

"When we're done here, you'll be giving a statement to Cpl. James. He's an investigator out of Williams Lake. I gave mine this morning and filed a report, while you were at the hospital and so did Gwen. It's important that we not discuss what happened this morning with you beforehand. It's standard procedure. Anything you can remember may help us catch who did this to you."

I nodded. "You may find talking about it what happened difficult. Just take your time — all the time you need. And if you're not able to finish here, don't worry about that. We can always arrange for you to give your statement in Vancouver."

Moments later, an officer appeared at the door, carrying a notebook and a sheaf of papers. He nodded hi to Alex.

"You must be Morgan O'Meara," he said. "I'm Cpl. James. I've been assigned to interview you regarding your rescue at Gustafsen Lake. I've been in touch with Det. Sgt. Fernice of the VPD. She's leading the investigation into your abduction in Vancouver and she'll want to interview you when you get back. I won't be working your case though. Sgt. Desocarras and Det. Fernice will be working your case jointly."

I looked at Alex. He nodded. Alex was on my case. That was good news.

"I'd like to get a statement from you now, if you're up to it."

I nodded and rising, slowly followed James out the door to an interview room further down the hall. Once inside, he closed the door and gestured to a table and several chairs in the room.

"Can I get you some water?" he asked.

I nodded yes and sat down at the table.

Lifting the wall phone handset, James asked someone at the other end to bring us water. Then he switched on a recorder, stated the time and day, Thursday, October 9, 2015 and our names.

"Ms. O'Meara, I'm going to keep this interview short. We can stop at any time if this becomes too difficult for you."

I nodded.

"Okay, let's start at the beginning. Your full name is Morgan Ailis O'Meara." When I nodded yes, James asked me to speak my answers, so that the recorder could capture them.

"Yes and no answers are fine."

"Yes." My voice was a soft whisper, so he adjusted the recorder levels.

"Should be okay now. It's a sensitive mic." He consulted his notes. "You live in Vancouver, with Lucas Arenas."

"Yes."

He watched the input level as I spoke. "Good. We're capturing your voice now. Mr. Arenas is your husband?"

I shook my head no. "Partner."

"And are you employed in Vancouver?"

"Yes, filmmaker. Also, TA, SFU, film; part-time."

"Teaching Assistant in the Film Department at SFU?"

"Yes."

"Where is the film department located?"

"SFU, Woodward's campus." The long answer is I'm a teaching assistant to Sophia Paridopolis, an associate prof of Film at SFU. Sophia lectures for FPA 130, an intro to film studies. I worked for her, the same course, as an MA student a few years back, so when one of the TAs fell ill the first week of classes, she asked me to fill in. I said yes because I need the money. I'm an independent filmmaker and my personal joke is that at any given time, I'm in need of hundreds of thousands, if not millions of dollars.

After glancing briefly at a report in his hand, he continued, "Are you a runner?"

"Yes." I took another sip of water. This was going to be harder than I thought. My throat feels like sandpaper.

"I know Det. Fernice will cover this as well, but before we get to the events at the lake, I want you to think back to what happened to you in Vancouver. You live on Trinity Street. That's in the East Village, near the Burrard Inlet, near the Ironworkers Bridge, right?"

"Yes." I paused for more water.

"I know Vancouver pretty well. I was stationed there for a few years. New Brighton Park is close to where you live."

"Yes." The last part of my sentence was lost in a surprise fit of coughing, which I had trouble getting under control. James paused here and looked at me, his concern obvious. "If this is too hard we can stop."

"No," I whispered.

"Okay. If you're sure." He looked doubtful, but I waved for him to continue. "It is helpful for us to get the details from you while they're still fresh in your mind. According to your partner's statement, you drove to New Brighton Park for a run. That would be the early evening of Tuesday, October 7th?"

"Yes." I'd driven to New Brighton Park, after the film lab ended. It was the last thing I clearly remember before coming to, on the shore of Gustafsen Lake.

"So, after the film lab, you changed into your running clothes and then drove to New Brighton Park."

"Yes."

"You didn't change into running gear at the park itself?"

"No."

"What time did you arrive at the park?"

"6:30 pm." I paused for another sip of water.

"Where did you park?"

"Pedestrian entrance." A flash of disconnected images and voices swirled in my head, but when I tried to pin them down and make sense of them they slipped away.

James noticed. "Is there something you're remembering?"

"No," and I made a circular motion with one hand. I said no more as I couldn't remember anything that happened after I left the car.

"Okay. You locked your car?"

"Yes."

"How close were you to the pedestrian entrance?"

"10 metres." I held up ten fingers as well.

"Was there anyone else in the car park area?"

"Couple," and I mimicked two people walking in front of me.

"Okay, couple walking. Anyone else?"

"Yes. Man, bent over trunk, my left." More gestures.

"Do you remember actually going for a run?"

"No."

James made a note. "Did you recognize the man leaning into the trunk of his car?"

"No."

"Did you notice what was he wearing?"

I thought for a moment. "Jeans, shirt, boots; freckles on arms; long hair; brown."

"And did you see his face?"

"No."

"Were you really close when you walked past him?"

"Yes." I remember the guy clearly; I could have reached out and touched him."

"What colour was his car?"

"Red-orange."

"Did you see the license plate?"

"No."

"Anything distinguishing about the car itself?" I thought about that a bit.

"Dull paint." I paused again, but this time, didn't resume talking as I couldn't remember anything else.

"Okay" he said, more scribbling in his notebook. "You have a good memory."

I nodded. I'm a filmmaker and physical details are important. I appraised Cpl. James now — the small scar on his chin, brown hair, clean shaven, light blue eyes.

"Do you remember anything about your abduction?"

"No."

"Okay Morgan, let's move to Gustafsen Lake and the events there. What's the first thing you remember?"

"Lying in water. Night. Hands taped." I moved to mimic my hands behind my back. Just saying the words, '*hands taped*', and I was back at the lake. Frightened. I'm frightened here, now, I thought, but didn't tell him that. I was glad that talking was so hard.

"Are you okay?"

He did notice. "Yes ... Got up. To woods. Hid."

"Your hands were taped behind you and you got up and"

"climbed bank"

"and hid in the woods?

"Yes." I reached for my water glass, but it was empty.

"Would you like a cup of coffee, or tea?"

I nodded yes. "Coffee. Water."

"Sugar, cream?"

I nodded yes, and James made a phone call requesting both.

"Okay Morgan. What else do you remember?"

"Morning ... to lake. Boat came."

"You hid all night?" said James, surprised.

"Yes."

"No sign of your abductor at this point?"

"No."

"Okay. Did you see his face, the man at the lake?"

"Yes."

"Do you know him, or have you ever seen him before?"

"No."

"You're quite sure you don't know him?"

"Yes."

James continued to look at me after I had finished speaking, holding my gaze. There was a knock at the door and my coffee and water were delivered. I immediately took a sip of both.

"What physical characteristics can you remember about your assailant?"

I thought about this, visualizing the man as he made a grab for me in the water.

"Big. 6′3″, 4″. White. Cap. Shirt, pants, shiny green."

"Anything else?"

"Red face." I remembered how he slipped and fell in the water. "Big hands. Crooked finger." I indicated the middle finger of my left hand."

"Middle finger of his left hand is crooked?"

"Yes."

"You're doing great, Morgan. We're almost done. I have just a few more questions that I have to ask and I want you to think very carefully before you answer. Is there anyone known to you that would want to harm you, in any way, perhaps an ex-boyfriend or lover?"

"No."

"Are you getting on well with your partner?" he asked, looking at his notes.

"Yes."

"Have you ever cheated on Mr. Arenas?"

That question caught me by surprise. I looked at Sgt. James, trying to make sense of where he was coming from. I guess he had to ask.

"No. Love him," I finally whispered.

"Well, you can be in love and still not mind getting a little extra on the side?"

I remained silent and stared at him.

"Unfortunately, Ms. O'Meara, I have to ask these questions. In most assault cases, the victim knows her assailant. I need to know if you gave your partner any reason to be jealous, to want to do you harm."

"No."

James tried another tactic. "Try to understand my position. We get a lot of native girls in here. Now, don't get me wrong. You seem to have really made something of yourself, beat the odds, if you know what I mean." I was instantly enraged.

"A native girl might be getting a little on the side because she's a native girl and that's what we do! And this might upset her boyfriend, who might hire a hit man to kill her." Everything I said came out as hoarse, unintelligible whispers and it was obvious James hadn't understood a single word. I was racked by another violent fit of coughing and grabbed the water glass.

Stupid bastard. I'd come so close to joining hundreds of my sisters — the ones that don't end up sitting across the table from guys like Cpl. James or anyone else. Found dead or gone, vanished, never to be seen again. Thinking that, I was suddenly frightened — felt a chill race up my spine. I shuddered and the fear must have showed on my face.

"Ms. O'Meara, I'm not trying to upset you. Like I said, I have to ask these questions. Unfortunately, most of the time, we have to look first at the husband, or boyfriend, because they are most often responsible."

I quickly went from being frightened to angry again and I glared at him.

James didn't miss the glare and maybe thinking I'd had enough he chose that moment to end the interview.

"If you're up to it, I'd like you to look at some mug shots of criminals with a history of this kind of assault."

Despite how tired I was, I nodded agreement — happy to get James out of the room. Something to do while I waited for Lucas.

"Is there anything else I can get you?" he asked, before fetching the binders.

I shook my head and sat back with a sigh of relief and closed my eyes, happy to be finally silent.

A short while later, James returned with the binders and quickly left the room. I began to look through them. It wasn't easy. There was something about the eyes of a lot of the men staring up at me. Page after page of men with vacant eyes, watchful eyes, mean, piercing eyes. Some eyes were kind, even reproachful. Often though, these eyes stared the camera down. I flashed on the desperation and anger in the eyes of my attacker as he reached for me. His mouth set, hard and grim when he realized I was slipping through his fingers. I would never forget his face and I didn't find his picture in any of these binders. When I was through, I put my head down on the table and fell asleep.

"Where is Morgan? Where is she?" Lucas was here! His voice so loud it woke me up. I struggled to my feet. As he burst into the room, I leaned on the table for support, then sank back into my chair.

"Morgan! What happened to you? I've been so worried! Who did this to you?" he cried out in anguish as he rushed to my side, tears brimming.

"I'm fine."

"Honey, I can't hear you. What's wrong with your voice?"

"I'm fine," I said again, right in his ear.

"No, you're not fine! Look at you! Sweetheart, what happened to your face? Your voice? You can't speak! Don't try to talk." He sat down beside me, completely oblivious to James who'd followed him into the room and was standing behind him.

I was facing James. It was childish, but I really enjoyed ignoring him, but he was having none of that.

"Mr. Arenas, I have a few questions for you. If I could speak with you alone."

Lucas turned to look at him. "Yes. Of course, officer."

"Ms. O'Meara, you can wait for him down the hall, in Sgt. Desocarras' office, where you were before," and he pointed in that direction.

"I'll take her there," said Lucas. We left the room and he walked me slowly back to Alex's office, me leaning on his arm. I wasn't in any pain, thanks to the meds, but I could only manage a slow shuffle. Once I was seated, I indicated to him to lean over and when he did, I whispered in his ear.

"Watch him. He's a racist jerk," but Lucas didn't understand a word I was saying as my voice had all but disappeared.

"Don't try to talk now sweetheart," he said, patting my arm. "We'll talk later."

Lucas returned to the interview room. James shut the door after him, turned on the recorder and gave the date and time for the benefit of the transcriber.

"What is your full name?"

"Lucas Stefan Arenas."

"And what is your relationship to Ms. O'Meara?"

"I'm her partner."

"And where do you work sir?"

"I'm a criminologist. I work as a researcher and writer and lecturer in the Criminology Department at SFU."

James didn't hide his surprise. "You teach. At SFU?"

"Yes."

"Is that where you and Ms. O'Meara met?"

"That's correct."

"And how long ago was that?"

"We met in 2006, in the fall. So, seven years ago. I met her through a mutual friend, Kate Brennan, whom I've known a few years longer. Kate's in the same department. She started a few years after me."

"Okay. I have a copy of your statement from the VPD. You first called to report Ms. O'Meara missing at 9:45 pm on Tuesday evening, October 7th. What you were doing that evening, prior to your phone call to the VPD?"

"I was making dinner. Morgan texted me that afternoon to remind me she planned to run after her film lab at the downtown campus was done. She's usually home by 8:00 pm. Trinity Street, where we live, is only a few blocks from New Brighton Park where we like to run. She wasn't home by 8:45 pm, then 9:00 pm, so by then I was very worried. She hadn't called and she was already an hour late. I called her cell, but she didn't answer. I thought maybe she'd fallen and twisted an ankle. So, I ran over to the park."

"And when you arrived there?"

"I went to the pedestrian underpass that leads to the pool and the running paths. She usually parks close by."

"Can a car drive through that underpass to the park?"

"No, the way is blocked. My car was parked close to the pedestrian entrance. Morgan wasn't in the car. I checked and the car was locked. There was no other car in the parking area. I took the pedestrian walkway, past the pool area and checked the trails along the beach. I didn't see her anywhere, so I climbed a small rise in the park itself, thinking I would get a better vantage point. Still, I had no sign of her.

Then I returned to where she had parked the car and headed up to Bridgeway Street. You follow along there for a few minutes and you come to a trail that runs along the inlet to Burnaby. Now I'm running, because I think maybe she's twisted an ankle, or she fell and broke her leg; something terrible like that. But still there's no sign of her anywhere. When I reached the Burnaby trail I took it, ran all the way to the Burnaby turnaround and back, looking everywhere for her. By now, it's been dark for several hours and I'm thinking: Why are you looking here? She wouldn't run the Burnaby Trail in the dark. She would have run along the beach, where there's light and I returned to the park. It's a completely open area and there's no sign of Morgan anywhere. I already know she's not there and by then, I was really scared."

There was a long pause. Lucas rubbed his face with both hands. Sighing audibly, he continued.

"I left the car that night because I thought, what if she returns to the car and it's not there. Then I ran home as fast as I could and called the police because in my heart, I knew she was gone. But the VPD wouldn't take a missing person's report, because Morgan hadn't been missing for 24 hours. I knew they wouldn't, of course! But I tried to anyway because she would never, just, not call!"

"And after you called the police?"

"Then I called our friends, Kate and Bart.

"What is Kate's last name?"

"Brennan."

"Bart has the same last name?"

"They're married, but no. Morris; Bartholomew, Bart Morris. The three of us returned to the park and searched again with high powered flashlights, both the beach trails and the wooded trail. I went back alone early the next morning. Then, the three of us searched again, a few hours later. I called the VPD that evening, and filed a missing person's report."

"Okay. So, it's probable that Ms. O'Meara was abducted sometime Tuesday night between approximately 6:00 pm, when she arrived at the park and 9:15 pm, when you say you arrived at the park for the first time."

"Yes. I would say that's right."

"Can anyone vouch for your presence at your house on Trinity Street, before you came to New Brighton Park, or your presence at the park itself?"

"No. I was alone at the house. I don't remember seeing anyone at the park after I arrived."

"So, all I have is your word?"

"Yes, my word only."

"You said earlier you've known Morgan for seven years. How would you characterize your relationship with her?"

"Ours is a close relationship. She means the world to me. I love her very much."

"You aren't seeing anyone else?"

"No."

"Has Morgan cheated on you recently, or in the past?"

Lucas looked at James.

"Answer the question please, Mr. Arenas."

"No."

"You're sure about that?"

"Yes. I'm sure."

"That's all for now, Mr. Arenas. Thank you for your time." He ended the interview and rose from his chair. He was done with Lucas.

It was late afternoon when Lucas and I left 100 Mile House and headed home. It was unseasonably warm for the South Cariboo, an immense, rugged plateau, just above the Fraser Canyon. The afternoon sun was low and red in a cloudless sky. A few patches of yellow remained but most of the trees were resolute, brown skeletons, lifeless amongst the green pines.

Expecting cold weather and snow on the ground, Lucas had brought warm blankets, a pillow, my winter parka, gloves and an oversized toque. Over my feeble protests, he bundled me up.

Alex had suggested we avoid the Coquihalla, a high altitude, mountain highway, where weather extremes were common and there was always the threat of snow this time of year. More to the point, I'd suffered a concussion and the altitude wasn't a good idea. Instead, Lucas took the scenic route via the Trans-Canada Highway that wound its way through the canyon created by the Fraser River.

Lucas was grim and his hands clenched the wheel tight. Incapable of conversation, I dozed beside him, seat partially reclined so I could watch the scenery — sheer rock walls, a solid mass and below them the Fraser, muddy with silt. I'd taken some of the pain medication just before we left the detachment office, despite the breathtaking scenery, I was soon asleep, lulled by the rhythm of the car as Lucas took the winding curves above the river. We made it to the town of Hope in good time and Lucas got out of the car briefly to stretch his legs.

"We're less than two hours from home, sweetheart. Are you hungry?" he asked when he got back in the car.

I shook my head and patted his arm. "Home." All I really wanted was a warm bed and the oblivion of sleep.

Lucas gassed up and got a takeout burger at the *White Spot*. He pulled back onto the highway and that's the last thing I remember until I woke up as we were crossing the Alex Fraser Bridge coming into Vancouver.

We arrived at our cottage on Trinity Street by 11:00 pm. Lucas told me the next morning I fell asleep in my pajamas, sitting on the side of the bed. I don't remember him helping me undress or tucking me in.

7

Alex dropped Gwen at home and returned to the detachment. He found James at a computer in the main office.

"What's your take on this abduction, Alex?"

"I think it was a targeted hit."

"Do you think she knew the perp?" James asked.

"No, I don't."

"What about the boyfriend?"

"He seems genuine."

"Well, I thought he showed a lot of fear when I interviewed him. In fact," and James checked his notes before continuing; "at one point he actually said, '*I was so scared*' and when he first saw O'Meara, just after he arrived, he was crying."

"I'm sure he was frightened. The man's a criminologist and my bet is he imagined the worst. His partner was missing. He gets a phone call that she's been rescued, a long way from home. He gets here, only to find her banged up pretty bad." Alex regretted wasting his breath on James almost immediately.

"Yeah, yeah, I know all that, but I'm thinking maybe Arenas was afraid because he had something to do with the abduction."

Desocarras was getting the familiar feeling he often

got when dealing with James.

"Well," James continued, "she's native and the boyfriend's native." Alex noted James' emphasis on the word native.

"I only talked with him briefly, just before he took her back to Vancouver. My guess is he's from Central America, or Mexico. He could be Mayan, though he's too tall for a Mayan. I think his racial heritage is mixed."

"Mayan? Mixed?" James shrugged his shoulders dismissively, trying to hide his confusion.

"I'm mixed heritage. My mom's people are Spanish; my dad, Shuswap. I identify as Shuswap." He didn't use the traditional name of the Shuswap nation, *Secwepemc*. It'd just confuse James — in spite of the fact that he'd been working for years in their traditional territory.

"As for Arena's possible involvement, my gut tells me he had nothing to do with O'Meara's abduction. I think something else is going on. She could have been a random hit, but I don't think so."

James still looked dubious.

"Did she remember anything about her abduction?"

James consulted his notes. "No, but she did describe a man she walked past in the parking lot, just after she parked her car. He was bending over the trunk of his car. But she can't remember anything after she walked by the car and the only other people she remembers are a couple that walked past her. That tells us something."

"Yeah, it does. I had a clear look at her assailant at the lake. It's all in my report: red hair, his chin stubble too, so his hair isn't dyed. Big man, well over six foot. If the guy in the parking lot back in Vancouver is involved, we've got two different perps."

"Yeah. O'Meara said the guy at the lake had a crooked middle finger, his left hand. She said his face and hands were very red. Probably because he was pissed that you and your wife happened along when you did," he said, with a small chuckle.

"Could be the redness is due to a skin condition." Alex flashed to the scene at Gustafsen Lake and O'Meara's distress and vulnerability. "I noticed how unusually red and puffy his face and neck were. I said so in my report."

"Yeah. I saw that. So, you think he has a skin condition?"

"Maybe, or maybe he's allergic to something."

"Could be," said James, handing Alex the interview notes. "It's your case now. Good luck with it."

"Thanks," said Alex as he took the file.

"Your wife mentioned you've got a few more days off. Are you gonna try to get in some more fishing."

"Not now," said Alex, tapping the file and getting to his feet.

"See you," said James.

"Yup," said Alex. He left the room and went to his office. He checked but there was still no word on the blue pickup and that was worrisome. It'd been nearly eight hours since he'd called it in. The road leading into Gustafsen Lake was so badly rutted, just getting out to the main road would have taken the perp at least an hour, unless he'd put a lot of money into a new suspension. Alex doubted that. From what he could see, the truck was a run about. None of the roads in the area were high traffic. It was mostly locals this time of year. It was as though the truck had vanished. It was possible the perp lived locally, but highly unlikely, unless he was stupid enough to do his dirty work in his own back yard.

Sundown was in half an hour, so too late to pay a return visit to the lake. He'd take a few men there first thing tomorrow morning.

Lucas called Kate and Bart as soon as Morgan was asleep. Kate answered the phone.

"Tell me she's alright."

"No. She isn't. They hurt her bad Kate."

"Oh no Lucas," said Kate, starting to cry. She handed the phone to Bart.

"Luke, is she okay?"

"I don't know." No sooner were the words out of his mouth, when he started to choke up.

"It's okay Buddy." Bart put their phone on speaker. "We'll be right over."

Lucas pulled himself together enough to protest.

"Morgan's out for the count and I'm not far behind her, to tell the truth."

"You haven't slept for days and you must be exhausted from all that driving," said Bart. "We'll come tomorrow morning, then. Is nine too early?"

"No. That works."

"We'll bring coffees and snacks and I'll stay and help you take care of Morgan," said Kate. Then, to Bart: "What time are you at the hospital tomorrow?"

"Not till 1:00 pm," said Bart.

"Okay you two, tomorrow morning then. And I'm so glad you're coming."

After he got off the phone, Lucas went into the bedroom and sat quietly on the edge of their bed, watching Morgan sleep. When he first tucked her in, he'd elevated her head and shoulders with pillows to help her breathe more easily. He leaned over now and gently touched the bump on her forehead and examined the angry, puckered line that ran right into her eyebrow. It must have been a deep cut. They had to stitch it. Her beautiful face was covered in bruises. More bruises were visible on her neck. When he helped her undress, he'd nearly lost it when he saw the ugly bruises on her inner thighs, the mean welts on her back and stomach, the scratches on her hands. He tucked the blankets gently up under her chin, then went to the bathroom and closed the door. His gut heaved and he vomited, again and again until he was empty, then washed his face and rinsed his mouth.

Lucas returned to the bedroom and stood in the doorway for a long time, watching Morgan sleep. Thoughts of how she must have suffered overwhelmed him. He flushed with guilt and shame. No one with her. No one to help.

Checking carefully that both doors and windows were locked and secure, he moved to the living room and picked up a small armchair which he moved to the bedroom and placed close to the bed. But he was too wound up to sit still. He returned to the living room.

The rain had stopped. The wind had picked up and through the living room window, he watched the Northern Star swing by her anchor in restless circles. She was moored where she'd been for two days now, still heavy with wheat, waiting her turn to unload. The lights on the inlet twinkled peacefully. Mocking him.

The night Morgan was taken, Lucas had a dream so real he understood a door had opened on memory. All he remembered were fragments: a bloated carcass floating in a bloody stream; smoke and fire. Last night's dream. So vivid — a rhododendron bush, heavy with beautiful red blooms. A dream without sound. Lights on. Then off.

8

When I woke, the sun was trying to poke through thick dark clouds. I slipped my feet into waiting slippers and moved to the bathroom to pee, wash my hands, dab at my face with a warm cloth. My lip was still a little swollen, the swelling on my forehead was down. The stitches are itchy. The bruises are starting to fade, turning yellow. I try to imagine them gone. Like it never happened. I can hear Lucas and Kate talking quietly in the kitchen. I smell coffee and I have a headache. Coffee might help.

I joined them in the kitchen, the love from both is comforting, but I shrink from being hugged. They don't let on if they notice. Kate makes me a coffee and I drink a little. The headache eases off. They tell me it's Sunday afternoon. Lucas made me scrambled eggs and toast. I try, but I can't get it down.

Kate suggests a bath. She wants to help me undress and I'm instantly horrified and can't stop shaking. I don't want her to see the bruises on my thighs. She'll know what happened. I don't want to talk about it, not with her — not with anyone.

"It's okay lovey. You can manage on your own. Of course you can." I nod, mute; head down. She made sure I had everything I needed, then left, closing the bathroom door softly behind her. I undress and climb into the tub, holding onto the sides for balance as I drop slowly into the water. Immediately, the heat of the water stings the delicate and bruised vaginal skin. I try not to panic and grab the side of the tub to get out, but the stinging has already started to ease off. And then, it stopped. I settle back into the water. Take up washcloth and soap; start to wash myself: every bruise, every scratch, everywhere they had touched me. Knew then why I wanted to be alone for this, my first move to reclaim myself from the men who laid their filthy hands on me, beat me, raped me, tried to kill me. When I was done, I eased back onto the bath pillow and let the water hold me gently.

The bath made me sleepy and I guess I'd stopped moving around. Kate was at the door, knocking quietly, asking if I needed anything. I told her I was okay. I got myself out of the tub and dried off. I put on the clean night gown she had ready for me, then made my way to the bedroom and climbed into bed. The last thing I remember was Kate gently tucking me in.

When I woke again it was just after 9:00 pm. I put on the waiting slippers and my housecoat, lying on the bed where Kate had left it, then went in search of her and Lucas.

"Sweetheart, you're up."

I tried to smile back — felt the pull of my lower lip, not quite able to respond.

"Are you hungry? I made you something to eat. Want me to warm it up?"

"Not really." He tried to hide his disappointment. "Maybe later," I lied. I walked over to where he was sitting on the couch, books and papers stacked beside him.

"Where's Kate?"

"Bart took her home when it looked like you might

sleep right through." Lucas shuffled things around to make room for me.

"How're you feeling?" he asked.

"Pretty good. A sleep marathon will do that." It was the truth and it surprised me.

"It's what you need. Your voice is stronger." Lucas watched as my hand instinctively went to my throat.

"Suddenly vulnerable, I tried to cover it. "What were you doing?"

"Just passing time, till you woke up."

"We haven't talked much."

"It's hard to talk with someone who's fast asleep." It was meant as a joke, but his eyes were dead serious.

We were both silent for a bit. I picked at the couch.

"We can talk, whenever you're ready," he said.

"Did you call my family?"

"Yes. Your mom's brothers in Thunder Bay. Your cousin Tanaka offered to visit your Nokomis Effie and fill her in. We both felt it would be better if she heard this in person."

"I'll call Tanaka in a few days. Nokomis too." I looked out the window at the inlet and the night sky; the grey drizzle of rain. "I didn't think I'd make it home." He took my hand and held it gently.

"I was so scared Lucas. I've never been so scared. Gwen and Alex saved my life." Once I heard the words, I knew that's all I really wanted to say — out loud — so those words would stop bouncing around in my head. I was looking into his eyes when I said that and saw the fear. "I need to be able to talk, Lucas!" Shrill. Accusatory. What the hell was the matter with me.

"I want to hear everything you have to say."

Then it dawned on me, the truth plain enough.

"You thought I wasn't coming back." I watch as his eyes tear up.

"I should never have gone running, alone, at night." I hate the sound of those words and I'm immediately so pissed off. Never go running again, alone, at night. Never again?

"That's what you do. It's who you are, a free spirit who goes for a run before dinner. It's why I admire you, one of the many reasons I love you so very much." His voice broke and he was silent for a while before continuing.

"Now — after what happened to Carey Bolton, and now you."

A free spirit who trembles and shakes and is afraid. I feel like I'm bleeding inside. Bart would say, when you're ready, journal your feelings. Tanaka would say turn on your camera. Document what's happened to you. But I don't want anyone to see. Or know. I don't want to talk any more. I'm tired, but I don't want to go back to bed and I don't want to be alone. I curled up on the couch beside Lucas. He got up to fetch a blanket for me.

Lucas looked at Morgan, awake moments ago, now fast asleep beside him. Kate told him about the visits they'd made to the Franklin Street house. He talked again with Michael last night about the children in the car with Carey; the men — child trafficking — the attempt on Morgan's life a message to back off.

The room was cool. He pulled the blanket up over her shoulders. He didn't want to go back to sleep. With sleep came nightmares. Last night was different.

He is in the jungle, walking somewhere. His mother is with him and there are others but he can't see their faces. The Pintos are close. Soldiers. Pintos. Like the beans — brown and white, mixed bloods — Spanish and Maya. The dream shifts and women are crying. They cry and cry, their tears a flood. A bloated carcass floats in their tears. The dream shifts again and someone tells Lucas to look. His father, Rafael is there beside him. He'd been gathering firewood and he has a bundle of dry sticks strapped to his back. He's standing in front of a rhododendron, his shirt so white against its red blooms.

He woke up in a cold sweat, heart racing, gasping for air. He got up and had a quick shower. Waited a while before coming back to bed. He was almost asleep when he remembered the red rhododendron his mom had planted, after a few years, almost as tall as their hut.

9

It's Monday morning. I'm on the couch. Lucas is in the kitchen. I have to have him close, a coward now who can't be alone. Not a coward. I'm scared ... stupid not to be scared. We're too close. I was too close. They're afraid. Everything is so mixed up. My dreams are mixed up. My thoughts are so dark. Shit. I need to pull myself together. How do I do that? Slept so late. Just want to sleep. But I'm out of bed now. Dressed. Hurrah for me.

Lucas interrupts my thoughts to hand me a cup of coffee. I force a smile. Why do I feel like he's a stranger? He returns to the kitchen. I follow him, wanting to be in the same room.

"What were you writing, Morgan?"

Should I tell him? He already knows. Silent, I watch him carefully chop onions and garlic and hot peppers, move each pile to the waiting skillet. He says nothing. I have to speak. I can't go back to that place. Not alone. "There's something I remember. Lying on a hard floor, hard like concrete and something against my face that felt like wool. There was loud banging and men's voices. Angry. Yelling." I remember words. Try to shape them, give them air, but they're ugly and hard on my tongue. I don't want to speak them yet.

"More than one man?" I hear the anxiety in his voice.

"Yes. More than one." I'm relieved. I told him. If I don't tell the truth, I'll never get through this. We'll never get through this. Neither of us spoke for a while. Men's voices swirl in my head. Down a long tunnel, their voices echo back: *House. Bitch. Fucking. Native. Bitch. Close. It'* I make note of the words, but don't share them. Lucas doesn't ask what I'm writing.

The smell of browning onions and garlic and green chillies now fills the room.

I break the silence. "What are you making?"

"A frittata."

And yet another of my favourite dishes. His plan is to get me to eat. "I think I could eat a little." Can't believe I said that and I want to take it back because I'm not hungry. At least the smell doesn't make me nauseous. I should eat something. I know that. I'm trying to please him. He's so unhappy — because I was beaten and raped and nearly killed.

"Not too much for me?"

"Okay." A quiet glance in my direction. So much love in those blue eyes. What is the matter with me? It's like part of me *is* missing. Part of me is missing. I re-read my notes and they give me an idea.

"I going to do a timeline for Det. Fernice. She needs to know everything that's happened, up to when I was rescued."

"I can do the writing, if you like." He's chopping veggies now.

"That would help. We'll do it when Kate and Bart get here." Kate thinks Carey's alive and I hold onto that for dear life. As they say in her Irish homeland, she has *The Gift.*

I remember the year I met her. Such a long time ago now. A small plane went down somewhere in the Coastal

Mountains below Prince George — a father and two sons, returning home to Vancouver from a vacation up north. Rescuers couldn't find the plane and there was hope the men had survived. But Kate told us the men didn't survive. I was quietly skeptical at first — an inward rolling of the eyes — but only because I liked her far too much to roll them in her presence.

Kate went to the VPD and told them about her vision of the plane wreck and the police arranged to take her up in a small plane to do a search. Kate directed them right to the site of the crashed plane! There were no survivors, just like she said. Talk about a major shift in one's worldview — mine did a 360°. I didn't even know that the police used psychics.

"Kate called to say there's a chance they might be late and if they are, we should go ahead without them," said Lucas.

"I'd rather wait for them."

"Okay." Lucas had beaten eggs into a creamy froth and poured them over the veggies. He turned the burner down low, covered the pan and sat down at the table.

"Kate told me about the phone call to Carey's mom, the Friday before you were taken. The caller said Carey was seen entering the house on Franklin Street. She said that a detective from VPD followed up the same day, but told Rosaline that no one appeared to be living there." He looked at me closely. "Are you okay to talk about this?"

"I'm okay. When we went to the house, there was someone there. A young Asian woman answered the door. She insisted Carey wasn't there and that she lived there alone. She was definitely upset we were there, but also very stoned. Our showing up could have freaked her out because of the drugs. Still."

"The caller was very specific about the address. Then,

you were taken three days later." He returned to the stove and checked his frittata.

"Kate and I went back the same evening. I went back the next day. I left a note with my name and cell."

Lucas dropped the egg lifter and we both watched as it bounced across the floor.

He turned to me. "You went back. Alone."

"I did, the next morning, but the house was empty. I'm sure it was. It felt — desolate. It seemed such a useless gesture, to leave a note, but we were all so disappointed that it turned out to be a dead end."

"Of course."

"I thought, maybe if someone comes back to the house and they read the note, they might remember something that could help us find Carey."

He'd retrieved the egg lifter and rinsed it under the tap. Trying to be casual. "What did the note say?"

"I said we were looking for Carey Bolton and if anyone knew anything, please call me."

Moving to the stove, he checked the frittata again.

"If I'd been here, I could've gone with you."

"But you weren't." There was a knock at the front door — Kate and Bart. I got up to let them in. They had to park a block away and neither of them are aware that the umbrella has been invented. The rain was coming down hard this morning and their outer garments were soaked.

"How are you?" they chorused together.

"I'm okay. I'm even a little hungry." Maybe if I said it often enough, I might feel hungry. I fetched them towels from the bathroom.

"Sorry we're late," Bart called out in the direction of the kitchen, as the two of them removed their outdoor clothes and dried their hair. "Traffic was heavy, even for a Monday." Then to me: "You're hungry Morgan. That's a good sign!" He seemed relieved. Sign of what? Right. Eating. A return to the land of the living. Me. Normal. Pretending to be normal.

"You're appetite's returning. I'm so glad to hear that, Morgan" said Kate, towelling her black curls vigorously.

I'd definitely have to eat something now, even if I gagged on it. I hung up the towels and followed them to the kitchen.

"You're not late," said Lucas. "In fact, your timing couldn't be better." He'd dished up plates of food. They sat down and dug in with murmurs of pleasure. He offered coffee all around before sitting down.

I took a small bite, chewed and swallowed. I was kind of surprised that it went down okay. "It's good," I said and meant it, "but Lucas, you gave me way too much."

"Eat what you can, honey" he said, trying to hide the fact that he was completely elated.

"Thanks for this Lucas," said Kate. "It's delicious."

"You are the master," said Bart, reaching for toast.

"Morgan remembered something very important."

Kate and Bart stopped eating and looked at me.

"Morgan visited the house on Franklin by herself. She left a note, with her name and number."

"When, Morgan?" asked Kate. The gentleness in her voice scared me.

"The morning after we went. I was on my way to Cineworks, to do some editing."

"You didn't mention it when we saw you later."

"The house was empty Kate. It didn't seem important."

Kate looked at Lucas. "Best to buy a couple of burners."

"Yup. After lunch."

Kate caught Bart's eye, "We should too. Take no chances."

"We will. On our way home," said Bart. He turned to

me. "Someone had your schedule and knew that you'd be at the park on Tuesday, or they followed you there. And if they followed you there, they must know that you work at SFU. They may have gotten their information from someone at the university, maybe one of your students, Morgan."

"If they had her cell number, they wouldn't need much else. Maybe they, whoever they are, are keeping tabs on all of us," said Kate.

"We've lost valuable time, thanks to me," I said. "No one is going to get the drop on me again!"

"Morgan, you have no responsibility here!" said Bart.

"But she's right," said Kate." We're running out of time."

"Morgan wants to create a timeline: between Carey's abduction on September 18th, and her rescue, October 7th," said Lucas.

"I have an interview with Det. Fernice tomorrow morning. I'm taking it with me."

Lucas had a notebook and calendar on the table beside him. "It's been 24 days since Carey was abducted." We all let that sink in.

"It was a lucky break when Mike spotted her getting into the *Suburban*, behind the *Clarendon*," said Bart.

"Saturday, September 27th, nine days after she went missing," said Lucas.

"The VPD has a record because Michael reported it immediately and he was interviewed a few days later, so Det. Fernice will have the reports," said Kate.

"The day after Morgan was abducted, Michael and I talked. He called Gilbrauson at MPU."

"What did he say?"

"He didn't call back until Thursday and by then, MPU knew that Morgan had been rescued. Gilbrauson said he'd add Michael's concern that the abductions were linked to

Carey's case notes. He went on holiday the next day."

"We know at least one club member is involved," said Kate, or someone who's friends with a member."

"A club employee could be involved too," said Bart.

"For all we know, bringing children to the club is business as usual," said Kate. "The duty of care to children is a bloody fiction. Paedophiles and paedophile rings: The UK — Jimmy Savile, BBC, raped hundreds of kids; Savile dead now and never charged. His is only one of the historical cases still under investigation there. The Franklin horror in the US and Canada no better with its own abysmal record of convictions. I assume there are security cameras at the back of the club."

"There's a security attendant in the office at the back entrance, but he doesn't have a window facing the street and he doesn't have a view of the parking lot exit west of the club. When we had dinner with him, Michael showed us where he spotted the car and the closest street camera is about 20 metres away," said Lucas. "Michael assumed the VPD didn't request footage."

"A fair assumption," said Kate. "How long has he been a member?"

"Since he joined Bourdais Lambert," I said. "I'm not sure what year. His area is intellectual property, but you know that. Very interesting clientele: writers, musicians, people in film." Me trying to make a joke.

"All the best people," said Kate, with a smile.

"It's quite the place. It was modernized a few years back."

"The Hong Kong Shanghai Banking Corporation, HSBC — the second biggest bank in the world — many billions of dollars in assets, has a branch right next door," said Lucas.

"I think they might even be sharing a wall with the

club," I said.

"Oh, they do," said Lucas. "I checked."

"Right. HSBC," said Kate. "They're in the laundry business on the side. Must be so handy for some of the members to have them right next door."

"I'm sure it is, Kate," said Lucas with a grin. "The influence of money and power. You feel it the moment you walk through the door."

"I'll admit to feeling out of my element," I said.

"You looked beautiful that night," said Lucas, trying to catch my eye. "I always feel like an interloper and I've been there a few times now for SFU functions."

"I've been thinking a lot lately about power and the powerful," said Lucas. "You've seen Morgan's pictures of our visit to Guatemala."

"All of her pictures are incredible," said Kate. I tried to pass it off. "They are Morgan!"

"Do you remember the ones she took of the Catholic church in the town square in Nebaj? The Catholic Church, house of *their Lord* and the entrance to that house is a massive wooden front door, covered in Mayan religious symbols." He grinned at the thought. "The 40-foot ceiling, statues larger than life, like the black Christ with his crown of thorns — Spanish domination and Spanish money — but built by my ancestors, with their wonderfully rich Mayan religious and cultural touches everywhere — like hidden messages."

"But at the club, there are no hidden messages from the poor," I said.

"I'm sure not," said Bart. The club is for the rich and powerful. It's a mark of membership."

"Exactly," said Kate. "And in the real world, some of those bastards get away with murder."

"That they do," I agreed.

"After dinner and drinks, we moved about, here and there, somewhat surreptitiously," said Lucas.

"As surreptitious as four brown folks can hope to be," I said.

"Michael's been scouting around a lot since he saw Carey. There's overnight accommodation on the fifth floor. Fernice and Desocarras need to know just how easy it is to get up there and back down to the parking level, completely unnoticed," said Lucas.

"When they did their big reno, the public areas got the upgrades, and the private areas, like the stairways, were ignored," I said. "We went up by elevator, and back down by stairways along the walls of the building. We didn't see a single soul coming down."

"Members, their children, and guests all use the overnight accommodation on the fifth floor," said Lucas.

"Michael says once you're registered, you can come and go pretty much as you please," I said.

"You think it would be easy to bring children in and out, undetected?" asked Bart.

"Very easy," I said.

"Children are allowed at the club. If they're under 13, the General Manager is supposed to be informed that they're there, and they have to be supervised."

"'*Supposed to be informed*' are the operative words here," I said, looking a Lucas. "A member could rent accommodation and bring children into the club and no one would be the wiser."

"There's a staff lounge on the ground floor, near the back entrance and a gym as well," said Lucas. "There not much else on that floor."

"There's a lot of room to move, especially where kids are concerned," said Bart.

"There sure is. Parking lot patrons can't enter the club

unless they're members because it's a card key entrance. But club patrons can access the parking lot directly from the basement. And that's very important. You don't have to leave the club via the back entrance," Lucas said. "Once you're in the underground parking area, there's a short ramp about 30 metres to the left of the back entrance to the club. Michael saw Carey near the top of that ramp. We checked it out the night we were there. If somebody wanted to come and go without being seen, they could do so very easily."

"But if someone was to bring children into the club, or leave with them via the ground floor, wouldn't anyone taking a break in the staff lounge see them?" asked Kate.

"They would, if someone was there and they were paying attention to who was coming and going. But staff are encouraged not to question what goes on, and plenty goes on," said Lucas, looking over at me. "Someone at Michael's firm was a guest at a party in one of the private dining rooms. One of the guests belongs to a local bikers' gang and he brought a few bags of cocaine with him and literally dumped it in piles, right on the tablecloth."

"That's a bit excessive, to say nothing of wasteful," said Kate. "Wouldn't they have a hard time finding it on white?"

"The staff working the party stood at the back of the room like they always do and ignored the piles of coke," I said.

"And the sexual activity on the back stairs," Lucas added.

"The club website does claim the staff are famous for their discretion," said Bart.

"And they aren't kidding," I said. I got up to get more coffee for myself and offered it around.

"Michael left the club via the pedestrian entrance on

Cordova Street," said Lucas. "He'd reached the street when he noticed a silver *Suburban* idling, off to his left, about 10 metres away. He told us he was just about to head in the opposite direction, going east. Carey must have just reached the top of the parking lot ramp, where it opens onto Cordova Street."

"Isn't Cordova Street one way?" asked Bart.

"Yes, one way going east," I said. "The parking lot ramp is in shadow. The *Suburban* was between Michael and the entrance to the ramp. When Carey and the man she was with reached the street, they turned and walked towards Michael. She was a bit behind and to the left of the man, so she was partially hidden. But something about the girl got his attention. The man opened the passenger door and stepped back so that Carey could get into the car. She walked the last few steps and got in and the man followed her in and shut the door. Michael turned to head east when he realized that it was Carey who'd just gotten into the car. The *Suburban* drove right by him and he ran after it, yelling for the driver to stop, but it sped up, quickly turned right and disappeared."

"I feel so bad for Michael," said Kate. They knew the story. It didn't get easier to listen to.

"Det. Gilbrauson did the follow-up interview. He told Michael that the Terrace RCMP were notified about the sighting. But he also said that when a person goes missing, the police get a lot of reported sightings, most of which prove to be false."

"Gilbrauson didn't buy that Michael saw Carey at the back of the club," said Kate.

"He said he was concerned that Michael was getting his hopes up over what might turn out to be a false lead." Lucas sighed with exasperation.

"A false lead that happens to wind its way to the back

door of the oldest private members club in Western Canada!" Kate was indignant.

"Exactly Kate."

"Michael told the VPD that he saw more than one child in the car," said Bart.

"He saw three children," said Lucas. "That should be in Gilbrauson's report. I'll include that here, just in case.

"Have you spoken with Michael lately?"

"I called him on Friday to let him know you were home safe. We talked on Sunday too."

I said nothing. Home. Safe. Those two words were hard to put together. I didn't feel safe. Not even here.

"I want Fernice to understand that Michael is certain he saw three children, and one of them was Carey, no matter what slant Gilbrauson put on the sighting. The girl had a limp and Carey has a limp. Her walk is particular to her."

"Amelia said she's slated for another operation next spring to help correct her gait, which is uneven. It puts extra pressure on her knee and she has to rest after a lot of exertion."

"Erroneous sightings are probably not uncommon when a person goes missing," said Bart.

"They aren't, but Michael thinks it was the location Gilbrauson had trouble with," said Lucas.

"Of course," said Kate. "Protect the bastion of male privilege at all costs."

"Point taken," said Bart. "And especially chilling if it turns out that protection extends to a paedophile ring."

"For all we know, there may be people who are aware of what's going on, and for their own reasons, are allowing it to continue."

"Jesus Kate! You really think that might be the case?"

"I do. It's certainly possible."

We were silent for a minute, then I remembered something else.

"Unless Kate told you Lucas, Amelia and I went to visit a friend of Geoff, Amelia's dad. The guy's name is Ange Batlan. That was the day you went to Victoria, to attend the Restorative Justice Symposium."

"I'd forgotten all about that," said Kate.

"You caught the early ferry. I was in my office and Amelia dropped by. Her dad really wanted her to connect with Batlan and he'd been after her to do that. She called him from my office and he was home so she asked me to go with her. His condo's just around the corner on Cambie Street. Batlan's an executive with Northfor Tech, a mining company. They have an office in Terrace. I think that's how Geoff knows him. He told Batlan about Carey's abduction when he was in Terrace a few weeks back and he's worried about Amelia being here, in Vancouver, with no family close by."

"I'll bet he is," said Bart.

"Batlan told us he has a friend who works at the VPD, He's been in contact with him and he wants to be kept in the loop about Carey's case."

"The more people asking questions, the better," said Kate.

Lucas looked at the list beside him. "I think I have everything now. I've included the visits to 168 Franklin, first, by MPU, then by the three of you, then Kate and Morgan and then Morgan, alone."

"Kate didn't tell me they'd gone to the house till after, Luke," said Bart. "I'd have gone with them."

"Lovey," said Kate, patting his arm. "You were already at the clinic. I didn't know when you'd be home. Amelia got the call from her aunt and we wanted to visit while there was daylight. It gets dark so early now."

"You being there wouldn't have made any difference, Bart," I said.

"The young woman who answered the door was nervous, wasn't she Morgan?"

"She sure was. Then the two of us, a couple of hours later, banging on the doors again."

"The police know about the phone call to Rosaline," said Kate. "They have a record of the detective's visit. And they may know the three of us went, because after we left, Amelia left a message for the same detective."

"But they don't know that you and I went back that night Kate, and that I went back alone the next morning. And three days later. Well, if it weren't for Gwen and Alex, I wouldn't be here now." I could feel the tears, hot behind my eyelids. I started to shake.

"Too friggin' scary for words," said Kate.

"Don't hold them back Morgan. Tears are a good thing," said Bart.

"I know they are." But tears I can't control mean feelings I can't control. I have never doubted my ability to protect myself. Until now. By the time I was 16, I had a black belt in Karate. In the world of tournaments, I'd often won, but in the real world, I lost a battle I still don't remember having. Admitting this is hard.

The tears started and I hate this because it makes me feel so vulnerable and I don't know how to fix that. I'm afraid that I'll never be able to. I looked across the table at Lucas, looking for comfort — but was taken aback. Everyone's eyes followed mine.

"Luke. You okay buddy?"

Bart's question startled him and the look vanished. "I'm fine."

You are not fine. Not fine at all.

"Where were you Luke?" asked Bart.

"It's been a difficult week," said Lucas, trying to downplay it.

"And you, the tough guy," said Kate.

"Not a tough guy at all it seems."

"We're here for you, for both of you," said Bart. "You know that."

"I do know that," I said. "I love you both and thank you."

"Are you hearing me Luke?" said Bart.

"Yes. I hear you."

Bart let it go but I knew him well enough to know he wouldn't let it rest. Kate offered to make more coffee, but there were no takers. She got up and put the kettle on for another cup of tea.

"I'm hoping the RCMP have ruled me out as a suspect."

"I'm sure Alex doesn't think that!"

"You're talking about the guy that interviewed you at 100 Mile House, aren't you?" said Bart.

"Cpl. James," I said.

"If he had any people skills at all, he would have tumbled to the fact you're incapable of that level of nastiness."

"I appreciate the vote of confidence Kate. I'm just as concerned Alex might consider Morgan's abduction a random act of violence."

"Statistically, the police wouldn't be completely off-base to consider it random," said Kate.

"You think Desocarras may assume Morgan was in the wrong place at the wrong time?" said Bart.

"He might," said Lucas. "We need to convince him and Det. Fernice that's not the case here!"

"Before it's too late!" I said.

"We are touching evil itself," said Bart, with a shudder.

"We are," Kate said.

"I intend to be very careful from now on. We all

need to be."

"Abducting Morgan was a message — to all of us." Kate had sat back down.

"Until this is over Morgan, you and I are tied at the hip," said Lucas.

"No argument from me," I said, thinking how hard I was finding it to be alone right now, even if Lucas was in the next room. "It's a good thing we're the same height." He didn't crack a smile.

"Us too, Irish," said Bart. We're tied at the hip till this is over."

"But we're not the same height," said Kate.

"We'll make it work. Somehow."

The Belly Of The Beast

10

"The sound of my voice woke me up. Lucas was propped up on an elbow, looking at me sleepily.

"You just yelled: 'I can't get in!'"

"I was in the woods at Gustafsen Lake, running from the bastard who tried to kill me." That certainly got his attention. He was wide awake now.

"I was in the woods, trying to find a place to hide. There were these orbs of light, like beacons, in a thicket right in front of me. I was so tired my legs gave out and I collapsed in front of it. I thought I was done for, but once I was on the ground I could see the opening to an animal burrow and I shimmied in, feet first. It wasn't quite big enough and I had to push hard to make room for my head and shoulders. Just after I pulled my head in, he was there. His boots were this close to my face," and I showed Lucas with my hand, just how close. "He moved his flashlight back and forth, back and forth, trying to find me. And I remember that his boots had splatters of burgundy paint on them, and blue too, but fine, like a spray would leave. And another thing. I remember a chemical smell; really nauseating. It was like my clothes were soaked in it."

"Was that in your statement?"

"No."

"Fernice will want to hear about this. I'm betting forensics will notice the smell."

"I'll tell her about the paint on his boots, and the sickly smell, but I don't think I'll be telling her about the beacons of light."

"She doesn't have to know about the friendly orbs."

"I will tell Kate though."

"She'll be so pleased, knowing you had help — not of the worldly kind."

"Non-believer, be warned. I've joined the club."

"There's a club?"

"Kate's special club — for those of us that see and feel what others are blind to."

"I will be forever grateful to those beacons of light for leading you to safety," he said, dead serious now. He was thinking of the attacker's boots, inches from her face.

"I'm worried about Kate. Bart said she hasn't been sleeping well for weeks. She has to keep up with her work at the university and finish her thesis. It's due in a few months."

It was plain to me that Kate was exhausted. Within days of Carey's abduction, Kate connected with her psychically. What connection she had was sporadic and rarely for long periods of time, but it happened day and night.

"Are you sure you're up to working tomorrow? I really wish you'd reconsider and wait another week."

"I've had four days of complete rest and physically, I feel pretty good. I could have gone out today but I didn't Lucas. The truth is, I'm afraid to leave the cottage. For every day I stay here, I know that it'll be that much harder to go out. The only way I'm going to do this is to jump back in." Big words. The idea of returning filled me with dread.

"I'll drive you in and wait in the concourse coffee shop until you finish your office hours. Then I'll accompany you to the film lab."

"We should both try to get some sleep. We've got a busy day tomorrow."

For me, all roads lead to film, my first love. I can't remember when I didn't want to be a filmmaker, though it probably dates to when dad bought his first movie camera. I borrowed it so often, he finally gave it to me and bought another for himself. It had been fun to be back at SFU and work with the first-year students, already shooting their first shorts using 16 mm film stock and old style Bolex cameras, editing on flatbeds — getting to know, first hand, the beauty and the art of film — rows of tiny pictures, each one perfect, then carefully synching the sound track. These days that stark beauty and intimacy was everywhere overridden by the immediacy of digital images instantly shared. I work in video too, but for me, it will never replace film.

SFU still teaches the art of film in a world gone crazy with video. The bonus is you can walk through the door as a regular paying student, which was why I applied there. The film office is on the second floor of the SFU Contemporary Arts building — a modern temple of polished concrete and glass — which also houses dance, theatre, visual art and contemporary music departments and theatres, studios and labs. The SFU building, part of the Foursquare Complex, called Woodward's by most people, included apartments, shopping and restaurants. Woodward's, the original department store, which now housed community offices, was the only building on the block that wasn't demolished to make room for the complex.

The thought of standing in front of the film students tomorrow afternoon and pretending everything was okay had my stomach in a knot. I reached for the *Rescue Remedy* Kate gave me and took some.

11

The sun warmed Lucas' face and an arm flung carelessly outside the blankets. He surrendered to the warmth and consciousness; took in the details of their bedroom, familiar and comforting.

Another dream of Guatemala: the classroom in the jungle and his father beside him. Watched his father sharpen a pencil with his small knife. Watched the sun dance in the blade. It was strange that his father was in that dream. They lived in the jungle for months, hiding from the army. But that was after his dad was killed.

The drone of a float plane reached him from the Burrard Inlet. He closed his eyes and he was a boy, watching a small, noisy plane rise into the air, banking and turning above his head, flying, like a bird. Pure magic to a boy who walked everywhere. He hadn't thought of that plane in years, but the memory was so clear, it could have been yesterday. It was donated to his parents' cooperative by an American charity—a generous and important gift. There were few roads in the Guatemalan highlands and it was the only way the cooperative could bring in supplies or get the coffee and cardamom they grew for export to buyers on the coast. Against the odds, after only a few years, the cooperative had enough to feed its members and a surplus to sell.

He could hear Morgan in the kitchen, making coffee, the sound of running water, then the grinder, taking cups from the cupboard. Then silence. No singing from the woman who sang every morning. She isn't singing, he thought, because the bastards took her song. He surrendered to the dark place where he killed the men that had taken her, taken Carey, squeezing hard on faceless throats until they gave up fighting for air and went limp in his hands. The enormity of his anger washed over him. It was an effort to get out of bed.

12

When we arrived at the VPD on Main Street, Det. Fernice was waiting for us in the reception area. We shook hands.

"And here you are Ms. O'Meara, safe and sound. How wonderful!"

I warmed to her instinctively — the way you do some people and not others. She was a little taller than me, in her early thirties, sturdy build, ash-brown hair and startling blue eyes.

Lucas watched her closely, his face guarded. When she turned to him, he introduced himself and handed her our timeline, the title large and bolded; our intention clear.

"We think this will aid your understanding of what's going on."

"It's an event timeline," I added, between Carey Bolton's abduction and mine. Lucas didn't smile and he didn't shake her hand. It wasn't like him to be aloof.

"Thank you," she said, tapping the list. Lucas sat back down to wait and I followed her upstairs to an interview room in Missing Persons. We got settled and were soon joined by another officer, who Fernice introduced as Det. Adam Ignace. He had a pitcher of water and glasses with him. She turned on a recorder and stated the date, time and those present.

"First, Morgan, I'd like to talk about your abduction here in Vancouver and anything you can remember leading up to that."

"Okay."

"You teach at Simon Fraser?" she said.

"No, I have a job as a teaching assistant in the film department this semester. I'm subbing for someone who took sick at the beginning of the semester."

"You're not a professor then?"

"No, but my partner Lucas is an Associate Professor in the Criminology Department. I'm a filmmaker. I did my undergrad and masters in film at SFU. I'm working for one of the film profs, Sophia Paridopolis. She teaches the introductory film course. Half of her students are in my lab."

"Who leads the other lab?"

"Carl Baraniuk. He's an MA candidate in film." I spelled his name for her.

"Does your schedule at SFU follow the same pattern every week?"

"Pretty much. I lead a seminar every Tuesday from 3:00 pm to 6:00 pm. I have office hours on both Tuesdays and Thursdays from 12 noon to 2:00 pm. It's convenient to go for a run after my lab on Tuesday. I also run with Lucas, but those times vary, depending on our schedules."

"On the Tuesday you were abducted, was your schedule as per usual?"

"Yes."

"The film lab you lead is at the Woodward's Campus."

"The film department is part of SFU's School of Contemporary Arts on Hastings Street East. The school is part of a larger complex called Foursquare. The old Woodward's building is part of that complex.

"I moved here from Manitoba early this year. Still

getting to know some of the landmarks."

"I'm not from here either. I grew up in Thunder Bay, in Northwestern Ontario. I came here to attend university and never left."

"Fernice tapped one of the sheaves of paper sitting on the desk in front of her. "I read through the statement you gave to Cpl. James and I'd like to review it with you."

She walked me through the events of the day I was abducted. I filled in the parts that were sketchy, starting with my dressing for the run, going down to the parking garage, retrieving the car and leaving the campus to go to New Brighton.

"Did you speak with anybody before leaving?" I thought about that.

"I said goodbye to Odessa Tate as I was leaving. She's the office manager of Contemporary Arts. I took the elevator down to the parking level."

"Was there anyone in the elevator?"

"A couple of guys, and there was a young woman as well. I remember her because she said hi to me."

"Did she call you by name?"

"She did. She called me Ms. O'Meara. I told her to call me Morgan."

"Is she a student?"

"She isn't in my lab but I've seen her around. She's definitely a new student. We're not that formal in the film department."

"What about the men in the elevator. Do you remember anything about them?"

"I think I remember one of them, a young guy, leaving the elevator with me in the parking area, but I didn't notice much about him, or where his car was parked."

"Were you aware of anyone following you as you left the parkade?"

"No. I was distracted, thinking about Carey Bolton."

"We'll certainly get to that. When you arrived at New Brighton Park, you parked the car and since you'd already changed, you were ready to run."

"That's right."

"According to your interview with Cpl. James, you don't remember anything," here Fernice consulted the sheets in front of her, "after you locked your car and left it?"

"I still don't remember what happened to me at the park."

"Do you remember running on the trails?"

"I have no memory of running."

"You told Cpl. James there was a man with longish hair who was parked beside you. He was leaning into the trunk of his car and you indicated that you don't remember anything after you walked by him, is that right?"

"Yes. When I got out of the car and locked it, I was thinking about Carey. We'd been to the house on Franklin Street a few days before."

Fernice looked at me blankly.

"All visits to the house are in the timeline Lucas gave you. It won't be in the interview notes."

"Okay. Please continue."

"I must have been abducted in the parking lot." With the words came a wave of intense fear and panic and without warning, I started to shake and cry. Ignace fetched a box of Kleenex and gave it me. It took a few minutes for me to regain control.

"That's been happening a lot lately." I looked at Fernice and I saw compassion in her eyes.

"We talk with a lot of women, and men, who've been victims of violence," said Cst. Ignace. There are services available and we recommend you use them, to help you deal with what happened."

"We'll make sure you have the necessary forms before you leave today," said Fernice.

"Okay." I picked up my notebook and flipped it open. Carey's picture smiled at me. Carey. The children. Still not safe. I took a deep breath.

"I'm having memory flashes. I've written down everything I remember. There's a copy of my notes with the timeline."

"Tell us about your memories," said Fernice, flipping to that sheet.

"One memory is just sound: men arguing, not sure how many. Their voices are hollow, as though they're in a tunnel. I remember fragments of what was said." I read from my notes: "*Our fucking house; my call, not yours; do it now; fucking native bitch; do what you want.*" I took a deep breath. "I also remember a very strong smell, a chemical smell. It was on my clothes. It wasn't a friendly smell, for want of a better description. I know the smell. I should remember what it is, but I can't. This isn't a problem I normally have. My retentive and recall skills are excellent."

"Okay, we have concern about a house. We have men very angry with you and we have an unfriendly, chemical smell that you're familiar with, but can't remember the name of." She paused and looked at me. "And we also have you, at some point, held somewhere that echoes a lot."

"And last night, I remembered lying on a hard surface, like concrete and something that felt like stiff wool against my face."

"This is excellent Morgan. Can we return to the sounds for a minute? Is there anything else distinctive about them?"

"Besides the words, the rest is a jumble of sound."

"Try to describe it, if you can."

"Well ... There was a loud banging sound, very rhythmic, like a hammer; and there was a kind of humming sound too."

"Humming?"

"There was a humming that held all the sounds together, running underneath all the other sounds. I know that's an odd way to describe it."

"Not at all," said Fernice. "Is there anything else?"

It was a struggle to put my fear into words, without tears. I didn't want to start crying again. Crying made me feel worse. More vulnerable.

"You probably already have this in your notes, but I had trouble talking when I was first rescued. It wasn't that my throat was dry, although I was very thirsty. What I mean is, that my throat felt bruised, as though there had been something around my neck. The bruises are still there. I'm sure I was strangled or choked. To be honest though, I have no recollection of this actually happening."

Fernice nodded, her face serious. "The medical report from the hospital indicates that the bruising on your neck is consistent with strangulation," she said. "Is your throat still sore, Morgan?"

"No. But it was hard to eat. For days. My partner is a good cook and he kept trying. Yesterday I forced myself to eat something. Today as well."

"Was it easier this morning than yesterday?" said Ignace.

"It was."

"It gets easier. Don't push yourself too hard."

Fernice consulted one of the sheets in front of her. "It shouldn't be long before we have the forensics on the clothing you were wearing."

"Lucas told me he gave you a DNA sample, so that you can rule him out."

"He did. Is there anything else you remember since

you gave your statement last Thursday?"

"Yes. Last night I remembered that my abductor was wearing boots with a lot of maroon and blue paint spray splatters." I showed Fernice and Ignace with my hands, just how close my face I had been to those boots. They exchanged a glance.

"Anything else?"

"No." I didn't mention the glowing orbs of light but the thought of my conversation with Lucas last night made me smile.

"Is there something else?"

"No." No way I was telling them about the lights.

"Okay. There is one more thing I want you to know." Fernice paused before continuing. "The rape kit done at the hospital captured DNA evidence of two men. They haven't been identified. Neither was a match for your partner."

I saw Ignace worry his lower lip. Something about that was comforting. I nodded but didn't say anything.

"Are you okay, Morgan?" she asked.

"As okay as I can manage right now."

"Do you remember the rape?"

"No," I said, holding on for dear life. "But the bruising, and soreness. I could barely walk. It was plain to me I was raped."

"I'm bringing this up now because you may remember the attack when you're alone. A memory like that can be devastating."

Great. When I remember the rape, I'll feel even worse.

"It would be good for you to talk with someone," she said.

"I got it." It was an automatic response. I didn't mean it to be rude. I just wanted her to shut up about it. There wasn't anyone I wanted to talk to, not about this.

"We're treating this as an abduction, aggravated assault, forcible rape and attempted murder."

I nodded.

"You were born and raised in Ontario, right?" The question came from Ignace.

"Yes, in Thunder Bay, at the top of Lake Superior."

"Used to be Port Arthur and Fort William."

"Not many people know that."

"I'm a history buff," he explained. Morgan, do you mind if I ask you about your ancestry?"

"No. My mother, Eva and her mother and father are Ojibwe. My grandparents belong to Greenwood Lake First Nation. Mom died of breast cancer about 10 years ago. My father, Daniel O'Meara, was born in Ireland. His family moved to Canada when he was still a boy. Mom and Dad met in Thunder Bay. Dad died of a heart attack a few years ago." *'Love at first sight,'* dad always said. *'Listen to him! It was months before he won me over,'* mom would insist, laughing. I miss them. What I wouldn't give to have a cup of tea with mom and dad in our old kitchen; visit Nokomis at Greenwood; go out for a beer with my cousin, Tanaka.

"Must be hard. Losing both parents," said Fernice.

"It is." I looked at Ignace. "When people ask, I tell them I'm *Anishinaabe*, but my dad was Irish." I stopped there.

"I get it. I'm mostly *Cree* but I know there's some Scottish in there somewhere," he said. "Are all your family in Ontario?"

"Pretty much. I'm close with my mom's side and especially close to my Nokomis. My granny," I added, for Fernice's sake.

"Most of them live in North Ontario. Dad only had one sister, my Aunt Ailis. I haven't seen her since I was a child. She lives in Nova Scotia."

"Your middle name," said Fernice. "It's an unusual spelling. Alice: named after your aunt?"

"That's right. The Irish Gaelic spelling."

"Are your family aware of what happened to you?" Ignace asked.

"Yes, after my rescue was made public. Lucas has spoken with everyone and has been very reassuring, though initially, he was close to hysterical." I didn't smile and neither did they. I guessed hysterical was something they dealt with a lot.

"Your mother and father are both deceased and you have relatives but are not in close contact with them," said Ignace.

"That's about right."

"If you were missing, the only person or persons who would be immediately aware would be your partner and close friends here in town."

"Until news of my rescue hit the papers, no one knew I was missing. Lucas phoned everyone last Friday to let them know I was home."

"It isn't our intention to be intrusive or disrespectful but as police officers, we're aware that Indigenous women are more often targets of violence than other women. I want to be sure I have a clear picture of your circumstances and how close you are to your family. At this stage of the investigation, we don't rule out anything." Fernice picked up the timeline. She looked at Adam.

"I just got this." He nodded and she took a few minutes to read through it.

"You believe that the abduction of Carey Bolton from Terrace and your involvement with the family, showing a keen interest in her case, led to the attack on you."

"I do."

"There's reference here to activities that aren't in Cpl.

James's interview report. Regarding the phone call to Rosaline Bolton, Carey's mother: the caller told her that he'd seen Carey going into a house at 168 Franklin Street, in the East Village close to the South Port."

"Rosaline called the VPD first," I said.

"Det. Hermes visited the house. She told Carey's mother that no one was there," said Fernice.

"Then Rosaline called her niece, Amelia Boudreau, asking her to check again. Amelia called Kate and I and we went to the house with her."

"Kate Brennan."

"Yes. She's one of the teaching assistants for a first-year Criminology class that Amelia is taking. Kate is also a PhD Crim candidate."

"What's her thesis," asked Ignace.

"A comparison of the Canadian judicial response to violence against women generally, as compared to the response to violence against Indigenous women and other women of colour."

"Right," said Ignace, letting that register.

"Back to the visits to Franklin Street," said Fernice. "When the three of you visited, there was a young woman at the house who found your visit upsetting?"

"It was hard to tell. She was stoned and we thought her fear might have been drug related. Amelia left a message with Det. Hermes that we found her there."

She scribbled a quick note. "But to your knowledge, there was no one else at the house at the time of your visit, that would be the second visit?"

"We thought she was alone at the time. Otherwise, we would have heard voices if others were there, and none of us did. We were on the front porch so I couldn't say for certain."

Ignace and Fernice shared a glance. Hermes had given

a report of her visit to Franklin Street at a team meeting the following Monday morning—in passing, really, but no mention of the phone call from Amelia though. There was no active file on Carey Bolton or Morgan O'Meara—she hadn't been abducted yet.

"Then you and your friend Kate returned that evening."

"Early evening. The house was dark and very quiet."

"And you went back, alone, the next day, and left a note seeking information about Carey and including your name and number."

"Yes. The house seemed to be empty."

"And you were abducted three days later." She glanced at Ignace; continued reading.

"Michael Bolton, Carey's uncle, saw her getting into a car behind the *Clarendon*, nine days after she went missing in Terrace?"

"Yes."

"Bolton reported the sighting to us. He was interviewed by Gilbrauson two days later." Another shared glance with Ignace. She scribbled another quick note on the pad beside her and continued reading.

"Carey Bolton has a distinctive limp."

"She does, owing to a birth defect."

"Bolton said there were two other children in the car, and three men, including the one who got into the car after Carey."

"Yes."

"Okay." Ignace and I watched as she referred to Sgt. James's interview notes, found what she was looking for and compared it to Lucas's timeline. She sat back.

"I'll make a formal request that the investigation into Carey Bolton's abduction and your abduction are officially linked and that the VPD and the RCMP share all the information they have."

"That's great."

She continued. "Have you noticed any unusual activity near your home, strange phone calls — anything that doesn't sit right with you?"

"No, nothing, and Lucas has been hyper vigilant since we got back from 100 Mile House. We're always together."

"Always?"

"Always."

"If you don't feel safe for any reason or if you have any concerns or if you remember anything at all, I want you to call me. When I say call me, I mean immediately. Don't worry about the time of day, or night." She gave me her card. "Call my cell. If you get my voice mail, leave a message and I'll get back to you ASAP. If it's an emergency, call 911."

"Got it."

"Last, but most important, don't do anything on your own."

"Like I said. That's the plan."

"Good. Thank you for coming in Morgan. Det. Ignace will get you an application for Victim Services on your way out."

Fernice and Ignace watched Morgan and Lucas leave the station.

"I'll follow up with 168 Franklin Street," he said.

"See if you can get us contact info for the owner. We need to get inside that house."

Fernice stopped at the unit clerk's desk on the way back to her office and handed her the timeline.

"Rachel, would you make copies of this for everyone. Put one in Gilbrauson's basket as well. And I need a copy of the report Det. Hermes did on a visit to a house in the

East Village, 168 Franklin Street, on Friday, October 3rd. Rosaline Bolton, Terrace BC made the call that initiated the visit and that would have been about Carey Bolton, her daughter, reported missing in Terrace on September 18th. There's no file for Carey. Start one and put a copy of Hermes' visit to Franklin Street in it. I'm requesting the Terrace RCMP case files on Carey. And that the files of Carey Bolton and Morgan O'Meara be linked."

"Right away Jeri," said Rachel, keying the information into her computer.

"For Carey's file, I also need the notes of Cpl. Gilbrauson regarding an interview he did on September 29th with Michael Bolton. That interview regards a sighting of Carey Bolton behind the *Clarendon*. That interview should include the report of Bolton's initial sighting of his niece behind the club, September 27th."

She continued to her office. First, she completed the paperwork to have the cases linked and included Sgt. Desocarras in those who were to be notified of the request. She cc'd Cpl. James as a courtesy. She reread everything she had: James's interview with O'Meara; the interviews of Sgt. Desocarras and his wife Gwen on the rescue of O'Meara; and the timeline created by O'Meara and her partner, which spanned the period from September 18th—the date of the abduction of Carey Bolton—to October 9th, the date of O'Meara's rescue by Desocarras and wife.

Hermes wasn't in till tomorrow. Gilbrauson was on holiday, so there was just the three of them to work the O'Meara/Bolton case. Fernice scanned a copy of Arenas' timeline and attached it to a new email to Desocarras. She let him know he'd be copied on everything that came her way and she expected the same.

He called within the hour and they rehashed what they

had. She'd flagged the visits the women had made to the Franklin Street house and O'Meara's visit alone, the next morning, three days before she was abducted. He wanted to know if there were any leads on the reddish-orange car that O'Meara remembered in the parking lot the night of her abduction. She told him she was requesting CCTV footage of the SFU parking garage. One of her officers would review it and if anything showed up, she'd let him know.

Ignace had already emailed her what he had so far on the Franklin Street house. Donald. H. Garry bought it in 1973. Garry died in 2001 leaving it to his daughter. It was still in her possession. She had property in South Vancouver too. The house on Franklin was probably a rental. Ignace was trying to track down the daughter.

Fernice had just gotten off the phone with Desocarras when Ignace called.

"Jeri, I pulled a report you'll want to have a look at. Back in 1996, two young girls were reported missing from the reserve in North Van. A few days later, an eyewitness account has them getting into a car behind the *Clarendon*. A copy of a newspaper clipping is attached to that. It doesn't look like there was any follow up."

"Who's on the case file?"

"No case file. Rhodes took the missing person's report."

"What tipped you to that?"

"I went looking for it because that sighting is still talked about in my community."

"Okay. See what he remembers."

"I'm glad that's done."

"How'd it go?" Lucas asked.

"Fernice is requesting that Carey's file and mine be

linked."

"That's what we wanted to hear." He looked grim as he pulled away from the curb and headed into traffic. There were dark circles under his eyes.

"You're not getting enough sleep," I said.

"I'm fine. He'd only driven a few blocks East on Hastings when he had to detour to avoid road construction. He took a left, swearing under his breath. I looked at him in surprise. He'd only gone a block towards the inlet, when he swerved right, onto a side street. It's a light industrial area and there were supply trucks everywhere, loading and unloading. When he finally got a chance, he headed left down an alley and zig-zagged his way down to Powell Street. Once he got onto Powell, it was stop and go traffic all the way home. He had to slow down to a crawl and he was seething. It was so unlike him.

We're driving through thin fog and the air has a chill that's hard to dress against. I tightened my scarf, pulled on my gloves and turned the heat up. We were nearly home when I remembered the rape kit results. I glanced at Lucas. He undressed me and put me to bed my first night home. He must have seen the bruises on my body, my back, on the inside of my thighs. He knows what the bastards did to me. He hasn't said a word.

13

After lunch, I redid my makeup. If I looked closely I could see traces of the bruises. I wouldn't be giving anyone else the opportunity to do so. The bruises on my neck were an ugly yellowish purple. I hid them under a large, brightly coloured scarf. I re-parted my hair so that a swath fell over the stitches. I looked okay and that would have to do. I wasn't going to hide at home.

"You only have to get through the afternoon — only a few hours," I told the bathroom mirror. I would try to do that without tears.

Lucas headed up to Twelfth Avenue to avoid construction and then doubled back down Main Street to East Hastings. At the corner, he headed west. We slowly pass the lineup in front of *United We Can* — people waiting their turn to cash in bags bulging with empties. Others selling stuff, talking, sleeping. For some, the street is home. Their lives, the triumph of hope over despair. Lots of others, better dressed, are just passing through. A block later we enter another world when Lucas pulled into the underground parking of the *Contemporary Arts* complex.

He parked and we took the elevator up to the Film Department office on the second floor. I remember the old film department — in the portables at the far edge of the campus up on SFU mountain—in the forest. I loved it there.

Lucas looked around. Lots of people were in the office today. "I'll be back to escort you to the lab about 10 minutes to 3:00."

"That should be good."

"I'm not leaving the complex."

"I know, and I'm glad."

"Call me if you need me."

"I will." I watched him leave, then headed down the hall to my office cubicle. When I returned from the lake, Lucas and Kate kept the world at bay. I didn't give any thought to the stir that news of my abduction had caused. Just yesterday, I went online for the first time to find that every shred of public information on my case had been googled, tweeted and shared by hundreds, maybe thousands—who knew?

I made it to the door of my office when Odessa Tate, office goddess of the Contemporary Arts Department spotted me through floor to ceiling glass and rushed into the hallway to greet me.

"Morgan, we've all been so worried. It's good to have you back, safe and sound." This was a lot coming from Odessa, who is normally quite reserved. Now she was giving my face a very close examination.

"Odessa, I'll be as good as new in no time." Impulsively, I gave her a gentle hug. We weren't close and although the hug was a bit much for this very proper lady, she lived through my hug and even managed to pat me gently on the back a few times.

I'd arranged to meet with Sophia Paridopolis first thing. When she heard my voice, she was out of her office and down the hall in record time. Coming to an abrupt halt beside us, she folded me in a hug. Then she stepped back and looked me over.

"Morgan, let's go to my office," she said, leading me back down the hall to her sanctum and closing the door after us. She got right to the point.

"Are you sure you're ready to return? It hasn't even been a week! Carl is happy to fill in for you, as I'm sure you already know."

"I do. He got in touch. Honestly Sophia, I want to be here." I could tell she wasn't buying it. "I have lots of support, and I'm doing fine. Lucas and I are taking every precaution." At least that part was true. She still looked dubious. I was going to have to work on my delivery.

"It's up to you of course. Your friend Kate Brennan came to see me and told me that you were going to be okay. I really appreciated that. I was just sick with worry," She sat quiet, lips pursed. Instinctively, I hiked the scarf up a little higher on my neck.

"I don't know what I'd have done without her, or Lucas." Sophia knew Lucas, but only casually — as a fellow professor in another department.

"I don't want to pry, Morgan. Kate told me about the missing child and the help you've given the family. I assure you that information has gone no further. Kate and Lucas are both in the Criminology Department so they'll be privy to how investigations such as these are run."

"That's true."

"Morgan, I'm here any time you need to talk. I'm so glad to have you back safe. I'm just so glad!" She was thoughtful a moment. "I assume there's no news about the missing child?"

"Not recent news. We think she may have been brought to Vancouver, or has been here, quite recently." I stopped there. The less said the better.

Sophia nodded her head, started to speak and then stopped abruptly and fell silent. Odd for her; she was usually so direct.

"Is something the matter?"

"Yes Morgan, there is." Sophia took a deep breath. "These past few days, nasty gossip has been circulating on campus about you and your partner, Lucas. It seemed to come out of nowhere. Odessa brought it to my attention yesterday."

"Gossip? What kind of gossip?"

"None of it's true. Anyone who knows you knows that! Odessa is absolutely furious about it and so am I."

What now? "What's being said, Sophia?" It was obvious she was mortified to be in this position.

"You're a woman of easy virtue who used to work the streets. You still sleep around. Your partner is very jealous. He has shown his displeasure towards you in the past and on more than one occasion, has put you in the hospital."

"No!" Fucking hell.

"I didn't want to be the one to tell you, but I thought you should know before meeting with the students."

No one showed up during office hours. Should I read something into that? Who knew. Doesn't matter. Gives me time to think. Whoever grabbed me, they're trying to discredit us. They're afraid of us. Franklin Street ... We got too close ... I got too close. Those bastards. They're not going to win. We can't let them win.

I found out early that the world isn't a safe place for me. When things happened that hurt me or scared me, I had mom, who'd already walked that road, who cried with me and shared her hard-won strength and wisdom until I had some of my own. For the first time in my life, I had doubts that it would be enough.

Dad handled things differently. '*Your dad doesn't see*

colour', mom would say. He'd wring his hands instead, mystified that the world didn't cherish mom and me the way he did. Then one of the students at my school went missing. She was from a reserve further north, boarding with a family so she could attend high school. It was almost a week before her body was found, face down in the reeds beside the McIntyre river. Not the first child — seven now — my community heartbroken. Frightened. Still demanding an inquiry.

It was dad's idea that we learn to defend ourselves. Mom, ever inch the scholar and bookworm, refused to even discuss it. *'I'm too old to learn. Put Morgan in the class.'* I went to those classes for years. Fear pushed me and I worked hard. I learned my lessons well, afraid I'd end up like that poor girl. And the others. But you know what, dad. It wasn't enough to protect me. Arming yourself against the hate of others doesn't make you invincible and it doesn't stop the hate.

Lucas interrupted my thoughts. He was here to walk me to the lab. I decided to wait till after to tell him about the rumours. We walked up to the fourth floor and arrived just before 3:00 pm. Most of the students were already here. Lucas checked the area carefully before leaving.

I'd met with the students five times already, including the afternoon of the day of my abduction. They're a good group: diverse, frank and opinionated. I looked around now at their faces, wondering who had heard the ugly rumours and I noticed that some avoided my gaze except for a guy named Nick. He was at the back of room and was staring at me. An insolent smile played on his lips. Here was one who believed the rumours. I stared right back until others turned to see what had my interest. The centre of attention now, he quickly dropped his gaze.

Conversation buzzed. I expected questions about my

abduction and decided the best way to handle them was to insist that there was nothing I could comment on.

There were indignant outbursts about racist and misogynist news bias and sensationalism. Some students had pulled up examples on their tablets and phones, which they were showing each other and me. Others had gone to the trouble to print some of the articles and bring them here. These were waved around indignantly.

Native Cop Rescues Near-Dead Native Girl

That was an older headline, from the day after I was rescued. I'd seen it yesterday.

"Morgan, did you see this?"

Here was another from today's Province, which I hadn't seen. I read now, from the copy a student handed me:

Morgan O'Meara, an Aboriginal woman with dreams of being an independent filmmaker, who until only recently lived on and worked the streets of Vancouver's downtown eastside, came very close to having her life snuffed out by an unnamed attacker.

O'Meara, who escaped a difficult life on the Greenwood Lake Reserve in Ontario, was found bound and gagged on the shore of Gustafsen Lake near Hundred Mile House.

The smear campaign was having the desired effect, and also, it would appear, opened my story up to embellishment. If they knew about the reserve, they'd know I wasn't raised there. And gagged — I wasn't gagged.

I told them that I welcomed any information they thought might be helpful, thanked them for their concern, then I shut the discussion down. They weren't happy and there was grumbling.

"Let me at least give this to you, Morgan. I think it's

important." Shelby was at my side and handed me an article that had appeared in the 100 Mile Free Press, Saturday, October 11th. She'd also printed out a tweet that mentioned the same article. I quickly scanned the article while she filled me in.

"Stacie Smith, she's an MA candidate in the English Department and she knows you're one of the TAs for the first years' film lab. She brought the tweet to my attention, in case you missed it."

Someone had tweeted about the article in the 100 Mile House newspaper.

KaleATalk@banishedboy @SFU_W 100 Mile Free Press article on blue truck will be of inturest to Omeera

My name was misspelled, but I was sure it was meant for me. There was absolutely nothing in the article itself linking the truck to my abduction, which meant that the tweeter knew that the truck was connected to it and knew this was very helpful for me to know. Even here, in the safety of the lab, fear crawled up my back.

The pickup had been partially torched and abandoned about 2 km from Canim Lake Reserve. Later, I'd check a map to see how far that was from Gustafsen Lake. The fire attracted the attention of some of the folks at Canim Lake. No body was found in the truck or nearby and there was no license plate. For sure Alex must know about this. Shelby agreed to stay behind after the lab. I'd talk to her then.

While he waited for Morgan, Lucas sat on a bench at the main entrance to the Contemporary Arts building. When he'd tried to talk with people earlier, they seemed uncomfortable. Some avoided him altogether. Steve Winn walked by, someone he knew well enough to be direct with him. Lucas called him over.

"Steve, what's going on? People don't want to talk to me. It feels like they're avoiding me. I don't get it."

"Let's get a coffee, Luke." They got coffees from the kiosk at the building entrance and returned to the bench.

Steve got right to the point. "Look buddy, there's some nasty rumours circulating. I know they're not true. But I think you should know what's being said about you both — some of it's really ugly stuff." Steve looked grim.

"Go ahead."

"Okay. You're a hot-headed Latin with a quick temper and handy with your fists. Morgan has a colourful past that includes time spent as a prostitute on the streets of Vancouver. You got jealous of some guy Morgan was flirting with and you beat her up."

Lucas was completely blindsided.

"Anyone who knows the two of you doesn't believe any of it. The gossip is pure bullshit and we're saying so!"

"Do you have any idea where this is coming from?"

"No idea. What happened to Morgan — that was scary. It must have been horrible for you, Lucas. Her missing, not knowing where she was."

Lucas nodded, not trusting himself to talk about that. Instead, he said: "Steve, can you pinpoint when the rumours started?"

"Personally, I first heard the stories yesterday, so Monday. But they could have started circulating on the weekend and I wouldn't have known. I was skiing in Whistler."

They talked a while longer, then Steve left. Morgan wouldn't be finished for at least an hour. Lucas continued to sip his coffee, watched people come and go. He wondered if Morgan had heard about the rumours.

Lucas was waiting at the door when the film lab finished. Shelby joined us as we made our way to my office. I pulled out the newspaper clipping about the truck and handed it to Lucas.

"Check this out." He started to read it — stopped — looked at me, then Shelby.

"Stacie Smith texted me about the tweet and the article," she said. She pulled out her phone, accessed her twitter account and pulled up the original tweet. Lucas and I read it over her shoulder.

"Stacie texted Gary Sulzberger too."

"A student?"

"He's in Carl's lab," said Shelby. I'm not sure how Stacie knows Gary, but I saw him at the cafeteria this morning and he wanted me to make sure you knew about it."

"Call Alex and see if the truck's still there," said Lucas.

"Just about to do that." I pulled out my phone. "And Shelby, thank you for bringing this to me."

"I thought it might be important. Stacie sure wanted you to know about it."

"It's very important," I assured her as I dialled Alex.

Lucas jumped in. "How do you know Stacie?"

"I work at the student bookstore on Burnaby Mountain, mostly weekends. Stacie's masters' thesis is on Indigenous Canadian Lit and I've special ordered a few books for her and I watch out for copies of out-of-print stuff, that kind of thing. We have each others cell number."

I got Alex's voicemail and left a message.

"If there isn't anything else, Morgan, I've gotta run. I've got a class at Harbour Centre in half an hour."

"We're good, Shelby."

"Good luck," she called over her shoulder.

"You think this is the truck?" Lucas held the newspaper article in his hand like it was a treasure map.

"Yes. I do."

"We'll go tonight. That way we'll be able to see it first thing tomorrow morning."

"I have Alex and Gwen's home number. I'll call Gwen, too and let her know we're coming. You didn't get to meet her when you came to get me. You're really going to like her." Gwen was at home and she picked up. She knew about the truck. She said she'd let Alex know we were coming up tonight and told me to text him as soon as we arrived.

We left the university and picked up take-out burgers on our way back to the cottage. After eating, we packed overnight bags with the few things we'd need.

Bart called to check up on me, and Lucas filled him about the truck. Bart was worried that seeing the truck would be hard for me. He offered to take tomorrow off and come with us. Kate never had anything booked on Wednesdays and there was no way she was staying behind. Bart offered his *Prius* for the trip. It was more economical than Lucas's aging Toyota. Gwen had suggested we stay at the Red Coach Inn. I called and booked two rooms.

While we waited for Kate and Bart, I told Lucas about my conversation with Sophia and the ugly rumours that were circulating about us. He shared what Steve had told him.

"A lot of people believe the lies," said Lucas.

I pulled out the article from today's Province. "Have you seen this?" He hadn't. He read it silently.

"Someone is trying to shut us down. That's not going to happen," I said.

By 8:00 pm, we were on the Trans-Canada Highway heading East. Bart took the exit to the *Coquihalla Highway* around 10:00 pm. We'd shorten our trip by an hour and arrive in 100 Mile House by 1:00 am.

The *Coquihalla* is a mountain highway and elevated — 1,200 metres at the summit — so it can be mist one minute, light snow the next, then rain, then a sky full of stars. We were treated to all of these while I listened to the low murmur of the fellows up front and the occasional sound from Kate. Tomorrow, I would get a look at the truck up close. The chances were good that seeing it would be hard. That filled me with dread, but this was something I had to do, ready of not. For a few brief moments, I tested myself — went back to the lake, could see myself on the path going down to the water; remembered Alex and Gwen coming toward me in the boat and I was already shaking with dread. I quickly shut the memory out and pulled myself back to the car.

When was it going to be okay? What would it take? I turned to Kate, fast asleep beside me. Bart told Lucas she was so tired, she sometimes dropped off in mid sentence. He was worried about her. Exhausted. Not getting enough sleep for weeks now because of her connection to Carey. I didn't want to talk with her about what happened to me. Didn't want to add that to what she already shouldered. Not talking to Kate was an ache that sometimes made it hard to breathe.

14

Carey lay in bed, listening to men arguing in the kitchen. One of them was yelling at Melanie. Then there was the sound of someone being slapped, then stomping up the stairs. Moments later, Melanie stormed into the bedroom.

"You fucking bitch! It was you they came looking for! You brought this on us." She pointed to Marie. "Wake her up and get her dressed. You too. We're leaving in 10 minutes." Melanie moved to the next bedroom and started to yell at them.

Someone was looking for her? Who? If they left here, they wouldn't be able to find her? Carey quickly sat up and tried to rouse Marie, but she wouldn't wake up. Marie had wet the bed. Carey went to the bathroom and got a washcloth and towel. She removed Marie's nightgown and started to clean her.

Melanie was at the door again. "Forget about the fucking piss, just get the brat dressed."

"Yes ma'am," Carey said to Melanie's back. Then she quickly cleaned Marie as best she could because no one likes to smell like pee. Her brother Elwin used to be so embarrassed when he wet the bed. Thinking about him brought instant tears. She missed him so much. Somehow, she got Marie dressed, but she couldn't find her new rag doll.

Marie carried the doll everywhere and wouldn't let anyone take the tags off. Maybe Seth could bring it for her later.

Marie was still asleep and one of the men came upstairs to carry her down to the car. He walked in on Carey as she was pulling on a tank top and leered at her. "Maybe later."

Carey kept her head low and quickly pulled on her jeans. The guy picked up Marie and left the bedroom. She could hear Christopher pleading with Seth to let him dress himself. She heard Joy tell Seth he needed to get the doctor for him. They couldn't take Christopher to the hospital because then everyone would know what they did to him; to all of them.

Carey pulled on her socks and shoes and put on her jacket. She could hear Joy tell Georgina to get her jacket on and hurry. Georgina told her last night she was going to run away, but Carey didn't think she would. She did the white pills, even when she didn't have to. Seth said Georgina needed them now. She was addicted, just like some of the women mom worked with. *'Trying to kill their pain with anything that works,'* she'd say.

"If you don't do what they want they'll get rid of you and then your mom will never see you again." That's what Melanie said to Carey when she didn't want to take the pills or drink alcohol with the men. As if you wouldn't care what they were doing to you if you were stoned or drunk. She'd counted the weeks she'd been a prisoner here — almost four weeks — and in all that time, no one got to leave. It was just like Christopher told her the first day. She had to do whatever they told her to do.

She was going to keep checking the doors to see if they were locked and one day, one of them would forget and then she'd run away. She'd just have to get to a road and hitchhike to a police station, then everything would be okay. She'd take Marie with her. Everyone said Marie was retarded, but that wasn't true. She just hadn't learned to talk in true words. She had her own words. Carey was sure she'd made them up because she couldn't hear.

Seth was at the bedroom door. He helped her walk down to the car and get into the front passenger seat. Four of the kids were already in the car. One of the men drove Melanie and Joy in another car. They had the new girls from Abbotsford in their car. A woman brought them to the house really late last night. Carey could tell they were sisters. They had the same blonde hair and one was hugging the other one and they were crying and Melanie was threatening to hit them if they didn't shut up. Carey felt sorry for them because they didn't know what was going to happen to them. When it got really bad, at least they would have each other.

Carey checked to see if the car door was locked. It was. Seth never forgot. She always checked and he always pretended he didn't notice. Most of the children fell asleep soon after Seth started driving. Carey tried to stay awake, to see where they were going. He drove in the city for quite a while, then went over the Granville Bridge. Carey saw a sign that said Vancouver Airport, but they didn't get in that lane and then they were driving through another city. It didn't look familiar but she thought that might be because everything looked different in the daytime. She couldn't help it; she dozed off and didn't wake up again until the car was travelling downhill, into a tunnel.

Seth noticed she was awake. He told her they were going under the Fraser River and that the farm he was taking them to wasn't far from the other side.

"I used to live here," he said when he pulled into the long driveway. She asked him if he lived here with his parents.

"With Theo." Seth waited with the children in the car until the other car arrived. Georgina asked if they could go for a walk but he said no. Seth held her arm tight when he walked her to the house. Once everyone was inside, Melanie locked the door. Seth went to get breakfast for everyone.

Carey was in one of the bedrooms upstairs. From the window, she could see a horse, way in the distance. It shook its head and its mane danced in the wind. She imagined she could hear it snicker and whinny. Then it cantered off, out of sight behind some trees.

Seth had been gone a long time. The kids were all awake now and really hungry. She hoped he was getting the doctor for Christopher. Melanie said she was sick of hearing him whine and told Joy to give him something to shut him up. Joy gave him something for pain and put him to bed in the bedroom next to hers. She could hear him moaning softly.

Melanie made Christopher go to Jeff's last night. Jeff hurt everybody. He talked about her and the other kids like they wanted to be with him and let him do the mean things that he did. That was a lie. Everyone was afraid of him, even Georgina, who wasn't afraid of anyone.

Seth told Carey once that he was sorry that he'd taken her. He said he had to. After she'd been at the house a few days, she knew why. He was a prisoner too. He always did what they told him. She noticed that sometimes he froze. It was like he wasn't in the room anymore and there was nothing for him but his own thoughts.

No one else seemed to notice though, that he stopped sometimes, the way her mom's computer at Grandma's house on the reserve stopped sometimes, when there were too many programs open and it would freeze and mom would have to close them all and reboot the computer to get it working again. Mom said it was because the reserve was at the end of the line. Her computer in town never did that.

15

The next morning, we met Alex and Gwen at Barney's. The place was really crowded and they both stood up and waved us over when we walked in. Kate was at their table in a shot and before Gwen could sit back down, she grabbed her in an intense hug and breathlessly whispered her thanks for '*saving me dear friend as you did.*' Kate's hugs are legendary and Gwen was completely taken aback. I watched as Alex quickly offered his hand to her, forestalling a hug. He was a reserved guy and he obviously wasn't one to throw around hugs either.

Kate is the only adult person I know who operates without pretense or guile. She also hugs when she thinks it's time to hug and too bad if you're not ready. It's one of the things I liked best about her, right from the start. And another was if the words are coming out of her mouth, that was her honest opinion and you could take it to the bank. I steered her to a chair at their table and gave her arm a squeeze. '*I'm somewhat fucked up right now but I do love you, please believe that,*' I tried to say with my eyes, but I couldn't get her attention. She was gazing at Alex and Gwen like they were *God's gift.*

Over breakfast, Alex told us he first heard about the torched pickup the previous Monday from an officer who lived on the Canim Lake Reserve. The fact that it was blue and torched must have got his attention in a hurry. He estimated that the truck was about 40 km from Gustafsen Lake. It had been abandoned on a short, side track just off Forest Grove Road. That's where we were headed.

"How did you find out about the truck?" he asked me. I gave him copies of the tweet and the newspaper article. He read through the tweet, barely glanced at the article. I told him about the lab student who brought the article to me and about Stacie Smith, who'd sent a text to my student Shelby with the heads up for me.

"Stacie Smith wanted to be sure you saw this article?"

"She did."

"Do you know Stacie?"

"No, neither of us have ever met her. We'd like to talk with her though."

"Don't do that, Morgan. Det. Fernice or me will get in touch with her. Do you have her number?"

I gave him the number that Shelby had given me.

"Did you speak with her about the tweet?"

"Not yet."

"Don't worry about that either. I'll talk to her when we're finished here."

Something about his tone said he wasn't kidding and that pissed me off. I'm the one who got abducted. Not him. Lucas didn't miss my reaction. He caught my eye and gave me an understanding look.

Alex told us he'd arranged for a fire inspection and the RCMP forensics team from Vancouver were flying up today as well. We piled into Bart's car and followed Alex and Gwen out of town.

It wasn't far to where the truck had been abandoned. There was a side road, only slightly better than a dirt track, connected with Forest Road, the road we took from the highway. Alex pulled onto the shoulder and Bart pulled in behind him. We piled out and he passed out latex gloves, warning us, as we put them on, to avoid touching anything.

The pickup wasn't more than 10 metres from where we stood. Kate was a little behind me and didn't miss my reaction.

"You okay?"

"I'm okay," I lied. Here I go, ready or not. We walked over to the truck. The front left tire was up to its axle in a deep rut so it was nose down, forward and to the left. It looked like most of the fire damage was contained within the cab and under the hood. The truck bed was intact.

"Talk at the station is the young lads at Canim Lake are responsible for torching it," said Alex. "I know that's not the case. If it was abandoned and drivable, one of them would have taken it for a spin."

"Probably torched by the red-headed guy," I said.

"That's my thinking," said Alex. Gwen was standing beside me with a strange look on her face. I caught her eye but she looked away quickly. I wasn't the only one who had feelings to deal with.

"Remember. Don't touch anything," Alex warned. "We don't want to destroy any evidence that might still be here."

"Do you think this is the truck, Morgan?" asked Bart.

"Yes."

"Me too," said Gwen. "I've never seen a vehicle this color blue."

"Looks like a home paint job," said Lucas.

"Aha," said Kate. She was at the passenger door, leaning down. The fire had burned through the layer of blue paint and although badly scorched, a deep maroon colour could be seen at the bottom of the chassis. "The perp painted the pickup at some point." Bart groaned at her side, rolling his eyes.

"Please, Kate, a little less levity."

Awash in alliteration, I thought, but didn't feel the joy.

"Bart. Look!" she insisted. "It used to be maroon."

He leaned in to have a closer look. "Quite right, Kate. I think I prefer the maroon." I thought of the splatters of paint on the guy's boot; realized Alex would know about them now. Sure enough, he leaned in behind them, making a note.

Lucas had moved to the driver's side of the truck. I was on the passenger side, a few feet from Kate. Alex moved to stand beside me.

"Alex, can we open this?" I indicated the large, aluminum box, right behind the cab. "There's something about that box."

He reached over the side and with one gloved hand, gently grasped the outer edge. Lucas followed suit and reached over from the other side touching only the corner of the lid with a gloved finger. Together they raised the lid. Because the front of the pickup was lower than the back, the lid stayed open. We all peered inside.

"I remember that smell! It's awful, isn't it!"

"Acetone," said Alex.

A vivid memory flooded back — trying to push the lid of the box open with my shoulder and the rush of cool air on my face. Without thinking, and before Alex could stop me, I reached over and slid a gloved finger along the front lip of the box. I snagged the glove on a sharp piece of metal that protruded a few centimetres.

"I remember this," I said, drawing back in surprise. "I was trying to escape from the box and I cut my hip on this." I pointed to my left hip area.

"Morgan, please tell me that you didn't cut your finger just now?"

"No," I reassured him. "I just snagged the glove. See", I

said, holding it up. "It didn't tear."

He was relieved. "Good! There may be a sample of your DNA there."

"Sergeant, look at these stains," said Lucas, pointing at dark brown smears on the truck bed, closer to his side.

"Could be dried blood. Okay folks. Best if everyone steps away from the truck. Forensics will be here soon." We walked back to the vehicles.

But it was Bob Golden, a local fireman, who arrived next in a sporty red coupe.

"Hi all," he said when he reached us. Bob, a tall, jovial guy, was carrying a large black case. He was here to do the fire inspection.

"Hi Alex. Hi Gwen, he said, nodding hello to the rest of us.

"Everyone, this is Bob Golden," said Alex.

"Hi Bob," we all chorused. He took a notebook from his jacket pocket.

"How long do you figure the truck's been here, Alex?"

"Since midday last Thursday; maybe a little earlier."

"You said on the phone this truck is linked to a case you're working on — the woman from Vancouver who was abducted last week."

Alex nodded in my direction, and Bob turned to look at me, taking in the row of stitches on my forehead and what remained of the bruises on my face. No concealer today.

"Yikes," he said seriously. Lucas moved closer; protective.

"Well, I'd best get started." He put on overalls, booties and a pair of disposable gloves and got to work.

"The Vancouver forensics team will be here soon," Alex told him.

"Sergeant, I'm confused," Bart said. "Is the forensic lab

that's coming up part of the VPD?"

"No. This crime scene is within RCMP jurisdiction. I requested the RCMP Forensic tech guys from Surrey to fly up."

"Kate has explained policing jurisdiction in BC, in Canada actually, a number of times now. I get it, at least I think I do." Lucas and Kate exchanged a glance.

"It's a bit convoluted," said Alex. Policing in BC is covered by 12 police forces; the RCMP is one of them and the biggest. Of the other eleven, VPD is the biggest and they have their own forensics lab and Scene of Crime services. The RCMP is under contract to police all towns in the rest of BC who don't have a police department of their own. We're also the provincial police force for BC and the provincial umbrella includes those municipalities with their own police departments, including Vancouver. And we serve as Canada's federal police force. As part of our federal mandate, we run the RCMP Forensic Laboratory Services. We have five forensic labs in Canada. One of these is in Surrey because RCMP E Division headquarters — E Division is the British Columbia/Yukon Division of the RCMP — is in Surrey. The Surrey guys are on their way up."

"Okay" said Bart, "So VPD doesn't have jurisdiction here in 100 Mile House, even though they're also investigating Morgan's case."

"That's right," said Alex.

"But the RCMP and VPD are sharing results, right?" Bart asked.

"Yes, we are. The RCMP investigation of Morgan's rescue at 100 Mile House is officially linked with the VPD investigation of her abduction," said Alex.

I turned to Alex. "Det. Fernice told me she was going to request that the Terrace investigation into the disappearance of Carey Bolton be linked to my abduction."

"They're linked now. We're sharing those files as well."

"Finally, a step in the right direction," said Kate, never one to hold back.

Alex looked at her, surprised, but said nothing.

"Morgan barely escaped with her life. Carey, still missing—nearly a month now. Michael spotting Carey and the other children in the car behind the club, that sighting basically ignored by the VPD! I know Carey's alive, but ... Kate abruptly stopped speaking when she saw the look on Alex's face.

"What are you talking about? Have you spoken with Carey?"

"No, I haven't spoken with her. It's not like that."

"You should tell the Sergeant what you know," Bart said.

"What exactly *do* you know?" he asked.

Kate looked Alex in the eye and sighed. "Carey has been communicating with me. Not directly, I don't mean that. It's more that I feel what she's feeling."

Alex said nothing, his face skeptical. Kate didn't miss that.

"I'm a recognized psychic, Sergeant. I've assisted police investigations in the past, both here and in Ireland. My connection with Carey comes and goes. Something is interfering with the communication, but I'm not sure what. I know she's afraid, at some times much more than others. She is alive. I do know that."

"How long have you had this ... *connection*?"

Alex wasn't buying any of this, but if it bothered Kate, she didn't let on. She was used to dealing with skeptics, me included, once upon a time.

"It started less than a week after Carey was taken," said Bart.

"It's always been sporadic. There's been nothing since last night. It does worry me when it breaks off and that happens a lot."

"Kate isn't getting much sleep," said Bart. He put his arm around her.

"Oh Bart, I don't mind that!" It's just so frustrating that we're not moving forward."

"We wouldn't be here if Kalea Talk hadn't tweeted about the article. She might even know where Carey is!"

"She might be a he," I said, thinking of @banishedboy. What happened to me is the talk of the university right now. It didn't take much for Stacie Smith to put two and two together."

"We'd like to talk to Stacie," said Lucas.

"Absolutely not, Lucas! I will take care of that, or Det. Fernice. You do both understand why it's important the police are the ones to talk with Stacie Smith about this? At the very least, the tweeter has intimate knowledge of the truck and its link to Morgan's abduction. He, or she, is definitely in harm's way by leaking this information. Smith may be as well."

"Yes," we said together.

I watched as Alex strode over to Bob Golden and spoke with him.

"The child is still missing," said Gwen, with a glance at me.

"Children," said Kate. "We think she's been trafficked."

"Trafficked!" said Gwen. She didn't know. It seemed that Alex didn't bring his work home with him.

"When Morgan and I were in Guatemala earlier in the year, we heard a lot about women and children being trafficked and about the paedophiles who were showing up in Central America, more and more — *on holiday*."

"70% of trafficked victims worldwide are women and

girls," said Kate. "Here in Canada, if a child is kidnapped, or suffers aggravated sexual assault — or is killed — then the minimum sentence is six years and the maximum is life! Canada hasn't had many convictions and sentences to date have been minimal. Not much of a deterrent when there's millions to be made."

"There are holes and gaps in the fabric of societies everywhere," I said.

"Gender and racial inequality is what some call it," said Kate. Seeing the look on my face. "Shit Morgan. I'm so sorry."

"You're right though."

"You don't need me explaining that to you. I can be such a twit."

"You're tired."

"No excuse," said Kate.

"In Guatemala, the villagers are known to take matters into their own hands."

Alex had rejoined us and heard what Lucas said. "Rough justice?" he asked him.

"Exactly. If a trafficker is identified, the villagers kill him."

"How long have you been in Canada, Lucas?"

"Since 1982. My mother and I came here as refugees, during the civil war."

"I don't know much about that," said Alex.

"Guatemala's 30-year civil war about land and who gets to control it, farm it. Most of the good land in Guatemala is owned by the Spanish, or families from other European countries, or Ladinos, people of mixed European-Maya heritage. Ladinos are the largest group of landowners now. They have a lot of power. Luis Gurriarán was a Jesuit priest who saw land cooperatives as the answer for the Maya. He came here to Canada, to study the cooperative model and shared what he learned back home. My parents were among the founding members of Santa Maria Trejá, the first land cooperative in Guatemala to reclaim jungle for farming — that was in 1970."

"Your parents belonged to the first land cooperative in Guatemala," said Alex.

"They did and theirs was very successful."

I was surprised at Lucas. He rarely spoke about his childhood and then, only in a guarded way.

"When did you start your schooling?" Alex asked.

"As a small child. My father was my first teacher.

"And your people?"

"My mother's parents were Ixil-Maya, but on my father's side I am Ladino all the way back to my great-great grandfather — a Ladino who owned the plantation my father, Rafael was born on. Dad identified himself as Mestizo, as do I. That's what the Maya call those of mixed race. The Spanish prefer Ladino."

Alex nodded, a knowing smile on his face.

"Why do they prefer Ladino?" asked Gwen.

Lucas smiled his beautiful smile. "Near the end of the nineteenth century, Guatemala had a dictator named Rufino Barrios. At that time, there were the Criollos, the Guatemalan born Spanish elite, about 5% of the total population; the Indigenous Maya, about 75%; and the Mestizos, who were estimated to be about 20% of the population. Barrios recognized that the allegiance of the Mestizos was often caught between the minority Spanish elite and the Indigenous majority and he gave them the chance to better themselves economically: the chance to work in government, serve in the army, to become professionals. But to take advantage of this opportunity, the Mestizos had to renounce their Mayan heritage. If they did, they became Ladinos — honorary Spanish — and helped to swell the ranks of the ruling elite. My great-grandfather was one of those."

"I get it now," said Gwen.

What Lucas said got me to thinking about my mom. A few years after she finished her degree at Lakehead, she married dad, an Irishman. When she did that, she lost her Indian Status and was no longer a member of the Greenwood Lake Reserve; her home, where she was born and grew up. She lost all membership rights. When that law was challenged and finally changed in 1985, she applied and got her Indian Status reinstated. And mine.

The others are deep in conversation but I'm suddenly very weary and too tired to talk anymore. I slipped into the back seat of the Prius and leaned my head back. Through the side window, I can see Bob, going about his work. I'm so tired I can't keep my eyes open. Time for a quick nap.

I'm somewhere dark. My face is being pushed into rough carpeting and a man is yelling at me enraged and hitting me again and again and he is raping me and I try to push him off try to roll over but someone else grabs my hands and yanks my arms above my head and I can't move and a big hand covers my mouth with a cloth. Someone else is trying to hold me and I lash out hard as I can with a sideways punch and he's saying it's okay it's okay and I scream it's not okay it's not okay and I'm punching and punching and screaming and crying and then through the loud roaring in my ears I become aware of Lucas — his voice. So quiet.

16

Alex was at his desk nursing a coffee, the O'Meara case on his mind. She was having a bad time of it and he hoped it didn't get worse before it got easier. That she was alive was a due to a reserve of inner strength on her part, or great stupidity on the part of her attacker, or more likely both. If he and Gwen hadn't happened along when they did ... but he didn't allow himself to finish that thought. He'd seen too many women who didn't survive.

He'd just finished emailing Fernice with an update about the tweet and the truck. He passed along Stacie Smith's cell number. He could feel a window was closing. Something had to happen and it had to happen fast. He looked down at his notebook, open at the tweet.

KaleATalk@banishedboy: Kale or Kalea, masculine or feminine; banished boy, masculine. Alex opened the database and did a search for Kalea Talk. No one listed. He did a search using the initials KT. That brought up 37 names with a first or last name beginning with a K or a T. Thinking banished boy, he narrowed the search to males first, which gave him 11 names. Only three had the initials KT. Alex started with them. K. Turner, 37 years old, was serving time for armed robbery; K. Tandy, in his late 40s, reported dead of an overdose two years ago; K. Tamburino, 28 years old, got five years for dealing in

1996 and last known address Whitby, Ontario. He was interrupted by an email from Jeri. No one named Kalea Talk on their database. Alex emailed her back: No luck on ours either. A minute later, his phone rang.

"Hi Alex. Jeri here. What if the name's a pseudonym, or maybe a mashup."

"Yeah. I'm thinking male because of the banishedboy."

"Maybe the young man who took Carey Bolton," said Jeri.

"Could be. So, an older teen then."

"Yeah," said Jeri.

"Right off, if it's a mashup, I see the word lake in the first four letters."

"Lake. That leaves an 'a' and the word talk. Hmmn."

Both were silent a full minute.

"Talka," said Alex, breaking the silence. Takla. Lake Takla. There's a Takla Lake First Nations.

"Where are they?"

"In Prince George. That gives me an idea. I'll call you back, Jeri."

Alex plugged in a new search: male, Indigenous, 21 or under, Prince George — looked at the words: *banished boy* — added missing. 24 cases came up. The first three were resolved; the fourth, a boy, Jason, 11 years old, was still missing; taken by his mother, possibly in the States. Alex quickly keyed in: *unresolved*. Now he had six, including the boy Jason. Jordan was next. He'd been missing three years and was 15 years old by now; a little too young. Next was Scott, who'd been missing for two years. He'd be 10 years old now, so definitely too young. The fourth entry was Seth Boyce. He'd been reported missing in Prince George about eight years ago, eleven at the time, so he'd be nearly 19 years old; a possibility. He checked the last two search results. Harjo, six years old; a recent case; a parental abduction by the father; still missing. The last entry was a boy named Lance, missing for three years. He would be thirteen now.

Alex pulled up the record for Seth Boyce, noted the mother's address at the time, plugged her name into the computer and bingo, she still lived there: Tanya Boyce, 135 River Glen Road in Prince George, BC. Same address, same phone number. He made the call. Tanya Boyce picked up. It was about 5:30 in the afternoon.

Alex identified himself and explained as gently as he could why he would like to see her. He could hear the hesitation in her voice, but as he quickly found out, it wasn't due to his request. An officer from the Prince George RCMP detachment had dropped in on her the day before to ask how she was doing and if her son had been in touch. The hair on the back of his neck prickled.

"I told him I haven't spoken to my son since the day he disappeared."

Alex explained that he was pursuing another case possibly linked to her son's disappearance. Tanya Boyce remained silent.

"I know how difficult this request must be for you, Ms. Boyce, but I would like to talk with you about your son's disappearance, the circumstances surrounding it and so on. I'd really like to speak with you in person."

"Would you be coming today? I have a church group tonight that I don't want to miss."

"How about tomorrow morning? I can be there by noon." She agreed.

It was about five hours from 100 Mile House to Prince George. Alex didn't tell anyone that he planned on driving up to Prince George. Something told him that wasn't a good idea and he hoped to have a much better idea why it wasn't, after he spoke with Tanya Boyce. He told his dispatcher he'd be out of the office until late in the day. He emailed Jeri that he had a development he was going to chase down tomorrow and he'd fill her in as soon as he knew something. He left the detachment and texted Gwen he was on his way. He was already late and they were having dinner with friends.

17

Seth didn't bring the children back to the farmhouse till very late. Carey pretended she was asleep so Joy didn't give her a sleeping pill. By the time everyone was in bed and asleep it was almost 5:00 a.m. Carey knew that because Ange had given her a watch. It had a soft wrist strap with pink and white daisies printed on it. She hoped she could keep it. The kids weren't supposed to have watches or ever know what time it was but no one ever told Ange what to do. He was one of the ones in charge. Carey didn't understand why, if he was in charge, he told Seth it was okay to bring Christopher to the party. Joy was upset because the doctor said yesterday he needed time to heal. He was bleeding when they got back to the farmhouse and Joy did something to help that and gave him something for pain. He was in the downstairs bedroom with her, so she could watch him.

Carey heard the car leave. Seth must have gone somewhere. She could hear an animal scrabbling on the roof. Maybe it's a raccoon, she thought, or a squirrel. Then there was the sound of something heavy sliding, then the sound of squealing metal and then a scream. Then nothing. She waited, but there was nothing more. The scream had sounded so human, not like an animal. She jumped out of bed and ran to the next bedroom. Georgina wasn't in her bed and the bedroom window was open. She looked out and could see where the gutter had been pulled loose.

Carey ran downstairs and tried to open the front door but it was locked. She went to the back bedroom to get Joy.

"Please help Joy! I think Georgina fell off the roof!"

Joy put on her housecoat and shoes and ran to the kitchen but she couldn't find the front door key.

"Seth's not here. I heard him leave in the car," Carey told her. Joy returned to her room and called Seth on her cell.

"Get back here quickly. Georgina fell off roof. She might have escaped."

Carey looked at her watch: 5:27 a.m.

"Who gave you that?"

"Ange."

"Go back to bed Carey."

Carey pretended to go to upstairs to bed and stayed out of sight on the second-floor landing. Joy sat at the kitchen table until Seth returned. He unlocked the door and the two of them went outside. Carey looked at her watch: 5:42 a.m. She moved to her bedroom window, watched a flashlight moving in the dark, but couldn't see what they were doing. A few minutes later, she heard the front door open. She moved quickly to the landing in time to see Seth carry an unconscious Georgina inside, then disappear into one of the back rooms. Carey climbed into bed with Marie and held one of her hands and tried not to cry. A while later, Seth came upstairs and made sure the windows were closed and locked.

"Carey," he whispered, "are you awake?" She pretended to be sleeping. He went back downstairs. A while later she heard someone knock on the front door.

"What is it now?" She recognized his voice. It was

the doctor. She heard footsteps moving to the back of the house and a door closing. That was the last thing she remembered before she fell asleep.

The children were moved to the gatehouse the next afternoon.

"It smells nice here," said Amy. She was one of the sisters from Abbotsford. It did smell nice, like fresh lemons. The kids were afraid it would be a prison because of Georgina trying to get away, but it wasn't. Carey asked Seth if Georgina was okay. He said she was but Carey could tell he didn't want to talk about it.

"When is she coming back?"

"I don't know."

Carey knew Ange was away on business for a few days because he told her. You could see another, bigger house through the kitchen window. Seth told her Ange lived there and it was like a palace inside.

Joy was at the gatehouse because Melanie was sick. Seth said that was because she was a junkie. The children liked Joy. She was nicer than Melanie. She never hit anyone.

Ange returned from his trip on Thursday. Carey was in the kitchen and she saw the taxi drop him off in front of his house. He wasn't home long when he came over to the gatehouse to visit.

The kids were all watching *Madagascar*. Ange asked Carey to come sit with him in the kitchen. Marie followed them and sat close to Carey, holding her hand tightly. She thought that might make him mad, but he didn't mind. He even smiled at Marie. He told Carey he was sorry he hadn't been here to greet them when they came and hoped they were enjoying their holiday. She was pretty sure he meant that they didn't have to be with the men.

He was smiling and happy and she didn't want to make him mad but she really wanted to know if Georgina was okay. She didn't ask though, because Melanie was in the kitchen with them and then Joy came downstairs to make a cup of tea. Finally, they both left. She had just started to tell him about Georgina, when Ange got a call. She heard him say, '*Hi Mark*'. It must have been important, because he only listened for a minute and then he got up and left the gatehouse without saying a word to her and continued talking to Mark outside. Then he made more phone calls and it sounded like he was arguing with someone. Carey saw him walk back to his big house through the window, so she and Marie went back to watch Madagascar with the other kids. She knew Marie was enjoying it because she let go of her hand.

18

We got back from 100 Mile House around suppertime on Wednesday. Bart insisted on getting take-out for us before he dropped us off. Lucas went in with him.

"Now, you won't have to cook Luke. You can just feed her and let her talk."

"She won't let me hold her," said Lucas. The transaction was done. Bart put away his credit card. Lucas picked up the take-out bag and they left the restaurant.

"You'd probably feel the same, if you'd been through what she's been through," said Bart.

"I just want to hold her Bart."

"Not your call buddy." He put a reassuring hand on Lucas's arm; felt him freeze and quickly withdrew it. What a mess, he thought. Lucas, wound up tight as a drum and Morgan unravelling.

"Would you like to talk to someone about how you're feeling? I have a colleague," but Lucas didn't let him finish.

"I'm good."

Right. You're just great. "Okay."

"They dropped us off. We ate, then sat quietly. He waited me out. It was a long time before I started to talk. I had to talk. I was choking on the ugliness of what had happened to me. It filled me to overflowing, spilled out all around me, had taken over our little cottage.

Remembering is a gift, I told myself. Realized, even as the thought came to me, my Nokomis would say that. Still, the words didn't come easy. At one point, Lucas silently offered his hand and I took it. By ten o'clock, I'd talked myself out. I was exhausted. We got undressed and got into bed. I remember reaching for his hand. I don't remember falling asleep.

19

Lucas sat up, numb with fear, his heart racing, a train hurtling full tilt down a mountainside. Another nightmare, but all he could remember were red flowers, like the blooms on the rhododendron bush that mom planted by their bamboo cabin in Santa Maria. It didn't make sense, to dream of flowers and to be so frightened. He stayed in bed for a few minutes, breathing deeply, trying to get his heartbeat under control.

Morgan was asleep. He got dressed and went to the kitchen. He filtered some water, ground coffee beans, and started the coffee maker, then sat at the table. His jaw ached, he was clenching it so tight. He lay his head in his arms, trying to relax.

He thought of his mom and their small apartment on Rupert Street. The tenant before them had painted the kitchen a soft yellow and mom loved the colour. Nineth never said so, but Lucas knew how much she missed Guatemala. Vancouver is a beautiful city, but Guatemala is a tropical paradise. She told him lots of stories about Santa Maria in the early days, before he was born and stories about Finca La Perla, the plantation owned by his great-grandfather, Ignacio. Her family were seasonal workers at his plantation and when she was old enough, she worked there too.

He'd read about La Perla. Ignacio Arenas was a cruel man. They called him the Lion of Ixil with good reason. Workers guilty of infractions were imprisoned in bamboo cages. His mom never spoke of the cages or the horrible conditions the workers lived under: Living huts open to the sky during the rainy season; the floors a sea of mud.

I smell coffee. It's 7:30 a.m. I got out of bed, put on my housecoat and slippers and went looking for Lucas.

"How did you sleep?"

"Pretty good. What about you?" No answer. Not that he had to. It was obvious he'd gotten little sleep. He looked terrible. He poured coffee for us and I joined him at the kitchen table. I remember when we moved into the cottage, the table was already here, a gift from the previous tenants but badly scratched up and painted over. We'd sanded it down and refinished it with a mixture of turpentine and linseed oil, a finish my dad often used. A lot of the scratches were still visible. The distressed look, we'd joked.

Lucas watched as I ran a hand over the satin smooth wood. "I just remembered something: You know that smell, when you refinish old canoes. It's called spar varnish."

"You're on your own," said Lucas. "This table is my only woodworking project."

"Dad used to build canoes and he'd do upkeep and repair every spring. He used linseed oil mixed with turpentine to restore the wood, just like we did for the table. Then he'd finish with a coat of spar varnish."

I called Det. Fernice, reached her voicemail and left a message that I just remembered something about where I was held. She called back in minutes. I put her on speaker and quickly filled her in.

"I remember the smell of spar varnish. I think I was held in a place where wooden boats are repaired." And then, it clicked. "The docks. The hammering sounds I remember are the sound of the docks when they're operating! Just a minute." Lucas and I both fetched our laptops. Back at the table, I told her I was searching for boat builders on the Burrard Inlet.

"We live close to the inlet. When the wheat pool or the sugar refinery is operating, it gets noisy and we're blocks away. But the level of noise I remember was much louder. Way more intense."

"Okay I found a small boat builder on False Creek near Granville Island," Fernice piped up.

"False Creek is too far from the docks," I said. "That's the Inner Harbour. I remember the banging as really loud so the place had to be damn close to the docks."

"What about this one," said Lucas. *Seabreeze Marine Boat Repair.* It's on the North Shore, right on the inlet."

"Just a minute," said Fernice. "Okay, got it. But wait. It looks like they build and repair fibreglass vessels."

"No, they do wooden boats too! Click on Our Services, then Marine Boat Repair. See the subheading, wooden boat repairs. Looks like it's a smaller yard, close to the main one. I guess most boats are no longer made of wood, but in a port town like Vancouver there's probably still people with wooden craft who'd need maintenance and repairs done."

Fernice agreed. "I'm still searching for other likely builders around the harbour area."

"There aren't any others on the South shore," said Lucas.

"There are a few boat repair places in Richmond and Delta, but both communities are too far away from the docks. I think *Seabreeze Marine Boat Repair* is the most likely spot."

"I'll make a trip over there right now," said Fernice.

"I'd like to come along."

"Let me check it out first. If the site looks promising, I'll get a search warrant and I'll want you to have a look around as well. Right now, I need you to sit tight."

"Oh man," I muttered, but my indignation was lost on her.

"I'll keep you informed." she said, before hanging up.

"There are other things for us to do," Lucas said, "after we have some breakfast."

I'd just gotten out of the shower when I heard the land line ring and moments later, Lucas saying: "Grandma Effie. it's good to hear your voice." My Nokomis. I quickly dried off and put on my robe.

"You know Morgan. But she has to take me with her everywhere she goes." I was beside him now in the kitchen.

"Here she is," said Lucas. "That's my main job right now. Bye for now Effie," said Lucas, handing the phone to me with a smile.

"What's your main job," I whispered.

"Taking care of you," he whispered back.

"*Boozhoo Nokomis* Effie." (Hello Grandma.) I sat in the chair Lucas had just vacated. My grandma's given name is Ephigenia, but I've always called her Effie.

"Boozhoo Morgan."

"I'm sorry I haven't called sooner, Nokomis."

"That's okay. We know you're resting. Your man called and told me enough to keep me quiet for a few days. I like him, but tell him for me he's a terrible liar. I could hear the worry in his voice even as he told me you were going to be okay."

"I'm healing up nicely. My good looks have taken a beating, but I'll be good as new in no time."

"They beat you!" Oh boy. I'll have to be more careful what I say. "Morgan, I'm an old woman, don't play with me."

"They did rough me up some, Nokomis, but I'm okay. Really I am."

"Rough you up! Morgan. Please!"

"I'm sorry Nokomis. I didn't mean to scare you."

"Well you did! Did they hurt you bad Morgan?" I could hear the worry in her voice.

"Not too bad," I lied, contrary to everything that was reported, and most of it accurate, at least in that regard.

"Your man told us last week that you're trying to find a missing child."

"The police are looking for her. The girl is a cousin of a student at Simon Fraser who asked for our help."

"Did the girl run away?"

"No. She was abducted."

"Abducted." She was quiet a moment before she asked, "Who took her?"

"A young native man was seen driving her away."

"No!" Her distress was real. "Where is she now?"

"We don't know."

"She's a prisoner." Nokomis spent six years at Fort William Indian Residential School. Her sister, my great-aunt Mary, died there — of fever they told the family. Even then, Effie wasn't allowed to go home.

"The people who took you, they meant to kill you, didn't they?"

"Yes."

"Are you in danger now, Morgan?"

"Nokomis, we're being very careful."

147

"You're in danger." She was silent a moment. I said nothing. "I know you too well, Morgan. I watched your story on APTN. You—out running alone—at night. Your mother always worried that you were too reckless and wouldn't know when it was time to know fear and be cautious."

Nokomis was right. But that was the old Morgan. I didn't yet have the words to tell her, or anyone, that something had changed. The change had grown from the very real fear I felt when I woke up with my hands tied behind me; when I had looked at the cuts and bruises on my face and body; when I tried to speak, and didn't recognize the hoarse croak that was my voice.

"Please. Nokomis. I don't want you to worry about me." That sounded pretty lame. I tried again, a bit more truthful this time. "We're up against some very bad guys and you can believe me when I say I'm afraid of them and I'm being very careful."

"You're afraid?" Effie asked, quite surprised.

"I am afraid and I won't do anything foolish, I promise."

"I'm glad to hear that. This world is not safe for us. I'm an old woman and I know too well the terrible things that have been done to our children, our women, our people." She was silent for a moment, struggling for the right words. "They are unable to treat us fairly. This is woven in the cloth that holds this world together. It breaks my heart that this happened to you. I struggle with forgiveness Morgan, and even as I struggle, more wrongs are done."

I thought of Kate and Bart. "We have many white allies. Some of them are helping me now." Silence greeted my words. Then with a sigh, she spoke again.

"That may be so, Morgan, and I am grateful to them. But what can they know about us? What can you teach them about us in English?"

148

Nokomis had a way of getting right to the heart of the matter. English is my first language. Everything I am hangs better on that frame than anywhere else. I'm haunted by the fear I'm strictly a visitor to her culture, my mother's culture. It's mine too, but sometimes, I feel like I'm spinning in one orbit, and mom's family is right beside me in another. I don't want it to be that way.

"Your cousin Tanaka tells me what's happening with your case. She gets the information online, from one of those native bloggers." That made me smile. "But Morgan, some of the things the others are saying about you are not true!"

"I know, Nokomis. It's a deliberate smear against Lucas and me. We think the people who had me abducted are behind it. We aren't fighting back because we want them to think that their campaign is working. We're doing that because we don't want to endanger the child." I didn't want her to know, not yet anyway, that there were other children being held.

"Your secret is safe with me. I have to go now. I hear your grandfather calling me." A little poetic license here, as it sounded to me like he was in the same chair! "He was in the garden, putting it to rest for winter and he's probably hungry but too tired to make himself something to eat. He needs my help; we're getting old."

My time was up. I was being dismissed. "I love you both and I'll call soon."

"See that you do and take care of yourself granddaughter. Think about coming home for Christmas. I'm sure Tanaka won't mind if you stay with her."

"I will. *Giizagiin* Nokomis (I love you, Grandma.) *Minawa Giwabamin.*" (See you again soon.)

"Giizagiin Morgan. Remember, don't go anywhere without your man," she added, just before she hung up. I found Lucas in the kitchen.

"I'm thinking of going home for the Christmas holiday."

"That's a good idea. Visit your family, your cousins. Tanaka wants you to come."

"She does?"

"She told me when I called her last Friday. We can stay with them."

"You'll come too?"

"I'd love to."

My cell rang. It was Fernice. She'd been to the boatyard and absolutely nothing jumped out at her. I found that hard to believe and said so.

"I hear you, Morgan, but we're not done yet." I sighed with exasperation. She ignored me.

"Have you heard from Stacie Smith by any chance?"

"No, we haven't."

"Okay. Thanks," said Fernice, abruptly hanging up.

"Fernice says she didn't find anything at the boat yard."

"If she said there's nothing there ..."

"There's no other possible boatyard where I could have been held!"

"You could have been held in someone's private garage, close to the inlet, where a wooden boat was stored."

"What about the noise level? The sound of the docks?"

"Right. That's not as easy to account for, is it, unless you were right on the water."

"I'm going to check out the *Seabreeze* boat yard."

"Not without me."

"We'll be really careful. We'll tell Kate and Bart where we're going."

"We could do a car rental," said Lucas.

"We could, and that's an excellent idea."

"And we should wear disguises. We're a rather distinctive couple." We stood in the living room, nose to nose.

"You could wear your blonde Marilyn Monroe wig and lots of red lipstick and something to cover up the stitch marks and this bruise here especially," he said, touching my cheek gently. "And your big Sophia Loren shades. I love those on you."

"It's not a Marilyn wig. It's an Agnetha Fältskog shag. I do so love ABBA".

At his confused look, "Agnetha. ABBA."

"Right. She's one of the A's!"

"And what about you? You can't go like that," I said, taking in his faded shirt, jeans and sneakers.

"I'll wear black pants, black shirt and shades, and my new black blazer. I look great in black."

"You do."

"We'll be a nice couple, looking to have their old boat fixed up — my grandfather's boat, of great sentimental value."

"That's a nice touch."

"Maybe I should spike my hair," Lucas said thoughtfully. I'd followed him to the bathroom and he was eyeing his thick, black hair in the mirror.

I rolled my eyes behind his back as I reached for foundation to cover my bruises.

"I saw that, Morgan. I'll only use a little."

"Bart! You should have stopped them!" said Kate.

"You're kidding. Right? That would have been like standing in the path of a fast-moving six-wheeler and waving at it with a hanky." Bart gently waved an imaginary hanky. "Det. Fernice told Morgan she went to the boat yard and nothing was amiss. It's the only possible yard on the inlet, given everything Morgan remembers. You can't blame her for wanting to check it out for herself."

"Of course not, but we should have gone with them."

"We know they're going to be there."

"What if it's scene of the crime!"

"Kate, we don't know yet if it's the scene of the crime, not sure anyway. It'll be okay. They're going to stay in regular communication with us. And they're wearing disguises. And at the first sign of trouble, they promised me they'd get the hell out of there."

"Disguises. How do you disguise tall and gorgeous?"

"Not as hard as you might think. He pulled up the selfie Morgan sent him. Morgan was wearing a blonde, shag wig and enormous shades. A very colourful butterfly tattoo was visible on her neck.

"Oh, my god," said Kate. "She has worked her magic once again."

"Today they're in disguise as the odd couple — not a hint of urbane sophistication. Her breasts seem to have spouted. I'm no expert but I'm pretty sure her breasts aren't quite as large as that."

"The hell you aren't," Kate grinned, trying to give him a playful poke in the arm which he deflected.

"The makeup is great."

"She's so good with makeup, isn't she," said Kate.

"Lucas spiked his hair. I think that's a nice touch."

"I like the clip-on sun visor. He looks a bit like a deranged golfer, with his hair sticking out in all directions above it. He's wearing makeup too!"

"I've never noticed how beautiful his eyelashes are," said Bart.

Kate knew Bart was putting a lot of this on for her benefit. She moved in for a hug. Fernice found nothing at the boatyard. Morgan wanted to have another look. But what if they *didn't* find anything? Meanwhile, Carey, or someone close to her, had been badly hurt. Kate's sense of this was strong and it lingered, adding to her growing sense of futility.

"I think Carey's being drugged. That could explain why my communication with her is so sporadic."

"Of course. She's being drugged. I should have thought of that."

20

Melanie gave Carey a sleeping pill. She pretended to swallow it, then got into bed and closed her eyes. Melanie wanted to get back to whatever she was doing and left the room quickly. As soon as she was gone, Carey spit it out. She was still awake when several men came to the gatehouse a few hours later. Phineas was with them. She could hear Bobbie crying. He was downstairs tonight, in the front bedroom where Seth slept. There was talking, then she heard Bobbie crying again, then the front door open and close.

"We didn't charge enough," said Phineas., he's going to make plenty off him. A shame we couldn't sell Georgina."

"We should get rid of her. She's too much trouble."

"And expensive," said Phineas. "Can she still work?"

"Oh yeah. It's a walking cast."

"What about the concussion?"

"Doc says that could be a problem for us."

Carey thought that the only reason they didn't sell her was because Ange wouldn't let them. She wanted to escape and get help, but it was hard to plan because sometimes, when she was supposed to be awake she was asleep and sometimes, like now, she was the only one awake. Seth wouldn't answer Carey's questions when she asked him.

Not about anything. She was sure he didn't want her to escape, as though he needed her here. She knew that he got in trouble with Ford if he caught him talking to her. Bad trouble. Seth never did anything to stop Ford from beating him up, like Ford had all the power and he didn't have any. It didn't make sense to Carey. Seth was almost as big as Ford.

Seth asked her about her leg again today. It really bothered him that her limp was getting worse. She told him not to feel sorry for her. When she was older she'd be having one last operation, at least she hoped it would be the last one. This one would help her foot point straight ahead and that would take the pressure off her knee. It would be better if she could exercise, but they were never allowed to leave the house, even if they asked nicely.

21

Alex got an early start for Prince George. He'd been on the road an hour when his cell rang. It was Jeri.

"Are you in the office?"

"No. On my way to P.G."

"What's up?"

"Not sure yet. I might have found our tweeter. I'll call you soon as I'm done there."

"Okay."

As the miles rolled by, a worrisome unease settled over Alex. He didn't for a minute think that the visit from the RCMP officer to Tanya Boyce was routine. When, a few hours later, he finally pulled up and parked in front of her apartment complex, he checked the area carefully before exiting his car and moving to the main entrance.

Tanya answered the buzzer quickly and let him in. She was on the ground floor at the back. He was hoping the fact that his Indigenous heritage was evident would have some play with her. It did. The look of relief when she opened the door and laid eyes on him was unmistakable.

She showed him into her small but tidy living room, indicated he sit on a brown sofa and offered him a cup of tea and a sandwich. He accepted both and waited while she went off to the kitchen to prepare them.

He thought through what his approach was going to be. He'd have to tread very carefully.

"I hope you like salmon salad," Tanya said shyly as she placed his sandwich and a cup of tea on the coffee table in front of him.

"Oh, very much, Ms. Boyce; a personal favorite," said Alex, thinking of the hundreds, maybe thousands of salmon he'd caught and eaten. He took a bite and pronounced the sandwich delicious, smiling at the middle-aged woman in front of him. Her long, dark hair, streaked with grey, was loose on her shoulders. Cheeks once round and full had sunk in a little. The eyes that looked at him now were intense.

"You've lived here for a long time Tanya?" Although he already knew the answer, he wanted to put her at ease.

"Fourteen years. It's small, but it's my home."

"It's a nice place and has a real homey feel," he said truthfully.

"Thank you," she said, lapsing into silence. Alex filled up the space with appreciative bites of the sandwich and sips of tea. This wasn't going to be easy. She was quiet and presented as somewhat timid, was probably always this way with strangers, maybe everyone.

"I'm glad the local detachment still has your son's case in their active file."

She said nothing at first; just watched him eat.

"It was strange, him visiting," she finally said, very quietly. "It's been quite a few years since they last came. And now you're here," she said, looking at Alex quizzically.

He nodded, acknowledging that. "Can we talk a little about your son Seth?"

"Of course. That's why you're come." She paused, then quietly said, "He's been gone almost eight years."

"Yes, I saw that in the file. I know that it was a long

time ago Tanya, but is there anything that you remember, anything at all, that might have indicated that Seth was having a problem. Maybe he was in some kind of trouble. Thinking back, was there any reason for him to leave without telling you?"

She looked down at her hands which had been clasped tightly in her lap. Finally, after a long silence, she raised her eyes and looked at Alex.

"I didn't notice any trouble, until it was too late."

"Was he having trouble at school Tanya?"

"Yes, he was. But then he had the testing and they finally knew how to help him and that had just started. He was doing better. His grades were better." She lapsed into silence again.

"What was he tested for?"

"They said he had dyslexia. It was hard for him to read and write."

"Can I ask you Tanya what you meant by too late? You said you didn't notice any trouble, until it was too late. Are you talking about his dyslexia?"

There was another long silence. Alex remained silent as well, sipping quietly on his tea, giving her all the time she needed.

"There's something I want to show you," she said. She rose from her chair and left the room. He heard her go to another room, open the door and enter it. After a short period of time she returned. She was holding a sheaf of papers. She walked over to the couch and silently handed them to Alex, then returned to her chair. He was holding the yellowed drawings of a young child.

"Are these Seth's drawings?" he asked.

Tanya nodded.

He started to look through them, laying each one in turn on the couch beside him. One drawing depicted trees, grass, a house and a very yellow sun behind a dark grey cloud. Some of the drawings didn't look finished, although he knew this to be normal with some children, bored with one idea, on to the next one.

He moved the picture of a boy and an adult, which appeared to be finished to the pile on the couch beside him. Alex looked down at the next drawing in his lap and had to struggle for composure. He lifted it up carefully.

A man stared at him. He was wearing a shirt which Seth had begun to colour — now a faded shade of blue. But what caught his attention and held it was a yellow stripe down the side of one pant leg. Desocarras looked at the yellow stripe on his own pant leg and knew that Seth had drawn an RCMP officer. He felt like he'd been sucker-punched. In a box drawn to the right of the officer was a child, a partial figure only, with very large eyes, no nose or mouth. Beneath the box, Seth had printed: boy disapeering; disappearing spelled incorrectly.

Alex looked over at Tanya. She had her head down, her hands clasped so tightly, the skin of her knuckles showed white. He continued to hold the drawing, waiting for her to look his way, but she was caught up in her own feelings.

"Has anyone else seen these drawings, besides you and me?" he asked her gently. She glanced at the pile of drawings beside him, then with sadness at the one he was holding.

"No."

"You didn't show these drawings to the officer investigating your son's disappearance." It was a statement not a question.

Tanya shook her head no. "I didn't find them until I went through his things, quite a while after he was ... after he was gone," she finished quite resigned. "I was afraid to go to the police."

"I am so very sorry, Tanya," Alex said. What else could he say? He examined the last few drawings.

"With your permission, I'd like to borrow this one," he said indicating the drawing of the police officer and the boy in the box. "I'll return it when I'm through with it, but that might be awhile."

"I don't want it back."

Alex nodded in understanding. "Was Seth involved in a youth group of any kind say, at a recreation centre, or a church group?"

"He belonged to the boy's club at my church. They met once a week. He loved that group," she said, so softly he barely heard her.

"And which church is that Tanya?"

"*Coming to Faith Christian Centre*," she answered, smiling for the first time. It's downtown and easy to get to. We're welcome there. I go every week. I belong to the women's group."

"Tanya, do you remember the name of the officer who came to see you yesterday? I'd like to get in touch with him about my investigation."

"Inspector MacLeish, Ford MacLeish. He goes to my church. It's him that runs the boys club."

22

Seebreeze boatyard was tucked away on a small side street in North Vancouver, not far from the Lions Gate Bridge that connects downtown Vancouver with the cities of North Vancouver and West Vancouver. It was located about a block up the street from the parent company. We drove past and the front gate was unlocked. We parked our Mazda rental about two blocks away, then doubled back to the entrance and walked through.

Our story was simple. Lucas, now Maurice DeGris, had an uncle who had died recently and left everything to him, including an old wooden sailboat. Uncle had been sick the last few years of his long life and he hadn't kept up with the yearly maintenance. Maurice wanted to make the old boat seaworthy and was interested in getting an estimate. I was his wife, Tansy. The low murmur of a radio got louder as we walked toward the shop. There was no door on the south, gate side, so we started around one side of the building. A high, wide door stood part way open.

"Hello. Anybody here?" I sang out in my best falsetto as we entered the large shop.

"Lucky for us, Tansy, someone is here!" said Maurice, all ebullience as he caught my eye and nodded in the direction of a younger man, hard at work, scraping the hull of a boat.

"Hi, I'm Mitch. How can I help you?" His glance took us both in. I caught amusement in his eyes, so much better than suspicion.

Maurice jumped right in, introducing us and launching into the story of his uncle and the old boat. I'd never heard Lucas *plumb the depths* so convincingly. Even I was carried away by his desire to restore the old treasure. I simply kept nodding and gazing raptly at *my guy*. Mitch, clearly one who loved what he did, stuck out his hand at the end of Lucas's grand soliloquy.

"Your old boat sounds a dream," said Mitch. "Why don't you bring her round so I can have a look?"

"That would be wonderful," said Maurice.

"I have to warn you though, sometimes the older ones, if they're left a little too long they're beyond restoring and that can be quite a disappointment. But you say it's only a couple of years since she was maintained properly?"

"Yes, yes, that's right! Just a few years," said Maurice, jubilant. "When would you have time?"

"Next Monday would be good. Mind you, I'll have to charge you for the appraisal and it can take a few hours. I have to get inside the hull for some of the tests I need to do. Then, if it's a go, we'll talk price and an estimate of how long it should take. How does that sound?"

"Wonderful," gushed Maurice while I smiled demurely.

"This is such an interesting place Mitch," Maurice continued. "All of these beautiful tools. How long have you been doing restoration work?"

"About 10 years now. Would you like to have a look around?" He was obviously pleased with the interest and I got the impression he was here on his own a lot.

"We'd love to, wouldn't we darling?"

"Oh yes," I agreed. Needing no further encouragement,

Mitch lead us off to the left of where he was working, electing to begin the tour there. We spent the next half hour getting a first-hand account of how old hulls are prepped and repaired and then made sea worthy and barnacle resistant with the newest finishes. This yard also arranged for the restoration of cabins and decks as well. Lucas nodded and sashayed his way through the entire tour while I scanned every available nook and cranny for clues.

"Do you live here, Mitch?"

"Oh no," he said. "I've got an apartment up the hill on Eighth Avenue."

"You must have a nice view of the inlet then," said Maurice.

"Yes, I do have quite a view. And I have a boat moored nearby, at the marina under the bridge."

"Long hours?" I asked.

"Oh, no. I'm always gone by six."

"It must be lovely for you," I said. "The inlet is so beautiful in the evening."

"It is, yes, but it can get a little loud when the wheat pool is operating."

"Right. It's on this side of the inlet, isn't it?"

"About half a kilometre away," Mitch said. "Not nearly far enough! I have to wear earplugs sometimes, or I can't hear myself think." I smiled at Mitch, then looked at Maurice.

"Well, we should let Mitch get back to work."

"Thanks for the tour Mitch and we'll see you Monday. I'll call to confirm, of course."

Mitch smiled broadly at Maurice, who he was clearly quite taken with. "See you Monday then," he said.

I waited until we were across the yard and through the gate before broaching that I wanted to return that evening.

Lucas beat me to it.

"Did you hear that Morgan, about the docks being noisy!"

"I sure did. I want to have a look inside that office space."

"The room with the closed venetian blinds."

"Yes. That old wooden door doesn't look very strong. Quite a big space back there I think."

"We could use wire cutters to get through the fencing around back. But how are we going to get into the building? It'll be locked."

"There's a fairly low window on the same wall as the main door, single sash design, sliding tongue to lock it, no screen."

"We'd have to break the glass to get in. What about an alarm?"

"I didn't see any sign of one, which is surprising, but there you go — all good for us."

"You're sure? It'd be a disaster if we tripped an alarm and the police found us breaking and entering," Lucas said, matter-of-fact.

"Point taken. There were two conspicuous signs warning of a Catchem alarm system."

"I know that system. We had it at the outreach office downtown. Setting and disarming it is done close to the main door."

"There was no sign of an arming box near the main door, or anywhere else. I think the signs are a hoax. And that wide loading door with the long heavy bar can only be opened from the inside."

"Also, the fence around the property is eight feet high with a barbed wire roll around the top."

"I imagine that's an effective deterrent." We'd arrived at our rental car.

"We've got the car till tomorrow afternoon," Lucas said. "Do you think we'll need it longer?"

"Let's wait and see." I called Kate and she picked up. I filled her in and told her of our plan to return to the yard this evening. I listened patiently as she gave me all the reasons visiting the yard was a bad idea.

"Kate, I can't explain it, but something tells me I need to have a look inside that locked area."

"Why don't you get the police to go with you?"

"Lucas says they'd need a search warrant, and it'd be impossible to get one without good reason, which they wouldn't have!"

"What if someone catches you?" she countered.

"Only one guy works at the yard and he's gone by 6:00 pm."

"Bart and I should go with you."

"We need you off site, in case something goes wrong — which it won't of course!" I quickly added.

She finally agreed, but reluctantly. "You can text when you're going in, when you're safely out of there, and then show up at our place for a full accounting after, no matter how late!"

"Absolutely."

"I saw the picture you sent Bart. I see Lucas has spiked his hair," she said, changing the subject.

"It's growing on me."

We had about three hours until our planned return to the shipyard. On our way home, we stopped at *The Roundel* for burgers. Sergio, our waiter, loved our outfits. I told him I was filming. Maurice remained in character throughout dinner and I played along. It wasn't the first time it's occurred to me that Lucas may have missed his true calling.

We were back home by 6:30 pm. I changed into jeans, a hoody and sneakers with haste and very gratefully. The wig was itchy and the heels were killing me. Lucas wet his hair, combed it straight back and hid it under a black baseball cap. I made sure we had one of the burner cells Lucas had bought for us. We also brought heavy duty gloves and I grabbed the garden shears from the back shed, just in case.

While Lucas drove, I checked in with Kate to let her know we were on our way to the yard. Stacie had called the land line while we were out so I called her back. When I got through, I identified myself and put her on speaker.

"Thanks for calling, Stacie. We've got a few questions for you, if you don't mind. I assume you know what happened to me."

"Well, I know as much as anyone else, although what they're reporting lately is below the belt. I don't believe any of it, by the way."

"I appreciate that. Have the police contacted you?"

"Someone named Det. Fernice called and left a message. I haven't returned her call yet. She said she was working on your case."

"That's right, she is."

"She wanted to know about the tweet and whether I had any information about the tweeter. I don't. The reason I called you is I got a strange phone call from a guy who said he was with the student newspaper."

"The Pinnacle?" I said.

"Right. He asked me to put him in touch with the tweeter. He wants to interview him. There was something odd about the guy."

"How did he get your name?" Lucas asked. I had a pen out and was fishing around for something to write on.

"From Gary Sulzberger, the other person I texted about the tweet." Lucas and I exchanged a quick glance. "He's in the other film lab." I texted him and Shelby, because I wasn't sure which one you were leading, Morgan."

"Did you get the caller's name?" asked Lucas.

There was a long silence.

"Stacie, are you still there?" I asked.

"Sorry, I'm still here. I realise now I should've contacted you directly, but I was scared. Everyone is talking about what happened to you, and I do mean everyone. One of the security guards told me the number of women requesting an escort to their cars at night has skyrocketed. Who can blame them? There's a lot of fear. You know, bad stuff happens to women students all the time, but this is different."

"Because I'm Indigenous."

"Yes Morgan! That's what I'm talking about. I am too and I don't feel safe!"

"I totally get it," I said. "The guy who said he was from the Pinnacle, did he give you his name, even a first name?"

"He said his name was Mark."

"We'll let Det. Fernice know about the phone call. She might call you about it.

"Okay. I'll talk to her if she does."

We said our goodbyes.

We left the cottage. Lucas had made a quick detour to a *Canadian Tire Store* near us to pick up heavy duty wire cutters. He was in and out in minutes, then we were on our way. The trip back across the inlet to the North Shore was much faster this time of night. We arrived at the shipyard a little after 8:00 pm.

Lucas drove by the main gate, now closed and locked. The shop building was lit, especially the main entrance on the side, but the lighting was low wattage. We parked in the same area we had earlier, just up the street and around the corner from the yard, well out of sight. I texted Kate that we'd arrived at the yard and were going in. She texted back, reminding me to take the cell in with us. The plan was I'd text her once we were inside, and again when we were clear. She had Fernice's cell number, just in case.

Gathering everything we needed, including the burner, on vibrate, we made our way to the north side of the lot. I had a *Nikon* tucked into a jacket pocket — just in case.

We decided to go in through the north side as there were only a few houses on that side. Getting through to the chain link fence entailed a bit of work. Blackberry bushes along the fence were quite overgrown and blackberry thorns are lethal. We found a relatively thin patch of bushes near the north-east side and I quickly cut a path through to the fence, using the shears to pick up and toss the snarly branches to one side.

Once at the fence, Lucas cut through the chain link, bending it back and creating an opening for us. I cut away a few more berry stalks just inside the fence. Then we slipped through the fence and into the yard on the shop door side.

There wasn't much moonlight, but there wasn't much laying about outside, so it was easy going, across the 30 or so metres to the building. We avoided the pools of light near the eaves and followed the wall to the left, where I'd noticed the small open window earlier. There was no eave light near it. The window wasn't open now and when Lucas put his shoulder to it, it wouldn't budge.

"Locked. I'll break the bottom pane," he said and grabbing the wire cutters, he drew back and slammed the cutters against the window. Nothing. He looked at the window in disbelief, drew back and slammed the cutters against the window again. That did the trick — the window shattered.

Once stray bits of jagged glass were cleared away, Lucas reached in to unlock the window and push it up, then he hoisted himself up and through the window, me right behind him. Broken glass made a not very satisfying crunch underfoot. We quickly made our way to the back of the shop, to what served as a reception area and the door to the room that I wanted to search. I tried the door — it was locked.

"The key might not be on site, especially if the room isn't used for boat repair purposes."

"Okay then, stand back," I said. I judged the distance from the door to my hip, leg extended, raised my leg to waist level, chambered my hip and let fly with a heel kick to the right of the lock. I felt it give, but it took one more kick before the panel gave way. I reached through and fiddled with the catch, unlocking it easily.

"Nicely done, Morgan," said Lucas as he pushed the door open and we entered the room, really an office.

"There are no outside windows in this area. I think it's safe to use the flashlight."

Lucas set it down on a desk and switched on the lamp function. I texted Kate that we were in.

There were a few filing cabinets and we tried them but they were all locked. We checked the shelving units, complete with small cylindrical locks on each door. There were two units and both were locked.

My dad had a similar lock on one of his cabinets in the shed where he kept his tools. After many years, the tumblers had worn so badly that he used to unlock it with any of his house keys. I tried dad's trick and used one of our house keys to turn the tumbler. It didn't work on the first cabinet, but to my surprise, it did on the second.

Print material — professionally done calendars, and

books of photographs were neatly stacked on the shelves. The first book I examined showed children at play, or innocently posing for the camera. My guy was not so lucky and he let out a cry of horror when he realized the book he held in his hands pictured children of all ages, even babies, being raped.

"*Madre de Dios!* Every picture is a crime scene. The bastards!"

I looked over his shoulder. The pictures were horrific. "Holy shit! What do we do?"

"We can't take these. If we do, they'll be useless as evidence. But we're not police, so we can tell them where we found them and then they can get a warrant to search and they can seize all of this."

"Okay. But we need proof that we found them. I'll take pictures: of the locked cupboards and of the calendars and books. We could open a book next to a closed copy of the same book, like this," and I showed him what I meant, propping one of the books open, next to the spines of a stack of the same, for reference. I can take a few sample pictures of the contents of each book."

"We'll need the overhead lights," he said, locating the light switch.

I quickly unzipped my camera. Lucas moved ahead of me, quickly setting up the shots. I took care to photograph the cover pages, which gave cryptic information as to the creation and distribution of this material. There was also a handwritten list and beside each item, ever decreasing numbers were crossed out and replaced.

"Maybe the handwriting can be identified," said Lucas. I took a picture of the list.

We were done in fifteen minutes. I relocked the cupboard. He shut off the overhead lights and we got out of there as fast as we could, through the building, out the window and a mad dash across the yard and back through the fence — and not a moment too soon.

High beam vehicle lights lit up the yard beyond the building.

"Someone's at the gate. Let's wait for a minute," said Lucas. "Maybe we can get a look at him."

We waited, crouched in the shadows beyond the fence, ready to sprint. A young man in a jacket and baseball cap made his way around the building to the door, quickly unlocked it and let himself in, closing the door after him. It wasn't long before lights went on in the shop area and not long after that, we spotted the guy at the broken window, only because he leaned out of it briefly to have a look around.

"Let's get out of here," said Lucas and we sprinted back to where we'd parked the rental.

Once we were back in and buckled up, Lucas turned to me.

"If we hurry, we might be able to get a picture of the guy's license plate."

"Right." I pulled out my camera.

Lucas started the car, but kept the lights off. We left the side street and he turned onto Rickard Street, where the gated entrance was located. He drove past the gate and pulled in behind a silver *Suburban* parked just beyond the open gate in the yard. The driver was nowhere to be seen. I hopped out, moved to the back of the car and took two pictures of the license plate using the flash before I turned, adrenaline racing, and dashed back to the car.

Then we were out of there, down the road and around the corner. The Lions Gate Bridge was only a few minutes from the yard. It wasn't long before we were over it, through Stanley Park and heading down Georgia Street.

I texted Kate that we were done and would arrive soon.

Their apartment, a funky, older walk-up, is in Vancouver's West End, close to English Bay. I called when we arrived in the alley behind their place and Kate came down to let me in. Lucas went looking for a parking spot for the rental.

Kate put the kettle on for a pot of tea. I sat at their kitchen table, still overwhelmed with our discovery of the pictures.

"Jesus lovey! After that text from inside, we didn't get another for almost 45 minutes. We were worried sick."

"We were on our way out the door," said Bart. He'd joined us at the table.

"Then you texted you were out. Thank God!" said Kate.

"Morgan. You look like you've seen a ghost," said Bart. He shared a glance with Kate. The apartment buzzer sounded and Kate jumped up to ring Lucas in.

"I ended up in the lot behind the tennis courts."

"Okay you two," said Kate. "Out with it."

They listened carefully as we filled them in: getting through the fence; breaking into the building; my kicking in the door; gathering the photographic evidence; our getaway and the *Suburban* at the gate.

"The silver *Suburban*," said Bart. "Wonder if it's the same one Mike spotted at the back of the *Clarendon*?"

"We should make copies of the pictures you took," said Bart. "I'll do that now."

"Some of them are horrific," Lucas warned quietly. "They'll be with me for a long time."

Bart nodded solemnly as I handed him my camera.

Moments later, Lucas's cell phone buzzed. It was Michael, wanting to know if we were at home.

"It's Michael."

"Invite him over," said Bart, and Lucas texted him

the address.

Within the hour, Michael was sitting with us at the kitchen table. We filled him in on our visit to the boatyard. Bart had loaded the contents of my camera onto his laptop and made two copies of the photos. He pulled up the shots of the *Suburban's* license plate and showed them to Michael. He studied them carefully.

"The cops will have access to the DMV data base," he said.

"There are other photos, Michael," Lucas said quietly. "We found child abuse materials, calendars, books, obviously meant for distribution. We couldn't take copies or we would have betrayed that we'd been there."

"So I took pictures of some of it, book covers, title pages, materials in the locked cupboard and so on, to show Desocarras and Fernice."

Michael nodded. "She called to let me know that your case and Carey's case are linked."

"Did she mention whether the VPD have followed up in any way at the *Clarendon*?" asked Lucas.

"She didn't. I did ask that they be very discreet. In truth, I suspected their version of discreet would be to sit on the file. Colour me skeptical, if you like. But I've been busy. As you know, the club has a distinctly boys club charm. Women — other than family that is — couldn't become members until 10 years ago. Don't get me wrong," he said, with a nod to Kate and me. "A lot of the women members are movers and shakers, but their numbers are still small. And ditto with the brown people. Take my firm, Bourdais Lambert. I'm the only brother working there, but I was at the top of my graduating class, so they're getting their monies worth. But I digress."

"Not at all," said Kate. Bart nodded agreement.

"Something is going on at the club and as a member, I'm in a position to investigate and that's what I've been doing. I've been casually talking up the staff, especially anyone who works the evening functions. The story I've been using is my family live out of town and my aunt and her daughter would like to come to Vancouver to do some shopping. I'm going to put them up at the club as I don't really have room at the condo and do they think my niece, who is only twelve, will feel welcome.

The information I'm after was quite specific: which members use the overnight rooms for guests; are the guests local people or are they more often from outside Vancouver and; is it common for young children to be at the club in the evenings."

"What have you found out?" asked Kate.

"A couple of things," said Michael, glancing around the table.

"I just know something is going on there," said Kate. "I can feel it in my bones."

"One of the waiters, his name's Marvin — bright red, bed-head hair and piercing blue eyes. He was working the night you joined me for dinner."

"The redhead. He's hard to miss. He was working a dinner party that we passed on our way to the bar."

Michael nodded. "Marvin works mostly private parties and banquets. I've heard he deals drugs at the club. I overheard someone ask him yesterday if he was working a banquet one of the members was hosting this Friday. I heard him say he couldn't do the Friday banquet, because he has papers due, and he's already booked to work a dinner party for Ange Batlan Saturday night.

I was right at their elbow, so I asked Marvin where he was studying and he said SFU. The thing is, until yesterday evening, I didn't know that, and considering what happened to you Morgan within, what was it — a week after our dinner at the club, I think it's worth noting."

"Worth noting," I agreed.

"What's Marvin's last name?" Lucas asked him.

"I'll find out. There's one other thing, but this is just a feeling really, that something isn't quite right. I was up on the top floor, in the accommodation area, snooping around. One of the housekeeping staff was leaving one of the rooms. She asked me if she could be of assistance.

I told her I was checking out the accommodations to make sure they would be appropriate for my visiting family who are quite religious. Is there a lot of partying and such that goes on? Well, she got the strangest look on her face. We were standing adjacent the door of the *Mackenzie Suite*. The reason I even noticed the name was that she looked from me to the door of the suite and back to me, so of course I looked at the door as well.

All she said was, '*I don't know, sir.*' Funny thing though. I could tell she couldn't wait to get away from me. And there was something in her eyes, not fear exactly. It was more like sadness. I'm quite sure she didn't mean to expose herself like that and I was careful not to let her know that I'd noticed. I thought it best not to ask her any more questions. I didn't want her to suspect anything."

"Fear and sadness; I doubt she'd feel that way about an excess of partying," Kate said.

"The *Mackenzie Suite*. How can we find out who rents the accommodation? And wouldn't it be great to get the membership list," said Lucas.

"We could get someone to hack into the club's server," said Bart. "I'm dead serious about that." He'd completed a third CD of our evidence pictures and plopped it onto the kitchen table with the other two, all of them couched in plastic cases and labelled simply 1, 2 and 3.

"I'm all for it," said Michael. "It would have to be someone we trust completely."

"Milhous Farthing!" said Lucas, looking at me for confirmation.

"Just the guy," I agreed.

"Milhous?" asked Michael.

"He prefers Miles actually," I said. "No one calls him Milhous except his wife, Verna. We were undergrads together at SFU. He's a filmmaker too, a wonderful actor, a brilliant, crazy guy. But wonderful as they are, it's not his acting skills we're thinking of," and I explained. "Miles hacked the university database as research for a film script he was working on about ethics and morality in our wired reality. He changed Verna's grade in calculus from a B+ to an A, to prove that no database is safe from being hacked. Once he got a screen shot of the changed mark, he immediately dropped her back down to a B+, so no one caught on. She was horrified."

"His hacking skills are pretty advanced," said Lucas.

"Verna did get him to promise no more hacking."

"Do you think he'll make an exception for us?" asked Michael.

"Lucas is texting him," I said, nodding in my guy's direction. He looked up at Michael and smiled.

Kate wasn't as carried away as the rest of us — wide-eyed with alarm was more like it. "Shouldn't we ask Det. Fernice to do this for us? What you two are suggesting is against the law." For her, there was a right way to do things, and then there was the wrong way. There was no in-between. She had to be convinced that there was no other way, or she'd never agree to this.

"I don't think Fernice will go for it, Kate."

Michael jumped in. "Kate, I would have asked for the

list weeks ago, but I was afraid of raising suspicion with the wrong people. We still have no idea which club member, or members, are involved; or staff for that matter."

"Fernice may have the same concern," I said.

"She might, but I think that the only reason the VPD didn't shut me down when I reported seeing Carey is I'm a lawyer at a prestigious law firm. I'm *Gits'ilaasu* and I know the score. My job gave me credibility with the VPD that I might not have had otherwise. They were polite; they listened to me. They went through the motions. Actually, the officers at the VPD were a lot more receptive than the RCMP up in Terrace. When I went to the detachment up there to ask about the investigation into Carey's disappearance I got nowhere with all but one of the officers — and I do mean nowhere."

"I think Fernice is frustrated that there's so little information. And if she thought they should be linked, that means she's looking very carefully at you reporting Carey's presence at the club. Your club!"

"But both cases are linked now," insisted Kate.

"Yes, they are, Kate, but there wasn't much to link. I don't know about the investigation into Morgan's abduction, but up in Terrace, the investigation into Carey's seems to have completely stalled out. There's no new information and now — well that's another story." Michael was quite disgusted.

"What do you mean, Mike?" asked Bart.

"Rosie called me last night, really upset. Cpl. Cumberland dropped in to see her. It wasn't an official call. He came because he felt obligated." Michael stopped, anger getting the better of him.

"Cumberland told her that rumours have been circulating at the detachment that Carey is something of a wild child and that Rosie isn't there for her and can't control her behaviour. This pisses me off so much! It's all lies!"

"Someone's trying to stall the investigation into Carey's abduction," said Lucas, with a glance in my direction. "Probably the same source as the smear campaign against Morgan and me at SFU."

"You guys too? ... Right. Cumberland doesn't buy it and that's why he went to see Rosie. He's sure the story didn't originate with the cops. He asked Rosie if she knew Paul Revier. He's one of the crown prosecutors up there; works the triangle which includes Smithers, Terrace and Prince Rupert, but his office is in Prince Rupert. Cumberland saw Revier having dinner with Sgt. Willis in Terrace. No court that week; nothing coming up on the docket; no reason for them to be meeting. Cumberland thought it was odd because he wasn't aware that they were friends. It isn't conclusive evidence, but it's a small town and everyone knows everyone's business. Willis is in charge of the investigation into Carey's abduction and the nasty rumours about Carey and Rosie started to circulate almost immediately after."

"Does your sister know Revier?" I asked. Michael nodded.

"She knows him and she hates the guy — with a passion! There are lots of people who don't like him because Revier doesn't treat all folks equally, or fairly. Up in northern BC — just about anywhere, for that matter — that kind of prejudice doesn't always get noticed."

"He's prejudiced against Indigenous people?" asked Bart.

"Yes," said Michael. "But there's another reason Rosie doesn't like him. Revier has a past and it's definitely relevant to this case. There was a paedophile that lived in Kitimat for years. The guy was a real pillar of the community; a businessman who won awards for community involvement. He was a coach for various sports including hockey and did a lot of volunteering with the youth. Over the years, his position made it possible for him to prey on a lot of young boys. For a long time, no one came forward. Then, one young man found the courage. There was an investigation, which eventually led to the paedophile being charged. When the word got out, others came forward too. There was strong evidence that he had sexually abused a lot of boys."

"Bastard," said Kate.

"It was Rosie's observation that Revier dragged his feet on the case. Nothing you could put your finger on really. But remember, Revier was the crown prosecutor for the case and he was supposed to be acting for the victims. There were a few people who said — openly — that he was working for the defence, if you know what I mean: lots of continuances that seemed contrived; important evidence disappearing. But there were other things.

One young man withdrew his statement. It was never publicly stated why, but the word in our community was there had been threats against him and his family. There was no proof, but Rosie remembers that kid and his family were scared. Another victim, a white boy, another defence witness, died under what were reported as mysterious circumstances. There was an investigation, but it went nowhere.

The boy who went to the police first was white. His family supported him 100% and he never wavered. It took almost four years from the time he came forward and the investigation began, to the actual trial. The verdict was guilty. But the night before he was to be sentenced, the paedophile committed suicide."

"Paul Revier. We should look for a link between him

and someone down here," said Kate.

"Absolutely! After talking with Cumberland, Rosie thinks that Revier's involved somehow in Carey's abduction."

"Jesus! Really?" this from Bart, who seldom swore.

"Really! Rosie's in a position to know more about him than a lot of folks. Her job at the women's shelter brings her into contact with women and children who have been victims of violence, or are at risk of being sexually exploited. There's been talk around town about Revier and has been for years. If my sister says Revier is a bad man — take it from me, he's a bad man."

"We need the membership list," said Kate, decisively, "and booking details on the club's accommodations. And anything else we can get our hands on! Good grief, listen to me! No one must ever know!"

"Don't worry Kate. We won't tell anyone," I reassured her, not trying too hard to suppress a grin.

"Get away with you, Morgan O'Meara," she grinned right back.

"What about banished boy," said Lucas.

"He's put himself in real jeopardy." Kate's grin was gone, replaced with a worried frown.

"I think he wants to be found."

"I agree with Morgan. And he wants to help," said Bart, "or he wouldn't have tweeted the truck location."

A perplexed Michael was looking from one to the other with raised eyebrows. "Who is banished boy? The truck. They found the truck?"

"I wanted to call you last night when we got back from 100 Mile House, but it was very late," said Lucas.

"Call me anytime. Day or night. I'm not getting much sleep these days."

"I'll remember that," said Lucas. "Someone who calls

himself banished boy tweeted about a blue truck that was spotted close to where Morgan was rescued. Belongs to the guy that tried to kill Morgan. We drove up Tuesday night and viewed it Wednesday."

"Okay," said Michael. "Let's keep a fire under this. I'll get Marvin's last name. You'll have it the minute I have it."

At that point, Kate wisely suggested that everyone check that they had the cell numbers of everyone else present. "We need to be able to communicate quickly."

"Wouldn't it be great if we could just speak with the tweeter. But of course, we can't."

"I hope he used a burner cell," said Kate.

"It doesn't matter if he did, he's still in danger. Only the thugs' inner circle would know about the blue truck," I said.

"None of them are safe. Not him. Not Carey or the rest of the children," said Bart.

"I think I need to book some time with you Doc," said Michael, trying to pass it off as a joke.

"Anytime," said Bart, and at Michael's dubious look he insisted, quite earnestly, "Really Mike. You've got my number. Call me, anytime."

Miles sent a text just before we reached home saying he wanted to talk about our request tonight. Lucas continued heading east and fifteen minutes later pulled up at Miles' and Verna's place at the foot of Capitol Hill in Burnaby. Verna was fast asleep when we arrived and Miles ushered us into his small, cramped office space, a converted second bedroom at the back of the apartment.

Lucas and I sat patiently, watching Miles fidget his way through a cup of tea and a smoke. We had declined a cup ourselves. I filled him in on our request.

"Sorry about the cigarette."

"Don't worry about it Miles."

"I'm working on a screenplay. Got stuck. you know how that is, Morgan. Damn cigarettes. I hate them."

I smiled with understanding. He'd been trying to quit for good as long as I'd known him. "When I get stuck, I eat. Easier on my lungs. Not so easy on my waistline."

"You want me to hack the server at the *Clarendon* and get the membership list." He gave us both a look. "And you also want to know who's booking the overnight accommodation." We remained silent while Miles sucked away on his cigarette between sips of tea.

"Morgan, you know there's nothing I wouldn't do for you. I'm not worried about getting caught. I mean, I won't get caught. This one's too easy! But what if having this information brings more heat on you." At this, he appraised my stitches and the yellowish blue ghosts of bruises.

"We're being very careful, Miles," I insisted.

"Right." Miles wasn't the least bit reassured.

Lucas tried another tactic. "We are being very careful, Miles. I'll get you a computer to work on from that can't be traced back to you, or Morgan. And believe me, we're going to be very careful how we use any information you're able to get us."

"A throwaway would be helpful, Lucas. From where?"

"The Kinesiology Lab at the university. They're upgrading and there's a few computers up for give away. People from other departments have already helped themselves. I can get one tomorrow. You can do a disc wipe after."

"Of course."

"No one will know or care that I've taken it. I'll get it to you and once you're through with it, we'll dispose of it," said Lucas.

"It's not like it's a bank," said Miles stubbing out his cigarette.

"Exactly," said my guy, reassuringly. "Piece of cake for you."

"How long has the girl been missing?" he asked.

"Four weeks," I said.

"That's a long time. And you say there's other kids as well?"

"We're sure of it," said Lucas.

"When can you get the computer to me?"

"Tomorrow, by noon."

"Okay then."

"Are you going to tell Verna?" I asked.

"Not right away. I did promise her, no more hacking. If it was for anyone but you Morgan, she'd be furious."

23

It was Thursday night, a little past 7:00 pm, when Adam Ignace and Jeri Fernice pulled into the alley behind 168 Franklin Street. They'd finally gotten through to the owner in Florida and she'd arranged for a key to be dropped at the station. They slipped on latex gloves and made their way up wooden stairs to the front-porch landing. The door had seen better days, but featured a serious deadbolt. She tried the key she had but it didn't work.

"Maybe it's the back-door key," said Adam. They made their way back down the stairs, around the house and up to the back door. Jeri tried the key. It didn't work. She shared a look with Adam, pulled out a set of lock picks and released the lock. The door opened onto the kitchen.

"It's been shut up for a while," said Jeri, sniffing. The kitchen was heavy with the smell of old cooking grease. A long kitchen table and chairs took up most of one wall. They split up to examine the house. Adam went down to the basement and Jeri headed upstairs.

The basement was damp and mouldy. He didn't find a light switch at the landing, so continued down the stairs, hoping for a hanging pull. He was rewarded, but the overhead bulb wasn't more than 40 watts and its meagre light dissipated quickly into the gloom.

The walls were original stone and had never been

updated. Some light from a lamppost in the back alley fought its way through grimy curtains. He made his way around the circumference of the basement, looking for a storage area. Finding none, he cut across the basement to the stairwell.

An ancient furnace sat in the middle of the room. He was ducking under one of the heating ducts that sprouted from it, intent on not hitting his head, when he stumbled over something soft, directly in his path. His flashlight revealed a small rag doll. He picked it up. The price tag and the manufacturer's tag, both the worse for wear, were still attached to one of the doll's arms.

There was little else of interest. Adam made his way to the stairway. He noticed a small mattress under the stairs and when he bent to examine it closer, the acrid smell of urine rose to greet him. It was covered by a thin sheet, urine stains clearly visible. Satisfied there was nothing else of interest, he made his way up to the kitchen and living room area, which took up a good deal of the first floor.

Adam was still carrying the doll and he put it on the kitchen table. Keeping his flashlight beam low, he examined the cupboards and found an assortment of kitchen gadgets, mismatched dishes, all clean, basic food-stuffs, cereal and the like. One of the drawers held cutlery, a few knives — one of them surprisingly sharp — a spatula and not much else. Most of the drawers were empty.

He moved to the living room. There was a small child's pullover, stuffed between the arm and the cushion of one of the chairs. He found a hair barrette, the kind that young girls wear, under a couch cushion. There was a small room off the living room, an enclosed porch area. This room contained a single bed and mattress and a small night table and lamp. The drawer of the night table was slightly ajar. He pulled it open, revealing nothing, but when he tried to close the door, it jammed and wouldn't budge.

Jeri had arrived on the same floor.

"I'm in here," Adam called out quietly, as he continued to struggle with the drawer.

"What's this then?" she said, arriving at his side.

"Not sure. This drawer opened fine, but now it won't close. I think there's something caught between the bottom of the drawer and the right side." His flashlight beam was trained on the small rectangular object that was causing the problem and he dug it out with a pen knife. He shone his flash light on it.

"A flash drive," said Jeri.

"Yup," said Adam.

"I found a few pieces of children's clothing upstairs, a young girl's, all of it was soiled with urine."

He told her about the small palette in the basement, really only big enough for a child or small adolescent, also urine stained and the few items he found in the living room."

"I saw the doll in the kitchen."

"I found it in the basement."

Jeri nodded. "It looks new. The tags are still attached."

Determining there was nothing else, they left the house and headed down the stairs, waiting quietly in the shadows until a group of teenagers passed before getting into Jeri's car. Once in the car, Jeri fired up her laptop and Adam handed her the flash drive. She plugged it in and pulled up the file. On her laptop screen, a jerky home video played. A man with his back to the camera was raping a small boy, whose cries could be clearly heard. It was over quickly and the man turned toward the camera, as if he was going to speak with someone else in the room. The video ended abruptly.

"Jesus! I wasn't ready for that," said Jeri.

"Me neither."

I'd only been asleep for a while and wasn't sure at first what woke me up. The clock said 5:30 AM. Lucas was talking in his sleep, then moaning and suddenly, flailing his arms and gasping for breath. I spoke to him quietly and kept a reassuring hand on his shoulder. I told him everything was going to be okay, not sure if it was him or me I was talking to. I guess it was both of us, because in my heart, I wasn't sure if anything would ever be okay, ever again. He didn't wake up and after a few minutes, his breathing slowed and he settled down.

It's funny how, when you least expect it, something you've always known and accepted — even if you didn't understand the why of it — will become clear. I remembered the deep sadness in my father's eyes. It lurked there, just behind his mischief, his jokes, his ready humour and funny stories.

The sadness in my Nokomis Effie's eyes had always been there too, even when mom made her laugh. Mom had a great sense of humour and she was always trying to make Effie laugh. Maybe mom was afraid the sadness would be hers as well. I wondered now if they'd ever talked about the years Nokomis endured at residential school, losing her sister there, or mom leaving home — leaving Greenwood Lake Reserve for high school and then to attend Lakehead. Mom stayed in town after she graduated and it only a few years later that she married dad — *married out.*

24

Friday morning, Lucas woke up bathed in sweat. He tried to remember what he'd been dreaming about, but it was all a jumble. His dad was present again. He was dreaming about him a lot lately.

His mom had told him so many stories about Rafael: he was the man who loved her; who taught her to read when no one around her could; who gave up a life of privilege so that she could escape a lifetime of poverty, of bondage. Her gratitude and love for him were immense and she'd always painted him as larger than life. Lucas admitted to himself that he wanted the impossible: to know his father as a man, a Mestizo, like him.

It was the smell of coffee that lured me from our warm bed. Lucas knew me too well. I was curled up on the couch, enjoying a cup.

By 9:15 am, we were on our way to SFU's main campus at the top of Burnaby Mountain. We went directly to the Kinesiology department and were shown to the room where the giveaway computers were being stored. Lucas checked them over and helped himself to one, letting a clerk in the office know he was taking it. She didn't check it off a master list, just made note that there was one less computer to give away.

I texted Miles that we had a computer for him. A few minutes later he texted me to bring it. We dropped it off on our way home. Miles told us he'd call as soon as he had something for us.

"Michael just texted me Marvin's last name, the SFU student who works at the *Clarendon*," said Lucas. "It's Roche — Marvin Roche. I'm checking the student database."

I'd just finished Skyping with the other TA, Carl Baraniuk, preparing additional reading material for the students on handling and using 16 mm and 35 mm film. The students wouldn't be using digital equipment their first semester. It's a glass wall though, given the digital universe in which millions of us swim every day, our cameras at the ready.

"There is no Marvin Roche enrolled at SFU now, or in the past," said Lucas. "If he isn't enrolled, why would he say he was?" I left my desk to come stand beside him.

"It's a good cover on campus if you're nosing around looking for information, or if you have other activities you don't want to draw attention to. He could go anywhere, talk to anyone. Who would suspect?"

"Sure, but why use the same ruse at the club? Why say he's a student, when he's not?"

"If he's a student, it lets him be selective about how many shifts he works. If he's dealing drugs, that could be very helpful."

"Point taken. No word from Miles?" Lucas asked.

"Not yet."

We were both exhausted, having got so little sleep the night before and decided to take a nap. I woke up after a couple of hours, but Lucas was still asleep. I didn't want to disturb him, he looked so peaceful, so I slid quietly out of bed, gathered up my clothes and went to the bathroom to wash up. After I got dressed, I went to the kitchen and raided the fridge in search of something to put in a sandwich.

I was at the kitchen table finishing up, when I heard the water running in the bathroom, so I started a sandwich for Lucas. He'd be hungry.

I heard something drop to the bathroom floor, then yelling.

"What happened?"

No answer. "I'm making you a sandwich. Bet you're hungry."

Still no answer.

"Hey, you okay?"

"Get it off," he yelled!"

Okay. That was strange. "Get what off?"

"So much blood!" So much blood!" he was screaming by now. That's when I ran to the bathroom.

Lucas was at the sink, anguished, tears streaming down his face, oblivious to me.

"Sweetheart. What blood? There's no blood!"

He paid no attention to me. It was a few beats before I realized that he couldn't hear me. It was as though he was asleep. His razor was on the floor. He had his hands in a sink full of water and I could see the hint of pink. A few drops of blood oozed from a tiny cut on his chin. He must have cut himself.

Lucas was bent over the sink, horrified, looking at his hands in the water like they belonged to someone else. He watched as his blood spread like a cloud in the water, until the basin was filled with blood. His mother, kneeling beside him, washing the blood from his hands and face. She was speaking, but he couldn't hear her. She looked scared. He was scared too. Then he became aware of a hand on his arm, felt the pressure of fingers at his waist.

"Sweetheart, there is no blood."

Lucas stared at me, completely perplexed. "The stream ... it's in the stream!"

"Whose blood is in the stream?"

"I don't know," he screamed.

Then I understood. I walked him to the living room and sat him on the couch, then grabbed the phone and called Bart. One of Lucas's nightmares had crossed over into reality.

Miles checked online and found the Westward Inn on Chelsea Boulevard in Surrey, booked a unit online — one well away from the front desk entrance — and was at their door in under an hour. The bored clerk paid no attention to him as she handed over the key.

He'd packed what little gear he'd need into an overnight bag. There was a desk of sorts in one corner of the unit. He switched on the desk lamp and quickly set up the computer equipment he had brought with him and established an internet connection. *Veresinumeris*, one of Miles' favorite nicknames, got to work.

The uncle of the missing girl had provided his membership information, including his username and password in case he should need it but Miles doubted that would be necessary.

No information in this world was completely safe from being hacked. Miles shook his head at the absurdity of it — the elephant in the room of a now gargantuan, wireless universe. He had snacks and a thermos of coffee with him, just in case.

Got what you need. A text from Miles.

"Yes! Yes! Yes!" I yelled out in glee and immediately texted back: I can come now.

Moments later: I'm at home.

"Hey," I said, spotting a sleepy Lucas as he emerged from the bedroom. "I thought you were napping."

"I heard you yell."

"I am so sorry honey," I said. "Miles has the lists!"

Sleep forgotten, Lucas was at my side in a few strides.

"Great! When can we see him?"

"You sure you're up to this? How 'bout you stay here and rest and I'll go pick them up?"

"Give me ten minutes."

"Lucas?"

"I'm fine," then, after registering my skeptical look, "I'm okay, really! I'm just a little tired."

After the earlier episode, I'd talked him into lying down. He tried to protest, but I wasn't having any of it. He caved and once I got him to bed, he fell asleep almost immediately.

Bart called back and I told him what had happened.

"I'll come over right after work," he said. But Lucas continued to sleep, so I let Bart know. He told me to call if we needed him and he'd come right over. I told Lucas about my conversation with Bart as he got ready.

"There's someone Bart wants you to see; a colleague of his."

"I'll call him when we get back."

25

We got to Miles and Verna's place about 9:30 pm.
"Where's the computer?" Lucas asked him.

"Wiped clean and dumped," said Miles.

"It was so brave of you to do this Milhous." Verna was clearly thrilled by what he'd done. He'd caved and told her.

"We can't thank you enough," Lucas said, as Miles handed us the lists and a flash drive.

"I took the liberty of printing them for you. I assume you'll be keeping all of this in a secure place?"

"Most definitely," said Lucas.

"Tea or coffee, Verna asked?" watching with undisguised interest as Lucas and I immediately started in on the lists.

"Herbal tea if you have it," said Lucas, and I nodded agreement.

Lucas started with the list of members and I had the list of guests using overnight accommodation for the past year.

"That's as far back as it went." Miles said, indicating the stack of paper I was holding.

"This is one list we're very interested in."

"The member's list is like a who's who of commerce and law and not just in British Columbia," said Lucas. "Here's Michael. There are judges, lawyers, Queens' Councillors, members of parliament, associate members from other Canadian provinces, even other countries."

"How much is membership?" asked Verna.

"$9,000 for full membership and half that for an associate membership." She whistled.

"Here's Ange Batlan, the guy that you and Amelia went to see."

"Batlan is a friend of the abducted girl's uncle. He offered his help to us early on."

"And here's a couple of VPD higher ups; and RCMP Inspectors, and the Deputy Commissioner, E Division. At Verna and Miles puzzled look, Lucas explained. "E Division is an RCMP designation, basically the province of British Columbia. The E Division Deputy also oversees M Division which is the Yukon." Lucas, always the patient teacher, could see that confusion still existed. He was about to launch into a detailed explanation of the multi-layered policing system in BC, but Miles held up his hand.

"That's okay man," said Miles. "Another time."

"Ange Batlan uses the overnight accommodation a lot. That's odd, isn't it? He lives in Vancouver, has that great condo downtown. It's only about ten blocks from the club. He could walk or take a taxi home in minutes, literally."

"He's signing for accommodation, but that doesn't mean he's using it. It could be for business guests, meetings, maybe even family members," said Miles.

"Right. Of course. He works for Northfor Tech. It's a mining company. They're in a number of countries, including Canada. Lots of visiting business interests and hence the need for overnight accommodation, especially if he wants to give them the VIP treatment. It looks like Batlan always books the *Mackenzie Suite*."

I picked up another list: *Gratuities List: Member Functions and Servers.*

"I grabbed that too," said Miles. "I didn't know if it'd be helpful."

"I'll ask Michael. He'll know," I said, texting him with our question about the gratuities list.

Michael called a few minutes later to tell us the *Gratuities List* would be very helpful. All club members have to host at least one function a year. It was a requirement of membership. Staff members working member functions share a gratuity—a set percentage of the final sales for that event.

"Can Michael make it for breakfast tomorrow?"

I checked. "He is and he's bringing Amelia and George." Kate and Bart had already confirmed. Verna wasn't one to stay up much past 11:00 pm and was nodding sleepily. We left soon after. We were nearly back home when I remembered that Alex hadn't called me back.

"Alex called this morning and left a message. I called and left a message but he hasn't gotten back. He said it was important he speak with me as soon as possible."

"Maybe he has the results of forensics on the truck?"

"Or my clothing." I'd had another flashback, this one about me in the back of the pickup. After I escaped from the box, I was trying to steady myself so I could jump from the truck. It was lurching all over the place because the road was so badly rutted. I remember the truck coming to a halt and the red-headed guy coming up over the side of the truck in a fury, his hands on my throat, squeezing tight. I must have blacked out before I stopped breathing. The puzzle was coming together for me, piece by piece and some of the pieces were damn scary. Maybe trauma counselling wasn't such a bad idea. I wouldn't be telling Lucas any of this yet. I was afraid of his reaction. And Bart, well, he'd be beside himself if he knew. Knowing what Lucas was going through, he was liable to try and sideline the both of us and I wasn't having that. Lucas either was my guess. I wouldn't be telling Kate. She'd feel she had to tell Bart.

It was empowering to remember why I couldn't talk those first few days after my rescue. I'd tried to escape, and maybe not for the first time either. And I had escaped at the lake. If I hadn't, there wouldn't have been a rescue. Lucas interrupted my thoughts.

"I hope they've got the forensics results back," said Lucas. "Maybe they've identified the guy at the lake."

The guy at the lake. Part of a brutal dimension about which we know so little of. Business in the shadows: the sale of human beings. I'm intimate with that world now. An oil on my skin that won't wash off.

26

Det. Sgt. Rhodes from Sex Crimes ran into Det. Hermes at VPD's Main Street office. They often did as Sex Crimes and MPU shared a large wing upstairs. Hermes never failed to notice how handsome Rhodes was, tall and fit and always well dressed.

"Det. Hermes, good to see you. How's it going?" he asked.

He was always the perfect gentleman, she thought. Unlike a lot of the guys.

"Not bad, thanks," she said. "And you, sir?"

"Can't complain." He smiled engagingly. "Any good news on the Carey Bolton case?"

Everyone was talking about the Bolton case, especially now that it was linked with the O'Meara abduction. "Not yet I'm afraid. The cases are linked but we're not so sure that'll be helpful."

"Why is that?" asked Rhodes, genuinely surprised.

"The word is that Carey Bolton is pretty wild. Dad lives in Powell River and he's not that involved in her upbringing. Her mother can't control her behaviour, a single parent and all that. Could be that the kid just decided to take off with her boyfriend. Looks like he was in the picture for a few weeks before she disappeared. If that's the case, we're back to where we started with the O'Meara abduction — a freak incident, just some nutter.

Who knows what we're dealing with there."

"Well, that does put a different slant on things."

"The media has picked up some pretty interesting background on O'Meara as well. She's no angel, and ditto with the boyfriend."

"I was out of town for a few days, so I missed that," said Rhodes, giving her his full attention.

"Det. Fernice isn't buying it though. She thinks that O'Meara's a straight shooter and she thinks the stuff about her sleeping around and working as a prostitute in the past is," Hermes stopped abruptly; then continued. "Well, not that it matters. I mean, the woman was forcibly abducted, beaten, nearly lost her life — but you know what I mean. And then, there's the intel we're getting that her boyfriend is a real hothead. He's put her in the hospital in the past. He's Latino."

"Lifestyle choices can have repercussions," Rhodes said. "However, having never met O'Meara, it isn't for me to comment. It's certainly a shame about Carey Bolton though," he said, shaking his head. "So young; taking off and not telling her mother. Anything could have happened to her. I deal with a lot of runaways. It's sad when young kids end up on the street. It's such a waste."

"Maybe if Bolton's mother had spent more time with the kid; trying to understand her better; making sure the kid knew there were limits," said Hermes.

"We often see people at their worst, don't we?"

"We sure do," Hermes agreed.

"People make mistakes and they suffer enough for them without us adding our judgment. It can be hard at times, not to judge, but I've come to realize that it's important to try and keep perspective. We serve them better when we do."

"Quite right sir," said Hermes, somewhat chastened.

27

The men started coming to the gatehouse around supper time. Carey remembered one of them was at Ange's club the first time she went there with him. Ford was here. He was sitting at the table drinking with Ange and the other men. He wasn't wearing his uniform tonight.

Marie sat next to Carey, holding her hand. It hurt, she was holding on so tight, but Carey didn't mind. She found it comforting. After a while, one of the men came over to where they were sitting. He'd been at the parties many times before. He signalled to Marie to follow him. She let go of Carey's hand and followed him, walking on her tiptoes, how she walked most of the time. Like she was treading water. *She's trying not to drown*, thought Carey. She wanted to grab her and run away with her. She watched them as they went upstairs.

Seth was in a chair across the room, reading. It looked like he was ignoring Ford, but when he signaled for Seth to follow him upstairs, he did, as though he'd been waiting. Ange left the men and came over to her.

"Carey, I want you to come with me now. Don't worry, I'm not going to hurt you, I promise." But he always said that, like what he did was okay if he told her he wouldn't hurt her. He held out his hand and she took it and followed him to a room on the main floor under the staircase. No one else used that room. After, she was going to ask him what happened to Georgina. Seth wouldn't tell her.

Seth came down the stairs dead slow and limped across the room. His lower lip was cut and one of his eyes was starting to purple. He made it to a doorway off the main entrance and retreated into the room there, closing the door behind him.

Ford came down a few minutes later. He helped himself to a drink from a bar set up on the kitchen counter, before sitting down with the others. He brought out a baggie of cocaine, set up some lines on the polished table top and started snorting.

"Hey MacLeish, where's Melanie?" someone asked.

"I don't know," said Ford.

"Who's taking care of the kids," another asked.

"What's to take care of? They take care of themselves," said Ford.

"Just making conversation," the guy said, a little unnerved by Ford, who now got up from the table, picked up the baggie and walked to the door of the room where Seth had retreated.

"Hey Seth," Ford bellowed from his side of the door. "I got a present for you buddy." There was no answer from the room.

"Come on, open up, you know you want it," he cajoled, but he was answered by silence.

"Seth, open the fucking door now!" he yelled, just as Ange returned to the living room with Carey.

"Ford, please, can't you leave the boy alone."

"Fuck off Ange! It's none of your business." But Ange wouldn't be put off.

"You're in my home and while you're here," ... but that's

as far as he got.

"He's mine and I'll treat him any way I want!!" Ford screamed as he rammed a beefy shoulder against the closed door. The wood splintered and with a small sigh, the door opened a few inches. Ford burst through the door and into Seth's room.

Ange moved quickly across the living room and through the wrecked door in time to hear Ford sneer, "don't play possum with me." He was oblivious to the fact that Seth was unconscious. Not even an eyelid flickered.

"Leave him alone, Ford," Ange said. "Can't you see that he can't hear you?"

Carey was the only child in the room. She watched as one of the men crossed from the kitchen and entered Seth's room.

"Is he alive?" She heard him ask.

"Yes," said Ange.

"He's just stoned," Ford said.

"He's bleeding Ford," Ange said. "What if he doesn't make it this time?"

"He'll be fine," he said, dismissively. "He just needs to sleep it off." Nothing more was said. No one argued with Ford. The three men left the room and returned to the kitchen. Carey tried to bury herself in a chair, praying that Ange would stay at least until Ford was gone. It scared her whenever Ford looked at her, but she knew as long as Ange was here, Ford wouldn't touch her.

Ange could see that Carey was afraid. He walked her over to his house. He made them cocoa and they sat in his living room and he told her about his plans for the two of them. He wanted her to live with him and he was going to get her a tutor so she wouldn't fall behind in her schoolwork.

Carey didn't know what to say. It knew it was important

to him that she want to come and live with him, so she told him she did. When he was finished, she told him about Christopher being hurt, then she told him about Georgina trying to escape and Seth carrying her into the house, unconscious.

He listened carefully to everything she said, even putting his arm around her when she started to cry. He told her the doctor had operated on Christopher and he would be fine, but he didn't know where Georgina was and didn't seem to know that she tried to run away. Carey could see he was upset by that. He told her he was going to make sure Seth was rewarded for taking such good care of the children. Carey was very tired now. Ange got her a blanket and she fell asleep on the couch.

Much later, Ange woke Carey up and brought her back to the gatehouse. All the men were gone. Ange took her upstairs and tucked her in with Marie. He told her he was going to be away for the day tomorrow but that he would see her in the evening. Tomorrow night, he told her, she was going to sleep over at his house.

She pretended to fall asleep and listened to his footsteps as he left the room, descended the stairs and a little later, heard the back door open and close again. Carey waited a few minutes, then returned to the room where Seth lay. She sat on the bed beside him. He was still unconscious and his breathing didn't seem right. The bruise on his eye looked bigger and she could smell blood but was afraid to put on the light.

Carey had only been in the room a few minutes when she heard someone at the back door. Two men came in. One of them was Ange. When she realized they were walking toward Seth's room, she got under the bed, just in time. The floor creaked softly as they entered Seth's room. One of them turned on the light.

"Phineas, you have to do something. Ford beats Seth up every single week. Every time he sees him. He can't take much more. Ford's going to kill him one of these days, I just know it. I see him looking at Carey. I won't have him touching her Phineas." His voice was hoarse with fear.

"Oh, for the love of Christ, Ange. Carey isn't yours. You can't keep her! You know that." Ange said nothing. Both men moved to the side of the bed.

"Where's Ford now?"

"He's at the club."

"And the judge and his pals?"

"Everyone's at the club; just the children and I are here. Why did it take you so long to get here? I told you I needed to see you. I really don't think Seth's going to make it, not this time."

"Relax Ange," said Phineas impatiently, "You worry too much. He's breathing."

"Look at him, Phineas," Ange implored. "He's barely breathing. His pants are soaked with blood. He's been unconscious for nearly five hours."

"I think soaked is overstating the case a bit, don't you? I talked with Ford and he said he got him stoned and that's why he passed out."

"Ford's lying! What if Seth dies here?"

"It's not a dead body yet," Phineas said. "I say we wait and see."

"Phineas, I told you before, I didn't sign on for murder!" said Ange, fear choking his voice. "You know this isn't the first time Ford has ... has lost his temper and done something stupid. We're the ones who have to cover for him. What if he dies here. In my home!"

"No. It isn't." said Rhodes, a hint of resignation in his

voice. He shook it off quickly. "But the money's good, isn't it? And I know you don't mind the money. None of us do."

"It's not about the money for me Phineas. You know that!"

"Ange, give me a break!"

"Are the children going to be here for the rest of the weekend? I want to spend more time with Carey," said Ange, the young man on the bed temporarily forgotten.

"Only till Tuesday, then they all go down to the States and that's final, Ange. We need to rethink this whole operation."

"Who's going to drive them to the airport?"

"If Seth's not up to driving by Tuesday, Melanie will be back from Whistler by then. She can drive them to the airport."

"I'd really like to talk to you about something," but Phineas interrupted him.

"Did you get the judge what he wanted?" he asked, changing the subject.

"He took a lot of stock and we're out of several of the videos. The log's up-to-date."

"Good. I'll have more stock printed. Videos too. What about the photo shoot this Monday? Might as well take advantage while the kids are here. The sisters who just arrived are very pretty, don't you think? Danlever is going to shoot this one. He's really good with the kids. It should be a good session."

"It'd be easier for us if we got everyone to sign up for the web portal," said Ange.

"That's the first sensible thing you've said all night. And yes, it would be a lot easier for us. But some of these guys have been customers for years. Print, something they can hold in their hand; that's what they want." There was a brief silence.

"There is something else Phineas. I've been meaning to talk to you about Marie," Ange said.

"What about her?"

"She's not eating much and she's wetting the bed every night. Melanie is furious with her most of the time, which doesn't help."

"I know, I know, she told me," said Phineas. "It makes more work for her."

"She doesn't care about the children. Joy is much better with them. Melanie doesn't even try to get Marie to eat. None of us speak her language. I'm ashamed to say I don't know what it is."

"She's been a problem since we bought her. Probably why we got her for such a good price. I should have known there was a catch." Phineas couldn't keep the exasperation out of his voice. "Anyway, that's a problem soon to be solved. I've made arrangements to sell her tomorrow."

"Tomorrow! Phineas, she's been with us for four months! Her and Carey are very close. There's always room for kindness."

"We're not a family Ange! This is business."

"Yes, Phineas, I know that. All I'm saying is," but Phineas interrupted him again.

"We have other, far more important matters to consider, like that bitch, O'Meara. It was dumb luck that Fred Norse didn't get himself arrested at Gustafsen Lake. He just barely managed to get away, from the report I read by the Sergeant up there. He blew the axle on his truck and ditched it. Told Ford he was trying to get back home by a back-road route. The stupid jerk, trying to dump the body in his own back yard. If he'd shown some sense and called right away, we could've got the truck out of there. Now we have a hell of a mess."

"Why don't you have the truck towed? Who would know?"

Phineas shook his head at Ange's stupidity. "Are you kidding? Vancouver forensics has been up there. And if they can place O'Meara in Fred's truck ..." He didn't bother to finish the sentence. "Apparently, she's back at the university, and so is that nosy Latin boyfriend of hers."

Ange was embarrassed by the turn the conversation had taken. "Maybe I was hasty in expressing a concern about the O'Meara woman. I felt I had to talk with Amelia Boudreau. I promised her father I would. It would have looked very suspicious if I hadn't, surely you can understand that. How was I to know that O'Meara would be with her! Sure, she was asking questions, but not the right ones. I think it was a little premature to deal with her in that fashion. It was deReesen who jumped on it. Ford can't think for himself, always so quick to act." Phineas cut him off angrily.

"I was in complete agreement with them. I made it happen because it had to happen. Christ Ange! That bitch and her girlfriends made a visit to our Vancouver safe house ... our safe house! And Melanie said she was back the same night with another woman and again, early the next morning. She left a fucking note! I'd like to know who gave them that address? I had a chat with Hermes in MPU and the call to Carey's mother came from a family friend in Vancouver who didn't identify himself."

"Do you think it was Seth? Ford thinks it was."

"No, I don't. Ford has complete control over him. I checked his phone log and the call definitely wasn't made on his phone."

"Maybe he used another phone."

"Seth's not bright enough to do something that clever. Besides, why would he. These kids mean nothing to him.

It's possible it was a chance encounter: someone connected with the family happened to see her going in or coming out of the house. A bad break for us, that's all, just one of those things. Anyway, it's taken care of. The Franklin house is history."

"We can use the gatehouse for the children, for as long as we need to."

Phineas continued, as though Ange hadn't spoken. "All Fred had to do was dispose of the body, the stupid fuck!"

"O'Meara must have been alive when Fred took her up to the lake," said Ange.

"Do I have to remind you that it was you who brought this unwanted attention on us Ange? If you'd kept your big mouth shut with that uncle up north, none of this would have happened. Then arranging to see O'Meara and the cousin and not clearing it with me first — what the hell were you thinking!"

"Neither O'Meara nor Amelia were a threat. I think we should just leave O'Meara alone and wait for things to die down. They will. Children disappear all the time and no one pays that much attention," said Ange.

Phineas relented a little, "Good point. Anyway, I think we're okay. The smear campaign your boy Marvin started at the university has taken off like wildfire. Both O'Meara and her boyfriend have lost all credibility."

"It has been effective."

"Although Hermes said that Fernice isn't buying it. She's had the O'Meara case linked with Carey's abduction. Fernice is tough. We might have trouble there."

"I thought that the Terrace RCMP was refusing to do that?"

"They didn't see the point, until she convinced them. They agreed to link the cases, but its more politics than anything. You know: native woman; native kid. Makes the police look like they're doing something. Linking the cases won't have any impact.

Revier is helping us out up in Terrace. Just to make sure the investigation goes nowhere, he put the word out that Rosaline Bolton is a troublemaker and has no control over her daughter. Carey is quite the wild child. Our Seth has been painted as the boyfriend that's been around for a while. What's important is Revier's story has been given a lot of credence by the Terrace RCMP. I hear from Revier that the investigation is stalled up there, just as we hoped. It's all good for us."

"Revier's not very bright," said Ange.

"He's the one who recommended we add your precious Carey," Phineas reminded him. "And he's the one that's been helping us cover our tracks and your mistakes."

At that, Ange fell silent. He didn't like Paul Revier. Never had. He was a braggart and full of himself, but he had to admit that Revier had been helpful.

As crown council for Kitimat, Prince Rupert and Terrace, Revier was privy to a lot of information of value to them. He'd suggested children that wouldn't be missed too much. He had good connections in other provinces too.

Ange knew Phineas was right. He should be grateful for Revier's hand in this. Carey was the most wonderful thing that had happened to him in a long time and he didn't want Phineas to know that he was secretly scheming how he could keep her for himself. It would be just the two of them. A family. Admitting to the depth of his feelings for her both surprised and delighted him. He would hire a tutor to teach her — once he had won her over and had her complete trust. That would take time. He understood that and he would be patient and give her all the time she needed. In the meantime, she could continue to live with the other children and when the rest of the children went to the States, Carey would stay here with him. Joy could take care of her. It was perfect really.

All Carey needed was time to get used to the changes in her life. Time to grow to love him. Phineas didn't have to know any of this — to hell with Phineas and to hell with the rest of them. They were like animals really. They didn't understand how beautiful the children were. He was different. He was not like them.

"There's one other thing, Phineas. I sent Seth to pick up stock the other night, and someone had broken into the boat yard."

"What!"

"It's okay Phineas. Relax."

"Relax! For Chrissakes Ange!"

"Seth saw the broken glass. Called me immediately. Someone got in through a small side window. They broke into the inner office, but they didn't get into the locked cupboards, he's sure of that. All of the stock was there. He brought what was left here."

"How'd they get into the yard?"

"They cut an opening in the fence at the back of the property. Theo and I found it the next morning," said Ange.

"You're sure Seth got all of the stock?"

"It all adds up."

"It's possible Seth's arrival surprised a thief, maybe an addict, looking for cash, or something to sell. It *is* near the reserve. Why isn't the place alarmed?"

"Penderman didn't think an alarm was necessary. Obviously, he's rethinking that," said Ange.

"And Seth brought the remaining stock here?"

"Yes, all of it. There wasn't that much at the yard and after tonight, there's very little. I thought Gregori was coming this weekend?" Ange said, changing the subject abruptly.

"He's flying in tomorrow," said Phineas.

"Is he angry?"

"He'll be fine, once everything's been taken care of."

They left the room shortly after, but Carey waited until she heard them leave by the back door before she crawled out. She sat down carefully at the end of Seth's bed. He didn't look like he was going to wake up but she decided to wait a while, hoping he would.

Someone was taking the children to Washington on Tuesday. It seemed like Phineas was the boss and if he didn't let Ange keep her, she'd have to go with the other children and be sold.

The police weren't looking for her and didn't really want to because they thought she was a bad girl and that she ran away. That made her angry and scared at the same time. It wasn't true, not about her and not about her mom, who was so kind, and loved her and Elwin and really cared about the women she worked with.

The woman named O'Meara was one of the ones who came to the dark house trying to find her. She remembered how upset everyone was. After that, Seth drove them to Theo's farm. Then they tried to kill the woman named O'Meara. But they failed and she's still alive. They were telling lies about her too. Maybe now, the women were afraid and had stopped looking.

Phineas was wrong about one thing. No one ever saw them going into the dark house because Seth always pulled up to the back door in the lane. He always made sure no one was around. Carey was sure it was Seth who called her mom and told her where she was. That's why the women came to look for her.

She leaned over and asked Seth to wake up, but she

knew he couldn't hear her. She had to get away and get help. For him. For all the kids. She was the only one who knew that they were going to sell them all.

Carey was tired now and knew she couldn't let anyone find her here. She whispered in Seth's ear that she was going to get them out of here. She just had to figure out how.

She went upstairs and climbed into bed with Marie and took her hand. They were selling Marie tomorrow and she didn't know how to stop them. And the rest of the children in just a few days. Carey couldn't stop the tears.

28

Fernice sent Alex a text message late afternoon. The message was simple: What's up? He'd promised to call with the results of the PG interview and still no word. It wasn't like him. He purchased a burner cell on his way to the office in 100 Mile House and called her before he got there. She picked up.

Alex went over what he had. He was pretty sure he'd tracked down the tweeter: a young man named Seth Boyce who'd been missing for nearly eight years. It was his mother Tanya he'd interviewed earlier. Two days ago, Inspector Ford MacLeish had paid her a visit. Why, after nearly eight years of silence, would MacLeish want to know whether Seth Boyce had contacted his mother, unless he knew that Boyce was alive and maybe where he was? Alex had checked and there was nothing in the Boyce case notes that linked MacLeish to Seth. Then he told Jeri about the drawing. He was almost certain the Mountie in Seth's drawing was Ford MacLeish.

"An Inspector!"

"Yeah. Seth's mother is a member of the same church that MacLeish attends and as a boy, Seth was a participant in the boys' club that he led — still leads, according to Tanya."

"When are you coming to Vancouver?"

"We're short handed here. The best I can do is a late flight out tomorrow, that way I'll be on the ground for Saturday. I'll text you the particulars."

"Okay."

Alex was still at his desk. It was late and he was tired. He decided to wait before he brought his suspicions to his boss, Ian Kennedy. He and his wife were in Toronto, visiting their daughter. She'd started classes at York University last month and was away from home for the first time. Kennedy wasn't due back till Tuesday next week. Alex liked and trusted Kennedy, an intelligent man who ran the detachment fairly, but he it occurred to him that Kennedy would feel duty bound to report what he told him to the brass in Vancouver. He didn't want to give MacLeish time to cover his tracks.

Seth Boyce would be in his late teens and seemed to be reasonably savvy with internet technology. He had inside information about the abduction of Morgan O'Meara. He had conceived of a clever way to get important information to her, and in doing so, he'd put himself in real danger.

Someone tipped off MacLeish that Boyce had been successful at getting a message to O'Meara, but who? Someone at the university more than likely. Or someone here in 100 Mile House? Not a comforting thought.

Desocarras pulled out the burner again. He tried O'Meara's number. She didn't pick up so he left a message that he'd be in Vancouver Saturday morning and that he wanted to meet with her and Lucas.

29

Lucas sat up quickly, heart pounding. The clock said 3:18 am.

"Lucas. What's the matter?" Morgan mumbled, turning to him. He patted her arm and she snuggled down and went back to sleep. He slipped out of bed, put on a robe and retreated to the kitchen. His journal was where he'd left it last night. He opened it and picked up a pen, looked at his hand resting against the white paper, the lines. He began to write, the words tumbling over each other to get on the page.

Several hours later, Lucas returned to bed but couldn't sleep. Morgan woke up soon after.

"You're already awake."

"I've been up for a few hours. Writing."

"Last night you yelled something in your sleep: '*The pintos. They're everywhere.*' What does *pinto* mean?"

"That's what the Maya call the army, because it's made up mostly of Ladinos — like the pinto bean, brown and white — Spanish and Maya. They did most of the killing during the civil war. Killed the Ixil, burned their villages. Chased and killed the ones who escaped to the jungle to hide. Sometimes, they followed us over the border to Mexico and killed us there. Some Maya were press ganged into the army. All other Maya men and boys older than 12 that lived in areas under army control were forced to participate in civil patrols. They were killed if they refused. The civil patrols also participated in the genocide. Sometimes though, it was the guerrillas who were responsible for killing us. We called them *The Little People*, because they were predominantly Maya. Last night, I dreamt that my father was shot by one of the guerillas. I was only a few feet from him. His blood was pumping out. A fountain of blood. I tried to stop it with my hands."

My poor Lucas. What was there to say. Atrocity after atrocity and the aftermath continued — in Guatemala and here, in our cottage. I took his hand.

"I could use some fresh air," he said. "Want to go for a walk. It's not raining."

"Sure. I think I could manage a short run."

"You want to run." He smiled. "You're a crazy woman, but I love you."

"And I love you, dear man."

It was cold and the air was crisp as we made our way down to New Brighton and the running trails on the water. Night lights still danced on the blue-black water of the Inlet. The dawn's early foray had just begun to lighten the under tips of heavy cloud as we ran through the parking lot and took the pedestrian tunnel to the exercise paths along the ocean.

We ran the laps twice at a leisurely rate. It was wonderful to be running by the ocean as the city woke up all around us, to take back ownership of my park. By the time we looped back through the tunnel, the sun was up in earnest, rain clouds in check at least for awhile.

We came to a stop at the spot where I had parked the night I was taken, an innocuous parking lot, the pavement a little uneven, not a car in sight at this early hour. Incorrigible blackberry bushes remained green and lively in the train track area which skirted the inlet. High steel fencing, barbed wire coiled at the top, kept everyone out. The Americans had insisted that the entire dock area be off limits since 9/11.

"Let's walk the rest of the way home. You can wait till next week to train for the *Sun Run*."

Lucas was right. It did feel good to run, but pushing beyond my limit wasn't going to achieve anything. We headed back to the cottage.

30

Breakfast was going to be a feast. A platter of fruit already sat on the table and the pot of black beans which Lucas had soaked last night simmered on the back burner. He was making *Tamales de Elote* especially for me, with chilies and shredded goat cheese generously sprinkled over the top. A tray of sausages grilled in the oven and an oversized omelet was planned for our biggest skillet. 'Oh yum,' I thought and realized I was honestly hungry. My legendary appetite was returning.

"Something pretty important must be up or Alex wouldn't be making the trip," said Lucas, as he carefully added a little more water to his tamale dough.

"He said he'd be here by 9:30 am."

"We've got lots to tell him."

"I should have called Fernice. It just seems easier to tell Alex everything and let him tell her."

"So, you decided to take the easy way out," Lucas said, with a grin.

"She told me not to go near the shipyard."

"Yes, she did. But when she finds out what we uncovered, she'll be glad we did."

"They'll both be thoroughly pissed off with us."

"Oh well. Can't be helped," said Lucas. There would be eight of us, with Alex. Bart was joining us after early morning rounds at West Sanctuary.

Alex arrived a little before 9:30 am, looking very dapper in a black fedora. I'm big on hats and I loved the fedora. Amelia and George arrived next, with Michael and Kate only minutes after. I was introducing everyone to Alex when Bart arrived.

We used the extender, which got all of us around the table, pretty much elbow to elbow. I served up a pot of coffee, setting the table with cream, sugar, juice, cutlery and plates, then started another pot. Kate made herself a pot of tea.

Lucas's timing was great, as always, and it was stove to platter to table in record time, everything piping hot and smelling delicious. No prompting was needed and we all dug in. Lucas beamed with pleasure as gratified sighs of appreciation were heard all around.

Alex ate quietly. I had introduced him to everyone as Sgt. Desocarras, but he insisted on Alex. Michael jumped in first.

"Alex, it was you and your wife who rescued Morgan."

"Yes, we did." Alex said with a smile, as he reached for the omelet platter.

"Luke, could you pass the tamales please?" Lucas handed the platter of steaming tamales to Bart.

"Lucas, I hope you don't mind me asking. Where are you from? asked Amelia.

"I don't mind at all. I'm from Guatemala."

"Are you Indigenous?" she asked.

"I'm *Ixil-Maya* and Spanish." In Guatemala, the Maya say I'm *Mestizo*, which means mixed."

"*Mestizo*. Like *Métis*?" asked Amelia.

"Similar," said Lucas, with a smile. "How is everyone doing? Can we get you anything?"

There was a chorus of '*No thank you*', '*This is great*',

'*Where did you learn to cook like this*' and '*Awesome*'. Lucas basked in the limelight good cooks always generate.

"Lucas, did you find out what department Marvin Roche is enrolled in?"

"Well Michael, he's not enrolled in a department because he's not a student at SFU." Alex looked at Michael, then Lucas.

"Aha," said Michael. "I knew there was something fishy about that guy."

"Who's Marvin Roche?" asked Alex.

"He's a waiter at the *Clarendon*." said Michael.

Alex nodded and kept eating.

I jumped in. "Lucas and I think he might be a drug dealer. What better cover than to say you're a student, and he looks the part, don't you think Michael?"

"Describe this guy Marvin," Alex asked Michael.

"He has very bright, auburn hair, bed head, and electric blue eyes," said Michael. Amelia and George exchanged glances.

"Uncle, is he about 6 feet tall, on the slender side, very snazzy dresser?" asked Amelia.

"Yes to everything, except the snazzy dresser part. I've only seen him in his waiter's uniform so I wouldn't know," said Michael. "Why do you ask?" He looked at Amelia quizzically.

"Lots of freckles?" added George.

"That's right!" said Michael. At this point, everyone was paying attention. Alex fished out a notebook and opened it beside him.

"Mark," George and Amelia spoke together.

"Who's Mark?" Michael asked them.

"I'll bet he's a drug dealer at SFU," I said.

"That's right Morgan," said Amelia, beaming at me. "He deals pot, some pills.

"Lots of students are into pills, especially at exam time. Cocaine too and other things if they can afford it," said George, raising his eyebrows and looking at Alex.

"Mark or Marvin deals at the club as well. Lots of drug use there," said Michael.

"Drug dealer," said Alex quietly, nibbling on a tamale. "Really delicious, Lucas."

"Thank you, Alex."

"Let's just say that some club members do exactly as they please and the staff turn a blind eye. You could say it's part of their job description," said Michael.

"So, Mark is a drug dealer at SFU?" Alex asked both George and Amelia.

"He is," said George. "He's been pointed out to me. I don't know his last name."

"I don't think anyone does," added Amelia.

"Someone named Mark got in touch with Stacie Smith," I said. "He claimed to be working for *The Pinnacle*, the SFU student newspaper. He wanted to interview banished boy." It was difficult to ignore Alex — completely deadpan cop face, pointed look and slightly raised eyebrows — but I managed. He'd warned us off interviewing Stacie. I stole a glance at Lucas, who was studiously eating.

"Did Mark say how he came to know about the tweeter?" asked Alex.

"We think he found out through a student named Gary Sulzberger," said Lucas. "Gary's in another film lab; not Morgan's."

"We didn't actually meet with Stacie. I phoned Det. Fernice as soon as I got off the phone with Stacie and filled her in."

Alex looked at me, then Lucas and then around the table.

"I spoke with the tweeter's mother yesterday. He

disappeared about eight years ago. She hasn't seen him since. An RCMP officer is implicated in his disappearance."

"Do you have any idea who the officer is?" Michael asked.

"Yes." All eyes were on Alex. "That's one of the reasons I'm here. He appears to have strong connections to Vancouver. I think someone down here tipped him off about the truck tweet, Morgan. He visited the tweeter's mother a few days ago."

We all fell silent. I felt the hair on the back of my neck prickle.

"I believe that officer is either linked to the tweeter or people close to him and now, with what you're telling me, it appears that he may be connected to someone at SFU. The reason I'm here today is that I'm very concerned for your safety Morgan, and anyone connected with you. That would include everyone at this table," he said pointedly as he looked around the table at all of us, "to say nothing of Carey and other children that are most likely being held."

Alex gave Amelia and Michael an understanding look. Michael looked grim and said nothing. Silent tears slid down Amelia's cheeks. George put an arm around her.

"I need to clarify a few things. First, it's a good bet that Mark and Marvin Roche are the same person?" There were nods all around.

"Maybe Mark's the informant, or the Vancouver connection," said Lucas.

"The only connection that we're sure of is that Mark is Gary Sulzberger's dealer, and Gary is in the other film lab for my course."

"I've seen Gary and Mark together, a few times." George pointed out.

"We've both seen them talking," said Amelia. "And everyone knows Mark deals."

"Gary's in Carl's film lab. We have Gary's contact info."

"Morgan, tell me you didn't contact Gary?" Alex didn't hide his alarm.

"No, Alex, we didn't."

Alex didn't hide his relief either. He turned to Michael. "Do you spend much time at the *Clarendon*?"

"I'm there quite a bit. I'm a lawyer with Bourdais Lambert. The firm has a business membership and I meet a lot of my clients at the club for lunch and dinner. Most of them are in the entertainment industry. My specialty is intellectual property, all areas."

Lucas and I exchanged a glance. Time to spill.

"Alex, Morgan and I want you to know we had a friend hack into the main server at the *Clarendon*."

"You have a friend who can hack into secure databases?"

"Well, it couldn't be that secure or he wouldn't have been able to get in. I mean, he's good, but he's not a professional criminal." I said.

"That is comforting," said Alex. "What did he get?"

"Club membership list for the last three years, and we have the list of who has used the overnight accommodation this past year and a list of which club employees worked which member functions," Lucas said. "I have two copies of everything for you and Det. Fernice. We haven't had a chance to make a careful examination of the lists. We just got them late last night. He went to fetch them."

"We can't tell you our friend's name. We have to protect him."

"Morgan, I don't want to know your friend's name," said Alex. We all watched as Lucas handed him two large manila envelopes.

"And here's Gary's contact information as well," said Lucas.

"Anything further anyone would like to share?"

"There is some urgency now," said Kate softly. "Today has been very hard." Alex relented and gave her an understanding nod. Amelia and George looked perplexed, having no idea what Kate was talking about, but said nothing.

"There is something else," I said.

"We intended to tell both you and Det. Fernice," said Lucas.

"We're not quite sure how you'll feel about it."

Alex resisted an overwhelming desire to roll his eyes.

"Morgan had a strong memory flash around her abduction. She remembered a loud and rhythmic banging and under that, a constant humming sound."

"It's the sound of the docks when they are up and running, so I thought, I must've been held near the docks. I also remembered the smell of spar varnish, which is used in the refinishing of wood boats. My dad was a canoe builder."

Alex nodded for her to continue. He already had an idea where this might be going. Fernice had updated him after she checked out the shipbuilders' yard.

"I phoned Det. Fernice and told her about the memory of spar varnish. While I was on the phone with her we located a small shipyard that does repairs to older wooden boats — *Seabreeze Marine Boat Repair*, a Division of Port of Vancouver Shipbuilders.

"Yes, I have that information. She visited the shipyard the same day and found nothing."

"We made a visit as well," I admitted.

"Two visits actually," said Lucas.

"Two visits." said Alex. These two were in a league unto themselves.

"The first visit was just to have a look around. I wanted to see if anything about the place was familiar, if it triggered any memories for me. Det. Fernice wouldn't let me go with her."

"We took every precaution, Alex," said Lucas. "We wore disguises and we rented a car." Amelia and George were shocked.

"Weren't you scared?" asked Amelia. We both nodded yes.

"You wore disguises?" said George.

"Morgan is very good at all things theatrical," said Kate, with undisguised pride. "She's in film."

"Really Alex, they were excellent disguises! No one would have recognized them," said Bart.

"Absolutely not," said Kate.

Bart pulled up the selfie and showed it to Alex.

It certainly wasn't the picture he was expecting. They were definitely incognito, which was very reassuring to Alex and he relented, a little.

"Okay, what was it about the first visit that made you decide to return?"

"The place was very familiar, Alex. I just knew I'd been there before. There was a locked office, just off the reception area. I really wanted to have a look inside that room."

"We went back the same evening," said Lucas.

"How did you get into the building?"

"I used wire cutters to get through the fence surrounding the property."

"We did have to break a small window to enter the building."

"You didn't set off an alarm?" asked Alex.

"I didn't see any sign of an arming box on our first visit," I said.

"Right," said Alex, clearly interested in this bit of information.

"The locked room was just off the reception area. We figured there wouldn't be a key close by. What would be the point? Especially if there was something that they were trying to hide."

"Morgan kicked in the door," Lucas added proudly. "She has a black belt in karate."

"What did you find?" Alex asked.

In answer, Bart reached into the breast pocket of his jacket. "They found some pretty disturbing evidence," he said, handing over two CDs. "I put a third copy in my safe deposit box. Everything has been deleted from my hard drive."

"What's on these CDs?"

"Pictures I took of images of children in books and calendars, all meant for resale." I didn't describe the photos, especially with Amelia in the room.

"Where exactly did you find this material?"

"In one of the locked cupboards in the room," Lucas said.

"And you broke into the cupboard?"

"We didn't have to. I used our house key. The cupboard wasn't very secure."

"Not at all, I'd say," said Alex. "What made you think to try your house key?"

"My dad had a locked cupboard in his workshop. When the tumbler wore down, he used his house key to open it. Don't worry Alex. We were careful to leave everything exactly as we found it and relocked the cupboard when we were done."

"That's good, but the evidence of a break in remains — the fence, the broken window, a kicked in door." He was grim. "Det. Fernice doesn't know about your visit."

"Not yet."

"Like I said, we intended to tell you today," said Lucas.

"That same night would have been far better," said Alex. "Is there anything else?"

"One of the pictures on the disc is the license plate of a silver *Suburban* that arrived at the shipyard, just after we left."

Alex looked at Michael and tapped the disc. "Have you seen that photo, Michael?"

"Yes Alex. It looks to be the same make and model and colour as the *Suburban* I saw behind the club. But I didn't get a clear picture of the license plate the night I saw Carey, so I can't confirm it's the same car."

"Where did you take the picture, Morgan?"

"Just outside the gate of the shipyard."

"I waited in the car while Morgan jumped out and took it."

"Where were you two when the *Suburban* arrived?"

"We were already out of the building and at the wire fence bordering the property where we initially entered the yard."

"Do you think the driver saw you leave?"

"No. We were on the opposite side of the yard, in complete shadow. The building was between us and the gate."

"Good." They barely missed getting caught, thought Alex.

"Okay. Morgan, Lucas and you as well, Michael. You all need to back off. Immediately! I need your promise that you will." He looked at us expectantly: waiting. We looked at each other. I nodded yes first and the fellas followed my lead.

"Okay. Anything else?"a

"There is one more thing, Alex," said Michael. "I don't know how important it is. Someone — we're not absolutely certain who — has started a campaign up in Terrace to discredit both Carey and her mother, Rosaline."

"How did you find out?"

"Cpl. Cumberland, he's at the Terrace detachment. He came to the house and told Rosie. He thought she should know. We're all pretty upset about it. Rosie's such a good mom and a very respected member of the community in Terrace, and Carey's a wonderful kid. Cumberland said some of the police have given the rumours a lot of credence."

"Any idea who started the rumours?"

"Cpl. Cumberland thinks it might be a lawyer named Paul Revier. He's crown counsel for the area up there. Cumberland saw him having lunch with Sgt. Willis and it was soon after that the rumours started to fly."

Alex noted his name and checked the spelling.

"Rosie believes that Revier is at least partly responsible for a known paedophile not being charged when he should have been and then dragging his feet on the case when the guy finally was charged. The paedophile committed suicide, the weekend before he was going to be sentenced."

"Go on," said Alex.

"Circumstances around the case were very suspicious. That's what some people said at the time — for instance, witnesses for the defense suddenly withdrawing their testimony; one died under circumstances that were never properly explained."

Michael looked over at Amelia. He knew Amelia was having a very hard time with all of this. It was comforting to him that George was in her corner.

"Speaking of tarnished reputations, someone is trying to ruin ours," said Lucas. "We joke about it to keep our spirits up, don't we Morgan."

"We try to. I worked the streets, then managed to get

myself off the streets, then went back to school and turned my life around. But I'm still kind of loose in the morals department and sleep around a lot on Lucas."

"And this makes me very jealous because I'm a hot-blooded Latin male who has no control over his temper."

Alex nodded. "Two smear campaigns: one in Terrace and one at SFU."

"Someone is trying to derail this case," said Lucas.

"They sure are," said Bart.

Alex left shortly after. But not before he got further assurances, especially from Morgan, Lucas and Michael, to back off. He had a feeling his words were falling on deaf ears. In the end, he did get them to promise not to do anything without telling him first. They agreed to that. He texted Fernice he was on his way.

31

Alex headed to a small diner in Port Kells, once a thriving port town but now part of the sprawling city of Surrey, on the south side of the Fraser River. Jeri lived in Langley, a community bordering Surrey, so it was a quick drive for her to meet him there. It was also well away from VPD turf. He got tied up in weekend traffic heading east over the Port Mann Bridge and by the time he arrived, she was finishing up a sandwich and salad. She spotted his fedora coming through the door and raised a hand in greeting. She stood when he reached her table and they shook hands.

"Jeri Fernice."

"Alex Desocarras."

"As you can see, I didn't waste any time. Sit, we'll get you something to eat," and she turned to signal the waitress behind the counter."

"I just finished breakfast. I'll have water for now, maybe a coffee." Alex went to the counter and placed his order, then returned to the table. Jeri pushed her empty plate aside and reached for her coffee. The waitress brought his order, leaving his bill and Jeri's. She was going off shift.

"I'm all ears," she said.

"First, you need to know that I've kept my people in the dark about the involvement of MacLeish, the officer in PG I spoke to you about. He's second-in-command up there, in charge of general policing operations. He has full knowledge of all RCMP provincial initiatives — including anything to do with missing children."

"I noticed that," said Jeri.

"At least for now, we have to assume he's not alone and that other officers may be involved. That's why I didn't want to risk a digital trail, or a paper trail."

"I agree. If we're wrong, so much the better. MacLeish could be nothing more than a valuable point person in a civilian operation."

"MacLeish paid a visit to Boyce's mother the day that O'Meara came up to view the abandoned pickup," said Alex.

"He found out about the tweet and put two and two together. Someone in 100 Mile House could have tipped him off. Or maybe someone at SFU."

"I just had breakfast with O'Meara and Arenas. Amelia Boudreau and a friend George Evans, the uncle, Michael Bolton, Kate Brennan and her husband Bart; they were all there. I wanted to warn O'Meara and Arenas, in person."

Jeri nodded. "Good."

"They had new information for us. I have copies of everything for you." Alex quietly handed over a large envelope. Jeri pulled out the lists and a CD.

"How did they get these lists? What's on the CD?"

"An acquaintance of O'Meara's hacked the club's server. The CD's another story.. You're not going to like it."

"What say we adjourn this meeting to my place? I live close by."

"Good idea."

"I'll let my partner know we're coming. She hates surprises but loves company," said Jeri as she got out her cell. "What did you tell your office?"

"I'm visiting a sick uncle in Mission." Norm Ferguson married Alex's Aunt Marissa 30 years ago. They lived on the Chehalis Reserve, on the banks of the Harrison River. Norm was *Sts'Ailes*. He was a gifted singer and one of over five hundred who still spoke *Halqeméylem*.

"Okay nephew, I got it," said Norm, making note of the burner cell number Alex wanted him to use if he had to get in touch. "If anyone asks, I'm sick as a dog." Alex called Gwen next. It went to voicemail and he left a message. No change in plans. He'd be staying in the lower mainland at least one more night. If anyone asked, he was visiting his Uncle Norm who was having some health issues. He hoped to be back in 100 Mile in time for his Monday afternoon shift. He had called the same story into the duty officer at 100 Mile House.

Alex followed Jeri out of the parking lot. She headed south, toward the US border and then east to her place in Langley. Jeri and Jasmine, her partner of six years, had a small, well-kept bungalow on Rees Lake Road, a quiet, out-of-the-way setting. To make it perfect, Anderson Creek meandered through a few lacy, white pines and one tall oak tree, right in their back yard.

Jasmine came out to greet them, offering her hand to Alex and a '*Hi Sweetie,*' to Jeri.

He followed them into the house and through to their kitchen, a bright room with south facing windows and a sliding door which led onto a deck and a nice view of the creek. Jasmine, who preferred Jas, was a caseworker with the Ministry of Children and Families. Jeri and Alex pulled out their laptops and lists. Jas excused herself, leaving them to it.

Alex pulled out a few sheets of blank paper. "I like to do a diagram when there's a lot of detail. It helps me organize my thoughts."

"Good idea." She left the room and quickly returned with a handful of markers. "I like colour." She plunked the markers down on the table.

Alex listed the four police forces involved: VPD, Prince George RCMP, Terrace RCMP and 100 Mile House RCMP. Each got a separate box. Jeri sat beside him, computer open.

"A box for SFU and one for the *Clarendon* and another for *Seabreeze Marine Boat Repair*." She pulled out the CD and the lists. "Did the hacker use his own computer?"

"No. Arenas said the hacker wiped and disposed of it when he was done."

"Good," said Jeri.

What's on the CD?"

"Images of child sexual abuse," said Alex and watched as Jeri struggled for composure.

"Who took the pictures and where?"

"O'Meara took the pictures Thursday night at the Boat Yard."

"What!? They've had these pictures since Thursday night! Does anyone know they took them?! Shit. The boatyard. I had a good look around. *Absolutely nothing jumped out at me*."

"Morgan and Lucas visited the same afternoon in disguise. Pretty good disguises actually. I saw a picture this morning. They had the employee give them a tour. That was their first visit. The place seemed familiar to O'Meara and she had a gut feeling about the office in the main reception area."

"Right. Window blinds closed. The office."

"They returned that evening. They got into the yard by cutting a hole in the wire fencing and gained entry to the shop through a small window at the side of the building."

"Where was the evidence?"

"O'Meara kicked in the office door and they found books and calendars in one of the locked cupboards in the office. They got out just in time. A young man arrived as they were leaving the yard and parked by the main gate."

"Tell me he didn't see them!"

"They're certain he didn't. By the time he was in the building, they were beyond the fence. They retrieved their car, then drove past the gate entrance. A silver *Suburban* was parked there. O'Meara got pictures of the license plate."

"We've got the CDs and club lists."

"License pics are in a separate folder," said Alex.

"Got it." She went online and accessed the DMV data base and plugged in the plate number: 863 MAL.

"The lists from the *Clarendon* include: paid up members each year for the past three years; members who booked the clubs' overnight facilities during the past year; and a third list of banquets, dinners and other functions that members have hosted at the club. That list includes the names of club members attending each function and the staff who worked it. Waiters and bartending staff share a percentage of total sales for any function they work."

"*Suburban* is leased to Northfor Tech. Principal driver is Ange Batlan."

"Batlan is a friend of Amelia Boudreau's father."

"Amelia; Carey Bolton's cousin. She visited the house on Franklin Street with O'Meara and Brennan."

Alex did a search for Northfor. "Northfor is a large mining consortium. Head office is in Vancouver. They have mines in northern BC, Alberta, Manitoba, Ontario, Saskatchewan and Brazil, Columbia and Guatemala."

"Let's start with MacLeish, for reasons we already know." Alex found his name on the membership list. "He's been an associate member for at least three years. You should see this. He handed her the drawing Seth Boyce's mother had given him.

"Did MacLeish ever see this?" Jeri studied the drawing closely.

"No. I don't think she's shown it to anyone. She found it after she reported Seth's disappearance. I think she has always suspected MacLeish. She's afraid of him."

"Poor woman."

"He belongs to her church," said Alex, to himself.

"The bastard. Next, we have Ange Batlan. He leases the *Suburban*. That connects him to the boat yard and photos of child abuse. And if it's the same car that Michael Bolton saw at the back of the *Clarendon*, that's connects Batlan directly to Carey Bolton."

"And he has that connection to her family through the uncle, Geoff Boudreau."

"Right. Then we've got Theo Penderman. He owns the boatyard. That puts him in the frame," said Jeri.

"He's a member of the club," said Alex, consulting the list. "This morning, I heard about two smear campaigns, one at SFU, discrediting O'Meara and Arenas and another up in Terrace, targeting Rosaline and Carey Bolton. Paul Revier's name came up in connection with the Terrace smear campaign. He's crown council for Terrace and Kitimat. Bolton told me that his sister thinks Revier's involved in Carey's disappearance." He filled Jeri in.

She consulted the functions list. "Tracing back, Revier's been at two of the most recent seven parties Batlan has hosted, about once a month. He's on our list." She continued flipping backward. "Wait." She returned to the most recent functions and working backwards, began to highlight another name.

"What's up?"

She looked at Alex. She was grim.

"Phineas Rhodes," said Alex, reading the highlighted name.

"VPD ... Sweet Jesus," said Jeri. She rummaged through Carey's file until she found what she was looking for: the single page report that Ignace had given her two days ago. She handed it to Alex.

"1996. Two Indigenous girls seen getting into a car behind the club? It was Rhodes who did the follow-up."

"Det. Sgt. Phineas Rhodes now. Adam Ignace from my section remembered the story and went looking for that. He spoke with Rhodes. His story was that a call came in, someone did a call log sheet and he did the follow up. According to him, there was nothing to follow up. He couldn't reach the woman who called it in."

"Number not in service. He said it was a prank call!"

Alex was instantly livid with rage. He got up and started to pace, working hard to get himself under control.

"Rhodes works in my Section — Special Investigations — he's in Sex Crimes. He's been to 18 dinners that Batlan has hosted and that's since May of this year. Shit. I work with the bastard! I would never have guessed. Never. Not in a million years!"

Alex sat back down and drew heavy square boxes around the Prince George RCMP and VPD with the same colour. They read in silence for a few minutes.

"Okay. Back to Batlan," said Alex. He's connected to another person: Marvin Roche, a club employee. According to Bolton, it's a well-known fact that Roche supplies some of the members with drugs. Even more interesting, the description of Marvin Roche given by Bolton matches that of a guy named Mark, last name unknown, who's well-known as a drug dealer at SFU. Amelia and her friend George Evans described Mark this morning — a perfect match for Bolton's description of Roche. It seems that Mark and Marvin are the same person."

Jeri picked up the functions list. "Roche works a lot of the parties that Batlan hosts."

"If he's dealing at the club and SFU, we could have our SFU connection," said Alex.

"Mark wanted to interview the tweeter."

"That's right. The call to Stacie Smith. George Evans told me this morning he's sure Mark is Gary Sulzberger's dealer. Gary's the other film student who got a text message from Stacie Smith about the truck tweet."

"Sulzberger could have shared that information with Mark," said Jeri.

"And Mark gave it to Batlan, or MacLeish."

"And one or the other of them told Mark to call Stacie."

"We're going to need backup, but who?" said Alex, as he drew connecting lines between the VPD and Prince George RCMP, the *Clarendon*, SFU and *Seabreeze*.

"That's the million-dollar question. Let's have a look at the photos. Maybe they'll tell us something. I'd like you to watch the video on the flash drive. It's hard to watch." They opened the photo files. Alex inserted the flash drive and waited for the video to load.

"You said there were three copies of the pictures?" Jeri asked.

"We have two of them. The third is in a safe deposit box."

"Jesus Alex! These are hard to look at."

The video had started playing. Alex watched it to the end. "Shit." A lot coming from Alex, who rarely swore. "It's definitely MacLeish. This was left for us to find." He opened the photo folder.

Jeri was clicking through the pictures. "One thing does jump out. I don't think these weren't taken by an amateur.

They're using a professional photographer — the lighting, the different settings. Some look like they were taken in a home environment."

"If they're still using hard copy for distribution, it means they've been doing business for a long time."

"Before the internet," said Jeri. "They must have a website by now."

They were silent as they clicked through the pictures.

"I've identified fourteen children, boys and girls," said Jeri, "and I'm not finished. "These poor kids, Alex. Where are they from? Where are their homes — their families?" She closed the folder.

"Something interesting came back from the forensic analysis we did on O'Meara's clothing. I sent you the link late Thursday night, when I got back from PG," said Alex.

"I saw that."

"The techs found fibreglass fibres on her running pants and hoodie."

"The North Vancouver boatyard is strictly wooden boat repair. I didn't notice any fibreglass work being done when I was there. Unless O'Meara was held somewhere else."

"Or it could mean one of the perps was involved in fibreglass work. Remember my description of the perp at Gustafsen Lake?"

"Red face ... fibreglass allergy! Right."

"We're close," said Alex.

"We are," Jeri agreed.

"Looks like we have two important questions: Who can we trust and what do we do next?"

"It's going to be a long night. Jas made a stew. Let's eat while we strategize. As for who we can trust, I suggest we trust no one just yet."

32

I paced back and forth across the living room, or tried to. Our cottage is small and that seriously cramped my style.

Beside Lucas now, I leaned over his shoulder. He was reading through the member functions list.

I sat down beside him and he laid the pages on the table. We would be staying at the club tonight, as Michael's guests — his cousin Yolanda Compton and her boyfriend Cedric Forno, in town for the weekend. Michael booked the *Burrard Suite*, directly across the hall from the *Mackenzie* — a corner suite and Ange Batlan's regular booking. Batlan hosted a weekly dinner, usually on Saturday. Marvin Roche was booked to bartend.

"Michael's meeting us at the back entrance. He'll make sure the coast is clear, then we'll take the elevator up to the fifth floor."

I would be wearing a curly, light-brown wig. The short curls dropped to my brows in front and would cover my stitches. Only traces of the bruising on my face remained; easy enough to cover with foundation.

"When are we going to tell Desocarras and Fernice?"

"I'll call after we get there."

"They're going to be so pissed."

Kate and Bart were coming at eight, posing as Michael's

clients—film producers from out of town. "I gave Kate a reddish-brown wig to hide her dark curls."

"A guy named Ford MacLeish frequents Batlan's dinner parties."

I did an online search. "MacLeish is an RCMP Inspector. He's in charge of the RCMP detachment in Prince George. Prince George is a thriving city and BC's second capital, according to this."

"He's at the top of the ladder," said Lucas. Prince George—that's where Desocarras went to interview the mother of the missing boy."

"Maybe MacLeish is the bad cop?"

"Here's another frequent guest of Batlan, Ronald deReesen, small 'd'. He's a judge; an associate member."

I googled the judge. "deReesen is a circuit court judge in Prince George."

185

"He seems to host a lot of parties as well, for a guy who lives out of town. But when he's here on Saturday nights, he's in Batlan's entourage."

"You think that's a coincidence?"

"No, I do not Morgan," Lucas grumbled. One of these days, I'll remember there's no such thing.

"Gregory Crothers had been present on Saturdays once a month, until late last year, when he started showing up bi-weekly."

I googled Crothers but nothing significant came up.

"Sgt. Phineas Rhodes, VPD—he's at the club a lot, often attends Batlan's dinners," said Lucas.

"VPD."

"Uh huh."

"Ange Batlan sure pops up a lot: He's a club member; he knows Marvin Roche at least in passing; he's a friend of Carey's uncle Geoff Boudreau; and Amelia and I went to see him just before my abduction. Jeez Lucas. Batlan's such a nice guy. It's hard to believe that he's mixed up in this."

33

A lex's throw away cell vibrated. It was Gwen.

"Alex, Cpl. Alfonse with the VPD just called here looking for you. I gave him your work cell number, told him about your uncle being so sick that you might not get right back to him. He said it's important that he speak with you tonight."

"Thanks Gwen," said Alex and disconnected.

"Was that your wife?"

"Yes. Someone named Cpl. Alfonse called from the VPD. He spoke with Gwen; wanted to talk to me."

"Cpl. Alfonse?"

"He told Gwen it was important that he speak with me tonight."

"I don't know anyone named Alfonse at VPD," said Jeri. "Why would he call you?"

"Something's up," said Alex, when his burner rang again. It was Gwen.

"Inspector MacLeish just called here looking for you. I told him you were visiting your Uncle Norm. He left a number where he can be reached."

"Thanks Gwen, I'll call him back. You okay?"

"I'm okay. Worried sick about you." She didn't usually tell him that.

"No need to be, Gwen. I'm taking every precaution."

"I know you are, but I can't help worrying." Alex talked with Gwen a little longer, his personal voice of reason in a sea of chaos. His work cell buzzed. As soon as he hung up with her, he checked it. MacLeish had just called. He pointed to the video, then to his cell.

"MacLeish," he said quietly.

"Shit," was all Jeri said.

"Gwen told him I was visiting my sick uncle."

Alex called his Uncle Norm first. He was watching the news on *APTN*.

"Uncle, are you okay."

"I'm fine Alex.

"I thought you were going to cultural night?"

"I did. I just got in. I'm getting old and I let the young ones keep the late hours."

"Uncle, if anyone calls for me, tell them I'm having a nap and take a message. If you need to call me, use the new cell number I gave you."

"I've got it right here beside me, nephew. Don't worry."

"Remember uncle. You're not feeling so well, you think it's the flu and if you're not feeling better by tomorrow morning, I'm going to take you to the hospital."

"I remember," Norm said, and then, in a deep, throaty voice, "I'm half dead." He was clearly delighted with his role.

"Love you, uncle. I'll keep you posted." He ended the call. "I'm going to call MacLeish now."

Jeri nodded and shut her laptop and made sure her phone was on silent. He turned on his work cell and dialed the number Gwen had given him. It had a 250 exchange, which is used everywhere in BC except for Vancouver and the lower mainland. MacLeish answered on the second ring.

"Inspector MacLeish," Alex said, making no effort to

stifle a big yawn. Sorry I didn't get back to you right away. I turned off my cell so I could get a little shut-eye."

"Where exactly are you, sergeant?"

"With an Uncle. he's sick with the flu, vomiting, diarrhea. I may have to take him to the hospital tomorrow morning to get him re-hydrated. We'll see how it goes tonight."

"Sergeant, where exactly are you?"

"I'm just a little east of Mission."

"You're not at home?"

"Wish I was," made its way through another big yawn. "My wife and I felt it best that I come down and check on the old guy. Very independent, wouldn't ask for help if he was on his death bed. You know how they are when they're getting on. I'm the only family he has left."

"Yes, yes, of course. I assume you have permission," he said in a snotty, aggrieved tone.

Permission? Alex was livid on the other end of the phone, and it wasn't easy to keep his voice even. MacLeish must not suspect a thing.

"I notified the office, of course."

"Well, attend to your personal business and give me a call when you're back in 100 Mile House. It's nothing important and can wait till you return." MacLeish hung up abruptly.

"Ass," Alex muttered softly. "Something's up, but MacLeish didn't share. I think he bought my story."

"Maybe they're on to us."

"I was looking at Boyce's file," said Alex, "at least the little that was online. MacLeish could have got wind of that." He was interrupted by the buzz of his burner cell.

"Alex, it's Morgan. You told me to call on this line if anything should come up." He put her on speaker.

"I wanted to let you know we're at the club."

Jeri leaned in. "You're where?"

"The *Clarendon* and so is Michael Bolton. Bart and Kate are joining us. They'll be here soon."

"Morgan, why are you at the club?" asked Alex.

"Well, we were going over the lists and we noticed that a few men always show up when Ange Batlan hosts his parties. Michael checked and Batlan was having one tonight, so he rented accommodation, across the hall from the suite Batlan always rents. We just want to observe."

Jeri and Alex shared an alarmed glance. Alex shook his head.

"What suite are you in?"

"We're in the *Burrard Suite*. Lucas and I are staying here, so we won't be spotted."

"Which suite does Batlan rent?" asked Alex.

"The *Mackenzie* at the end of the hall and furthest from the elevator, on the left. We're right across the hall."

"Morgan, which men are you referring to, when you say the ones that always show up?" Jeri asked.

"Ange Batlan, Ford MacLeish, he's RCMP from Williams Lake, Ron deReesen, he's a judge, Sgt. Phineas Rhodes, VPD, a guy named Crothers."

"What exactly do you intend to do?" Jeri asked."

"We don't intend to do anything, honest. We're just going to observe."

"Observe?" she repeated.

"Morgan, you of all people know how desperate these men are," Alex cut in. He flashed back to her struggling, hands taped behind her, wading into the water of Gustafsen Lake. Gwen and him screaming at the guy.

"Lucas and I are staying in the suite. When Kate and Bart get here, they're having drinks and dinner downstairs with Michael."

"So not much happening there at the moment?"

"Nothing."

"Just a minute Morgan," Alex said, taking her off speaker.

"We could park in the underground lot beside the club. That way, we'd be moments away if there's trouble. But first, I want to check out the boat yard. Do you think we have time? And how far is it from the club?"

"About fifteen minutes. We could visit the yard and be back at the club by 9:30 pm and that still gives us lots of time to check it out."

Alex put Morgan back on speaker and told her they would call when they arrived at the club, around 9:30 pm.

"Morgan, if you need us for any reason before 9:30 pm, call me on my burner cell and we'll come running."

"Got that," said Morgan.

"Do you intend to stay the night?" he asked.

"Probably not." Which was a lie. We all had overnight bags.

"Be very careful. We'll be close by." Fernice said, ending the call. "Let's get going. They grabbed what they would need and left the house.

"It's going to be a long night," said Alex, as they climbed into his rental.

Lucas and I would eat dinner in the suite and keep a watch on the comings and goings across the hall. We were both frustrated that we couldn't be out and about. I had to remind myself that it'd only been 10 days since my return from 100 Mile House. Michael went downstairs to wait for Kate and Bart. They were posing as Trish and Brendan Moreland, producers of a new Canadian sitcom that was in the works.

The Morelands arrived about 8:15 pm. Kate, as Trish,

was stunning in a midnight blue, off the shoulder silk dress. Her abundant black curls were hiding under a straight, silky cut wig. She'd darkened her eyebrows and went with theatrical makeup. Bart was delighted.

"You do know that I married you because of your great beauty," Bart said as they walked up the steps to the club.

"Ah, but I should have told you. It won't last," she countered. "The women in my family age very poorly," she added, with great relish, flashing him a beatific smile.

"Fortunately for me, intelligence and wit never grow old."

She squeezed his arm a little tighter. "I'm scared," she whispered in his ear.

"Me too," said Bart.

They'd parked in the underground lot beside the club. When they walked up the steps of the front entrance, Michael was waiting for them and signed them in. They took an elevator up to the suite.

"We're in luck," said Michael once everyone was gathered. "Batlan's dinner party is in the *Hamilton Room* tonight. It's close to where we're eating and it'll be easy to keep an eye on them."

"Where is the *Hamilton Room*?" Kate asked.

"On the second floor. It's a sub floor of sorts, tucked away and very private."

"I wish I could get a look at these guys?" said Lucas.

"Marvin Roche is serving. He'd be able to identify you and Morgan."

"What about me?" Kate asked.

"Absolutely not!" said Bart, surprising us all. "They know who you are and these guys are dangerous, Kate. Besides, you're wearing stilettos. You wouldn't be able to run."

"I've got my sneakers with me!" said Kate indignantly.

"You can't wear sneakers with that beautiful dress."

"Sneakers would be a dead giveaway," she said, laughing. It was good to hear her laugh. The last few weeks had been a great strain on my normally ebullient friend.

"Not to worry everyone, said Michael. "I've got it covered. I'm going to pay a visit to Batlan's little party. I'll be looking to buy some weed and while I'm there, I plan on taking some pictures. I have a lapel camera," he announced with glee.

"Oh Michael. What a great idea!" For me, with all cameras it's love at first sight.

"I bought it yesterday in a shop on Hastings Street — a spy shop." He was clearly delighted with the purchase and took a few snaps of us. "As soon as your dinner arrives, we'll go down."

"Does Batlan usually book the *Mackenzie Suite*?" asked Bart.

"Always," said Michael.

"This room is perfect," said Lucas, looking out the peep hole. "No one can get by us."

Into The Mist

34

The air was cool and damp. Everything shrouded in a thick blanket of mist. Seth, hot and flushed with fever, didn't feel the cold. He stumbled towards the garage. Wanted to get Ange's car, to take Carey home, a surprise for her. Georgina wanted to go home. That's all she wanted. What they all wanted. What he wanted. Too late for him. Too late now. He'd done so many things. Bad things. Too many.

When he turned back to look for the gatehouse, it had disappeared. He moved in a slow circle, but it was gone. Completely disoriented now, he kept going, trying to find a landmark. He heard the distant, muffled sound of a dog barking close by. Ange didn't have a dog. His house was up high, the last house on the street, such a beautiful house. He slept there sometimes, when there were no children to take care of; to pick up food for; to drive to the clients; so many children, Ange's beautiful children. Their faces in his dreams. Always in his dreams.

Walking was easier now. He was going downhill. He didn't think he should be going downhill and thought he must be going the wrong way. He kept moving; stumbling into trees and tripping over rocks. Aimless now, and near exhaustion, he lost his balance and he was sliding, over the edge and falling, down, down. Suddenly came to an abrupt stop. Too tired to get up, he leaned back; rested his head. His mom was beside him. She covered him with a warm blanket. '*Don't need it mom*,' he tried to tell her. '*I'm so hot*'. Her hand on his cheek was cool and gentle.

When Alex and Jeri arrived at the boat yard, no lights were visible in the yard or the main building. They parked a few blocks away and made their way to the outside perimeter of the property. A dense blanket of fog hovered higher up the mountains. Only their tops were visible.

It took a few minutes to locate the entryway that Arenas had cut through the fence. Jeri used wire snips to quickly cut through the makeshift fix someone had rigged up.

"Did they really think this would keep anybody out?" she said, as they made their way through the fence into the yard and approached the building from the back. The broken window had been boarded up. They followed the wall around to the entrance. Jeri picked the lock and once they were inside, they pulled out flashlights and made their way to the front of the shop. It was so overcast that no light filtered through the windows in the reception area.

"They didn't get the door fixed," said Alex as they entered the office.

"No windows in here. We can risk putting on the overhead."

Alex, flicked the light switch with one gloved finger. Jeri got to work picking the cupboard locks. The shelves were empty.

"They must have moved the merchandise that night,"

said Jeri.

They moved to an unlocked door along the back wall. It opened onto an empty, windowless room, as long as the main room was wide. There was no light source here. They had to make do with what light penetrated from the main office area and their flashlights.

"Notice the smell?" said Jeri. "Acetone."

"The smell of acetone was strong in the truck box too." Alex hunkered down to examine the floor area and a patch of wall in one corner. "It looks like blood staining here."

"There's a small spray up the wall there as well," said Jeri, following it with her flashlight. The floor, which had the hard, unforgiving feel of concrete, was covered with threadbare, low nap carpeting.

Alex continued to focus his light on the floor, slowly traversing it, inch by inch. "What's this," he said, as he carefully fished a tiny blue pill from the carpet's low nap.

"Can you read the imprint?"

"*Barr*," said Alex.

"*Diazepam*. It showed up in O'Meara's tox screen. She said she'd taken nothing that day, not even aspirin. *Valium* plus acetone fumes in the strength indicated by their presence in the room — O'Meara wouldn't have been able to put up any kind of fight," said Jeri.

"And if she'd never experienced the effect of either substance before, she wouldn't have recognized her symptoms for what they were." Alex returned the small blue pill to a spot not far from the blood stain and moved further along the wall.

"The smell is stronger over here. It could be a spill. The odor wouldn't be able to dissipate in a small, closed space like this; no window or ventilation."

They completed their examination of the room, but found nothing else. They had barely returned to the office area when a loud, rhythmic banging started up. Jeri moved back into the smaller room and listened carefully.

"The banging is much louder in here. That's the sound that O'Meara described in her statement."

Alex's burner cell buzzed. It was Morgan, texting them an update. Michael, Kate and Bart had gone downstairs to have dinner. She was upstairs with Lucas. Alex texted that they were on their way and would let her know when they were at the club.

35

Lucas was in the washroom when I heard the unmistakable thump of a suitcase against the door across from us. I got to the peephole in time to see a man in a suit and overcoat open the door to Batlan's suite and enter. I saw him in profile, left side, as he moved his briefcase to his right hand and pulled the door open to enter ... clean-shaven, sharp nose, pale complexion, medium height, ash-blonde hair, worn longish.

"Damn it," he said, loud enough for me to hear. He must have banged his hand on the door jam.

I watched the door close, then returned to my roast beef dinner. Lucas was back. I told him that someone just entered the room. "I heard him swear. He banged his hand. I got a good look at the guy from the side." More noise from across the hall and I jumped up to look.

"Same guy. He left his suitcase and overcoat in the room."

"Maybe he's staying the night?"

"I want to get a look at the room? Everyone's at dinner — this will probably be our only chance." The suites all had original carved doors and the hardware, including the locks, all in surprisingly good shape, were original as well. Which may be why the locks hadn't been fitted with deadbolts when the club was renovated. I'd been playing around with the lock on our door and found that, while it wasn't easy, it could be disengaged with a plastic card.

"I'll bet the doors all have the same type of lock. They really should consider dead bolts on these doors."

"Where'd you learn to do that?"

"A cousin."

"Okay. I'll keep watch outside the suite. If you hear one sound from me, get out of there, and quick!"

I grabbed my camera and my credit card, already the worse for wear from practise. We left our room door off latch. Lucas kept watch beside me, while I fumbled with the door lock on Batlan's suite. It wouldn't budge and I was about to give up when it quietly opened and I was in.

Batlan's suite was more like an apartment and it was beautifully decorated. A king-size bed filled a nook at the far end. One of the windows provided a stunning view of the lights on the inner harbour. There were several couches, a beautiful lacquered armoire, occasional chairs, quality side tables, cozy carpeting. A textured silk lamp and wall sconces provided soft, intimate lighting.

I took some photos and was just about to have a go at the suitcase at the foot of the big bed when I heard Lucas whistle. I got out fast, pulling the door shut behind me. Lucas was holding our door open. I dashed through and he quickly followed.

"I heard the elevator ding," he said.

"There wasn't much lying around. I took some pictures. I didn't have time to check the blonde's suitcase."

We stood, side by side, me looking through the peephole. Whoever had just arrived went into a room further down the hall.

We'd just started on dessert when there were sounds across the hall. I jumped up in time to see a woman in uniform push a cart stacked with fresh towels and linens into the room.

"I couldn't see her face. Don't cleaning staff usually leave their carts in the hallway," I whispered. We finished dessert and were enjoying coffee when we heard more noise at Batlan's door. This time, I got a good look at her face.

"She was at the back entrance when we came in. Michael nodded to her."

"She could have been up here checking on supplies."

"There were six stacked towels on the cart, same as when she went in. I think she came up to Batlan's suite for a reason."

"Maybe someone sent her up."

The elevator chimed, indicating yet another visitor to the floor, but they entered a room further down the hall.

"I want to check out the suitcase the blonde guy left."

"Wait Morgan. Just a few more minutes. The woman may return."

"Honestly, Lucas, this is so frustrating."

"I know honey, but we can't afford to let those bastards know that we're here. Let me see the pictures you took of the room."

I knew he was trying to mollify me but I handed him the camera and he pulled them up. I heard some noise and glanced through the peephole in time to see a man enter Batlan's suite. This latest visitor was medium height and quite stocky.

I quickly motioned to Lucas, but too late.

"Another guy," I said, describing him.

We hovered close by and it wasn't long before there was more action at the door. Lucas was at the peep-hole when the thick-set man emerged.

"Thick set guy; probably the same guy you saw.

"I wish I could take pictures of these people."

"These guys are probably at dinner with Batlan. We'll have pictures when Michael gets back."

It was close to 10:00 pm when Fernice and Desocarras parked beneath the club. She called Morgan.

"How's it going?"

"Batlan's room has had a few visitors." I gave her a brief rundown.

"Who's with you?"

"Lucas."

"Check in with us every 10 - 15 minutes, okay, even if nothing's happening."

"Okay."

Kate, Michael and Bart showed up soon after. Michael downloaded the shots he took of Batlan's guests to his laptop. Kate slipped into the bathroom to pee, while the rest of us gathered around to have a look.

"I made sure Marvin Roche wasn't in the room. Then I went in, pretending I was drunk, asking for Marvin. I wasn't sure if I was getting decent shots. I walked to the head of the table, patting guys on the back, trying for different angles. They tolerated me for a bit but boy, they got pissed off fast. Then Roche arriving with the dinner trolley and I made arrangements to buy some dope, which I did, twenty minutes later. I figured I had to or they'd be suspicious."

"You did great Mike," said Bart.

"Some of these pictures are a little fuzzy," said Michael, peering at his laptop.

"Oh no, they're fine, really!" I reassured him. "We can see everyone."

"I count ten men," said Bart.

"This guy was up here," I said, pointing at a guy

probably in his 30s with ash-blonde hair."

"Him too," said Lucas, pointing to a close-up of a thick-set man raising a glass to his lips.

As Michael scrolled through the pictures, I thought I recognized one of the men after the fact and asked him to scroll back.

"That guy, the one sitting to the right of the heavy-set guy. I'm sure I saw him at the VPD, when I went in for my interview. He was at the front desk."

"I don't remember seeing him," said Lucas.

"I noticed him because he was talking to someone. He has a beautiful voice; a deep baritone."

"He's definitely a person of authority," said Bart. "His face, his whole demeanor. He's used to being in charge."

"What about the blonde?"

"Him too."

There was one particularly good shot of the entire room. Marvin Roche could be seen, just inside the frame, close to the dumb waiter.

"Look at that," said Bart. "Those two are in a pissing match. The blonde is glaring across the table at him," he said, pointing to the VPD guy, "and he's ignoring him. The blonde is royally pissed off."

"I'd love to be a fly on their wall!" Kate was back.

"We need Batlan's guest list," said Michael. I'll try to get it from one of the staff."

"Oh Michael. What if Batlan finds out?" Kate didn't like the idea one bit.

"Don't worry, Kate. I'll be careful. I'll make sure Roche doesn't get wind of it," he said, glaring at his computer screen."

"We should get these pictures to the sergeants. They're in the parking lot below us." I called down, put her on speaker and told her what we had.

"You said you were only going to observe!"

"I was very careful," Michael assured her.

She gave us an email address and Michael sent her the pictures.

"I'm going now. Is the coast clear?" Michael asked Kate, who was on watch at the door.

"Yes — Oops, no!" she hissed. "Wait."

"A woman in uniform just arrived and she's very distracted," Kate announced in a stage whisper. "Okay. Now."

Michael slipped out the door and was down the hall in a shot.

"Let us know when she leaves, Kate, and look to see if she's carrying anything." She nodded.

Lucas had turned on my camera. "These are pictures Morgan took in Batlan's suite," he told Bart.

"What? You broke in?!"

"No, not me — Morgan. I kept watch by the door."

Bart feigned heart palpitations, took the camera and scrolled through the pictures, while the two of us looked on.

"Tall man leaving," Kate whispered from the door.

"Kate, did you see him enter?"

"No, not while I've been watching."

"Then where'd he come from?"

"Maybe he entered the room before the cleaning woman," said Kate.

"Maybe we just missed him," I said.

"Or maybe there's another way into the suite," said Kate, eyes wide. "It's a heritage building. Who knows what went on here in the past. It's downtown, in the heart of the business district, and so close to the harbour. For all we know, there could be a maze of secret doors and passageways. Maybe there's an underground entrance that no one knows about!"

"Kate's got a point," said Lucas. "Batlan's suite is the last one on that side of the hall. We should check out the area beside it."

"Let's go," said Bart.

Checking first that the hallway was empty, Bart and Lucas slipped out, leaving Kate and I were alone in the room. We sat in tub chairs near the door. Kate slipped off her heels and wiggled her toes.

"What's directly beside us?" Kate asked.

"Facing our door, a suite on our right and on the left, a storage room." There was noise at Batlan's door. We both jumped up.

"The woman's leaving," whispered Kate. "You look."

I took a peek at her as she locked up. "She was here earlier," I whispered back.

"She's carrying a plastic bag."

We both heard the elevator ding. It was Michael. Moments later, Kate unlatched the door and he slipped into the room.

"Did you see that woman, the one with the dark hair pulled back in a bun?" he asked us. We both nodded.

"She's the woman I talked to one night when I was up here checking things out, the one I got a sad vibe from, kind of scared. Remember Morgan, I told you about her."

"I do. She's been up here a few times."

"Maybe I'm reading more into it than was there."

"No, Michael, I think you're right," said Kate. "The second time she entered empty handed and when she left, she was carrying a small plastic garbage bag."

"I was in the room earlier and there was no garbage anywhere. She must have been in there for at least ten minutes? What was she doing?"

"You were in the room, Morgan?"

"Just briefly, Michael. Lucas stood watch."

"Where's Lucas and Bart?"

"They went to check out the landing at the end of the hall. They should be back any minute now. Did you get the list?"

"I'll have it shortly." He flipped open his laptop and pulled up his pictures. "Which guys have been up here?"

"First, the guy we're calling the blonde came and went. Then the housekeeper came and went. Then the heavy-set guy came and went. That one there," I said. Then the housekeeper returned and she just left. Kate saw a tall man leave, before the housekeeper left, but no one saw him enter the room. We could have missed him going in."

"That's the guy I saw leaving," Kate said, pointing to the man I remembered from VPD headquarters."

"VPD," I said.

She looked at me, eyes wide. "VPD!"

Michael handed the laptop to Kate. "I'll go see if the list of Batlan's guests is ready. Then I'm thinking we should round everyone up and get out of here."

Kate and I looked at him. "We can't leave yet Michael!"

"Besides, we're perfectly safe here," said Kate.

"She's right, Michael. I'd like to stay a little longer, but I'll check in with Fernice first." I called her with an update which included what Lucas and Bart were up to.

"It's 10:20 pm," she said. "How long have Lucas and Bart been gone?"

"Only a few minutes."

"Call me back the moment they return. Then we'll get all of you safely out of the club." A vindicated Michael gave us *the look*.

"Michael, put me on the guest list as your uncle, Manuel Deroche and text me when that's done," said Alex.

"Okay," said Michael.

The sergeants were grim. They'd had a close look at Michael's photos.

"MacLeish called me from here," said Alex.

"Rhodes certainly looks like he's right at home! What I'd like to know is who's the guy across the table from Rhodes that he's so angry with?"

Jeri noticed that Alex had his hand on the door handle. "Maybe wait until Bolton has you on the guest list," said Jeri. No use tipping our hand unless we have to."

He nodded reluctantly.

36

Carey stared at the dark red stain, almost invisible in the dark plaid of the blanket. Seth's blood. Maybe he was in the bathroom. The door was slightly ajar and she knocked on it very quietly because she didn't want to scare him, but there was no answer. She pushed it open, slowly. He wasn't there.

She went back to the living room. She could hear a car making its way up the mountain below them, the sound fading and dying away when it parked. Someone was snoring upstairs. It sounded like Melanie.

Carey felt a flood of relief that Melanie was back. She'd been gone for two days. It was always harder when she was away. It was especially hard if Joy wasn't here either. Then there was no one to take care of the younger boys and girls. Not that Melanie liked taking care of them, but she did take care of the basics. She was probably sick. She was always sick when she got back from being away. There was no use asking her to help find Seth.

Carey checked the little room under the stairs. The door was ajar but the room was in darkness. She closed the door and turned on the overhead light. Everything was just like it always was. Photos of Ange's daughter Winnie were everywhere. Ange told Carey that she wanted to live with her mother, and that at first, he missed her very much, but he didn't care about that now because he had Carey and he hugged her tightly, which always scared her. It felt like he was never going to let her go.

Ange wasn't going to give her back to her mom. And he wasn't going to keep her either. She didn't know what to do. Seth was gone. The men would be back from the club soon. She turned off the light and went back to Seth's room and stood by the bed. That's when she noticed the night stand. She opened the drawer and there was Seth's *iPhone*, attached to the recharger. He was never without it. She remembered what Ange had said last night: '*Phineas, I didn't sign on for murder!*' Maybe Seth had died. Thinking he might be dead made her heart hammer in her chest. She tucked the phone and the recharger into the pocket of her hoodie and left the room.

The house was quiet and the front door right there. She decided to go for help and reached for the door knob, when she heard the crunch of tires on gravel as a car pulled into the driveway. She ran as fast as she could across the room and up the stairs. She went into the bathroom and closed the door and locked it. Then called her mom's landline. Her mom didn't pick up and it went to voicemail.

I'm sorry I went with Seth mom. Please don't be mad. Ford hurt him badly. He's gone. They're going to sell Marie and she needs me to feel safe. They're going to sell all of us. We're at Ange's house up high. They're taking us to the States. Mom do you still love me? Please come and get me. I don't

Carey was nervous and scared and she hung up before she was done. She made sure the phone was on silent and slipped across the hall her bedroom. The sisters were fast asleep. She climbed into bed and reached for her stuffie. She hid the phone in it's secret compartment and hugged it close. Pulled the comforter up to her chin.

Michael had just returned with Batlan's guest list when his cell rang. It was Rosie and she was close to hysterical. Carey had called her a short while ago and left a message on the landline. Rosie, exhausted from lack of sleep, had laid down for a nap. She didn't hear the phone ringing in the next room.

"Rosie, honey, it's okay. It's okay. This is great news! When did she call?" Morgan and Kate snapped to attention. Michael walked quickly to the other end of the suite and put Rosie on speaker, Kate and Morgan right on his heel.

"Rosie, was there a name displayed?"

"Seth. I have the number. And the message."

I'd already started a text message to Fernice.

"You're sure the name Seth displayed," he said, looking from Morgan to Kate.

"Yes, I'm sure. I wanted to call her back, but I was afraid of getting her in trouble."

"You did the right thing Rosie."

"What did Carey say?"

Rosie started to cry and the trio listened in silence to her sobs. When she got herself under control, she read back Carey's message. As she read, Morgan put the message in the text and sent it.

"Oh Michael! Why would she ask if I still love her! Of course I still love her! And she hung up suddenly, like she was interrupted. What if someone caught her making the call?"

"Two officers are close by. They're investigating Carey's case. We'll get this information to them immediately. I'll get one of them to call you and tell you what to do next. Rosie honey, ask Estelle to come over and stay with you."

"I'm calling her next."

"Rosie, it's going to be okay. Det. Fernice or Sgt. Desocarras will call you very soon. I need you to hang up now."

"Okay." We heard the disconnect. My phone rang. It was Fernice. I put her on speaker.

"Michael, did your sister call Seth's number?"

"No. She didn't want to get Carey into trouble."

"Thank God. Michael, listen carefully: No one is to call this number. Are we clear?"

"Yes, we're clear. I told Rosie one of you would call and tell her what to do next." He gave her Rosie's home number.

"We will. Right now. Sit tight." Jeri hung up and turned to Alex.

"Right now, we're the only ones with the number. Hopefully it's still live," and she typed in the information for a trace.

"This is great, Jeri! A link that no judge can dispute."

"VPD!" Jeri shouted at the screen. "The number traces back to the VPD! Shit, shit, shit! That bastard is really pissing me off! It's Seth Boyce all right, but it looks like the phone is a line item for Special Investigations." Alex looked at her and in answer to his unspoken question, "Phineas Rhodes, Sex Crimes. Rhodes signed the phone out to Seth. He could have a trace on the phone right now if he knows that Seth no longer has it." She pulled up Ange Batlan's address.

"Batlan lives on Marion Way in North Vancouver. Looks like he's at the end of the road, fairly isolated. His road connects to a trail heading further up the mountain. North Vancouver is basically on a mountainside."

"We need to get over there now!"

"We get the civilians to safety, then we go. Jas's parents are away. We can use their house in Mount Pleasant. It's close."

Alex called Rosaline to reassure her and make sure she gave out no further information. Jeri was calling Jas, when her cell phone rang. It was Morgan.

"Det. Fernice, I just found a link between one of the photos we found at the shipyard and the suite here that Batlan always books." I'd been scrolling through the room photos I'd taken. I remembered one of the photographs from the shipyard was of a young girl, sitting on the arm of a chair, looking peacefully over the photographer's shoulder. He'd taken the shot so that the red armoire in Batlan's suite, framed her.

"Batlan's suite has definitely been used for photo shoots. I'm willing to swear that the red armoire you can see in several of the long shots I took is the same armoire that was used in at least one of the pictures we found at the boatyard."

"Which suite?"

"Shots I took earlier in Batlan's suite." Damn. I wasn't going to tell her just yet.

"You were in Batlan's suite!" Jeri looked at Alex. He had just finished his call to Rosaline.

"For the love of Christ," she muttered, putting Morgan on speaker.

"Where is everyone right now?"

"Kate and I are here. Lucas, Bart and Michael aren't back yet. It's been a little more than half an hour since Bart and Lucas left. Michael has gone to look for them."

"I'll get right back to you. Get ready to leave!"

Fernice hung up and messaged Michael that everyone was to prepare to leave the club, but before she finished, Alex added.

"Tell Michael I'm coming in and to meet me at the front desk," said Alex.

A minute later, Michael texted back: At front desk.

Desocarras was out of the car in a shot and up the underground parking ramp to the street behind the club, then quickly jogging the short block to the front of the club. Michael was at the front desk and signed him in. Alex pulled his fedora low and followed Michael through the main concourse and up a short flight of stairs to the mezzanine, then on to the elevators at the back wall. Michael rang for one. The club was animated and busy and it was getting late. No one paid any attention to the two men as they slipped into the empty elevator and pushed the button. They got off at the fifth floor and Michael led them down the hall to the *Burrard Suite*. He opened the door and followed the Sergeant into the room.

"Where's Lucas and Bart?" Alex asked.

"They're not back yet," said Kate. "I'm worried."

"No one has come or gone across the hall either, not for quite a while," I told him.

"I couldn't find them and I'm pretty sure they're not on this floor," said Michael.

"What were they planning to do?"

"They went to check out the stairwell area at the end of the hall, right beside Batlan's suite. We thought there might be another way into the suite.

"Are you familiar with the layout of the club?" Alex asked Michael.

"Yes."

"Good. Come with me. Let's see if we can find them. Once we do, we're out of here."

He called Fernice and quickly filled her in, then turned to Kate and Morgan.

"Stay here until we return." Checking that the hallway was clear, Alex and Michael left the room and made their way quickly to the stairwell, then entered the landing.

"This would be the end wall of Batlan's suite," said

Michael quietly.

"Let's have a look around," said Alex and he led the way down to the fourth-floor landing. Several large swing doors led out to banquet facilities. They descended to the third-floor landing. Similar swinging doors led to meeting and banquet rooms. But there was an additional door, marked with an EXIT sign. They took that one and found themselves in a narrow passageway, dimly lit by old fashioned wall sconces. Without a word, Alex started down the passageway, Michael right behind him. The murmur of indistinct voices could be heard. They seemed to be coming from the floor above them.

They reached another door, which opened directly onto a narrow flight of stairs going up. The air was dry and very close; the lighting dim.

Alex closed the door and turned to Michael. "Have you seen this passageway before?"

"No. I didn't know it was here."

"Where is Batlan's party?"

"Second floor."

"I want you to return to your suite and stay with the women. If I'm not back there in ten minutes, phone Det. Fernice."

Michael nodded, but he hesitated.

"Go back to the suite. I'll meet you all there." He waited until Michael went back through the door that led to the main landing, then started to climb.

The stairwell was steep, the treads were narrow and there was no handrail. It wasn't much wider than Alex. He counted twelve steps to a small landing, then up again to another small landing which joined with yet another stairway going up. He judged himself to be at or near the fourth floor. There was no exit to the club proper on this landing. He continued up to the next landing and judged himself to be halfway between the fourth and fifth floors. There was a sound now that he hadn't noticed before. He crossed the landing and stopped to listen. The sound of laboured breathing reached him. He continued to climb.

As Alex neared the next landing, the first thing he saw was a pair of expensive Italian loafers, then the man wearing them. Gun out, he stepped over the man's legs and bent to check his pulse. Fast, but steady. He was wheezing heavily. He stepped over him and examined the small, narrow door behind him, slightly ajar. It was impossible to get the door open because the man was blocking the swing side. There was just enough room to roll him over onto his right shoulder. He propped him in that position with one foot and was able to pull the door open a few feet and slide through sideways.

He found himself in a small storage room. A few feet ahead of him was a half open door, its edges illuminated by light from the next room. Alex let the door to the landing close behind him and stood motionless in the closet, gun out, listening for signs of life from the room beyond. Hearing none, he stepped into the suite. It was something of a shock after the narrow passageway. Vancouver harbour was picturesque through a bank of windows to his right. He checked the bathroom. The suite was empty.

Alex made his way to the door. No one was visible through the peephole so he opened the door and checked the hallway — all clear. Michael Bolton's suite was directly in front of him. He stepped into the hallway and closed the door behind him but as he raised his hand to knock on the door to Bolton's suite, it opened and he slipped inside. The scene that greeted him was bizarre.

Morgan and Lucas were at the door. Lucas looked like he'd seen a ghost. Kate and Bart were sitting on the couch.

A child, about seven years old, sat between them. She was wearing a red velvet dress. Long, dark curls framed her delicate face. Her eyes were frozen wide, her face solemn.

"We found her in Batlan's suite," said Lucas. "There was a man on the landing. He was unconscious. Our guess is he and the child came up that staircase. The unconscious guy must have doubled back through the passage door for some reason. We left the guy where he was and entered the suite and we found the girl."

"When did you get here?"

"A few minutes ahead of you."

Alex walked over to the couch and knelt in front of the girl.

"Can you tell me your name?" he asked her gently. The child was holding on tightly to Kate's hand. She stared at him, mute.

"Has she spoken at all?"

"No, she has not, poor wee thing." said Kate.

Alex called Jeri. "Lucas and Bart rescued a child from Batlan's suite just a few minutes ago."

"Do you think they know the child is gone?"

"I don't think so."

"You're coming out now."

"We're on our way."

"I'll move to the top of the ramp."

"Copy that."

He turned to Michael. "What's the best way out?"

"Down the elevator to the bottom floor and from there to the underground parking via an exit door that's close to the members' gym. The gym is on the right and the exit door is just beyond it, on the left side."

"Michael, go and hold the elevator. We'll watch from here. If it's clear, I'll bring the others and we all ride down."

"Okay," said Michael. "It just got this. It's a list of

Batlan's guests." He handed it to Alex, grabbed his coat and overnight bag and took off down the hall to the elevators. Alex stuffed the list in his vest pocket. He followed Michael to the door and watched as he made it to the elevators and pushed the button. A ding was heard and the doors opened. Alex quickly ducked back inside the room and pulled the door shut.

MacLeish barrelled down the hall and Alex, finger to lips, watched through the peephole as he entered Batlan's suite and closed the door. Everyone stood at the door behind him. Bart was carrying the girl. Kate had their bag. Morgan was wearing her short, curly wig and Lucas carried their bag.

"We go now," Alex whispered. He opened the door and crossed the hall to the door of Batlan's suite, gun out. Kate left first, then Bart, carrying the child, then Lucas and Morgan. Michael, ashen faced, was inside the elevator, holding it for them. Alex backed down the hall, keeping his eye on the door to Batlan's suite as everyone quickly boarded the elevator. Alex slipped in, the door closed and they were on their way down to the basement.

"Bart, where's your car parked?"

"Level B, one down from the street."

The elevator reached the basement and they all got off. This late on a Saturday night the gym area was in darkness. A few staff could be heard talking in the lounge area further along the hall. They took the exit to the parkade, emerging on Level A.

"Det. Fernice is waiting at the top of the exit ramp, this level, at Cordova Street. I'll take Morgan, Kate, and the child to her car. Michael and Lucas, go with Bart to get his car. We'll wait till you're behind us on the ramp, then I'll hop in with you. We all leave together. Go! Now!" and they did, running.

Fernice was waiting at the top of the ramp. Morgan got in front, Kate and the child tumbled into the back seat.

"Where are we going?" Alex asked Jeri through the driver's window.

"Jas's parent's house in Mount Pleasant. They're on holiday. She's on her way with the spare key." She gave him the address.

Moments later, Bart pulled up behind Jeri and Alex hopped in the back beside Lucas. Jeri spun out onto Cordova and cut over to Hastings Street before heading east, Bart right behind her.

Bart and Michael talked quietly. Lucas watched the car in front. He could see Morgan's curly wig in the passenger seat. She was sitting up front. Kate was behind Fernice, the child beside her. Lucas leaned back and closed his eyes, his chest tight with tension.

"You okay there, Lucas?" asked Alex.

"I'm good." It was plain that he wasn't, but there was nothing Alex could do about that now.

37

"Where the fuck is the girl!?" Gregori Kirigin — well practiced at ridiculing those around him — was livid with rage.

"I don't know." Rhodes was flustered; a difficult position for a man who prided himself on always being in control.

"You don't know!"

"Maybe Penderman took her," said Rhodes, grasping at straws.

"Why would he do that? And where's the buyer?"

"I just called the front desk and Delacroix hasn't checked in yet. Penderman was supposed to join us after the sale." Then something occurred to Rhodes. He walked over to the closet, stepped through and tried to open the door to the stairwell. Gregori was right behind him.

"The door won't open."

"Check the landing — now!" he hissed.

Rhodes turned on his heel and left the suite, seething with rage, but doing his best not to show it. Kirigin was the wunderkind who took care of their online presence and a myriad of other things as well. He was very important in their operation and Rhodes couldn't afford to get on his bad side. He knew Kirigin wouldn't pull out of their deal over this — whatever it turned out to be — but it gave him a chance to treat Rhodes badly. Something he loved to do.

Kirigin and his partner, Eric Severall lived in Baltimore, MA. With the social and economic collapse of Russia in 1991, Severall saw an opportunity and over the years, had developed excellent trafficking connections in Russia, the Baltic States and East-Central European countries formally under Soviet control. Those connections served him well.

The partnership with Severall and Kirigin put them in the big league. Their BC operation was small potatoes in comparison: the distribution of books and calendars; arranging local parties; managing a few kids. When they joined forces with them, they became part of a very lucrative human trafficking ring operating right across North America.

Rhodes took the stairs and descended to the third floor, exited at the landing and entered the seldom used side stairwells. He climbed to the fifth floor and found the unconscious Penderman sprawled across the landing adjacent the suite. He rolled him onto his side and rapped on the small door leading to the closet of the suite. Kirigin opened it.

"Christ! Tell me he's alive."

"He's alive. We need to move him into the suite."

"Brilliant idea." Rhodes ignored him.

Penderman was a big man, well over 200 lbs and unconscious he was dead weight. Rhodes pushing and Kirigin pulling, they managed to get him through the door to the closet area. That done, there was enough room to roll him onto a small rug and pull him through to the suite. Rhodes moved the unconscious Penderman onto his side and arranged his arms and legs to keep him there.

"He does have high blood pressure. Maybe he had a stroke."

"Surely not surprising. Better questions right now:

Why was he out there and where the hell's the kid? Call an ambulance for this," and he waved a hand disdainfully at the unconscious Penderman, "then find the girl!"

Rhodes dialed 911, arranged for an ambulance at the back entrance and called the front desk to let them know it was on the way. Then he texted MacLeish to come to the suite.

"We'll find her. She can't be far and is probably just frightened by all this," said Rhodes. "And even if someone does find her, there's nothing to tie her to us and she can't speak English."

Kirigin glared at him. "Who saw her last?"

"Probably Joy. Marie wets herself. Penderman phoned Ange earlier and he sent Joy to the room to deal with it."

"And who is Joy?"

"One of ours. We bought her last year. She helps with the kids and Ange got her a job here, to help smooth things with out of town sales."

"Penderman must have called from here."

"Probably."

"Where the hell is Joy? Find out who was here when she came to the room. We need to find that kid. She can't have gotten far." Rhodes dialed Batlan.

"Don't worry; she won't talk. She hasn't spoken a word in the four months we've had her," said Rhodes. "That's another reason we decided to get rid of her."

"She doesn't talk. Period?" Rhodes nodded.

"Perhaps she's dumb." At Rhodes blank look, "maybe she's unable to speak."

Rhodes was speechless. It hadn't occurred to him. "Maybe she is," he said, flustered at his own stupidity. "Anyway, she won't be giving us up then, will she?"

"Phineas, are you there?" It was Batlan, his voice tinny and distant on Rhodes' cell phone speaker. Rhodes talked with him briefly before turning to Kirigin.

"They were both here when I came up. I left before Joy arrived. But apparently, when she came up the second time, both Penderman and the girl were still here. Ange wants to know what's going on."

"Ange wants to know what's going on!" Kirigin bit the words out through clenched teeth. "Phineas, has it occurred to you that someone has taken the girl from this room? Maybe they've already left the club."

"Of course it has," Rhodes blustered, but that's not at play here, I'm certain. No one is on to us!"

"Really? You think the kid just got up and left?"

Traffic was light and twenty minutes later, they pulled into the alley behind Jas's parents house. Jas was taking the 90N. She'd be here pretty quick.

Marie was fast asleep between Kate and Bart. The sergeants were out of the cars and talking at the back gate.

"No one saw us leave," said Alex.

"But they'll know by now the child is gone."

"Unless they're complete idiots. We can't put her with child services, at least not yet. They'll be looking for us to do that."

"Jas has someone in mind." Jeri called Det. Ignace while they waited for Jas. She brought him up to speed and told him they needed a trace on the cell phone Carey had called from. Ignace left immediately for the Main Street Station.

"We'll need search warrants."

"Batlan's house, the boatyard and Penderman's house. We can use knowledge of the civilian search for Penderman's warrant," she said.

"But we don't know where the materials are now. The guy who showed up at the boatyard must have taken everything." Jeri was silent for a moment.

"Maybe everything was taken to Batlan's place? We won't have a problem getting a warrant for his place. Not with Carey's phone call."

When Jas arrived at her parents' place, she parked in the alley, quickly exited the car and motioned for everyone to follow her as she headed up the sidewalk to the house and unlocked the back door to the kitchen. Bart carried the sleeping child in from the car and laid her on the couch in the living room. Jas turned up the heat and found blankets and a pillow.

"She's out for the count," said Jas, checking the child's pupils. "Looks like she's been drugged." She lifted her carefully and tucked a folded blanket under her. "I smell pee," she said.

"Jas, did you find a safe place for her?" asked Jeri.

"I did, but I want to talk to you first and get my story straight."

"Tell your caregiver that the child's mom is in an abusive relationship. The husband beat her up and threatened to abduct the child. We can't put her in the system yet because the husband has access to the MCF database. We need to insure the child's safety for the weekend at least."

Jas nodded and called her contact. After a short conversation, she got off the phone.

"She's waiting for me. She'll keep the girl for the weekend, no questions asked."

"That's great," said Jeri.

"I'll go with you," said Kate. "I can help with the little one."

"I'll go too," said Bart. Can you bring us back here after?"

"I can do that."

"Make sure you park in the alley when you bring them back."

"Sure thing boss," said Jas, with a good-natured wink to Jeri.

"I just want to keep you safe, keep everyone safe," said Jeri, her voice sharp.

"I know you do, Jeri," said Jas, much more seriously. "I'll be very careful." Bart picked up the child, Kate wrapped her in the blanket and they followed Jas out to her car. He got into the back seat. Kate climbed in after them. Jeri watched the car leave and returned to the kitchen.

"Let's go Alex."

Alex turned to Michael, Lucas and Morgan, sitting around the table in the kitchen.

"I'm sure you all understand how important it is that you remain here, for your own safety."

38

Carey heard the front door open and close, the clomp of heavy steps cross the living room to the kitchen, chairs scraping against wood as the men sat down at the big kitchen table. Everyone was talking at once and it sounded like they were mad. She recognized the voices of Ford and Ange and Phineas.

"We need to get rid of the kids tonight!" She didn't recognize that voice — a bossy man who talked like a teacher who's angry with his students.

"We've already made arrangements for Tuesday." That was Phineas.

"And for a good price," said Ange.

"You're delusional, both of you. We can't wait. Not now!"

"Greg's right. We get rid of them tonight," said Ford. "I called Cecil. He's on his way. Norse too."

Carey reached for the stuffie and hugged it close. Her mom didn't know they were selling them tonight. She was tired and scared and tried to stay awake, but was soon overcome by exhaustion. She didn't hear the sound of shoes on the wood floor downstairs moving from room to room, then their heavy clomp on the open stairs up to the bedrooms. She didn't remember that they tried to wake her up, to ask where Seth was.

"We tipped our hand when we took the girl," said Alex. They were approaching the Marion Way cut off that led up the mountain to Batlan's place. "They'll try to move the kids ASAP."

"Yeah … Take a right here," said Jeri. "You don't see fog this bad very often. It's like a blanket!"

The higher they went, the thicker the fog and Alex was forced to slow down. "We need to pull in the North Van detachment."

"I vote we wait till we get there," said Jeri. "I'll feel a lot more comfortable if we're on site, controlling the situation."

"Agreed. Once we're at Batlan's, I'll make the call to North Van and get them to move on search warrants. It shouldn't take long, once they find the duty judge." Alex looked over at Jeri. "You'll have to take a back seat once we're there," he said. "I am sorry about that, Jeri."

"Don't be, Alex. Let's just get the bastards."

"How much further?"

"We're close," said Jeri.

"We don't have to just sit here! There's nothing to stop us from doing a little surfing," said Michael, booting up his laptop. "Good, someone has internet."

"Where's Batlan's house?"

"He's at 8985 Marion Way," said Michael. Lucas and I watched over his shoulder.

"He's close to the end of the road and his place borders a wooded area."

"It looks like his street becomes a trail."

I asked Michael to switch to satellite view. Batlan lived right at the forest edge, very secluded, which gave him lots of privacy.

Michael zoomed in. "It looks like there's two buildings on the property, and a smaller one, probably a garage."

"Seth must know the area. If he left the house, which way would he go?" This from Lucas.

"He could be anywhere. If he's hurt, he could be disoriented. Chances are he might not have gotten very far."

"He could be unconscious. They may have people searching for him right now. What if he's dead?" Lucas fell silent, his face stricken.

"Lucas, are you okay?"

"I'm all right and I'm going. We need to find Seth, before they do."

"Okay," I said.

"Lucas is right and we can't ignore the possibility that they may have killed Seth. Remember Carey's text, *Ford hurt Seth.*"

"Maybe he got away somehow," said Lucas.

"I hope so. How long before Jas gets back with Kate and Bart?"

"She said round trip, about half an hour."

"We should go now! We should be searching for Seth!" said Lucas impatiently.

"We can't do this without Kate and Bart's help. We'll leave when they get here." The three of us bent over the images on Michael's laptop — forest, forest and more forest."

Michael pulled up the weather forecast. "Damn. All of North Vancouver is under very heavy fog," he said. "If anyone does find us, we can pretend we're hikers and we're lost."

"We'd have a hard time passing as hikers," I said. "Especially you, in that suit."

In answer, Michael grabbed his overnight bag on the floor beside him and said, "hiking pants, hoodie, sneakers."

"We really do need Kate for this," I said, "especially with the fog."

"And Bart."

"Yeah, him too, but what I really mean is that Kate has special skills. I put the words in air quotes to make my point. The VPD have used her in the past to find missing persons."

"Irish magic," said Lucas.

"Magic is good," said Michael.

"The fog will work to our advantage. It's good cover for us," said Lucas.

"We don't even know what Seth looks like?" said Michael.

"How many single males do you think are lost up there tonight?" I said with a smile.

"Right. I'm not thinking straight."

"Understandable," I said.

"Desocarras and Fernice are going to be so pissed with us." said Lucas.

"Much more so, if we showed up at Batlan's house," I said.

"Which is where I want to go right now!"

"Michael, you know we can't do that."

"I know."

"My money is on the Sergeants," said Lucas.

Michael looked at Lucas. "Do you think we should tell Jas we're going to look for Seth?"

"No. Jas won't go for it," I said. "She'll feel she has to tell Jeri. Let's leave Jas, Jeri and Alex out of this. They'll just worry. They don't need that right now. We wait till Jas brings Bart and Kate and when she's gone, then we go."

Carey woke up the sound of Joy's voice. She was in the next room and it sounded like she was getting the kids dressed. Downstairs, everyone was talking loud. They were really mad because someone took Marie from the club. She heard a man say they'd have to move them all tonight. Two men were out looking for Seth. She went into the upstairs bathroom and took Seth's cell from the secret compartment in the stuffie and called her mom again. Her mom answered, but then she started to cry and ask her where she was and wouldn't let her talk. She had to whisper, everyone was so close to the bathroom and her mom couldn't hear her very well. But when she told her they were taking them somewhere and please stop crying she did. Mom gave her the number for the cell her Uncle Michael was using. Then Christopher wanted to use the bathroom so Carey hung up and hid Seth's cell in the stuffie and waited in her bedroom until Christopher was done. She shooed him out and went back into the bathroom and locked the door.

She'd had to keep Uncle's number in her head, saying it over and over because she had nothing to write it on. She pulled up the texting screen and right away put in the number and then she was so nervous she pushed SEND before she typed a message.

The men downstairs were angry, which scared her and then she couldn't remember the number and she wanted to cry, but then she remembered she could pull up the SENT message. She told her uncle to please help, they were taking them away tonight and she hit SEND again. She put the phone back in the stuffie and went back to the bedroom.

Melanie was in the hallway, talking like she had marbles in her mouth. She could hardly stand up and had to lean against the wall. Joy was with her and one of her eyes was black and there was a big red mark on her face. That made Carey mad but it scared her too. The kids were crying. Joy asked Carey to help get the children dressed.

"Michael, Carey just called! I talked to her! I gave her your cell number. She said they're taking the children somewhere tonight. Oh Michael, she was so scared," and Rosie burst into tears. Michael waited till she got control before he spoke.

"Did you call anyone else?"

"No, Michael, only you."

"Is Estelle there with you?"

"Yes. Geoff too."

"Good." His next question was interrupted by a text message. He put Rosie on hold to check it, but there was nothing there, just the number. He switched back to his sister, but didn't tell her about the blank message screen.

"The police are on their way to where the children are being held." He was interrupted by another text message. He put Rosie on hold again to check it.

Please help they are selling us tonight we are at Anges house up high

"Rosie. I just got a text from Carey. I've got to get this to the police.

"As soon as you know anything, anything at all, call me!" she said, before hanging up.

Michael called Jeri. "Carey just texted me. The children are at Batlan's. They're moving them tonight."

"Okay. We're nearly there. Don't respond to the text." She hung up and told Alex.

"How far away are we?"

"Less than two kilometres. Ignace should be at VPD by now. We'll soon know where exactly the phone is."

"Rhodes could be tracking it."

"And Carey probably has it close," said Jeri. "Shit."

Ignace arrived at VPD, Main Street and took the elevator up to Technology and Communications. He wasn't the only one working tonight. A woman sat with her back to him, at a computer across from him. She looked up briefly when she heard the door open.

Ignace logged in, pulled up the tracking program and entered the phone number Jeri had given him. He watched the small, pulsing strobe on the screen. It was stationary and in moments, he had the coordinates and the address. He moved to the hallway outside the room, pulled out his cell, got Fernice on the line.

"There's two houses on the property. The phone is in the smaller house near the garage. I'll let you know if it moves." He hung up and returned to the room. Something about the screen the other tech was watching caught Ignace's interest, so he wandered over and asked her if she knew where the blank log book sheets were, giving him the opportunity to get a good look at her computer screen.

As he suspected, they were looking at the same corner of North Vancouver geography. The woman barely paid attention to him, so intent was she on the screen.

"They've got you working late tonight."

"Yeah ... Det. Rhodes, Special Op."

"You been here long?"

"Just got here."

"Don't think I've seen you around here before. Adam Ignace, nice to meet you."

"Wendy Caruthers," she said, smiling back, then

"Sorry, have to get back to work."

"Of course," said Ignace, returning to his work station. He moved out to the hallway once again and called Fernice.

"Bad news, Jeri. There's a civilian tech up here, says she just got here. She's tracking the same cell phone. She said she's working for Phineas Rhodes."

"Keep me posted," she said, hanging up and turning to Alex.

"Rhodes has a tech tracking the same cell."

Alex had driven up to the turnaround just past Batlan's and back down a few blocks before he pulled well onto the shoulder and cut the motor.

"Give me a minute," said Alex. He called Kennedy and let him know that he and Det. Fernice, VPD MPU, were working a joint case, missing person, a child named Carey Bolton, abducted by a suspected paedophile ring. At least two police officers were implicated, Ford MacLeish RCMP, Prince George and Phineas Rhodes, VPD. They were doing recon on Ange Batlan, another suspect, and gave the guy's address in North Van. His next call was to bring in the North Van detachment, warning that there should be absolutely no sirens within one kilometre of the address. Officers were to park two blocks below the address and wait for instruction. It was Saturday night and North Van was dealing with very high call volume including two bad accidents due to fog; one with fatalities. The only available car had just finished a domestic call near Squamish, on the Sea to Sky Highway, and was dispatched immediately. More cars to follow as soon as they were clear.

"We've got a wait ahead of us. They're dealing with two traffic accidents; one with fatalities."

Fernice's phone vibrated in her pocket. Ignace had texted:

Just lost cell signal same location.

Her cell phone buzzed again: Ignace.

"I can be there pretty quick."

"I want to bring in Ignace," Jeri whispered."

"Do it."

"How soon can you get here?"

"About fifteen minutes. I'll use the siren."

"No siren within one kilometre. Park below the address and stay alert. We just got here and don't know how many perps we're dealing with."

"Is North Van coming?"

"They are, but we've got a wait ahead of us."

"Okay," said Ignace, hanging up.

"We could disable their transportation while we wait for backup," said Alex.

"Let's do it." They exited the car. The hollow clicks of car doors closing an eerie sound in the dense fog. There was a gravel pathway beside the road, part of the trail that led to the other side of Batlan's property. The house closest to them was identifiable only by its mailbox at the foot of the driveway, the house itself invisible.

"This house is the closest neighbour," she said, consulting her phone. "Batlan's address is on the other side of these trees."

They continued, past a thick stand of trees and stopped at the foot of a wide, red gravel driveway.

They had just started up the drive when a car door close by creaked opened. The sergeants quickly drew their guns and stepped off the gravel into a deep layer of cedar chips. They stopped to listen. Half a minute later, they heard the car door slam shut. The sound decayed quickly. The chips rimmed a hedge of tall laurel trees that lined both sides of the driveway. No sooner had they moved behind the hedge when a cell phone rang close by.

"No," said a gruff voice. "Don't worry. We'll find him."
There was another pause. "I've got her. She's in the car."
The sergeants looked at each other.

"I told you. We'll find him!" Then, after another pause,
"Cecil's driving the kids."

Footsteps crunched the gravel and stopped near the
end of the driveway.

"I told you. I've got Melanie." After a short pause, "The
older one too. That'll be extra." The crunch of his footsteps
receded quickly as he made his way back up the driveway.

Jeri and Alex headed quickly up the path beside the
laurel hedge.

Ford found Seth's cell phone in Carey's stuffie. Ange tried
to stop him, but Ford shoved him aside and punched
Carey hard, knocking her out cold. When she woke up,
she was in Ange's car in the garage and her head hurt.
All the kids were with her. Except Georgina. And Marie.
She remembered that Theo came after dinner and took
her away. They were selling the kids to somebody from
Nevada named Dirk. She heard Phineas say they were
going to fly the kids out of Langley. Carey knew they
weren't going to let Ange keep her or she wouldn't be in
the car with the other kids. As soon as her head stopped
hurting she would go for help.

The big man with the red face came into the garage.
He was talking on his phone. Another man was with him.
Carey quickly shut her eyes and pretended to be asleep.
She didn't know his name but Ange said he was one of
Ford's thugs. Whoever he was, Joy was afraid of him. They
were talking about Seth. When they found him, they were
going to deal with him.

39

Jas returned with Kate and Bart, but didn't come into the house. She gave us the keys and told us where the closest corner grocery was. Once she was gone, we brought them up to speed on the plan to look for Seth, then suited up as best we could before we took off.

Traffic was light and Bart pushed it until we were over the Ironworkers Memorial Bridge and climbing Mountain Highway. Visibility steadily declined the further up we went and I couldn't help wonder how the hell we were going to find Seth. I looked at Kate. We were in her hands now. She didn't speak until shortly after Michael announced we were about two kilometres from Batlan's address.

"Pull over here Bart," she said.

He immediately pulled onto the shoulder, tucking neatly into a mailbox pull out. The box read 6553.

Without a word, Kate was out of the car and heading up the road.

We piled out of the car and took off after her, walking fast to keep up. She veered off the road into a small clearing. Bart and Michael flanked her. Lucas and I followed close behind.

A short while later, Kate veered again. Now we were in the forest behind the houses on the east side of Marion

Way. She seemed to be heading north, although I was just guessing at this point. We were going uphill.

Beside me, Lucas moved like a cat, constantly scanning the area around us and I did the same, alert to the fact that someone else might be out here looking for Seth. Lucas was right at home hiking anywhere, but then he'd spent his childhood climbing among the Cuchumatán mountains and he loved to hike. Michael was another guy who'd been raised in the mountains. Bart was already panting a little, though it sure didn't slow him down.

We were still moving uphill when Kate veered again, this time to the right. We were descending now. This terrain was very steep. Kate was forced to slow down. We all struggled to maintain our footing on slippery rocks and tree roots. We continued downward for some time when Kate again veered off, this time to the left, then abruptly stopped. We gathered behind her. She turned to us and pointed down. She had reached a cliff. It was impossible to judge how high it was.

We fanned out to the left and right, looking for a possible pathway to the cliff base. Michael had gone left and was the first to find a path down. He quietly passed the word along.

"I vote we take it," he said, after we were all gathered around him at the top of the path. "What do you think Kate? We can always cut back."

Kate nodded, and moved to start down, when Lucas held up his hand.

"Let me go first, Kate. I'm more sure-footed and you need the insurance. When we get to the bottom, you can take the lead." She nodded and waited for him to start down then followed him, Bart after her, Michael after him and me last.

It was one of the weirdest experiences I've ever had,

watching as one by one, my friends disappeared into a blanket of fog, until it was my turn and I too descended. The path down was treacherous and we had to take it very slow. It was close to a metre between footholds in some places and at one point, I couldn't find one. Then, I felt Michael's hand gently and carefully place my left foot on his shoulder. I continued to hold on tight, resting as lightly as possible on his shoulder, until I found a pocket for my right foot and eased my weight into it. Not long after that, Michael tapped me on the leg, then he reached up and lifted me to the ground. Kate had already taken off to the left, Lucas and Bart behind her and we started after them.

I could hear water rushing by, fairly close. It was eerie not to be able to see the water, only hear it. Large boulders covered the landscape. I kept Michael in my sights as first he, then I, scrabbled around, or over, one boulder, then another.

All of us heard Kate's loud whisper. "Here."

Bart, Lucas and Kate were huddled around an unconscious young man. I recognized him from the boat yard. Seth Boyce. His back was against a small section of rock face. It looked as though he'd sat down, then his body slid sideways a little, coming to rest against a smaller outcrop of rock. One leg was tucked under him and the other stuck out awkwardly to the side. Bart was checking him over. "He's alive, but his breathing and heart rate are slow — hypothermia. His face is badly bruised. He may have fallen down the cliff face so another concern is the possibility of a spinal injury. We need to get him to a hospital."

I texted Alex on his burner and let them know we had Seth and that he was alive, but unconscious.

Seth was wearing a lined jacket, but it was undone. Bart carefully held Seth's head, while Lucas zippered up his jacket.

I removed my mittens and pulled them onto his cold fingers, then, as Bart held his head perfectly still, I pulled my toque onto his head.

"We can't call Search and Rescue," said Bart.

"It might put the kids in danger."

"Or the police," said Michael.

"Or us," I added.

"We'll carry him out," said Lucas.

"Lucas is right. We can do it and there's no time to lose," Bart said. "But I'd feel a lot better if we could stabilize him in a sitting position, from the head to the base of his spine. We can carry him out on a human chair."

I had an idea. "How many scarves do we have?" We had four between the five of us.

"If we could find a length of wood, we could secure his head and torso and hips to that with the scarves. Then, we all lift him up and two of us form a chair under him and carry him out."

Kate stayed with Seth while the rest of us searched for a piece of wood that was long enough to do the job. Lucas found one, about eight centimetres in diameter covered with wet leaves. He tested it and it was strong enough. We cleaned it up as best we could, then set about the difficult task of tying Seth to our makeshift spinal support.

While Bart held Seth's head, keeping it aligned with his spinal column. Kate, Bart and I carefully moved him away from the cliff face, just enough to ease the wood support down to the base of his spine. The brace was a little too long; it extended above Seth's head a little, but that was better than too short. Then we moved him out from the face of the cliff a few more centimetres, just enough to ease one long scarf down his back to his hip area, another to the chest area, just below the armpits. Kate and I worked together on the torso scarves, pulling them as tight as we could. Bart continued to hold Seth's head completely still, his wrists just above his ears on either side, his long fingers fanned out over his neck, while we secured his forehead and then the chin area to the wood brace. We were ready to go.

I sent Alex another text, this one to say we were bringing Seth out and the mailbox number where we were was parked. Kate plugged 6553 Marion Way into the Maps app on Bart's phone and called up the directions on foot — 1.5 km across some very rugged terrain.

Somehow, the five of us raised Seth up off the ground. It was harder than I thought it would be, but we used the cliff behind him as leverage and that helped. Bart and Michael were about the same height. They would be Seth's chair. The rest of us held him steady while the guys locked wrists below and behind him. Kate and I would lead the way, while Lucas walked behind them.

Jeri and Alex found the garage at the top of the driveway and went in through the side door entrance. They found two cars — a silver *Suburban* and a Fiat. She moved to the *Suburban* and he headed for the Fiat. She pulled out her flashlight and shone it into one of the windows. She couldn't believe her eyes.

"Alex," she hissed. He was at her side quickly. She moved her flashlight around, as the two of them gazed at the vehicle full of sleeping children. They tried the doors but they were all locked.

"I count seven," she said. "If we flatten the tires, they won't be able to drive it away."

"But they'll know we're here and that could put the kids in jeopardy."

"Right. We need to take out the. driver and get the key,

then one of us can drive the kids out."

Alex's phone buzzed and he checked his messages. They found Seth Boyce, and he's alive! They're carrying him out to the road."

"They found Seth Boyce! They're here!"

"No. About two kilometres below us."

"Thank God. No mention of Search and Rescue."

"No."

"Nothing we can do now, except pray they make it out safe." Jeri called Ignace and updated him about the children, gave him their position, a warning about possible perps on foot in the driveway area and the garage and instructions to come up the driveway on the right side, staying behind the laurel hedge. The sergeants left the garage and took up a position close to the side door, alert for the driver and for the approach of Ignace.

Joy stood outside the gatehouse, shivering in the night air. Ange told her to wait there for Fred. He was taking her somewhere. Ange had promised her she would work for him, even after the children were sold. He told her he wanted her to help him raise Carey. He said he'd help bring her boy to Canada and that they could both become Canadian citizens and there would always be enough work for her and enough money to educate her boy. Her boy, only two years old when she was sold. He was nineteen now. All young men at home had to serve in the army. Maybe he was already a soldier.

Fred came through the front door of the gatehouse and grabbed Joy roughly by one arm, forcing her to stumble along beside him until they got to his car. He opened the back door and shoved her onto the seat. She struggled to sit up but he stuffed a rag over her nose and mouth, forcing her to breathe the fumes. She quickly lost consciousness.

We slowly made our way along the base of the cliff, then came to a fork and took a path uphill. Once we cleared the cliff face, there were no more boulders, although we did have to navigate our way across several fallen trees. One was so big, two of us straddled it and we passed Seth, hand to hand, up, across and over to the other side. It was hard, and it took a while.

We were on this path for ten minutes or so when it levelled out a bit and we all noticed the sound of rushing water. The path veered this way and that and finally it connected with a gravel walkway. The sound of running water, not as loud now, was still on our left.

"We're heading south," Kate said, consulting Bart's phone. "If we can find a decent path heading west, to our right, that should take us to the road."

After a while, Kate and Lucas took over for Michael and Bart who were exhausted and I took over navigation. We continued in a southerly direction for what I judged to be about 200 metres and then the walkway seemed to veer west, zigzagging in lazy arcs between north and west.

We wouldn't have realized we were as close to the road as we were but for a car going by, the glow from its headlights a shimmer of pastel yellow; quickly disappearing.

"What now?" Bart asked. "We can't risk the road, at least not for long."

"Go ahead of us and look for an address," said Kate. "That'll give us our bearings."

"Okay" He moved to the shoulder and headed uphill. He was back quickly.

"There's a mailbox close by with 6163 Marion Way on it."

"Lucky for us, someone was kind enough to paint the street name on their mailbox," said Lucas, grinning. It warmed my heart to see that grin.

"The *Prius* is at 6553, so we're only about four blocks away from it," said Bart. "I'll call an ambulance," which he did, noting the address where he'd parked, and stressing the danger of the situation.

"Tell them no siren once the ambulance reaches the cut-off to Marion Way," warned Michael, beside himself with worry.

"Right," said Bart, relaying that information as well.

We started up the road now, keeping on the footpath to the side of the road.

"I want to stay with Seth. Bart and I'll go to the hospital with him," said Kate.

Ignace let Fernice know he'd arrived, then moved silently up the driveway behind the laurel hedge. His footsteps made no sound in the layer of soft cedar chips which rimmed the hedge. Desocarras and Fernice were waiting for him close to the side door of the garage. They all moved into the garage. Fernice introduced Ignace.

"North Van is on the way," said Alex. "We're hoping in the next 10 minutes. They're busy tonight."

"How many perps?"

"We don't know," said Alex.

We do have seven unconscious children in the *Suburban* over there," said Jeri.

"We've got the kids!"

"We're not sure if we have all of them. I'll go now and check out the other buildings," said Alex.

"They plan on moving them tonight and very soon," said Jeri. You and I will cover the children and wait for the driver. When he arrives, we'll subdue him and get the keys. Our priority is to get them to safety."

Joy regained consciousness, but when she tried to sit up she couldn't move. She pushed up, hard as she could. An arm flopped down and a body rolled over and landed in a crumpled heap behind the front seats. Melanie's eyes stared up at Joy, glassy and vacant. Her first instinct was to scream. She knew she had to get away. She struggled to sit up, but was overcome by nausea and weakness. Silent tears slid down her cheeks into the cushion. Melanie was dead and she would be too.

The car was old and the air close and thick with the acrid smell of mould and stale cigarette smoke. She grabbed the armrest near her head and pulled herself close enough to the door to try to open it. Hearing a click, she nudged the door open a few inches. Fresh air rushed in from outside, and she gratefully turned her face towards it. Now a stranger was opening the door and peering in.

"Ma'am, are you okay?"

"Please. No more!"

"Shh," said Alex, finger to his lips. "We're here to help ma'am." He bent over and looked closely at the body on the floor of the car, inert, eyes staring, sightless.

"How many men are here, on the property?" he whispered.

She looked at him, dazed. Alex pointed at himself. He mimicked a person walking with two fingers pointing down, gestured in the air around him. Then she realized what he was asking.

She counted to herself. "Eight men."

"What's your name ma'am?" Alex asked her.

"Joy," she barely got out before she slipped into unconsciousness. Moments later, Alex felt the hair on the back of his neck prickle. Too late. Felt the sucker punch to the side of his jaw, felt himself airborne the short distance to the bushes beside the car. Dazed, he listened as the car started up and crunched over something ceramic before it hurtled past him down the driveway.

Fernice and Ignace heard the car start up. "Stay with the kids," said Jeri. I'm going to check on Alex."

She found him in the bushes, about five metres from the garage.

"I'm fine," he insisted as he struggled to his feet. "Let's get back to the garage."

"What happened?" she said, once they were inside the garage.

"I found two women in a Honda, close to the gatehouse. One was deceased. One was conscious, at least long enough to tell me there are eight men on the property."

"Eight."

"That's when someone landed a punch," said Alex. "I'll be fine. Give me a couple of minutes."

We arrived at the *Prius*. Bart fetched a mat and a blanket from the trunk. The mat went on the ground and we lowered Seth onto it. Then Bart knelt behind him, supporting him while we tucked the blanket around him.

It was a while before the ambulance arrived, but once they did, the attendants took over. They did an assessment, moved Seth to a striker board and onto a gurney and then into the ambulance. Bart handed me the keys to the car. He'd pulled doctor status and they were letting him ride in the back of the ambulance.

"I need to be with the boy," said Kate. She looked at Michael. "It's okay. Everything's going to be okay." She got into the cab. The driver did a U-turn and the ambulance disappeared into the swirling fog.

Lucas, Michael and I climbed into the car and the boys

settled gratefully into their seats. I could well understand;
I was tired and I hadn't done any of the carrying.

Michael broke the silence. "She said everything's going
to be okay."

"She did."

"I hope that means the kids are okay."

"We could go up to Batlan's, park a couple of blocks
below."

"Morgan, you know we can't do that!"

"Lucas is right. I want to go up there too, Morgan."

"Well, what do we do now?"

"We could follow the ambulance to the hospital and
wait with Bart and Kate," said Michael.

"To the hospital then," I said, as I started the car up
and turned on the lights. I was about to start a U turn
when a burgundy Honda careened past us, far too close
for comfort. There was something about the driver's
face — then it clicked.

"That was him!"

Michael was lost in his own thoughts and Lucas was
on his cell phone, texting Alex that Seth was on his way
to the hospital.

"Who?" asked Lucas.

"The guy at the lake!" I shouted, as I did a U-turn, "The
one who tried to kill me!" I took off after the burgundy
Honda.

"Holy shit!" said Michael.

"Get as close as you can, Morgan!" Lucas yelled, "so we
can get the te number!"

It was eerie, coming up behind his taillights, elongated
beacons of red-orange that disappeared and reappeared
in the heavy fog. They were my only point of reference.

The car was giving us a GPS readout and Michael had
his phone out as well. I'd come down the Marion Lake, Rice

Road extension and turned onto Lynn Valley Road, one of the main connectors to Mountain Highway, the Hwy 1 extension that would take us over back the Ironworkers Bridge.

The Honda was pushing it. "He must know this road really well," said Lucas.

I didn't and I found that oddly comforting.

As we descended further down the mountain and closer to the Burrard Inlet, our visibility slowly started to improve. This area was more built up and I backed off, concerned for unseen traffic and possible pedestrians.

"I don't see him!"

"There he is!" Lucas yelled. "The lane beside us."

I changed lanes and edged closer. He gunned it and pulled away from me.

"He knows we're onto him — he's getting away!"

"It's okay Morgan, I got the plate number: 383 HIR ... or 385."

"I think 5, 385," said Michael, who was nearly in the front seat with us, craning his neck to read it.

I'll text Alex the plate number," said Lucas.

"Tell him we're on Lynn Valley Road. Close to the 29th Avenue intersection."

Our visibility had improved. As we approached the intersection, I could see I had the green light. I slowed a bit and had just started through when a bright red, compact car shot out of the fog on our right. I had to swerve hard to the left to avoid it and the other driver swerved right, both of us squealing to a stop.

The car missed us by inches. I quickly pulled around the guy and got the hell out of the intersection. I drove along for several minutes but the Honda was nowhere to be seen.

"Maybe I should backtrack."

"He knows we're following him. Maybe he pulled over somewhere and is waiting for us to go by," said Lucas.

We'd traveled less than a kilometre when Michael spotted the front end of the Honda as we sailed past the far side of the William underpass.

"There he is! Keep going and turn off as soon as you can, but not too soon." We were at a lower elevation now and visibility was a good 20 metres.

I spotted my chance and pulled off into a mini-mall parking lot. There was parking at the front and side as well. I pulled into the side parking lot, did a U turn so we were facing Lynn Valley Road, pulled up to the outside wall of a 24-hour convenience store and shut the car off. We didn't have to wait long. The burgundy Honda shot by a few minutes later.

"There he is!" we all yelled together. I started the car and I took off after him.

"No word back from Alex?" Michael asked.

"Not yet."

"He'll have to go through the intersection at the next cut-off and take a left onto the highway," said Michael, consulting his phone. "It's a steep downhill all the way from here. There's a couple more exits, a few kilometres from the Ironworkers Bridge."

"I'm going to hang back a bit. Maybe he'll think he lost us."

Lucas was first to spot him a few minutes later. "I think that's him in front of the Mercedes, two cars up. See him, Morgan? He's trying to pass the SUV in front of him."

"I see him." I stayed behind the Mercedes and sure enough when he got his chance, he gunned it around the SUV. Now there were two cars between us.

"Do you think Fernice got your text?" asked Michael.

"I'm sure she did. Something must be up."

Cecil Green sauntered into the garage. Ignace took him to the ground and Fernice cuffed him. She found some lengths of rope hanging on the end wall of the garage and bound his feet.

"I'll get you, you fucking bitch," Green shouted as Fernice pocketed the keys to the *Suburban* and the perp's cell.

"Unfortunately, a favorite of mine," she said as she quickly gagged him with her scarf. Working together, they took the last piece of rope and tied his hands to his feet, behind him.

"That should hold him awhile," said Jeri. She handed the keys to Adam. They approached the *Suburban* and he unlocked it. Fernice noticed a young girl in the front passenger seat was watching them. She quickly closed her eyes when she saw that Jeri had spotted her.

She opened the passenger side door a few inches. "It's okay. You don't have to be afraid of us. We're here to help."

The young girl opened her eyes and studied Fernice carefully.

"Who are you?" she asked her.

"We're police officers."

Carey had watched the man and woman subdue Cecil. She decided she could trust her and informed her solemnly, "They'll kill you if they find you."

"I'll keep that in mind," said Fernice, just as seriously. "What's your name?"

"Carey."

"Carey Bolton?" The girl nodded. "Well, it's my pleasure to meet you Carey. You're a very brave girl."

Carey didn't say anything. She didn't feel very brave.

"Are there more children in the house?"

"No. We're all here. Except for Georgina. She's

somewhere else. Because she got hurt trying to escape. And Marie. They were going to sell her tonight. And Seth. I don't know where he is. Does my mom know you're here?"

"Your mom knows we're here. We'll let her know you're okay. Right now, we're going to get all of you out of here as quick as we can. "Does Marie have long dark curls?"

"Yes."

"Then she's safe."

"Carey's face lit up in a   smile, which quickly disappeared. But what about Seth?"

"He's on his way to the hospital."

Alex was a block down from the foot of Batlan's driveway, waiting for North Van. Jeri called to let him know Ignace was coming out with the children. Carey Bolton was one of them.

"He's driving them down the mountain to the Lynn Valley connector. Ambulances will meet him there."

"Two cruisers just arrived," said Alex.

"Good. Ignace is coming out now."

"Once he's in position, we'll move on the gatehouse and the main house."

Fernice turned to Ignace. "They're waiting for you. Text me once you're at the connector, and again when all the children have been picked up." She opened the garage door. Adam started the car and pulled out of the garage. The car was quickly enveloped in mist as he headed down the driveway to the road. She closed the garage door then checked on Cecil Green. She didn't want him interfering with their plans. She then quickly left the garage and joined Alex at the foot of the driveway.

"Arena, O'Meara and Bolton are chasing the burgundy

Honda," he told her when she reached him.

"Give me strength," he muttered, furious.

Whitaker had just joined them. "Whitaker, advise your dispatch that we have three civilians in a dark blue *Prius* chasing the burgundy Honda I just called in. We need to intercept that Honda. They were at Lynne Valley and 29th Avenue about four minutes ago." Sending cruiser to intercept Honda. Where are you now? Alex texted.

It was a full minute before the text came back.

Close to last cut-off from Upper Levels Highway before bridge.

Whitaker passed that along to the North Van dispatch. The call had gone out to a cruiser on the Dollarton Highway.

"They could get themselves hurt," said Whitaker. "Are they crazy?"

"A little, yes," said Alex.

"More than a little," said Jeri.

Alex texted Lucas: Why are you chasing Honda?

Lucas texted back: Driver is Morgan's abductor.

"Morgan, the police are going to try to stop the Honda."

She had just rounded the curve and was looking for the last exit ramp from the Upper Levels Highway. They were about eight km from the Ironworkers Bridge and there was no cruiser in sight.

"Where are they?"

"They didn't say."

Morgan moved into the passing lane to keep an eye on the Honda.

"Look! said Michael. "Isn't that Joy in the back seat?" Joy disappeared from view briefly. A few moments later she was visible again.

"There she is again! What's she doing?"

"She's got something in her hand. She's trying to hit him. He's swatting at her." The Honda swerved from side to side. "She's trying to stop him!" yelled Michael.

"She's going to get herself killed," said Lucas, teeth clenched, as I swung back into the right-hand lane.

"She knows it's her only hope. The man's a deranged psychopath!"

"Morgan he's exiting!" said Michael. The Honda had swung into the Exit 22 lane, tires squealing.

There was no one behind me as I careened down the exit ramp right behind him.

"I don't see Joy," said Lucas.

"I don't either. He's going east on Fern," said Michael.

"What the hell's he up to?"

"If he catches Lillooet Road and heads north, if I remember correctly, there's a lot of bush," Michael said. "It's been a while but I've been up here before."

Sure enough, a few minutes later, the Honda turned onto Lillooet Rd. I followed. We were heading north now. We were going up again and it wasn't long before we entered fog as thick as it had been on Marion Way. The Honda had disappeared. Without warning, we arrived at an intersection and I had to brake quickly. Lillooet Road seemed to come to an abrupt stop.

"It's a roundabout," said Michael. "If we go right, we head further up the mountain. Left takes us into the roundabout and back the way we came.

We decided to go right. We were still heading uphill, a much steeper climb now. Now and then, we caught glimpses of pine boughs hanging close to the road, but little else.

"How long have we been on this road?"

"Ten minutes," said Michael, checking his phone. "There are no intercepting roads shown on the map."

"This car is in a lot better shape than the Honda. We'd have overtaken him if he'd gone this way. I vote we return to the roundabout." The guys agreed.

I turned around and headed back down. By the time we made it back to the turnoff, over twenty minutes had gone by. I started into the roundabout.

"Morgan, there's a hiking trail that connects with this hub," said Michael. I cruised slowly around the circle, but we saw no sign of the trail entrance.

"It's here, somewhere," he insisted.

I headed back into the curve again. Lucas saw the exit first, almost hidden because it formed a backwards V with the hub.

I hung a sharp right onto a dirt trail. We were heading downhill, but I stopped quickly when we dipped into a large pothole.

"We're better off on foot," said Lucas. "We can travel faster."

I backed out of the pothole, pulled over and killed the engine. We climbed out and I locked up, securing the key in a zippered pocket.

Without a word, we fanned out across the trail and headed slowly down the path, Michael and Lucas on either side of me.

We hadn't gone far when Michael came to an abrupt halt. A woman was sprawled in his path. He knelt beside her and checked her pulse.

"It's the housekeeper. She's alive, but unconscious. She must have gotten away somehow."

I bent to have a closer look. She'd been doused with acetone.

"I'll stay with her," said Michael. He cradled her with

one arm while he wrapped his jacket around her. "I'll call for help. You two be careful," he whispered, as Morgan and Lucas disappeared into the fog. Then he called 911 and quietly explained who he was, described the scene as best he could, gave the coordinates from the GPS app on his phone and explained that there was at least one cruiser already looking for a burgundy Honda and them.

We found the Honda about 20 metres further down the trail. The left back passenger door was wide open. We approached the car carefully. The driver's side was empty. I leaned into the open door. A young woman stared up at me.

"It's the women we questioned at the Franklin Street house," I whispered. Even as I bent to take her pulse, I knew she was dead. An intense wave of anger pulsed through me and my adrenaline surged. I stood up.

"Let's get the bastard."

We both heard it then: the distant chink of metal against rock came from somewhere below us. As we descended, the sound grew in intensity until I was sure we were close. We stopped and listened. The digging had stopped. Moments later, the silence was broken by a thin, tuneless whistling. My hand shot out and I grabbed Lucas's forearm.

"That's him." I'd spoken out loud and slapped a hand to my mouth — too late. Lucas gave my arm a squeeze, put a finger to his lips and started a slow 360° turn. I kept my back to him and scanned from left to right.

The whistling had stopped and there was only that silence peculiar to being enveloped by fog. We stood quietly, straining to hear, when I felt the air whoosh as the shovel came down behind me. Lucas let out a surprised grunt and pitched forward into the bushes to my right. I whirled to face our attacker, risking a quick glance in Lucas' direction. Just his legs and feet were visible.

When he raised his shovel again, I let fly with a roundhouse kick that connected with his left arm. He wasn't ready for any kind of defensive move and he whirled with the kick and stumbled backwards. I heard the shovel fall to the ground. I looked again in Lucas' direction, but he'd disappeared.

"Lucas, are you okay?" No answer.

The bastard was up again, without the shovel this time and shook off the kick. Both of us watched as Lucas came into view briefly on my right, then stumbled away and disappeared. Red face barely glanced at him before advancing on me. He meant to put me down first.

"This time I'll kill you bitch!" His big hands reached for me and I waited till he got close before I let fly with a knife kick to his right shin.

Stumbling, he grunted in surprise. I pressed my advantage and tried to disable his right knee, but he backed off out of range. He was strictly a grab their throat and choke 'em kind of guy.

"What's the matter asshole?" I said, adrenaline pumping. He came at me again, hands raised in front of him and I let fly with a roundhouse kick to his right hand. He howled in anger and I knew I'd done some damage. I immediately followed that with a vicious kick to his right thigh, but he managed to side step and deflect it. Then he stormed me, grabbed my left arm and made a grab for my throat. I blocked the throat grab and delivered three fast punches to his nose, throat and one to his ear. He grunted in surprise and let go of my arm. I stepped back quick. Waited.

He came at me again. Dead on. I feinted left, then right,

then spun around and delivered a sharp kick to his right knee — heard the satisfying crunch when I connected.

"Shit! You fucking bitch! I'll gonna kill you!" He limped off, barely able to put weight on his right leg and disappeared into the fog. I knew I'd caused some serious damage.

"Lucas, are you okay?" Still no answer. Maybe he was unconscious. I had to assume I was on my own.

I circled, slow and continuous, scanning the fog for any sign of the hulk. He wasn't gone long. He emerged from the fog on my left. Oh shit, he found the shovel, which gave him reach. I'd have to be careful. He advanced on me slowly, limping — kept coming — eyes bulging with rage. I stepped to the right, looking for an opening. He swerved in my direction. I stepped left, waiting for him to get in close enough to try another kick to his weakened knee. He swerved toward me and kept coming, the shovel up over his head now. I'm about to feint right, when suddenly, he has the most surprised look on his face. I watched in amazement as his body lurched sideways, the shovel flew from his hands, clanging loudly as it hit the ground, and he collapsed in a heap, face down in front of me.

"Yes! Way to go Lucas!" I yelled.

Behind him, Lucas is clutching a good-sized rock. He held onto it as he came to stand beside me. We bent over the hulk. The only sound was my rapid breathing.

"I thought you were unconscious. Where'd he hit you?"

"He got me across my shoulder blades. Knocked the wind right out of me."

"That's why you didn't answer me."

"I couldn't get any sound out!"

Then I remembered Michael. "Hey Michael," I yelled. "Can you hear me? We got him!"

Seconds later, Lucas' phone buzzed and he put it on

speaker. It was Michael.

"I hear you! You got him!" came out, loud and clear.

"Morgan fought him off and I finished him off with a rock."

"You guys are amazing! The cops are on the way." Sirens could be heard on the road near us.

"Correction. They're here!"

It wasn't long before we could hear the slamming of car doors and the distant voices of the cops.

"A squad car will be down here soon. They'll take us up to the car and you can rest."

"Rest. Are you crazy! I'm totally stoked and ready for a run!"

"That was amazing Morgan, the way you fought him."

"Thanks honey. It's like riding a bicycle. You never really forget how."

40

The cell phone Jeri had taken off the skinny perp in the garage vibrated. Have you left yet?

She texted back: On the way. Where to?

A full minute later: Mountain Air in Langley. Dirk will meet you.

She showed the text to Alex. "Let's surprise Dirk." Alex turned to Cpl. Whitaker.

"*Mountain Air* in Langley. What do you know about that outfit?"

"Not much. Mostly lessons. Some short-haul cargo."

"The arrangement is to bring the children there and hand them over to someone named Dirk." Whittaker got on the phone with the Langley detachment and filled them in.

Shortly after Ignace arrived at the Lynn Valley cut-off, the ambulances started to arrive for the kids. The first one took away Carey and she insisted Christopher come with her. The second ambulance arrived soon after and two more children left. Not ten minutes later, the third and fourth arrived together. Once all the children were on their way to the hospital, Ignace texted Jeri. She called him back.

"We need you to drive the *Suburban* to *Mountain Air* in

Langley ASAP. We want to nail the perp who'll be waiting there to buy the children. He'll be looking for it. Langley RCMP have your number. They'll fill you in."

"On my way," said Ignace.

Cpl. Whitaker had started the ball rolling on search warrants.

"We'll have to move fast—very fast. These guys are well connected. Might even be good friends with the judge you get to okay the warrants," said Alex.

Whitaker smiled at what he thought was a joke, but Alex wasn't kidding—he didn't crack a smile. Whitaker's smile quickly disappeared.

"Yes sir."

The North Van officers were very interested in the tall, blonde woman with the VPD badge. Jeri answered their unasked question. "I'm Det. Sgt. Fernice, VPD MPU. Sgt. Desocarras and I have been working this case jointly."

"We came here tonight on a fishing expedition," said Alex. "Then things heated up."

"Is this the only entrance to the property sir?" asked Cpl. Menard. Corporals Clement and Brookside, who'd arrived in the second cruiser, flanked her.

"That's the information we have. There's two houses. One is a gatehouse. It's close to the top of the driveway, just beyond the garage. Firsthand information is that there were eight men on the property. At least two are hires."

"One of the hires is bound and cuffed on the floor of the garage," said Fernice. "Your dispatch has been informed that another perp escaped in a burgundy Honda with two women abducted from the property. One is deceased and it's assumed the same fate is planned for the other. A cruiser is in pursuit."

"So are some civilians," said Whitaker, with a grin. Fernice and Desocarras looked at each other grimly.

Whitaker lost the grin and Alex continued.

"Which leaves six men. All of them are suspected of being involved in a human trafficking ring of unknown size and scope. At least one man, Ange Batlan, lives at this address." He looked at the corporals, one by one.

"Two of the six men are police officers," he continued. "We don't know if they're in uniform. One is an RCMP officer out of the Williams Lake detachment — Inspector Ford MacLeish."

"The other officer is Det. Sgt. Phineas Rhodes of the VPD," said Fernice. The officers looked at each other, at Desocarras, then Fernice. No one spoke.

"Everyone on the property is to be arrested," said Alex. "Any questions?"

There were no questions.

Desocarras would take Whitaker and Menard with him to check out the main house and Fernice, Clement and Brookside and would check out the gatehouse. Desocarras would buzz Brookside once his team was in position, then both teams would move. They had walkie-talkies as well, but there would be no live communication unless necessary. It was just after 3:30 am when they started up the driveway and disappeared into the fog that hovered, damp and cold. Once they were in position at the Gatehouse, Brookside motioned Clement to go around back. He waited for Desocarras' signal, then he and Fernice moved to either side of the front door. It was unlocked. They entered quickly, guns drawn.

Across the room, five men seated at a large, polished oak table stared at Fernice and Brookside in surprise.

"Stop now!" could be clearly heard from the back door. Clement entered, gun drawn.

At the table, a short, beefy guy was pulling out his gun when Brookside yelled: "Drop your weapon now! Put it on the table. Slowly!" His face red with rage, Ford MacLeish put his Smith & Wesson on the table in front of him.

Fernice advanced on the table, her SIG Sauer trained on MacLeish's torso. Images from the video flashed in her head — the horrible rape of the little boy. It was him all right — the bastard. Brookside had moved to check the room under the stairs.

"Someone slipped out the back door," Clement told Fernice. "Should I pursue?"

"Not much point in this fog. Did you get a look at him?"

"Not really. As I stepped onto the porch, he jumped off it and literally disappeared."

"All clear back there," said Brookside as he started up the stairs to the second floor.

"Everyone on your feet, hands behind your head, walk away from the table to the middle of the room."

The men looked at each other.

"Now!" yelled Fernice.

"Jeri. Clearly, there's been some mistake. I'm sure if you just give us a few minutes to explain," said Rhodes. He started to walk towards her.

"Shut up!" said Fernice. "Now!" Her repugnance was growing by the second.

"On your knees. All of you! That includes you sergeant! The lot of you, hands behind your head!"

"All clear," said Brookside, coming down the stairs from the second floor.

"We should bring the skinny guy in from the garage. He's in the corner by the side door," said Jeri, watching Rhodes.

"I'll get him," said Clement and left the gatehouse. Fernice loved the barely concealed look of alarm on Rhodes' face — watched the wheels turning — felt a great satisfaction when nothing came out of his mouth. Desocarras, Whitaker and Menard came through the front door.

"Main house is clear," said Alex. He watched as the officers cuffed each man in turn and sat them on the floor.

"We have a perp on foot," said Jeri. Clement said someone escaped out the back door as she was approaching the porch."

"Identify the man who escaped," Desocarras demanded of the men on the floor.

"There's no one else here," said MacLeish contemptuously. Alex shook his head.

"The woman had the count right," he said to Jeri. Mention of the woman caused MacLeish and Rhodes to share a quick glance.

"We have the right to remain silent," piped up a dapper, silver-haired guy.

"What's your name sir?"

"Ange Batlan."

"You watch too much American TV," said Alex. Brookside turned to him. "I called for the van to transport them to the detachment."

"Excellent," said Alex.

41

Kirigin was at the fridge getting milk for tea when he heard the front door open. He turned, saw the gun at the other end of someone's arm and quickly stepped out the back door and nearly into the arms of a cop coming up the back stairs. He took a quick step left off the end of the porch, right into the fog, nearly falling flat on his face. He headed for the road, trying to remember the layout of the property and found the end of the garage, a lucky break. From there, he quickly made his way down the driveway to the road. He scuttled left downhill and passed three empty police cruisers at the side of the road. He had to get away; fast. And not from Vancouver Airport.

He moved to the shoulder of the road and stuck to the footpath that wound its way down behind the mailboxes. He needed a taxi, but decided not to call till he was at least a kilometre away from the shambles up the road. Take no chances. He'd need an address, and a story. He began to shiver with the cold and hugged himself for warmth. His suit jacket was hanging on the chair in Ange's kitchen. Briefcase lost to him too and his valise at the club. Best leave it — too risky. Nothing incriminating in either. He always made sure of that.

42

I drove to Lions Gate Hospital so that Michael could see for himself that Carey was safe. Hospital staff let him see her briefly. He took a picture of her, fast asleep in her hospital bed and texted it to Rosie so she could see with her own eyes that her girl was safe.

When he hopped back in the car, Michael was still on the phone to his sister, talking and laughing, enjoying the moment with her. Rosie wasn't on speaker but we could still hear her cry and sob and scream out her happiness, Michael laughing and crying right along with her.

As soon as he got off the phone, Michael booked Rosie and Elwin on the first flight tomorrow morning to Vancouver. Estelle and Geoff and Beth were coming down too. Then he called Amelia and left a message with the good news.

Next, I drove us to the RCMP detachment office in North Vancouver. The media caught up with us there: a journalist from The Province, juggling coffee and a notebook and TV media including CBC, CTV and Global. The media scrum spotted us as we approached the front entrance and there was no getting around the tightly knit pack.

They jogged alongside us, microphones extended, while their respective cameramen hoisted big shoulder digitals, jockeying with each other for the best angle.

"Ms. O'Meara, what can you tell us about the children who were rescued from the home in North Vancouver?"

"There were seven children rescued. Was one of them Carey Bolton, the child abducted from Terrace, BC?"

"What can you tell us about the unconscious hiker who was admitted to Lions Gate Hospital earlier this morning?"

"Is he tied to this investigation?"

Just a few days ago, I'd watched Candy Kristoferi of Global TV happily tarnish my name, and Lucas's, with what appeared, at least to me, to be a good deal of relish. She wasn't the only journalist who jumped on that bandwagon. She stuck out a microphone as she jogged along beside me.

"Ms. O'Meara, do you know the name of the young man suffering from hypothermia who was admitted to Lions Gate early this morning? Is he connected to this case?"

I caught her eye, too tired to even attempt to hide my dislike. Lucas dished out some cold shoulder of his own. As we made our way resolutely through the reporters, Kristoferi turned to her cameraman and soldiered on:

"Morgan O'Meara and Lucas Arenas have just arrived here. One of the officers involved with this case informed us that this brave couple apprehended, single-handed, a known felon involved with what we recently learned is a suspected paedophile ring that has been operating for some time right here in Vancouver. While it's too soon to speculate . . ."

The last of her words were lost as the detachment doors swung shut behind us. Hospital staff told Michael that Bart and Kate were already here. They were giving their statements when the three of us arrived. It was about 7:00 a.m. but things were sure humming. We found seats in the waiting area and settled down to wait our turn. Lucas sorted the players out for us.

There were the RCMP who worked out of the North Van office, two plainclothes from VPD — Lucas recognized one from a seminar he had attended and guessed the woman with him was plainclothes as well. There were two more plainclothes whom Lucas guessed were attached to the North Vancouver office. Things are usually busy after a Saturday night. This morning, it was a jurisdictional and logistical nightmare.

"Both the RCMP and VPD will be investigating police misconduct. Maybe that's why he's here," said Lucas, pointing out a grim looking RCMP Inspector from E Division headquarters. "And at some point, the Vancouver Police Board will be involved — civilian oversight."

Kate emerged from an interview room and spotted us. She was at my side in a few quick strides. I got up to hug her.

"We heard someone here talking about the big guy they brought to the hospital. I heard them say your name. Is he the one — the bastard at the lake?" she finished through clenched teeth.

"The one and only."

"Morgan, are you okay? Tell me everything."

I looked at Kate, trying to figure out where to begin. "Maybe you should sit down Kate. This is one story that you'll find hard to believe. I'll start at the end."

"Morgan O'Meara, don't you dare." She refused to sit.

"You'll like the ending," I said with a grin because I do

so love teasing Kate. "I fought the bad guy. He has a badly messed up knee, courtesy of me, which I hope never heals properly, and what we're hoping is the worst concussion ever, courtesy of Lucas."

Kate grabbed me up in another fierce hug. Two hugs back to back. It did feel so good to be hugged by Kate. We sat down together, kitty corner to the guys.

"He hit me with a shovel and knocked the wind out of me," Lucas was telling Bart.

"Are you sure you're okay, Lucas!"

"I'm fine. Really! Morgan fought him off. She was on fire! The creep didn't have a chance! Then I found a big rock. Actually, I tripped over it," Lucas admitted with a grin. "Then I put it to good use and hit the bastard over the head."

"A shovel?" asked Kate.

"He was digging graves," I said. "One was for the young woman, the one we tried to talk with a few weeks ago, at the house on Franklin Street."

"Oh, no Morgan. She was just a kid!"

"He also planned on killing the woman from the club. The one we saw go into Batlan's suite a few times. She's at the hospital too."

"Sweet Jesus!" said Bart.

"What do you know about Seth Boyce?"

Kate and Bart had been at the hospital nearly two hours before an officer brought them here. They'd given what little information they could to hospital staff regarding Seth and his mother, sharing his name and the fact that she lived in Prince George.

"Seth's in pretty bad shape," said Bart. "They had to induce a coma. His mom knows he's been rescued and a number of agencies — including a liaison with the RCMP, are arranging transportation to get her down here."

"Have you told anyone about Marie," I said quietly to Kate.

"Not yet. We thought the poor wee thing should get some rest and quiet. Or, we could just say nothing and let Det. Fernice or her partner Jas tell them."

"I like that idea," I said.

"Me too," said Kate. "We should get going now."

"There's nothing more we can do here," said Bart, standing up to leave. We're hungry and some of us really need to sleep," he said with a smile. Lucas, so alert a few moments ago, was nodding off beside him.

Lucas and I still had our statements to give. I moved to Bart's chair and linked arms with him. We dozed while we waited.

43

A lex and Jeri stood at the big oak table in the gatehouse. Both were wearing latex gloves. They'd been tracking messages between Rhodes' phone and the driver, a guy named Cecil.

Langley had arranged a welcome for the buyer from Nevada, full name: Dirk Likely. Ignace was on his way and would meet them at an industrial complex about a mile from the airport.

The rest of the cell phones taken from the men were bagged and sitting on the table. One of them buzzed. Alex slipped it out of it's bag and turned it on.

"MacLeish's", he said. "A message from someone named Paul:

Kids gone? Tell Ange not to cry. I'll get him another cutie.

"Revier. Crown counsel, Terrace/Kitimat. I wonder if he's in town?"

Alex pulled out the list Michael had given him as they left the club. "He was at Batlan's dinner party earlier."

"Maybe he's staying at the club?"

"Probably," said Alex. "That'll be a VPD arrest warrant."

"Where'd you get the list?"

"Michael Bolton, as we were leaving the club." He handed it to her.

"We'll need warrants for Paul Revier, Prince Rupert. Penderman's in the hospital. Plus, Danlever and Smyth, I don't think they're members and Marvin Roche."

"Have you reached your boss?"

"I left a message. Shouldn't be long." He is gonna be so pissed with me, she thought, but didn't share. "Don't worry Alex. Revier's not going anywhere. No plane to Terrace for at least a few hours is my guess."

"Where's Whitaker?" Alex asked one of the uniforms.

"Just outside sir, at least he was a few minutes ago." The sergeants found him on the front porch.

"Have we got the warrants yet?" Alex asked.

"Any minute now. Homes and work environments of everyone present."

"That's a good start."

"What about Dirk Likely, our perp at the airport?" Jeri asked. "Langley will need an arrest warrant."

"It's likely he won't be getting away," said Whitaker. Jeri smiled.

The crime scene techs arrived just before dawn. They started with the gatehouse. More uniforms arrived from North Van. They were herding the perps out the gatehouse front door and into the police van waiting in the driveway.

MacLeish turned to Desocarras: "I'll have your badge before this is over," he said, low and vicious — no trace of fear.

"No. You won't," said Alex, very quietly. He stared him down. Something dawned in MacLeish's eyes. He was the first to look away.

The sun struggled to cut through the dense fog that continued into the early morning hours. You could feel its presence. The air was noticeably warmer.

44

If it had been up to him, they would never have done business with MacLeish — little better than the Wild West really, but it was Severall's decision to make and Eric was all for it. MacLeish was the big draw. Rhodes sweetened the deal. Having them on board guaranteed better access to Western Canada. Very lucrative for everyone. But as time passed, what little veneer MacLeish had managed to grow in his rise to the top was wearing thin and the crazed animal who didn't seem to have an off switch poked through, more and more often. Not that Kirigin wasn't used to the type.

He'd assured Eric there was nothing incriminating in the briefcase left behind at Batlan's house — just his initials on the case — the pseudonym, of course. The room at the club was in Batlan's name and he was a guest under his pseudonym. That preening idiot wouldn't dare give him up. He wouldn't live to see his next birthday if he did — they'd see to that. There was the overnight suitcase at the club, but nothing incriminating there.

He couldn't risk flying out of Vancouver, or Seattle. His Gregory G. Crothers passport was in the suitcase at the club and useless to him now. He'd need another to cross the border into the States. Eric would make it happen. A contact would cross the border into Canada and meet

Kirigin at an all-night *Tim Hortons* in Abbotsford, BC with the passport, a briefcase, and a coat. That would put them close to a US border crossing in Sumas.

Kirigin had called a taxi and waited for it, freezing in the damp. Once the driver arrived, he pretended to be a little drunk, pretended to be leaving the residence of 7092 Marion Way to avoid a disagreement of some sort. But the man barely batted an eye. Used to all kinds. He hung onto the taxi with a considerable tip up front and had the driver head to Abbotsford. It had been twenty-five minutes since he made his escape from Batlan's residence. Time was on his side. He had a window of three to four hours at the most before the cops would be looking for him. The contact would bring him back across the border into Sumas, Washington and drive him down the coast to Oregon. From there he would rent a car and drive to Nevada. Eric was going to meet him for a little gambling.

Dirk Likely had flown to Vancouver, BC on American Airlines. He wouldn't risk taking the kids out of the country through Vancouver. Ladner airport was a much better choice, small and quiet. He could see the pilot was ready to go. A small flight of stairs had been pulled up to the door of the plane. The guy wasn't that happy working a Saturday night, but his turnaround was about three hours for the usual hefty fee.

They'd be flying the kids to Rosario, another small airport, not too far from the US border. The driver and a truck would be waiting for him. They'd take the kids over the Rockies to Idaho then East to New York State and the buyer. He wasn't flying these kids all the way to New York state. He'd done that before and it cut too deep into his profits. Overland was better. He'd feed them a couple of times and put them to sleep for the rest of the trip.

Likely watched as Rhodes' driver pulled through the main gate and made his way down the road to the main building. He stepped onto the tarmac and signalled the driver, pointing to the small Cessna just beyond the last building. Turning, he headed for the plane. The driver headed for it as well, getting there slightly ahead of him. Dirk walked up to the car and around it. The driver got out.

"You're new," said Dirk.

"Cecil couldn't make it."

"No one told me."

"It just happened. You'd be Dirk."

"That's right. Best we get moving."

"Not tonight, Mr. Likely. You're under arrest."

45

Insp. Brandeis had been assigned to coordinate the overall investigation of the trafficking ring. He sent two officers out to search the area where Fred Norse had been apprehended the night before. One of the officers, Lassiter, had been present there last night.

O'Meara and Arenas both said they heard Norse digging close to where his car was parked, somewhere to the right of the trail. The officers found a few boot prints where Norse had landed in a patch of soft earth at the side of the trail, leading in, so it was easy enough to find the freshly dug grave from there, about five metres in from the road; in just enough and no more.

"People walk the trail. They didn't necessarily walk in the woods. Still, you have to wonder at the brazen nature of the guy," said Lassiter.

"No kidding. Just looking at that grave creeps me out."

"Me too," said Lassiter.

They fixed the position of the grave and for the next few hours, slowly traversed the area.

"I marked two areas that I wouldn't mind checking out," said Lassiter, "within a 25-metre circumference. Both sites are sunken in a little."

"I found one that looks very recent. We should get

Ryder and Pax out here." Cpl. Ryder was the officer who handled Pax, a shepherd trained to find human remains.

"Officer corruption. Shit. It's our worst nightmare," said Whitaker. He and Alex were headed out to a local drive-through for something to eat.

"Wish I could have played it differently," said Alex.

"I don't see how," said Whitaker.

Alex shook his head. "I guess."

"Are you kidding Alex? How else could you have played it? You'll probably get a promotion."

That'll be the day, he thought. "After lunch, I'm on my way to the Surrey office to meet with the brass at E Division." The adrenaline rush of the last 24 hours had left him exhausted. A nap would have been more welcome.

"Did you talk with Brandeis yet?" Whitaker asked.

"Yeah. Earlier." It was his headache to make sure the case against the ring was air-tight and no mistakes were made. He'd be working closely with the VPD as well. Alex wondered idly how good his liaising skills were. The history of cooperation between the two forces wasn't stellar.

Jeri Fernice was at VPD headquarters on Canada Way. Her report was done. She was being interviewed and it was tough going, but she'd expected that, especially because of her decision not to inform her superiors of her suspicions regarding Phineas Rhodes.

Superintendent Portchanal, who oversaw Special Investigative Services at VPD, sat across the table from her, along with Inspector Antoine, who was leading the investigation into the ring for the VPD. VPD Chief of

Police, Jim Chan was there and Ravinder Singh from BC's Office of the Police Complaint Commissioner. OPCC was a civilian oversight body and the fact that Singh was already involved meant that the Chief had brought him in. The RCMP had their own oversight body.

Phineas Rhodes was one of three sergeants in the Sex Crimes Unit. Jeri was the only high-ranking officer in MPU. They were both under the Special Investigative Services umbrella. No one — including her — knew for certain if the blot was going to spread within the VPD, or if it started and ended with Rhodes. The three men in front of her were grim.

"And you and Sgt. Desocarras, reviewing the evidence you've given us here, made a decision to investigate on your own?" Portchanal asked her.

"Yes sir. That's correct."

Portchanal was obviously pissed off. "Sergeant, you're telling me there was no one in Investigative Services you felt you could trust."

"It wasn't a lack of trust, sir, as much as it was that I, we, didn't know who we could trust. Believe me when I say, neither Sgt. Desocarras nor I wanted to handle the situation the way we chose to. We're both team players. I certainly am and I think my record reflects that. We were concerned — as I've already stated — that if we alerted the wrong party, or parties, we would blow whatever advantage we had to rescue the children. That was our first concern. After the phone call from Carey Bolton, we both felt the window to rescue them was very, very small." Fernice saw the first glimmer of understanding. She pressed her advantage.

"We'd just intercepted the sale of one child or that's what we assumed."

"The child at the club?" asked Chief Chan.

She nodded yes.

"What happened to that child?" Chan asked.

"My partner, Jasmine Ray, found a safe place for her." She didn't miss that Portchanal and Antoine shared a glance at the mention of Jas. She ignored them and continued.

"When we found out about the phone call from Carey Bolton, I had Det. Ignace go to the Main Street station and track the phone — a cell that I'd already determined Rhodes had signed out to Seth Boyce. As suspected, it was on Ange Batlan's property. Within minutes, Ignace reported that Rhodes was having the same cell phone tracked by a civilian tech. Sgt. Desocarras had already uncovered that Boyce disappeared almost eight years previous. We had the evidence to link that disappearance to Insp. Ford MacLeish. That, and concern for the safety of Morgan O'Meara and those close to her brought Desocarras to Vancouver to meet with me."

"Desocarras didn't report his suspicions to his commanding officer."

"Not immediately. At that point, MacLeish was the only suspect that was a police officer. By late yesterday morning we had some proof of Vancouver connections. Once we had access to the club lists yesterday afternoon, we began to narrow the field. That's when Phineas Rhodes first emerged as a suspect. We still didn't have the complete picture. What we did have was evidence of a paedophile ring and officers from two police forces incriminated. Then, last night, the phone calls from Carey Bolton that the children were at Batlan's and were to be moved."

She paused briefly and took a sip of water before continuing. She'd been up 30 hours and counting and was feeling it.

"Shortly after we arrived at Batlan's residence,

Desocarras pulled in the North Van RCMP. He notified his superior of what we hoped to achieve. I notified you as well, within half an hour of that. Shortly after that, we found seven children, dressed to travel, in a *Suburban* parked in Batlan's garage. All but one, Carey Bolton, were drugged. The plan was to fly them to the US out of Langley. We still didn't know for certain there weren't other children on site. We still had no idea if anyone else at VPD, or from another RCMP detachment, was involved in the ring — besides those we'd already identified as potential members. Our situation was a difficult one, but once we were on site, we felt we could control the outcome to the advantage of both police forces."

Deputy Comm. Carl Pendergast sat across from Alex, reading his report. Insp. Brandeis, who'd debriefed him at the North Van office was in the building somewhere. Staff Sgt. McCormick, PG detachment, was scheduled to join them via teleconferencing.

McCormick had dispatched a team to MacLeish's home in PG to do a search and an assistant to Brandeis had flown up mid-morning to accompany them. Alex was willing to bet the PG RCMP would find incriminating evidence at MacLeish's home, or on his workplace computer. He was arrogant, sloppy and careless and that would be his undoing.

In BC, the burden of proving guilt and the possibility of conviction rests squarely with the police and the Crown has to be convinced they can convict before they'll lay charges. The evidence had already started to pile up. Any heat that might have come Alex's way had cooled considerably.

It had been luck really, finding the children asleep in

the garage. A half hour later might have been too late. Kate Brennan, against all odds, finding Seth Boyce in the fog. He'd read the reports and that certainly wasn't luck. Alex made a mental note to rethink the whole psychic thing. Hospital staff had induced a coma, but Boyce's chance of survival was slim due to trauma, blood loss and hypothermia. And the two women — one dead, the same fate intended for the other — that just barely averted. They had O'Meara and Arenas to thank for that. In the search of Batlan's main house, police found remnants of a cache of child abuse materials, among them, some of the items O'Meara and Arenas found at the boatyard. Most distribution was on the net now. Keeping hard copies on hand was a holdover from earlier days, indicating they'd been operating for of years. He remembered the report that Ignace had found — the sighting of the two girls behind the *Clarendon* — that was back in 1996. No case file on them. No follow-up. It had been almost 20 years. How many children had been grievously harmed over the years, right under everyone's nose?

When interviewed, O'Meara and Arenas admitted breaking into the boatyard and taking pictures of what they'd found there. They didn't mention hiring Miles Farthing to hack the *Clarendon's* server. Bolton told the police that he paid a staff person for membership and other lists the civilians had shared with the sergeants. The police secured further copies when they presented the club manager with a warrant.

Everyone arrested at Batlan's that night had been questioned. Everyone else at the dinner, including the bartender, Marvin Roche, was being pulled in for questioning. Jeri had arranged arrest warrants for the lot, including Paul Revier. They assumed he'd be at the club, but when VPD got there, he was gone. He'd slipped out of Vancouver on an early morning *Central Mountain Air* flight to Prince Rupert. He was to be flown back down to Vancouver later today, accompanied by a uniform from the Terrace detachment.

When interviewed, Bolton gave police the camera he used to take pictures of the men present at Batlan's party the night before. They had the guest list. The names had sent a shock wave right up the line — RCMP, VPD, a few heavy hitters in the business world and one man, deReesen, a sitting judge up in Prince George. The big guy he'd found on the back stairs was Theo Penderman. He was at the Vancouver General. Diagnoses: stroke.

There were officers on the trail of the guy who got away. Initially, GGC was all they had, from the briefcase the perp had left behind at Batlan's Place. Then the VPD found Greg Crothers overnight case in Batlan's suite and his passport.

Police also had the picture that Michael Bolton had taken at Batlan's dinner party. Once they had a good shot of the guy, it went out across Canada and the US. Crothers didn't show up on any database, anywhere. Then they caught what they hoped was a break.

Crothers had called a taxi about a kilometre down the road from Batlan's place. 5-0 Taxi dispatch said he was dropped at a 24-hour *Tim Horton's* in Abbotsford. He'd had almost three hours lead time. They figured he'd managed to get across the border on foot. Or he might still be in Canada.

Everyone was furious Crothers had given them the slip, but they had another lead — a dry cleaning receipt from *South Village Dry Cleaning*, still attached to a blue, merino wool sweater in the suitcase he left in the suite at the club. The business was in Bethesda, Maryland. It was Sunday and it took a while to locate the owner. Gregory Crothers was Grigori Kirigin. He'd given the cleaners a cell number. More important, the cleaner offered a delivery service and they had an address. Bethesda was following up.

Last update from the hospital indicated all the children were awake, except a boy named Christopher. He'd undergone surgery this morning and was still sleeping. Hospital staff were feeding the children. Social Services staff were on-site, but everyone was taking it slow. The child they rescued from the club was to be transferred to Lions Gate Hospital. Carey Bolton told staff her name was Marie.

They knew about Georgina, the young girl who was hurt attempting to escape but had no idea where she was. Carey had talked about a doctor, but he hadn't yet been identified. Techs were examining computers from all residences. They should have some answers soon.

"Do you think the kids are going to be okay?" Whitaker had asked him. Like all of them, he was pretty shaken by the horrific implications of what they'd uncovered.

"I hope so," said Alex. The image of MacLeish raping the small boy leapt immediately to mind. He promised himself that he would talk with somebody about the video, sooner than later. It wasn't something he would share with Gwen. He couldn't bear to burden her.

The media were in a frenzy and police media spokespersons had their hands full. The TV news at noon had featured reporters at the front entrance of the *Clarendon*, more out front of 14th Street RCMP Headquarters in North Van and someone covering the main branch of the VPD on Canada Way. There was a media van outside of E-Division headquarters in Surrey when Alex arrived.

46

Lucas was falling asleep over the late lunch I made for us, so I insisted he go back to bed. He was asleep almost immediately.

I peeked out the front window. We'd had strange cars parked outside the last few hours. I figured they were journalists, but I needed to get out of the cottage and decided to make a run for it. I slipped out the front door, car key ready, and sprinted for the Toyota. A woman a couple of doors down was out of her car and after me. I jumped in the Toyota and took off, losing her in the mid-afternoon traffic on Wall Street.

Half an hour later, I found myself parked at the turnoff to the trail, just up the road from the scene of last night's faceoff. What if I'd been alone, and I was the one with that rock, and the bastard was on the ground? I wanted to grab that rock from Lucas and I wanted to cave his head in and when I looked at Lucas, I saw my anger and fury reflected there. What stopped us? What does it take to cross the line and kill another human being?

Lucas was devastated by what we'd been through, separately and together these past few weeks. Right now, I wasn't okay, but I knew that somehow, eventually, I would be. I wasn't so sure about Lucas.

He'll talk about things when he's ready. That was Bart's advice. Good advice, but it didn't seem like it was enough. I wanted to do more but didn't know what more was. And I had a suspicion that there was nothing I could do, just as there was nothing more he could do to help me. It was up to Lucas now and it was up to me.

The trail looks so different in the light of day. It's thickly wooded on either side and the North Shore Mountains make a beautiful, backdrop. A memory surfaces. I'm a child, squatting on the shore of Lake Superior, water lapping at the toes of my runners. The sun, a bright red ball hovered just above the water line, right in my line of sight so I had to squint. Infinite water stretched out before me, not like glass because Superior was never like glass; too big to be home to only one spirit.

I was wearing one of dad's jackets, more like a blanket really, the cuffs rolled up, the back so long it pooled on the sand behind me. I'd probably refused to wear my own jacket, always running, always too warm, too constrained, even then. I stretched out my arms and slowly, carefully, placed my palms on the water's surface — a child's wonder at the grandeur of this water universe; a toddler, trying to understand the mighty spirits of Lake Superior.

But my memory of crouching on the shore is a memory of a home movie dad took, because he had brought his *Super8* along as he so often did and captured my awe and wonder. I watched that movie with him again, only a few years before he died. It was a very real memory for him and he sure loved that clip, but does it count as a real memory for me? I think so, because they say we remember every single thing we lay our eyes on and store that remembrance somewhere. I like to think that dad's clip helped tease out the memory for me.

The photographer's lens is the eye of my time and my

parents' too. It's the tool I chose a long time ago to tell my stories. In a way, we allow it stand in for memory; we don't even question that it does. The camera lens becomes our eyes. It sees so much better than we do. We record what it sees. But if we want to, we can choose one angle over another or a long shot over a closeup. We can change, transmute, enhance, even disfigure our photo memories and where is reality in all that? I didn't have an answer for that question. If I was to be honest with myself, I don't really like asking it.

All the times since that I had crouched on the shores of that incredible lake, swam in it, floated on it, and yearned to understand its majesty, its mystery — did I get any closer to it than the two-year-old child in Dad's home movie? Maybe not. All my life, I've been entranced by the stark power of the photographic image, it's near perfection, the beauty in those perfectly caught moments. But so much about the intrinsic truth of things does not lie still in your hand and let you peer at it. Maybe understanding and knowledge emerge from a place that we can never see, or name.

I left my camera in the car and started down the hill. I rounded a bend in the road and further down I could see yellow crime scene tape fluttering in the breeze. Even from here, I could hear a dog barking and thought maybe some hikers had brought their dog along with them. Two cruisers and a van with the RCMP logo were parked on either side of the track. As I approached the vehicles, three men emerged from the woods.

"Please ma'am. Come no further! This is a crime scene," said a uniformed officer tersely.

"Yes, I know that." I could hear the edge in my voice.

"Sorry Ms. O'Meara, I didn't recognize you at first. It was Lassiter. He was here last night. The team had arrived at the van, carrying a small black bag. Lassiter opened the back door of the van and the three of them placed the bag carefully inside. Lassiter turned to me.

"Why did you come?"

"I don't really know," I told him truthfully. "I guess I just want to better understand what happened."

"Of course, ma'am," he said, nodding sympathetically.

"Is that what I think it is?"

"Yes ma'am. It's a body bag."

"It's very small."

"Yes. It is."

"It's a child, isn't it?"

"I'm sorry. I can't say ma'am."

47

Sunday, October 19th

I watched the men carry dad's body and lay it beside the others, along the side of the shallow pit they'd dug at the bottom of the communal garden. Mom couldn't stop crying. Afraid she would give them away, someone had to cover her mouth and force her to silence. They had to pull her off him so they could bury him.

I couldn't bear to look at him on the ground beside the others, his sightless eyes fixed on nothing. His gaping chest wound now a deep black. I didn't watch as they put him in the grave. Didn't watch as they covered the bodies with dirt.

We took what we could carry and returned to the jungle. Some elected to try their luck over the border in Mexico, but the army sometimes followed. For months, we hid from the army, always on the run. There was never enough to eat.

Mom decided to return to La Perla. We were exhausted and there was nowhere else for us to go. She knew the guerillas had murdered my great-grandfather but she didn't know, until we arrived there, that my father's family asked the Guatemalan army to install a Garrison on La Perla land. She must have been terrified to find the army there.

About 5,000 Maya and a few Mestizos were living in two villages on La Perla. One village supported the Arenas family and the army, while the other supported the guerillas.

We stayed with a family that was pro-Arenas family and pro-army. That must have been hard for her too. It wasn't for me. I was afraid of the guerillas. One of them killed my father. I can remember the look on the boy's face when he realized what he'd done. An accident. They were there to ambush the army, not kill the campesinos.

The civil war was still raging and the guerrillas made constant forays onto La Perla land: against the army garrison, against the infrastructure of La Perla and against villagers known to oppose them.

The army had a special tactic they employed against the guerrillas: The civil patrols. Every Maya and Ladino male living on La Perla who was twelve years and older was forced to do civil patrol duty: looking for guerrillas and guerilla sympathizers. To refuse to participate was a death sentence. I remember the young boys, not much older than me and their civil patrol hats and their guns. It was years later that I found out that the La Perla civil patrol was the largest in the highlands. Some said they could be as brutal as the soldiers.

We had been at La Perla a few weeks when mom heard that one of my father's uncles, Enrique Arenas, had come to La Perla to oversee the coffee harvest. After Ignacio Arenas was murdered, the Arenas family lived in Guatemala City year-round. If Enrique was there, then an uncle of moms, Te'k Si'm, who always worked closely with the owners during harvest would be on site, in the workers' lodgings near the mansion.

Late one afternoon, close to sundown, we went looking for him to ask for his help. He was happy to see us. So many of mom's family had been killed in the civil war and she was his niece, and very dear to him. She told Te'k Si'm she wanted to get out of the highlands and go to Guatemala City, where she felt the two of us would be safer. He agreed that was a good plan, but knew we couldn't walk there. It wasn't safe for her to be on the road, alone, with me. It wasn't safe for any woman now. Rape by the soldiers was common, as was the abduction and trafficking of children.

Uncle worked for the Arenas family as a handyman a good part of the year and earned a little more than most of the Maya who worked at the plantation. A few evenings later, he visited, bringing the money we needed to travel. Somehow, he'd also managed to get identification papers for us.

We left La Perla very early one morning a few days later, crowded onto the flatbed of a supply truck with many others. The truck took us to the nearby town of Nebaj, the scene that day of a big civil patrol rally. We watched from the highest steps of the Catholic Church in the city centre as hundreds and hundreds of men and boys marched in front of us, wearing matching civil patrol hats and carrying guns.

One man stood close to us on the steps. He was tall and pale skinned and very imposing in mirror sunglasses and a different kind of army hat than the Guatemalan soldiers wore. I'd never seen an American soldier before and asked mom who he was. She told me he was a soldier in the United States Army and that his country supported the Guatemalan army. He had come to witness the great success of their campaign.

It was late afternoon before we left Nebaj and the highlands. I remember how excited I was when our camioneta, a brightly coloured and ancient school bus imported from the US, rumbled to life and took off at high speed down the road, a trail of smoke and evil smelling fumes billowing out behind it.

Our journey from La Perla to Guatemala City took four days. Each camioneta we boarded took us closer and closer to the capital. Sometimes we got seats, sometimes we stood. Always we were packed in tight.

Each time we passed through an army checkpoint, everyone had to get off the bus, show their papers and answer questions. Dad had taught both of us to speak, read and write Spanish and mom conversed easily with the guards.

Her story was always the same: We were going to live with her sister in Guatemala City. She'd been promised a job in a small hotel there. Maybe that's why we were always allowed to get back on the bus. Some weren't.

We reached Antigua the morning of the third day. Te'k Si'm told mom to go from there to San Juan del Obispo, a small Maya town nearby. He had a cousin there, a jeweler who worked in jade and went to market in Guatemala City once a week to sell. We walked from Antigua to San Juan in a few hours and found uncle's cousin easily. He was going to Guatemala City the next morning and he took us with him.

Morgan was back. Lucas listened to her drop the car keys on a small side table near the front door, then take off her boots. She came into the kitchen and put on the kettle before sitting down beside him.

"Sweetheart, did you get some sleep?"

"I got a little. I've been writing about my family. Our time in Guatemala."

"I'm here, if you want to talk."

"I know. I was just going to write about how mom and I escaped from Guatemala. Did I ever tell you about the day we came to Canada?"

"No."

"Remember when we visited Guatemala City and we stayed in that small hotel in Zone 10."

"I'll never forget that — gated houses in a gated zone."

"The Canadian Embassy used to be in Zone 9, right

next door."

"Zone 9 is very modern."

"With the help of an uncle of mom's, we made it to San Juan del Obispo, a Maya town just outside of Antigua. The next day, a jeweler that uncle had put us in touch with, drove us from there to Guatemala City. Our final destination was an area of poor *barrios* in the north of the city, Zone 1, the old city. Mom had heard that thousands of homeless were living there and she thought we could hide there and be safe, at least until the civil war was over."

"There'd been a major earthquake in Guatemala City seven years before. The government didn't have the capacity to deal with a catastrophe of that magnitude. Thousands died in the quake and it left over a million homeless. People were still living amongst the rubble. Add to that the thousands more, like mom and I, who had come from the highlands to escape the bloodshed. Flimsy huts covered every habitable square inch, made from everything imaginable."

"Had your mom ever been to Guatemala City?"

"No."

"It must have been overwhelming for her."

"I think so. So many people, the desperation of the whole scene and ours as well. We walked around and around for hours, looking for help, or someone who could give us some direction. There were people trying to organize the homeless. Mom found one couple and talked with them for a long time.

That first night, we slept with strangers, all of us huddled together in an alley against a wall. The next morning, with the last of the money she had, mom bought us tortillas. Then she told me we were going to go to the Canadian Embassy and ask to be admitted to Canada as refugees. She'd asked the jeweler to show her where the Embassy was, just in case.

"But why did she choose Canada?"

"Many went to Mexico and many went to the US. Both were close. But mom reasoned that since Father Gurriarán had studied the cooperative movement at a Canadian University, Canada would be a safe place to go."

"So, your mom told you that you were leaving Guatemala."

"Yes. That day."

"Your mom was a courageous woman, sweetheart."

"She was very brave, Morgan. So very brave."

"Then what happened?"

"We walked to the Canadian Embassy. Guatemala City was like being in another world, but all the signs were in Spanish and we were fluent in Spanish, thanks to dad." Lucas smiled at the recollection. By the time we got there, it was past mid-day. There was a security guard at the main entrance and he asked us what we wanted. Mom told him in Spanish that she would like to speak with an embassy official about an important matter and the guard waved us up. There was an elevator with only one button, because it only made one stop — the embassy offices on the top floor of the building. We arrived at the top floor and got off the elevator, which opened onto a waiting room. There were two more security guards, but these guys were in front of a heavy steel door. One guard was Maya, the other Ladino. They were Guatemala City police officers."

"Police?"

"Yes! They were standing in front of the door, guarding it. They had AK47s, and they were holding them at port arms."

"Ready to fire?"

"Ready to fire," Lucas said. "Mom asked so politely, in Spanish, to speak with an embassy official. Honestly,

Morgan, she showed no fear, but I knew how afraid she was. She'd already told me it was our only hope. I held her hand while we stood there. I could feel the urgency in her fingers, because usually her touch was so gentle, but Morgan, her face betrayed nothing."

"Then what happened?"

"Nothing happened. The guards ignored us. We just stood there. I can't remember how long, but a long time. Then someone else came up in the elevator, got off and walked over to the guards. I remember the guy, he looked like a government official, you know, wearing a suit and carrying a briefcase. One of the guards got on the intercom immediately, a buzzer sounded and the big steel door opened. We were standing a few feet from the guards and when they stepped to the side to let him in, mom and I ran through the door, right behind him."

"Did the guards try to stop you?"

"Oh yes. One guy shifted his rifle to one hand and made a grab for me. I was a little behind mom but she had my hand and she pulled me through. Mom had caught them by surprise and we were through the door!"

"Now you're inside the embassy!"

"We were inside, but not yet safe."

"Was your mom wearing her red corta? Her Ixil clothing?"

"Oh no! She was wearing her mestizo clothing. She'd been wearing that for weeks."

"What did your mom say to the embassy official?"

"It was awhile before we got to see him and when we did, mom told him everything: about Father Gurriarán and the founding of the cooperative, how the priest had studied the coop movement here, in Canada; about my great grandfather, Ignacio Arenas and his assassination by the guerrillas; how the army burned our cooperative to the ground; about the assassination of my father, Rafael, Ignacio Arenas' grandchild; how we fled to the jungle; then how we escaped from the army, again, and made our way back to La Perla; how she feared for my safety especially as I was also an Arenas. Then she showed the official her Ixil clothing and told him she had been afraid to wear it to the embassy; that if the guards knew she was Ixil, they might refuse her entrance."

I met Lucas' mother Nineth when I first started dating him. I remembered her as a beautiful, vibrant woman, full of life and love.

"Your mom was such an amazing woman Lucas and I loved her stories."

"That day, she told the story of her life," said Lucas.

"And you were accepted as refugees, of course!"

"We were, yes," said Lucas, and his beautiful smile beamed, full wattage. "Then we came to Canada, and you know the rest."

"I do not know the rest, but I'm a patient woman and I can wait."

Lucas looked at her now — very serious — the smile gone.

"Morgan, I've been thinking that I need some time to sort things out. I've decided to take a leave of absence from the university."

"That's a good plan."

48

It was Sunday evening. We'd just finished take out curries and were sipping on chai tea.

"Michael called to say that Carey's doing okay," I said. "He didn't know much about the other kids, but he did know that the boy who needed surgery came through it well."

"Poor wee thing," said Kate.

"They brought the girl we rescued to the hospital this afternoon. Her name's Marie," said Lucas.

"How is she," said Bart, exchanging a worried look with Kate.

"She was afraid, until she saw Carey. They're pretty close. I guess Carey tried to watch out for her. Michael said Carey gave quite an interview to the police and is something of a media celebrity."

"She spoke with the media? We didn't see that, did we Kate!" They were both horrified.

"Oh no! No one has been allowed access to the children. Michael thinks that someone at the North Van detachment must have leaked that Carey got her hands on a cell phone and called for help."

"If she hadn't made those calls ... I can't bear to think about it," said Kate.

"Carey told Michael that she found Seth's phone in his

room — that was after he wandered away. She hid it in a stuffed toy that Ange Batlan had given her. At first, the traffickers thought Seth took it with him when he left. Then they must've had the phone tracked so they could pinpoint where he was. That's when they realized it was still in the gatehouse."

"Then, I guess, no one could find it and it wasn't in his room. When they found the phone, MacLeish hit Carey so hard he knocked her out. The next thing she remembered was coming to in the *Suburban* with the other children."

"Lord love us," breathed Kate.

"Global did a feature on Seth, during a special noon broadcast. Did you catch that?" Kate and Bart hadn't.

"Someone from the media got hold of a picture of Seth Boyce, taken when he was ten."

"Just a boy," said Kate.

"Maybe they got the photo from his mom," said Bart.

"Did Michael say how Seth's doing?" Kate asked.

"He didn't know but Fernice called us late afternoon and said Seth's still with us. His mom arrived at the hospital this afternoon."

"I've spoken with the director at West Sanctuary," said Bart. "If Seth pulls through, she's agreed that he can stay with us there, as a patient."

"We're hoping the police will allow that," said Kate.

"The VGH operates an Indigenous lodge for out-of-town family members," said Bart. "His mom could spend time in Vancouver while he recovers."

Lucas's face lit up at the suggestion. "I hope you can make it happen."

"Me too," said Bart.

"This whole situation must be overwhelming for his mom … Carey's family is here from Terrace and Milton, that's her dad, he's here too. He drove down from up-island."

"Where is everyone staying?" asked Kate.

"Michael put them up at *The Georgia*." Bart whistled appreciatively. "This is a real celebration for everyone. They're jubilant to have Carey back. He didn't say much about how Carey is doing though and I didn't ask."

"Do we know anything more about Marie?" asked Kate.

"Carey told the police Marie doesn't speak and that no one in the gang had ever spoken a word to her, can you imagine!"

"Marie has never spoken? It's hard to believe that no one cared enough to find out why," said Bart. Kate's eyes filled with tears.

"I don't think the traffickers would care whether she could speak or not," said Lucas.

"So true, Lucas, but that's not what I meant. Children, all children, are very quick to pick up language. I'm thinking there's another reason she doesn't speak."

"We suspect she might be unable to speak," said Kate. "She may be deaf as well. We were with her for over an hour. We both noticed that she didn't react to sound. At first, I thought she might be in shock, perfectly understandable. But it got us wondering, didn't it Bart."

"She could be deaf and dumb," said Bart.

"Poor kid, what a nightmare for her."

Kate nodded. "Have you seen the clip of the men they arrested at Batlan's being led into the RCMP detachment in North Vancouver?" said Bart. "We recognized all of them from the club last night."

"The one from the VPD — Rhodes. The bastard's in Sex Crimes," said Kate, indignantly.

"Both Vice and MPU are in Investigations," said Lucas, with a glance in my direction. "And MacLeish, the RCMP officer from Prince George, he's second-in-command up there, in charge of policing operations."

"Including anything to do with missing children," said Kate.

That gave me a chill.

"And the guy, Derision?" said Kate.

That got a smile from Lucas. "Nice Kate." You mean deReesen; Appellate Court, Prince George."

"A judge!" said Kate. "The whole business is appalling. Where does it end?"

"We didn't see the blonde guy going into the detachment office with the rest," I said.

"We think he got away," said Lucas. "We've heard nothing on the news about him."

"I know who you mean," said Bart. "The one sitting across from the VPD officer. Even if he did get away, they have his picture. He's not going to get far."

"You can tell the media don't have much information," said Kate. "We know more than they do at this point."

"Has Alex called?" asked Bart.

"He did," I said.

"Did you ask him about the guy that got away?"

"I did. He said they have a strong lead. Wouldn't give me anything else. Changed the subject and asked how we're all doing. I told him we're okay. Are we?"

"I'm not," said Kate. "Not really."

"Neither am I," I admitted. It was then that I told everyone about my trip to the hiking trail this afternoon and watching the police carry out the body bag.

"I arrived when they were carrying it out. Someone small. I asked one of the officers if it was a child. He wouldn't confirm. Said he couldn't. They had a sniffer dog. I could hear him barking."

"I told the police I thought it was a burial site," said Lucas. "I just knew it!"

"Carey told Michael that a girl named Georgina tried to escape last week. She never saw her again."

"You're thinking that might have been Georgina that they found," said Kate.

"Maybe." I got up to fetch the teapot. While I was at it, I snuck a peak through the curtains of our living room window. There was a parked car I didn't recognize. It was already dark but I could make out a man sitting in it. The same guy that was there an hour ago.

"I think we have a media presence out there," I announced, returning with the teapot and offering it around.

"Trafficking in children; an international ring. It's so disheartening," said Lucas.

"But we shouldn't be surprised," said Kate.

"A shadow economy. Kate and I were talking about it on the way over. It has such an unbelievable ring to it, doesn't it? What shadow? It doesn't operate in shadow, it operates under our very noses. And there's nothing invisible about it."

"Do we know where the kids are from?" Kate asked.

"I heard on the news that two of the children, sisters who were in care, have been identified as residents of Quebec; two more sisters and Carey are from BC. As for the rest, they haven't yet been identified."

"So, we don't know where Marie's from," said Kate.

"Michael heard from one of the cops that she may be the daughter of a woman who was trafficked into Quebec from Eastern Europe."

"Where's her mother? Is she alive? And her father?"

"They've no idea. Carey told her family that Batlan was quite upset because he wanted to keep her and raise her."

"He wanted to do what!?" said Kate, nearly choking on her tea.

I was thinking about the children that had passed through the hands of Batlan and his gang. And the blonde man only a few feet from the door I hid behind — his cold, calculating face. He was still free. Kate intruded on my thoughts.

"What about the woman in the car?" Kate asked. "Did Michael know anything?"

"Her name's Joy. She suffered a concussion and they're keeping her in for observation. It's anyone's guess how long it will take for her to heal after what she must have witnessed, been forced to do. Michael said Phineas Rhodes is the fourth person Joy's been sold to. It's been seventeen years since she's been free. She's from Romania. She has a son. The last time she saw him, he was a small boy."

"Seventeen years!" said Kate. Her son's a man now."

"She can apply for a Temporary Residence Permit. The TRP will give her access to health care, trauma counseling and any other help she might need. She can also apply for a temporary work permit."

"Does she have to testify against these guys?" asked Bart.

"No, she doesn't have too; only if she wants to. And she can have her TRP extended before it runs out. Or she can return home, if that's a safe option for her."

"True humanity is precious indeed," said Bart.

"And continues to be somewhat illusive," said Kate sardonically.

"Ah Kate, you're right, but then, you're so often right," Lucas said, with a wry smile.

"Get away with you!"

"We helped rescue eight kids, a young man who hasn't been free for eight years, a woman who hasn't been free for seventeen years.

"And," added Kate, "we've made life extremely

uncomfortable for some very nasty bottom feeders."

"I'll say," said Bart, raising his chai tea mug. "To us then, and Michael, *in absentia!*"

"I'll second that!" I said.

"Me three," said Lucas.

"To warm words on a cold day," said Kate, raising her cup of chai.

49

The next week we had Michael, Bart and Kate over for dinner. Michael was worried about Carey. The family was overjoyed that Carey was back with them, but the carefree girl she'd been before her abduction no longer existed.

"Her eyes are so sad. She has a therapist. She's seen her twice and that seems to be helping, a little. She gave Carey her cell phone number and she can call her anytime. Rosie took a leave of absence so she can be with her full time. Carey refuses to go to school, rarely leaves the house, so Rosie is home-schooling her. They've moved back to Gitaus, our village. They're living in our Granny's house."

"It's important that she feels safe," said Bart. "Home-schooling is a great idea. It lets her take back some control over her life. Returning to her school in Terrace may trigger memories she's trying to avoid. Feelings of guilt are very common."

"She feels responsible for what happened," said Lucas.

"She does!" said Michael. "I don't understand it. She didn't do anything wrong, it was all done to her!"

"It's very common Michael. She feels that way now, but in the long term, with love and support, that'll change," said Bart. "Right now, though, the most important thing is that her feelings are validated by those around her and it sounds like Carey is getting lots of love and support. In time, she'll come to understand the great injustice that's been done to her and she'll find a way to live her life fully once again. I've seen this miracle happen many times."

"I sure want to believe you Bart."

"Believe him Michael," said Lucas, with feeling. "We have an incredible capacity to heal."

"You guys are the best, you know that, right?"

"We're stellar," said Lucas. Bart laughed.

"Carey knows the whole story now, doesn't she? It must be so hard for her, sorting it all out."

"And her dad wasn't much help. The first thing he said when he found out she accepted a ride with Seth Boyce was, '*What were you thinking, getting into the car of a stranger?*'"

"Oh no! What did she say?"

"She started to cry. She told him that her knee was hurting and her mom was working at the women's shelter till 9:00 pm and that she had already talked to Seth a couple of times and he was really nice."

"It's that simple, isn't it," said Bart.

"Milton felt like an idiot as soon as he heard Carey's explanation. He immediately apologized to her, but it was already too late; the damage was done. Carey was no longer the victim — he reinforced, at least in her mind, that she was partly responsible. I'm so pissed off at him right now! I think his words had an effect on her."

"Did he stay?"

"No. He volunteered to leave the same afternoon he got here. Carey didn't want him to leave, of course, and he didn't want to go, but she was upset and Rosie insisted he leave. It's just a mess, because Carey really loves her dad."

"You all have to heal too, Michael. Everyone who loves Carey is affected."

"And Milton as well," said Lucas. "He was just parroting what he's probably heard all his life."

"Sorry Lucas. I'm not ready to hear that, not yet anyway," said Michael, both hands up, palms out. "On the bright side, Carey would really like to meet Morgan and Kate," he added, looking at the two of us. We looked at each other.

"That would be lovely," said Kate.

"It would," I said. "When do we go?" It was decided. We would fly north to Terrace the next weekend to visit Carey and her mom.

50

November 28

I asked Ange, please, don't let those men touch me and he promised he would protect me, but he didn't. He pretended to be kind and gentle, but he wasn't. He said he would keep me and not let anything happen to me. But they were going to sell me, sell all of us, to strangers and he didn't try to stop that.

When I told Ange about how horrible everything was and how scared I was, he told me not to worry. That soon I'd be living with him and everything would be okay and I should just put it behind me. But how am I supposed to do that?

And Ange expected me to just forget that I had a mom and dad and a little brother and that I loved them all so, so much.

Everyone knows that I was abducted. That I was away from home and no one knew where I was. That very bad men had me and the other children and that terrible things happened, things I will never be able to talk about with my friends.

Julia gave me her cell number and told me I can call her anytime. But she doesn't understand, no one does. How can I talk when everything that happened makes me feel dirty and sick inside? How can I tell mom that I can't face going *back to school because everyone knows? I'll never be clean again. It doesn't matter what anyone says! I know that. I'm never going back to Terrace and I'm never going back to school!*

Dad called again. He was crying. He's so sorry for what he said. He really wants to see me and I really want him to come. Mom won't let him, because of what he said to me about getting into Seth's car.

I called Julia and told her to I want to see dad and that he's sorry and please tell my mom to change her mind. Dad isn't bad. He would never hurt me. He didn't say what he said to hurt me. It's what he always said to me when we talked about how young girls have to be careful about strange men and not to trust them. He was just trying to protect me and he feels bad because he wasn't there, picking me up from soccer practice. I know that, even though he doesn't say it. I know he feels guilty and thinks that what happened to me is his fault.

Uncle Michael is bringing his friends Morgan and Kate to visit us. I really want to meet them.

Julie's right. I do feel better when I write down what I'm feeling.

51

I'd never flown up to Northern BC and the view from the plane is spectacular. Hundreds of miles of pristine, snow-capped mountains and the Pacific coastline — surreal, cold and distant below us. Michael's in front of us, his head bent over work related stuff. Kate's beside me.

"What are we going to say to Carey," I said, not for the first time.

"Honestly love, I've no idea," said Kate. "I'm hoping that the words will just come as they're needed."

"Me too."

"There is one thing you could share," Kate offered. At my blank look, she said: "You both escaped. You could tell each other your stories."

I reached out a hand and Kate took it and gave it a squeeze, tucking my arm through hers.

"Bart says we don't have to have the answers, Morgan. We just have to let her know we care."

Rosaline opened the door at Michael's knock. He enveloped her in a big hug, then stood, one arm around her as he introduced the two of us. Kate wasted no time stepping forward to give Rosaline one of her famous hugs as well.

"Is Carey here?" I asked.

"She is and she'll be out in a bit. She's very pleased you decided to come, but ... you know," she said softly.

"Of course," said Kate. "We've no expectations. We're just glad to be here."

"And I'm so glad you could all make it. I've lunch ready for you. You must be hungry."

"I am," said Michael.

"You're always hungry," laughed Rosaline.

"Rosie's a great cook," Michael told us.

"Hi Uncle." We all turned to the doorway.

"Carey" said Michael going over and giving her shoulder a gentle squeeze.

"Carey, these are my friends, Morgan, and Kate."

"I'm Morgan. We're very excited to finally meet you Carey."

"That we are. I'm Kate."

Carey gave us a little smile.

"Here, let's get everyone to the table and get some lunch into you," said Rosie.

"I could definitely eat," I said.

"I'm as hungry as a wee army," said Kate, laughing.

"Where are my manners?" said Rosie. "Let me take your coats."

"I'll take their coats mom," said Carey, coming forward, her eyes on Kate and me.

We handed her our coats and the three of us shed our footwear. Kate and I had brought slippers. We got them out of our overnight bags and pulled them on. Michael had forgotten his so Rosaline got him a warm pair of socks to wear and we all followed her to the kitchen.

Carey took our coats to one of the bedrooms and quickly joined us in the kitchen. She took the chair on my left and I smiled. There was no return smile, but I sensed one lurking there somewhere.

"Smells delicious Rosaline," declared Kate.

"Oh please, Kate, call me Rosie."

"Rosie it is," Kate and I chorused together, then laughed.

Rosie had outdone herself. Our lunch menu included lasagna and fresh baked buns, all of it delicious. An apple pie waited on the back of the stove.

I liked Rosie right off. She was a no nonsense woman with a warm smile. I sensed that she was genuinely relieved that Kate and I had come.

"Can I ask you a question?" said Carey. I looked at her.

"You can ask me anything you want?" I said with an encouraging smile. Everyone at the table grew quiet. Continued eating.

"How'd *you* get away?"

"I tried to get away a couple of times actually. The first time, I was in a box on the back of a pick-up truck."

"In a box?"

"Uh huh, like a storage box. I got the lid open and I crawled out."

"Did you jump from the truck?"

"That was my plan, but no. The guy who had me saw that I was trying to escape and he stopped the truck."

"What did he do then?"

"He strangled me." I didn't really want to talk to her about this, but after the hell that she'd been through, I felt it best to be completely honest. Michael didn't know about that and he gave me a horrified look, which Carey didn't see.

"That must have hurt a lot," said Carey, her eyes full of concern.

"It was over pretty quick."

"Then what happened?"

"I must have passed out. The next thing I remember, I came to on the shore of a lake. I got myself up and escaped into the woods close by. I found a thicket and I crawled into it. Then I fell asleep."

"You fell asleep!"

"I was very tired," I said, smiling at her.

"And he didn't find you?"

"No, he did not!"

"They made us go to sleep a lot, even when we weren't tired. "They gave us pills. Lots of different kinds, said Carey. Whenever I could, I hid the pill in my cheek and waited for them to leave, then I'd spit it out."

"Good thinking!" I said."

"Yeah, well, I couldn't always do that," she said. Sometimes, they'd make us open our mouth so they could check. Then I'd have to swallow it and I couldn't help falling asleep."

"That must have made you angry."

Carey nodded yes. "They gave us other pills too, so we wouldn't be any trouble."

"Right. Me too."

That ended conversation for a while.

"So, how did you get away, Morgan?"

"I woke up the next morning and the guy who took me was nowhere in sight, so I crawled out of my hiding place and headed back to the lake to get a drink of water. Man, was I thirsty! That's when I heard a motor boat, so I hurried as fast as I could down to the lake to try to get the attention of the people in the boat."

"And they saw you?"

"They sure did. They rescued me."

"I wanted to save the other kids, and myself, but we were never alone."

"But in the end, Carey, it was you who saved them, and

yourself."

Carey gave me a dubious look. I was surprised that she wasn't buying her part in the rescue.

"You got your hands on that cell phone," Michael interjected with a grin. I could not believe it when you texted me!"

"I was so nervous Uncle!" She turned back to me. "The first time I hit send before I typed the message."

"Oh no!"

"But the second time, I got that message, loud and clear," said Michael.

Carey stopped talking and started eating in earnest. Rosie jumped in.

"Kate, Michael tells us that you have psychic abilities."

"He said you knew what I was thinking," said Carey — all attention — even as she made inroads in her lasagna.

"It's more that I knew how you were feeling, at least some of the time. It's the same as if someone is sitting right beside you and you just know that they're happy, or they're sad. You had me worried, more than once," said Kate. "Then I'd know that you were feeling better."

"I see," said Carey gravely. "But how did you know it was me who was having those feelings?"

"I can't explain that."

"How did you find Seth? Is that different?"

Kate nodded. "It is. There's no way to explain how I do that either. I don't even know how it works. It's a gift."

"I'm sure glad you found him, Kate."

"Me too."

"Do you know if he's okay, I mean, really okay?"

"He's staying in a place where they help people to heal from the kind of experiences that you and Seth had to live through. My husband and the team that he works with are helping Seth. And his mom is close by, so he sees her every day."

Carey gave this some thought. "Is your husband a psychiatrist?"

"He is."

"Julia's a psychiatrist and she's helping me."

"I'm glad to hear you have a helper," said Kate.

I happened to glance over Carey's head at Rosie and Michael, studiously ignoring us, heads down, eating. Carey was studying me very closely.

"That's a scar on your forehead?"

"Yes, it is."

"Did one of the men do that to you?"

"Yes, Carey. There were lots of bruises too. I'm healed up now, but I still feel them in a way I can't quite explain." That just popped out. Even I was surprised.

"I know what you mean," said Carey. The two of us shared a glance of understanding.

"There's something I'd like to show you Morgan. It's in my bedroom. Mom, can we be excused?"

"Of course, sweetie."

I got up and following her to her bedroom. She shut the door and we sat on the side of her bed.

"I don't really have anything to show you. There's something I want to ask you. I didn't want to ask in front of the others."

"Of course, Carey, anything. Ask away."

"You don't have to tell me if you don't want to." She was suddenly quite anxious. "I don't want you to be mad at me. I really like you Morgan."

"I really like you too, Carey." I laid a hand on her shoulder. "You can ask me anything you want," I assured her. "I won't be mad, I promise."

"I'm really grateful that you helped my uncle find me.

I'm so grateful to everyone who helped."

I nodded and waited for her to continue. There was a long silence.

"Did they rape you?" she finally asked me quietly, looking at her hands.

"Yes. Some men did. I don't remember much about the rape. I was semi-conscious. I'd been drugged. But I knew I'd been raped and beaten. I was sore after and there was a lot of bruising."

Carey turned quickly and looked me right in the eye.

"Are you mad I asked?"

"No, not at all," I assured her. You know Carey, you're the first person to ask me."

"Didn't your boyfriend ask?"

"No, he didn't. He knew though, even before I told him. He felt it was his fault."

"Were you afraid to tell him because then he wouldn't love you anymore?" Then I understood.

"No Carey. I had to tell him so that we could work through it together. I think that deep down, he still feels partly to blame because he wasn't there to help me. But he couldn't have stopped it from happening and there's nothing he can do about it now."

I opened my arms to Carey and she moved in for a hug. As soon as I put my arms around her, she started to cry.

"They raped me too," she sobbed into my shoulder, "and did terrible things that I can't get out of my mind. They made us take pills. They made us drink. We weren't allowed to say no. I haven't told anyone yet, not even Julie."

"You just told me honey."

She looked at me, surprised. "I did, didn't I."

"Yup. You know, I think, some day, we'll be able to put the bad experiences we've had behind us. I don't mean forget about them. I don't think anyone can ever do that. But first, we have to talk about what happened, so that it's not bumping around inside our head."

"That's what it feels like," said Carey.

"And we do need to forgive ourselves, not blame ourselves, so we can move forward with our lives. That's the hard part, isn't it?"

"I don't know how to put it behind me, or accept it, or forgive myself, like you just said we need to do."

"I'm still working on it myself Carey. All of it. I sure don't have all the answers. But I do know one thing. It takes as long as it takes."

"I like that," she said. "It takes as long as it takes. Mom wants me to hurry up and get better. Uncle Michael too."

"They want you to heal. They don't want you to be sad. That's because you're so precious to them."

"Yeah, and mom is used to making it better for everyone, but she can't wave a magic wand and make it better for me," said Carey, a very sage comment coming from an eleven-year-old. "I feel so much pressure, but I can't do it any faster."

"We know that we have to do this for ourselves, in our own time, don't we," I said.

"Yes, we know that."

"At first Carey, I blamed myself for what happened to me. If I hadn't gone for a run at night, just paid closer attention to what was going on around me, not been so distracted, you know what I mean. I wanted to turn back the clock."

"I still blame myself because I got in the car with Seth," she said quietly and in this child's eyes I could see that she did. It was so unfair.

"Carey, you did nothing, absolutely nothing wrong. There are bad people out there, and they do bad things.

One thing I do know for sure is there's no healing for us if we travel down that road."

"Part of me knows that. Really. And that's what everyone keeps telling me. But it's like having a tape in my head that says the same thing over and over: *It's your fault.*"

"Have you read any of the things people are saying about you Carey?"

She shook her head. "What things?" I looked at her. I was incredulous. It must have showed.

"You're a hero! You saved yourself and seven other children, and you saved Seth and Joy. You are so very, very brave. You're my hero," I said and she could see I meant every word. Carey was looking at me strangely.

"I don't feel very brave right now."

"From my own experience, the things we're most afraid of talking about get bigger and bigger if we keep them inside."

"Julia says the hardest wounds to heal are the invisible ones."

"She's right about that."

"She also says talking about the things that hurt us is a way of taking away their power so they can't hurt us anymore."

That resonated with me. "I really like that! You know what I'm going to do?"

"What Morgan?"

I'm going to tell everyone that I care about, exactly what happened to me: about the men who raped me; about the man trying to kill me; about everything. Talking with you today has helped me see that I have to do that. Thank you, Carey, for helping me realize how important that is."

That surprised her. "You haven't told your friend Kate?"

"No, not everything, But I'm going too, really soon."

"You know Morgan, you're my hero. Uncle said you took down the bad guy that was trying to kill you with karate!"

That made me smile. "Well, that's not exactly how it went down. I held the guy off for quite a while and I did bust one of his knee caps. That gave me a lot of satisfaction. Believe me! But it was my partner Lucas who hit him with a big rock and dropped him in his tracks. That was fine with me."

Michael chose that moment to call us back to the kitchen. "Hey you two — if you don't get back here, I can't guarantee there'll be any pie left!"

"He's not kidding," said Carey, matter-of-fact. "He loves mom's pies. He can eat two pieces."

"Two!"

"And its apple pie, my favourite and my mom is an awesome baker and we have ice cream."

"Apple pie and ice cream. That sounds good. We better get back to the party."

"Is it a party?"

"It's a celebration, absolutely!"

We were sitting in the living room, enjoying after lunch coffees.

"We have a surprise for you Carey," I said, looking over at Kate.

"You tell her," said Kate.

"No. You tell her," I insisted.

"We wanted you to know that Marie is living with my husband and me." Carey jumped up and threw her arms around Kate.

"You're taking care of Marie?"

"Yes, we are."

367

"But where's her mom?"

"No one's been able to find her."

"How long can she stay with you," Carey asked, suddenly worried.

"Until her mom is found."

"What if they don't find her?" she asked, her face apprehensive. Kate didn't want to tell her, not just yet, that Marie's mom was most likely dead.

"Then my husband and I are going to adopt Marie," said Kate.

"She's safe then, with you?"

Kate nodded and smiled.

"Has she spoken yet?"

"No, sweetheart, she hasn't. But that's because she isn't able to speak."

Carey thought about this. "She has her own words, but they're hard to understand."

Kate nodded.

"You know Kate, Marie understands things in other ways. She likes it a lot when you make really funny faces."

"That's good to know," said Kate, thinking briefly of Bart, all but standing on his head to make Marie smile.

"Maybe when you're feeling better, you can come visit Marie," Kate suggested, looking to Rosie for confirmation. She smiled back.

"And she could come here and visit me too, couldn't she mom?"

"Either is fine with me honey," said Rosie.

52

My last lab with the film students was the first week in December. Truth be told, I was glad my teaching time was over and done with. Teaching, I've discovered, requires a lot of patience and I'm more of a does. As I'd promised them in October, we had the no-holds-barred session on media treatment of my abduction and rescue.

It was interesting and instructive for me to listen to others discuss how, in the short space of a ten days, I went from professional, but careless woman who took chances and put herself in harm's way — to street prostitute who managed to extricate herself from that life and into another but continued to sleep around, for free — to the final incarnation where I was miraculously wiped clean of stupidity, carelessness, victimization and questionable morals and emerged as Indigenous woman, badass superhero.

My students come from many corners of the world and race, gender and class bias are alive and well in every corner. These are my struggles too; always have been. And while my Indigenous heritage is a green light to a twisted few to wreak their own sick havoc on me, it is also my strength and my power. More so now than ever.

I no longer cover my stitch marks and have taken to combing my hair the way I always did, off my forehead.

I'm tired of hiding them — from myself and from the rest of the world. I want to remember how I got them and watch them disappear. I don't want how I got them to haunt me for the rest of my life.

Lucas combs the papers and online press daily for news about that nasty crew. The body they were carrying out when I arrived at the trail was a girl named Georgina Carlisle. Carey's mom doesn't want her to know yet. Her healing is up and down and the family is worried about how it would affect her. I am too. Personally, I found it devastating. They found two other bodies in the area: an adult woman and a male youth. They haven't been identified yet.

The blonde guy hasn't shown up in the news which has caused us endless speculation and me some private worry. It doesn't help that Jeri Fernice calls weekly to check up on me. She's pretty slick about it, but I think they're worried about me because they haven't caught the guy yet. We're hyper vigilant now that we know he's in the wind, but we haven't noticed anything untoward.

Lucas noticed that Batlan was out on bail much faster than the others. Kate and him are guessing Batlan will be a key witness for the defense in the upcoming trial. It looks like they're going to throw the book at all of them. I wish the book was heavier. Trial date is set for this coming March.

About a week ago, I got word that my application for the Telefilm micro grant had been accepted. I was stunned at first; I guess because some part of me didn't think I'd get it, but that was quickly replaced with joyful delirium and my feet didn't touch the ground for days. I wanted a big party to celebrate and started planning a feast. That's as far as I got before I started to flounder a little. Lucas offered his help. Thanks darling. What would I do without you. We invited everyone and what a party it was!

Kate and I spent time together yesterday. We went for lunch and did some Christmas shopping. It was a real gift, because she has so little time now that Marie is part of their family. Kate and Bart are totally in love with her. She told me it happened on that Saturday night. The next morning, they decided over breakfast that they wanted to be her guardians.

I hadn't planned to, not right then, but I found myself telling her everything. She held me in her heart, just like she always does, while I stumbled through the whole sorry mess. Once I got started, I couldn't stop. She held me tight and we cried together. This was the second time and it wasn't as hard as I thought it would be.

After, she insisted Lucas and I come to their new place for dinner. Bart was making lasagna and we both love it. They've moved to a two bedroom in the east end near us which is great, and they're in the process of adopting Marie. It was confirmed that her mom died in Quebec a few years ago. As for her dad, no one knows and probably never will. If Marie is able to heal, it will happen with Kate and Bart. It was joyful and affirming for us to spend the evening with the three of them.

We're in pre-production now on the film and both feet are firmly back on the ground. It's exciting and a little overwhelming too at times, but I'm putting together a great team for this, including Miles, who came on board as Production Manager.

Tomorrow, Lucas and I are flying east to visit my family for the holidays and I'm excited about that. It's been too long. We're going to stay with my cousin Tanaka and her guy, which will be a lot of fun for us and great for them.

They're gonna love Lucas's cooking!

It will be December in Ontario's north and since this is his first time to cavort in that bracing a level of cold and now, I thought it best to check what he's packed for the trip. It's a good thing I did. I'm taking him shopping for snow gear today.

I plan on spending a lot of time with my *Nokomis*. Looking back on our lives, I don't think Effie ever kept secrets from me. It's more that I just wasn't listening close enough to what she *wasn't* saying. There's so much I hope she'll share with me, now that I'm a better listener.

Acknowledgments

West Sanctuary at UBC Hospital in Vancouver, BC does not exist. Nokomis Effie's home reserve, Greenwood Lake, is fictional. If it did exist, it would be East and North of Thunder Bay, Ontario.

La Perla Coffee Plantation does exist and continues to be owned by the Arenas family. I have fictionalized all members of the Arenas family, except for the original owner, Ignacio Arenas. He was given La Perla for his part in putting down the Guatemalan peasant land reformation movement started by Jacobo Arbenz. He was killed by guerrillas during the civil war. After his death, the Arenas family did ask the army to establish a garrison on their land.

Thanks also to Ronald Wright for his insightful book, Time Among the Maya. He made it easier to get at the truth, in plain sight and suggested the plot twist that got Lucas and his mom out of Guatemala. In Antigua, Guatemala, I am grateful to one Maya guide for his truth telling—nameless here for that reason.

Victor Porter of OCTIP gave generously of his time and the important loan of Benjamin Perrin's book on human trafficking in Canada. Whitney Sedgwick was generous with her time and helpful with the questions I had about the field of counselling.

Thanks to Rea Gosine and Catherine Hansen, careful readers of early drafts of the novel. Michelle Fornasier, read a later draft, and helped me get to the heart of the matter. Audrey DeRoy, singer extraordinaire, who helped with Anishinaabe words, but more important, started me on the path to a much deeper understanding of how language carries culture within it. Thanks to Dave Martin for coming up with the title, and my daughter Marcella Reay who believed in me and this book from the beginning. Any mistakes are mine.

Books

Bearing Witness, Violence and Collective Responsibility, Sandra L. Bloom, MD, Michael Reichert, PhD, Routledge, 1998

Invisible Chains, Canada's Underground World of Human Trafficking: Benjamin Perrin, Penguin, 2010

That Lonely Section of Hell: The Botched Investigation of a Serial Killer Who Almost Got Away, Lori Shenher, 2015

The History of Childhood, Lloyd DeMause, Harper/Collins, 1974

Time Among The Maya: Travels in Belize, Guatemala, and Mexico, Ronald Wright, Penguin, 1989

About Valerie Van Clieaf

I'm a woman of mixed Indigenous/East and West European heritage. I've lived in Vancouver off and on for many years. I've been an outreach worker, a carpenter's helper, a cook and a waiter. I have few fond recollections about my cooking jobs as I was a terrible short order cook. I once taught first aid part-time, worked as a bartender on the weekends (I loved bar tending) and worked on-call as a secretary, all during the same winter. I've worked in more offices than I can remember, on a few factory floors including a fish factory in Vancouver, BC and a packaging facility for saran wrap in Ontario. The second job ended when I stuck my hand in a pot of hot glue near the end of the third shift. Fortunately for me, I already had the first aid training.

As I found out, making a living can be difficult and tiring if you haven't lined up what you love to do with what you're actually doing. That's when I decided to go to university.

While I studied music and music composition, I worked at Octopus Books in Vancouver. I went back and forth between writing and music for a while, before music won out. For about 20 years, composing, arranging and teaching music was my life. A life filled with music is a wonderful thing, but there was something else I loved just as much and that was writing.

End of Innocence is my first novel. Part II, Sacrifice

Zone, will be published in the spring, 2018.

For more writing by me, including some background on End of Innocence, you can connect with me via my website: https://valerievanclieaf.com

CPSIA information can be obtained
at www.ICGtesting.com
Printed in the USA
LVOW10s1505090118
562394LV00011B/831/P